RESURRECTION

LISSA KASEY

Resurrection : Pillars of Magic: Dark Awakening

1st Edition

Copyright © 2021 Lissa Kasey

All rights reserved

Cover Art by Doelle Designs

Published by Lissa Kasey

http://www.lissakasey.com

Please Be Advised

This is a work of fiction. Names, characters, businesses, places, events and incidents are either the products of the author's imagination or used in a fictitious manner. Any resemblance to actual persons, living or dead, or actual events is purely coincidental.

Warning

This book is licensed to the original purchaser only. Duplication or distribution via any means is illegal and a violation of International Copyright Law, subject to criminal prosecution and upon conviction, fines, and/or imprisonment. This eBook cannot be legally loaned or given to others. No part of this book can be shared or reproduced without the express permission of the Author.

A Note from the Author

If you did not purchased this book from an authorized retailer you make it difficult for me to write the next book. Stop piracy and purchase the book. For all those who purchased the book legitimately: Thank you!

TRIGGER WARNING

Listed below are the trigger warnings for this book. If any of these things bother you, please proceed with caution:

- References to sexual assault on a minor
- Sexual assault and coercion
- Memories of child abuse/neglect
- Mental illnesses including OCD, Anxiety, Depression, Codependency, and Mania

CHAPTER 1

A sharp tug of death magic brought him to the surface. Not yet aware, more a hint of actual sleep as he fell into a dream about a handsome lover, he glided on the edge of the memory. For a while the images were sweet, if a little disjointed. Time made little sense as the scope of the dreams bounced from place to place.

The second tug dragged him out of the dream and forced a thump of life into his chest. His heart starting, as though it had been stopped for years, stuttering and wheezing back to life, aching in a way he couldn't recall ever feeling. Not that he recalled much.

He gasped, but instead of air, found dirt filling his lungs. He choked and flailed, reaching for anything to clarify his awakening. The surface was close, hands grasping at nothing, released from the soil and his imprisonment. He struggled to crawl free, drowning in earth, and a rolling chaos of mixed memories.

After reaching the top and extricating himself, he lay there, staring into the darkness, trying to put pieces into place. Spitting out dirt and sucking in musty air, he tried to understand where he was.

He'd crawled from a grave; that much was clear. But he was in some sort of stone tomb, walls thick and muffling any sounds of life from beyond. The door almost imperceivable in the pale light. Only the most delicate hint of brightness appeared around the edge of some square near the top.

A vent? The thought fell into place, giving him definitions and images, but no underlying structure. He knew *what* it was, the technicality of it, but not any recollection of seeing it before.

His heart beat so slowly he was tempted to crawl back into the earth, wrap it around him like a blanket, and return to sleep. Why was that a comforting thought? Did anyone enjoy being buried alive?

Though he didn't exactly feel very alive in that moment. More a pain riddled corpse, grasping for anything solid. Was he some sort of zombie? Another word that brought definitions and images to his mind. He hoped he didn't resemble the shambling, rotting corpses he could recall from movies. And further back, he vaguely recalled something very similar in real life, though much more horrific, yet still familiar.

He sucked in air, the feel of it cooling his throat, clean, but also heavy in his lungs. As if he hadn't breathed in a long time. Distantly he heard an alarm. Muffled and quiet, it was some sort of beeping. Just annoying enough to make it harder to think. He lay there for a while, trying to put thoughts into place. A thousand faces and memories ran through his mind as sharp as shards of glass, broken, scattered, and missing in some places.

He couldn't remember even the basics, his name, or the names of any of those faces. Why he'd been buried. Or how he'd been able to crawl free of the grave.

The smell of dirt, cool and earthy, eased a bit of his growing anxiety, but the hint of a scent, wafting through the vent high above, made his stomach growl. It wasn't even a delicate sound of passing hunger. No, it roared like some ancient monster needing to feed. The growl was followed by a pulse of hunger surging through him so strongly that even his teeth hurt. He touched his lips, wincing as one of his teeth cut the edge of his lower lip. He didn't bleed, it just throbbed with a dull ache.

Blood. That was what he smelled. What he craved. He groaned at the idea of the thick, hot liquid pouring over his tongue.

Voices approached and he listened hard to try to make out what they were saying. It was an unusual jumble of sound, with heavy accents he couldn't understand, even while straining to hear them. What he did catch was the smell of blood and the steady beat of at least one pulsing heart. He pushed himself up, ready to crawl toward the door, needing to feed.

It opened before he could do much more than turn his head toward it. Then it closed again, leaving one man inside. This one didn't have the steady heartbeat, his was slower. Nor did he smell as divine as whomever had been outside.

A lamp turned on, low, but still too bright for his eyes, and he flinched. Yet the man held something that made him crawl forward. The smell so good that he had a visceral need to get there, take it. Drink.

He swallowed hard, throat dry, his thirst begging to be quenched.

The man said something, but he couldn't understand it at all. He couldn't feel any fear from the man, more irritation, but the man held out a cup. And that cup was everything he wanted in that moment.

It was hard to hold, his hands—fingers stiff and unyielding—didn't want to move. The man actually pressed the cup to his lips, tipping it to let the heat slide into his mouth.

It was heaven. Everything narrowed to the liquid fire of that cup. The delicate flavor of chilis and chocolate hidden beneath the copper bite of blood. He couldn't remember how he knew what any of that was. Only that the warmth of it trickled down his parched throat, slowly awakening nerves, filling his body with growing sensation, and added aches. He hurt all over. Every part of him an echo of pain, as though he'd slept a thousand years and the joints and muscles were being forced to move, stretch, and function.

Then the cup was empty.

He cursed, tipping it, hoping for more. It barely touched the hunger; only began to awaken his senses. Not enough to clarify anything. Or give him much strength at all, though when the man took the cup away, he tried to fight it. But the man was stronger and set the cup aside before sitting down on the stone lip of the crypt beside the light.

It wasn't so terribly bright anymore, in fact, it didn't illuminate much about the man. Only that he was young, with dark hair and eyes, dressed in jeans and a leather jacket. All items that were boxes checked on a list of things that only partially made sense in his head. Words becoming images or vice versa, without an understanding or memory as to how or where.

He put his head back on the dirt and sucked in air as the heat of the blood trickled through him, a slow drip of living energy. Barely enough to touch each nerve.

"Boss says you'll need more blood," the man said. "But since my guy was the closest non-vampire supe, you'll have to manage on that tiny bit till we get you out of here. I don't share well outside our ménage." The man's words began to make sense, an almost secondary recognition, that the language he was hearing wasn't his first, but still something that had been learned. "You in there? Boss said it could take a bit to sort through the mess. And you've been down a long time. Glad you showed up back here instead of at the house. That could have been bad." The man sat with his hands in his lap, still enough that if he hadn't been speaking, he wouldn't seem to have been moving at all.

"Gabe?"

The name startled him. That too, felt visceral, his. A piece locking into place, his mind grasping it. He was Gabe. Had been Gabe for a very long time. Of that he was certain, though everything else was still a jumble. Almost overwhelming were the memories that rolled with the name. More faces, names, events, snippets of broken bits of his past, emotions dancing with an intensity that almost made him pass out.

Gabe teetered on the edge of darkness for a few minutes. There was too much. Too much everything, but not enough clarification.

"Luca tastes great, right?" The man said. "But it will be your only taste. If anyone else had been closer I wouldn't have shared. He's mine." The last bit was said with a deadly edge. "We get a bit possessive. He likes me getting all caveman. Says it makes me hotter and he loves being thrown on the bed, or against a wall, so I can screw his brains out." The man trailed off, staring into the distance. A voice crackled into his ear from an... earpiece. Something else Gabe wasn't sure how he recognized.

"Car is ready. Does he need a box?"

The man stared down at Gabe, expression mostly blank, but he reached up to push a button and said, "No. He's mostly mobile. How much blood does a vampire need when they come back? I don't need much."

"If it's not from his Focus, he'll need a lot. And he was down a lot longer than you ever have been."

"Ronnie is not going to be feeding him any time soon," the man said.

"No..." the headset crackled a slow response. *"We'll get him to Max. Get him fed and back on his feet. See where his head is before exposing him to the witch."*

"I'm not worried about the witch," the man said. "Give me a minute to get him moving."

"Sam, be careful. He's weak, but that doesn't mean he's not lethal."

The man, Sam, let out a sarcastic laugh. "I'd be thrilled to put him back in the ground."

"Not forgiven?" The voice crackled through the line. *"He might not even remember."*

"Too bad for him then. He's got a lot of bullshit to make up for. And I still fucking feel our bond. How is that possible when he cut me off?" Now he sounded mad, though he still didn't move from the ledge.

"Those sorts of bonds are never completely gone. Not until true death. It's similar to a past lover and how you always remember bits of them, good and bad."

"Ain't loving this shit," Sam said. "Fuck, things were going well. Why now?"

"Some things will always be a mystery."

Sam stopped chatting with the voice in the earpiece and stared down at Gabe. Gabe sucked in air, his chest aching as the slow beat of his heart steadied, though his hunger was barely eased. He felt more in control, though very disoriented and tired.

"I'm a vampire," he said, his voice little more than a raspy whisper. Not a zombie, but still undead, tied to the grave and death. The boxes in his head checked as he filled them with what he knew about vampires. The lists were long, but had a lot of holes. More missing pieces.

"I was disappointed, too. It's not all the phenomenal cosmic power that romance novels lead us to believe," Sam said. "But here we are."

Gabe tried to sort through his thoughts to clarify. "I went to ground."

"Yes," Sam agreed. "Better late than never, I guess. How much do you remember?"

That was a loaded question. "Too much? And not enough? Nothing fits together."

Sam let out a long sigh. "You look like shit. All zombie-like. But your eyes aren't red. They're black, meaning you need blood, and the revenant is close. If we put you in a car, will you attack anyone who's not a vampire?"

"I don't know," Gabe answered honestly. He felt as if his control was in place, but he knew that the hunger was intense enough to take over. "Maybe not?"

Sam reached for the button again. "Bring the box."

Box?

"Once I open the door, I'll need you to get in the box," Sam instructed. "We will add grave dirt to it." He waved his hands at the contents of the tomb. "I think you came back here because it's where your grave dirt is. I know Ronnie added most of it from your apartment after he moved everything out. I'm glad you woke here. Waking up in the witch's backyard would have meant war, I think. Especially with the kids there…"

Kids? Witch? "Vampires aren't allowed to touch witches," Gabe whispered, feeling something tug at his memory. The glimpse of a face, there and gone. Too fast to catch much of it.

Sam laughed. "Yeah? Maybe in the old days. I haven't seen that in a book anywhere, and Max insisted I memorize that shit. I've read them all. Maybe something from your sire?"

The woman's face popped up in his mind, clear, but with no name. The emotions, however, were potent, as Gabe felt himself lurch upward as if to attack. He stopped himself only inches from grabbing Sam, though Sam hadn't moved at all. The thought of her made him homicidal. Good to know.

"That's a trigger, yeah?" Sam asked after a moment.

Gabe cycled through a handful of memories attached to that face. "She was a monster."

"Who said you couldn't touch a witch?"

"Yes."

"Funny. Since you're married to one."

Married? Gabe grasped at the thought, again the flicker of a face, but not enough to really see it. "I don't remember."

"Ronnie will love that. Play dumb. He might forgive you sooner. Or put you back in the ground."

"Forgive me. What did I do?" A thousand things echoed through his head all at once. The noise becoming too loud. Too many things. Deaths even. Monstrous acts. He caved in on himself, rolling up into a ball and trembling in the wake of too many memories trying to find a place in his mind.

Before he knew it, he was in a box, the scent of dirt surrounding him, and the lid slid closed as Sam stood over him. "This is seriously bad timing."

Gabe wanted to ask questions, but the top closed and he felt sleep drag him down. The comfort of the small place, dirt and darkness, letting him chase back some of the scattered memories. He let it all flit away for a while, resting with the memory of a dark-haired stranger who'd been his first kiss.

Curious how clear that was. That moment, though obviously a different place and time. Gabe felt the box moving and the pull of his grave letting him go as he was carried away from it. Even with the dirt in the box, mixed with soil from the grave, he knew the distance meant something. A strain on his control, rising hunger, but total exhaustion.

He tried to follow the memory of the dark-haired man. Older than him, but only by a few years. Gabe sat on the edge of those thoughts, similar to a faint dream, watching the man grow and go off to battle, and finally watching him die.

That ached, similar to a wound to his chest, deep and piercing. Raw. He cringed away from it, trying to relax and ease the feeling, though he was lost in the sensation of dying all over again.

CHAPTER 2

Seiran Rou wasn't in the media enough anymore. That was why he kept ending up in situations like this. Apparently being the director of the Department of Magical Investigations within the Dominion, the ruling body of magic, wasn't enough to warrant him enough cool kid points that drunk frat boys knew him on sight.

Teaching classes on the University campus for almost a decade, and hundreds of lectures across the country, meant everyone should have known him. But it had been a few years since he'd been on a major network, mostly because the magical world had been calm and quiet. At least the public thought so. The few mishaps that did pop up each year he helped shut down before they could become major network news.

Of course, if Sei hadn't been all Sherlock Holmes, "Aha! Dear Watson!" to one of the researchers, and gone off on his own to pursue the lead they'd found, he'd not be stuck here, in a dorm room, strung upside-down in some precariously flickering rope trap.

It seemed to be on some sort of timer. Which didn't make sense. But every few minutes the ropes would loosen, and for a half second, he'd plummet to the floor, but it would catch him and tighten again, like a snake coiling and uncoiling.

However, it was fast bordering on becoming a problem. And none of *this* sort of shit should happen on his campus. Now he knew why his Aunt Lily had been so eager to retire and hand him the reins. College kids did a lot of stupid stuff, and he was often caught up in the middle of it trying to unravel their mistakes.

Unfortunately, he still often got the deer-in-headlight look from the non-magic masses, despite being a largely politicized figure by the media. Had the kid who'd let him in the door to the dorm earlier known? Who Sei was or what awaited him? Had this been planned, or had he just stepped in someone's bullshit?

Sadly, it was most likely the latter. Which meant not only had he been caught in a badly constructed magical booby trap, but he was also locked in with a somewhat concerning enchanted golem.

Technically, he'd been searching for the golem.

After a handful of incidents on the UofM campus had been brought to the administration's attention, he discovered that a couple of students were using a golem to take tests for them, or cover for them in lectures. Not smart, since golems were creatures of questionable magic who only spoke truths. It could memorize textbooks and answer quiz questions, but it could not rationalize essays with human morals and consequences. Golems would also do a lot to fulfill its commands. It made them easy to turn to darker things, including theft and murder.

No one had died. Yet.

The magic woven around it, making it look like a regular person, had begun to unravel. More than a handful of reports around campus of a guy with "his face falling off" had been the first indicator. Golems could only play human for so long before the blood magic began to fade.

Unfortunately, spells steeped in this sort of magic tended to go sideways fast. The golem had attacked a group of football players—who Seiran personally had always thought deserved a beatdown—

and ended up on a couple of uploaded camera phone videos. They'd taunted it and pushed it around, which normally wouldn't have a golem lashing out. But the fact that it had reacted, meant something had either gone wrong with the magic that created it, the players were interrupting a set of commands, or the bond the caster had to it was weakening. Possibly all three.

Four college kids were in the hospital. All would recover, but Sei needed to find the golem before the next batch of kids it crossed paths with didn't.

Kids... sigh. He was getting old. Thirty-six wasn't that old, was it? Most of the kids... students, he was trying to save were barely twenty. Many not old enough to legally drink alcohol. Seeing them made him think of his own kids, though they were much younger, and the need to catch this thing intensified. Just because it had stayed on the college campus so far, didn't mean it would forever.

When someone found or created power from killing something, they tended to forget the rules. Magical power needed balance, which meant the longer this golem lived, the more it would pull from the environment, and possibly its creator or creators. The more the creators exploited it, the more they would feel emboldened to do. Taking tests was a small thing, but how long before it migrated to revenge, or even murder as it unraveled?

Tracking the golem down should have fallen to one of the inspectors. But as usual, the department was understaffed. The fall season was always the worst. The warning stretch of winter coming, a sleepiness in the earth, and a reorganization of "who worked where" as people were promoted, demoted, or moved. A half dozen newbies had been welcomed a week earlier. All wet behind the ears, with stars in their eyes about saving folks and stopping magic crimes. Kids.

Sei sighed thinking back on the past few weeks. He was not about to send the first-year researchers into the field. Not after a golem. He wasn't even sure most of his new hires knew what a golem was. He had been fighting for years to have more diverse curriculum added to the magic studies programs. The Dominion had the idea that not teaching certain things could keep students from experimenting with them. A stupid philosophy that was disproven as a regular part of Sei's job.

There were a dozen ways to create golems, though the physical makeup was mostly the same. None of the rituals were particularly nice, and at least half of those required blood sacrifices. Usually death, unless the witch casting was extremely powerful. The Dominion didn't really recognize black magic as a thing, as intent mattered more. But killing someone to create a shapeshifting body double to take tests and attend lectures? That was a bit of a stretch on the positive intent spectrum.

It was more self-exasperation that kept him trapped in the rope trick, than anything else. Well, that and the fact that every time he tried to use magic, the golem began to move. Lying on the tiny dorm bed it looked like little more than a pile of sticks tied together in a sort of humanoid shape. A head, arms, legs, a torso, but nothing else definable. No current command or intent that required a human face. Either that or the magic had unraveled so far it couldn't be human.

The golem smelled of rot, dirt, and underneath, the edge of something green. Within all that decay was some bit of life.

Earth was Sei's strong point. But the ropes surrounding him were some sort of metal coated in plastic. Weirdly immune to his element. The tiny bit of power he'd used simply to discover the makeup of the trap bonds, and the haphazard spell controlling it, made the golem open glowing red eyes and turn its head his way. It seemed to grow a little in size, the edge of dark menace trickling from it until he stopped using magic. Almost as if it was pulling from Sei's magic. That could go bad very fast as Sei's magic was almost limitless.

Some sort of ward, perhaps?

Nothing he'd ever seen before, and he spent a lot of time studying the obscure—mastering wards and incantations—that could be construed as gray magic. Not because he planned to do nefarious things, but to recognize them before the danger grew out of control. He'd had a successful career out of doing just that. Apparently, today was to be his day of self-discovered inadequacies.

This golem might have been used for stupid things, but whatever spell it had been tied to for defense, was not benign. A golem could punch through concrete, or break a human into pieces, but it couldn't cast its own spells. It was a thing created by magic, but not one that could manipulate magic.

As the Pillar of Earth, the most powerful earth mage on the planet, Sei could have decimated the bonds and the golem all in one blow. But it would have damaged the dorm, and been an *excessive use of force*. Which meant lots of paperwork, and he'd be unable to question the golem about who had created it, and who might have died for it to live. These were not low-level spells, so even if some kid found a book of necromancy in their parents locked spells cabinet, creating a golem wasn't the same as microwaving a pizza—pop the disk in the box for five minutes and wait. It was a complicated list of ingredients, incantations, and required a high-level witch. This wasn't even a magic studies dorm; no one in the program, although a handful of them belonged to witch families.

How did a couple of jocks create a golem powerful enough to fool teachers, some of whom are witches themselves? How had no one sensed what they did? Or reported anything suspicious? Most of the magic students stayed in the dorms together, but he knew there were a couple dozen spread out across the campus, and the teachers were even more widespread, with almost every professor now having some sort of elemental strength. But no one noticed? Was that a spell, too? Something to mask the presence?

Sei would need to dive into the disaster of the Ascendance records again. The old cult of magic, though mostly disbanded, had collected a lot of questionable written works in their time. Their stockpile of reading spanned a more eclectic mess. But it was extensive, and Sei didn't have that much time to read anymore. Not with a fulltime job, a tenured teaching position at the university, and three kids to raise. He didn't think *Tales of Dark Magic* was ideal bedtime reading, either. Maybe he needed to remedy that.

He glared at the golem from his upside-down position. Blood rushing to his head was making it harder to think. Each use of magic seemed to be siphoned by the golem, even if it was only a hint, and then the binding spell sped up. Having spent years working on the balance of power around a siphon, Sei could detect the nuances of it. He wondered if Sam knew about spells to create siphon powers. Usually, those sorts of spells were temporary or lethal.

The inheritance ceremony transferred power from one individual to the next, but required the death of one caster. Sei couldn't think of any spells that siphoned small bits of power. That was more the act of a born siphon, like Sam Mueller. He hated the fact that he'd have to call the vampire as soon as he got out of this mess, maybe even sooner.

The golem was far enough away, a good ten feet, that it was hard for Seiran to make out the tiny inscription on its forehead, which of course, was in another language.

Latin? It didn't seem to be Latin, although Latin was still the language most commonly used in spell casting. Sei had been studying the language since he was a preteen. His mother had insisted that he memorize and master a lot of the original magic languages. Reading them was much easier than speaking them.

It didn't look Greek either. More Farsi, or something else from the Middle East. And Sei only knew that because Sam had spent a lot of time mastering the language for his work under Maxwell Hart. Max was the master of vampires, so when he demanded, all the little vampires had to follow. Not that Sam was a little vampire. The whole witch *and* vampire thing was a big deal, as it was rare for powers to remain when a person crossed the threshold between life and death. But Sam worked for Max first, only begrudging Sei's company when it benefited them both.

Would Sam know? It was an easy enough question. And a less messy fix to this entire situation. To control the golem and take it over, Sei needed its name. Too bad it hadn't been written in English and said something like "Spot," he would be done and gone. No need then to call the grumpy vampire.

Suck it up, Ronnie. Sei could hear Sam's sarcasm in his head even while it was his brain conjuring up the vampire's reaction. *You'll always need me. Some badass Pillar you are. Trapped by a couple of frat boys and unwilling to blow the place up.*

Asshole, Sei thought.

The weight of his phone dug into his back pocket. The devices were huge now, and his didn't like magic much, as he tended to short them out with magical bursts. Would the trap set it off?

Sei wiggled around to reach his phone, irritated that the ropes kept tightening each time he moved, and then did that weird, jerking, drop and wrap back up. It was not a fun ride at all, rather a startling drop that each time he thought he'd land face first, hands too wrapped up to catch himself, but it was a tease, never quite letting him go. And each trip back up, it wrapped up tighter, making it hard to breathe now. Plus the constant up and down was making him nauseous.

Finally, he got the phone and zoomed in on the forehead of the golem to take a picture. It seemed to be working, but the phone took a long time to send the image to Sam. Sei stared at it, hoping for a quick answer or callback. But he had no idea where Sam was. He could be halfway across the world.

The spell did its weird drop again, this time slapping Sei onto the floor hard enough to knock the breath out of him, and then yanking him back upward to slam into the ceiling. It felt a bit like being in a spider's web, gummed up tight and barely able to move. At least he hadn't dropped the phone. If he didn't get a callback soon, he was going to say screw it all and blast this fucking trap to pieces, property damage or not. Of course, that could mean a rampaging golem minutes later, after it absorbed the power of Sei's spell, but he'd cross that bridge when it happened.

He tried to navigate to a search, but it was hard to do that with one hand. His kids would have been able to do it. Ki was a master of phone stuff. Sakura too. Kaine didn't much care for technology, but could use it because his siblings could.

The phone rang. Sam! Thank all things green and growing.

It took a fun game of how far could Sei twist his fingers in the wrong direction to push a button to get it to not only pick up the phone, but flip it to speaker. Maybe he needed to become one of those douchebags always walking around talking into an earpiece and acting all snooty when someone turned their way. Though he'd probably have lost an earpiece by now.

Another drop, tighten, roll upward. He was not a fan. A few more of these and he would upchuck the bento box meal he'd had for lunch.

"Hello?" Sei called, hoping he hadn't accidentally disconnected the call. Or Sam hadn't hung up in annoyance as he often did.

"Ronnie?"

That stupid nickname would never go away. At least Sam was the only one brave enough to call him that. "Did you get the picture?" Sei asked. Okay talking was bad. Ropes tightened when he talked. He was so going to fuck up whomever created this spell.

"Yeah, why are you messing with golems? You know there are field inspectors to do the dirty work, right?" He sounded as annoyed and sarcastic as usual. Sometimes Sei really wanted to hit him.

Sei fought for air for a minute, trying to breathe shallowly so the ropes didn't tighten further. "Read name?" He gasped out. The ropes tightened again, leaving him breathless, and black spots dancing across his vision. He was running out of time. He had to either take over the golem or destroy it all before he passed out.

"It's stupid. Fucking thing is named Forest. Who names a golem

Forest? I mean, I get it looks like sticks, but it's gotta be mostly clay underneath…" Sam rambled on.

All Sei needed was the name. The second he heard it, he wrapped his power around it, feeling the winding strength of the earth narrow down to the link on the golem. His power grabbed onto the name, a claim and bond that tried to suck magic from him immediately. But he took over control, weaving his strength around it, and scrawling its name in the power. The swirling energy etched through the golem told Sei more than one had died to create it. That was disheartening.

The strangest part was that it felt like the golem wasn't an empty vessel filled with intent, but rather powered with actual souls. That wasn't possible though, was it?

His magic filling the room meant the ropes tightened as though they were going to sever him into pieces. He dropped the phone as his arm went numb, but he kept his power flowing, even while his sight completely blacked out.

The human form was so fragile sometimes. Even his.

He sank into the spells. It was a complicated weave not all that unlike a spider web as he'd thought earlier. Layers of spun design, rolling one on top of another. This wasn't a newbie's experiment. Nor was it some frat boy's wet dream of getting out of schoolwork. A practitioner had cast this mess. Not a mess so much as art.

And Sei memorized it as such. Locking it away, not just inside of his memory, as he'd spent years mastering his vault of internal knowledge, but also within the golem. He tied the creature to himself, taking over the bond to its previous master, and wrapping it in his magic to have a firm grip on the golem's power. With the shifting of the bond, the spell released, wards shattering like a glass window pane, and he hit the floor hard.

Okay, hard enough to knock him out for a minute or two, but not more than that. He groaned and tried to drag himself off the floor. His chest hurt from the compression. Since it wasn't the first time he'd had that feeling, he knew he likely had a couple broken or cracked ribs. By nightfall he'd be covered in bruises, stiff, and hopelessly sore. His phone, however, was going to need to be replaced.

He glared at the protective coating, just as shattered as the screen itself, and the dark screen underneath. "So much for gorilla glass, eh?" Sei said, growling at the phone that was supposed to be unbreakable. "Fuck, Jamie is going to be pissed."

At least the rope ward was broken. He was not a fan. Whoever created that mess really needed to be tied up in it for a lesson in what not to do with wards.

Sei turned to look at the golem who was sitting up on the bed now, looking at him with eyes that were far too alive to be that of the creature. It no longer looked like sticks, but a person, young and male. Sei hoped it wasn't the visage of one of the ones who died to create it.

"Forest," Sei called it by the name it had been given. Once they got back to the office, he would have it show him whose blood had been spilled to create it. Were their souls trapped inside? Was that what he was sensing? The underlying awareness of a soul?

Necromancy hadn't been an area he studied much. Most of the magic was hidden from the Dominion as it seemed to appear more in men than in women, and the women still controlled the Dominion. Though spells could be universal, the power wasn't. Maybe whoever cast this spell hadn't been a necromancer, which was why it had started to unravel? Sei only knew of one person to ask.

Which meant another call to Sam. The undead dealt with the dead. "Come with me," Sei instructed the golem. He gathered up the magic items he could find, the rope, a handful of basic books and spell supplies, but found nothing of real significance. If the casters had been living in this room, they kept their good stuff elsewhere. Though he suspected these frat boys had been given this golem. Perhaps they'd bought it? Or it had another means to an end? Since it was bound to Sei now, that meant he could ask a lot of questions. He prayed he could find the creator before they brought another to life.

CHAPTER 3

The box stopped and Gabe had no idea how long he'd been moving. Only that when the lid opened, the lights were too bright, and he smelled blood everywhere. The need to eat tore at his sanity, demanding he break free and devour them all. He was so ravenous he couldn't think straight, his mind focused on the pulsing heartbeats, following each rhythm to place exactly how close or far they were from him.

He growled, lurching for the first who loomed over him, not caring if it fed him or not, only that he was free and could ease the sharp ache in his stomach.

Someone grabbed him. Strong arms clamping down, unyielding, even while blood filled his mouth. He groaned, the flavor bitter and hot as lava going down his throat. This blood was not as strong as the first cup given to him by Sam, but it filled him just the same. Spreading out, bringing life to every vein and cell, he sucked down the hot fluid until the one holding him commanded him to let go.

It took real effort to release that first vein. Even while Gabe gagged on the aftertaste. The lingering hint of... dog?

"It is an acquired taste," the one holding him said. "Now drink from me to regain control." The blood he got this time was dead blood, and Gabe tried to spit it out. But he was held down, and the slimy coldness of it forced down his throat, replaced seconds later with warm fluid life which he gulped at until he thought he'd burst.

The cold blood seemed to circulate slowly, with an almost binding edge, taking a grip on the dark hunger inside him, and shoving it back. It wasn't pleasant, but it didn't really hurt. The heat of the other blood soothed the chill, coating over the bonded layer, filling him with warmth and life, and easing his hunger. It was a strange combination of hot and cold, fire and control, chaos and peace.

Finally, he lay exhausted, so full he couldn't move without contemplating throwing up, but warming as the blood worked its way through him. The aches began to ease, giving rise to a tingling sensation that almost hurt. More as though his limbs were actually awakening for the first time. The cold bond relaxed him, soothing some of the rising panic that had nearly taken him over, and making him sleepy.

"At least he doesn't look dead anymore," Sam said from somewhere to Gabe's left. "Maybe I'm getting old, but he doesn't look like he used to?"

"You don't age, baby," someone told Sam.

Gabe looked over to find Sam curled up on the couch with a pretty young man. Both looked barely legal, and gave him a mess of broken memories if he thought too hard about them. He blinked to ease some of the strain of memories.

"You don't either," Sam said.

"I do. Just not very fast."

Sam stared at Gabe. "He's still thin. Does he need more blood?"

"Time and his Focus will help," a voice said from behind him. That one still held him, the bond tying them together slowly weaving stronger, but not overwhelming. He wasn't sure he liked the feeling of being tied to another like this. It was restraining in a lot of ways, though it kept the dark lingering presence of his revenant quiet.

He flexed a little. Not physically, but with something that felt more intangible. Magic? The bond strained. Gabe felt like he could break it if he worked at it. But the man clamped a hand around his throat and whispered, "Leave that be or I'll have to put you back in the ground."

The hand cut off Gabe's air, and he knew deep down that he didn't really need to breathe, but that didn't stop his brain from freaking out. Gabe let go of the magic and stopped pushing at the bond.

"There you go," the man said. "You're not in control enough to function on your own. Once I'm assured of your sanity, we'll discuss removing it. You don't want to let the beast free to slaughter everyone, do you?"

Gabe shook his head.

"That's what I thought."

He sucked in air when the hand released his throat.

"I like that your steel hasn't been lost. When you went to ground, you'd become little more than a puppet."

"I don't remember," Gabe said. Though he did in small ways. His mind cycled with a thousand jumbled images he couldn't piece together. A broken jigsaw puzzle without a picture to guide its re-creation.

"You will in time."

The physical grip loosened a little, but Gabe wasn't fooled. That hold was unyielding, and ready to put him down if he lunged at anyone. There were actually a half dozen heartbeats in the room. He could clarify them now almost by species. Shifters, which explained the lingering taste of dog he had in his mouth, a witch and a dhampir, as well as Sam and the one holding Gabe, who were vampires.

In a chair across the room was the witch. This one was handsome, covered in tattoos, and trying really hard to keep his attention on a video game he was playing.

"Stinks," the witch said quietly.

"Vampires fresh from the grave do have a smell," said the one Sam was snuggling with. That was the dhampir. Gabe recognized his scent, and vaguely the taste of him. His blood had been in the cup. It made sense then why Sam would be so possessive. They were lovers. What had Sam said his name was? Luca? "I think I'm going to take Con out for a bit." Luca got up. "Pretty sure Max still has work for you," he said to Sam.

Sam growled. "I didn't sign up for vampire babysitting duty."

"You didn't," the voice behind Gabe agreed. "However, if you'll retrieve his witch, perhaps you can pass that duty to him?"

"Fuck," Sam said. "Ronnie is going to be pissed. He's already had a bad day."

"Rou accepted the bond. He must accept all that comes with it."

"Fucking vampires," Sam said, stomping his way to the door.

"*You* are a vampire. You know that, right?" Luca said.

"Not by choice."

Luca patted his shoulder as Con, the witch, took his other hand. The witch wouldn't meet Gabe's eyes. "Is it safe to have him around the kids?"

"He's fed," the one behind Gabe said. "We shall see his control soon enough. Sam will bring Rou, and Rou will decide if he goes back or is allowed to reorient."

"Can he be put back in the ground?" Sam wanted to know.

"Forcefully."

Gabe tried to get up as the idea of going back in the ground was too much at the moment. He recalled waking up and feeling like he was drowning in dirt. The arms around him tightened.

"If he resists, it can still be done. We will work on making him presentable, if you will retrieve his Focus." The arms around him were like a vice, keeping him down despite Gabe feeling like he could rip through walls.

Sam stared at him, not at all afraid to meet his gaze, even as Gabe found the memories too messy to sort through. He knew this man… vampire, whatever, from somewhere. Recognized small bits in his mind, glimpses of him, from different places, and times, yet none of them connected.

"I know you," Gabe muttered. "Somehow?"

"This amnesia thing isn't going to fly with Ronnie," Sam said.

"It's not amnesia as much as him needing to work through a thousand years of memories."

"It will all come back to him?" Con asked, lingering close to the door, but holding Luca's hand tight.

"In time," the voice behind Gabe agreed.

Gabe looked up, straining to see who held him, and mildly confused that the voice sounded familiar. He couldn't help but be a little stunned when he recognized the vampire who held him as the man from his memories of his first kiss. The one he'd watched grow, go off to battle, and die. Yet there he was, exactly the same as those final memories, though clean-shaven, and dressed differently.

Not dead. A vampire. How had that happened? Gabe couldn't even remember how he'd become a vampire. The woman flashed through his brain again. Her image bringing rage to the surface.

"Titus," Gabe whispered, as the arms around him held him down. The name felt right.

"Go get his Focus. I will try to help him find some clarity," Titus said.

"Fuck," Sam cursed again. "Anyone else wanna deliver the bad news to the witch? He doesn't take bad news well these days."

"Rou loved Santini," Con said.

"Past tense verb," Sam said.

"Those last few months were bad," Luca agreed as he opened the door. "Not sure if Santini will remember any of that. Once the revenant takes over, it's all a blur."

"I remember most of mine." Sam said as he followed his lovers out the door.

"Not all of them, but we keep you sane," Luca said.

The door shut behind them, and Gabe was left floundering, feeling weak and very lost. "I…"

"I know," Titus said. "Let's get you cleaned up and ready for your Focus. Perhaps he'll help you fit the puzzles back into place."

"You were dead…"

"I am dead. As are you. Undead. I am also no longer Titus, as you are no longer Gavriil. Not that either of those names are what history remembers. Your sire is dead by your own hand. And that was long ago. You belong to someone else now."

Gabe wasn't sure he wanted that. To be someone else, lost in a world he couldn't piece together. Titus hauled him to his feet and dragged him toward a bathroom.

"We'll start with the stink of the grave," Titus said. "Getting you clean will go a long way in appeasing the witch."

"We aren't supposed to touch witches," Gabe whispered.

"Sirenia had strange rules. Likely because her mate had a fondness for the blood of witches. I find the bite a bit intense, plus the upkeep is not particularly worth it as they are high strung by nature."

Sirenia. Gabe's sire. Those pieces fell into place. He even caught a glimpse of her death. His head throbbed. He heard water begin to run, and the steam of a hot shower slowly filled the room. Gabe concentrated on the growing mist, sucked the dampness into his lungs and tried to clear all the mess from his head.

"I'm married to a witch?" Gabe whispered. He was dragged to the center of the floor in the shower and left there. The water began to pelt him. But it eased to a gentle warm rain a few seconds later. His skin began to awaken, and he realized he was nude, and obviously very dirty as the water streamed off of him in muddy rivulets.

"You never actually completed the deed. Though he is your Focus. Human laws are unsigned, but the bond between you can only be broken by true death. You decide as to whether or not you're married."

"A male witch?"

"It is not as uncommon as you might think."

Gabe bowed his head into the torrent of water. The dirt streamed over his face, water warm and soothing. He touched his face, startled at the beard growth which seemed unfamiliar.

"Once you're clean, we can shave it if you like." Titus moved around the room, setting out clothes and some toiletry items. Gabe had to work to sort through the memories to place those things.

"Brain is slow..." Gabe muttered.

"And that is normal. You were down a long time."

He tried to remember the last time he'd gone to ground. It had been a few weeks during the plague. He'd been starving, but unable to find food that hadn't been infected. And the few vampires he knew who'd taken from the dying wound up suffering for days in agony. "How long?"

Titus appeared thoughtful. "Thirteen years or so. You'll have to ask your witch for certain."

Over a decade. That was a lot of time to miss. And he still had a lot of memories to sort through. He also couldn't recall feeling this weak the last time he'd gone to ground. "Why am I so weak?"

"You were absorbed back into the earth. Not all of us are down long enough for that to happen. I've heard the recovery time is longer."

"Absorbed by the earth..."

"Your witch's element is earth."

"Did he put me in the ground?" Gabe's right arm suddenly ached. He could vaguely recall it crumbling as branches or something ate away at it.

"No."

That was very firm. Gabe sighed. His head pounding. Too many memories trying to find a place at once. It hurt more than he thought any memories should, even scattered ones.

"It will all come back," Titus assured him.

"Does he hate me? This witch of mine?" Gabe wondered.

"Possibly."

That didn't bode well. "And he's powerful."

"He's the Pillar of Earth. None more powerful in the world. At least of the accepted magics."

Well, fuck. Gabe sank down to rest his forehead on the floor. He'd never been one to run away, but he felt like maybe now was the time to start.

"You and I were lovers once," Gabe whispered.

"In our mortal days. We tried briefly after being turned. Though, as most of our kind, that ended badly. Vampires rarely spend eternity with other vampires. Our cold blood and prickly natures don't lend well to relationships. We seek the living because they are life and warmth, rather than just blood. I go by the name Maxwell Hart now. You may call me Max. And you are Gabriel Santini, also known as Gabe. Once we experience our first death, we leave many names behind, but you've used Gavriil and Gabriel for most of the last millennia. Does any of that help?"

Gabe caught the image of a bar, a loft, an apartment, places, empty, and again that face, partially hidden from his memory. Long dark hair? His witch perhaps? "Bonded to a witch…"

"You loved him once," Max said. "Maybe you'd already been very far gone. Tresler's scheme had been building for years. It's likely he'd begun to take control of you before you met the witch."

Tresler. Another face. Vampire. And the memory of him dying, head severed as plants devoured every bit of him. Had Gabe's witch done that? It had snapped something inside of Gabe, awoken him to pain so intense that even now he gasped at the strength of it. The memory of his arm being so badly damaged, taken over by earth magic and slowly feeding on him as the earth often did. And emotionally, that was too much. His brain felt like exploding into a saturation of light, and leaving it all behind.

He didn't want to remember that kind of pain. Would anyone?

"Who killed Tresler? My witch?"

"Sam," Max answered. "Borrowing your witch's power, and awakening to his own."

Sam, the vampire with sarcasm on speed dial. He hadn't seemed all that powerful.

"Don't let him fool you. Sam is a witch as well as a vampire. A very rare type of witch. He is a siphon as well as a fire witch. And while he may breathe irritation and snark, Rou is a good friend of his. If you were to break bonds with me, Sam would put you down permanently to protect his friend," Max said.

"Rou is my witch." Gabe clarified.

"Seiran Rou, Pillar of Earth, head of the Department of Magical Investigations at the Dominion, is your Focus."

The Dominion brought up a handful of scattered and startling images. None of them good. "The Dominion is a cult?"

"In a lot of ways, yes. Though it is as accepted nowadays as Christianity."

"And as destructive?"

"Yes," Max agreed.

"Fuck."

CHAPTER 4

It took Sei longer to get home than he had hoped it would. Long enough that his stomach growled the whole way, and he ended up calling a cab because he hurt too much to drive. The department clinic had looked him over and found nothing life threatening, just lots of bruising. And he'd called ahead from the office phone to let Jamie and Kelly know he would be late getting home.

Sei would heal. Maybe he'd even spend a few hours napping in the arboretum to help the bruising fade faster. The space, which was a firm connection to his element, could heal just about anything. The memory of being shot in the head and landing on the ground of that very same arboretum flashed through his mind. He shoved it away, unwilling to deal with bad memories and unresolved emotions after such a terrible day.

Sakura had called back right afterward to promise dinner would be ready. Not that she cooked. She didn't have the patience. Though she'd help her brothers, and even if Sei was just eating a frozen pizza warmed in the oven, it was plenty of work off his plate to end his long day. His kids being old enough to do basic house stuff like clean and cook was both a perk and a bane. Sometimes dinner got burned or thrown in the trash. Clothes turned pink in washers, or groceries were left out too long. It was part of learning how to be independent people, so Sei didn't let it get to him too much.

The mothering he got from his own kids, however, was not something he enjoyed at all.

It was Jamie's fault. His brother treated him like a kid still, so his own kids had adopted the concern. That somehow, Sei didn't know how to feed himself and keep from going nuts thanks to all the magic he contained, while still keeping the world in balance. It was annoying to say the least.

When he walked in the door, Ki was scowling.

"What?" Sei asked. Ki's red hair looked a mess, standing up like he'd been pulling on it. Mizuki was Sei's worrier. And far too observant for a fourteen-year-old. All of them in their teens now, Sei had waited for the terrible teens to arrive. And they sort of had. Only not with boys who refused to shower or leave their room, or girls who kept secrets in diaries, but with them hovering over him. They also had a really bad habit of talking back to him. Karma, Sei's mother informed him. Though he thought she'd always deserved his attitude, whereas he didn't think he'd garnered the same level from his own kids.

"You got hurt at work again."

"Bruised mostly. Already been to medical. I'm fine. I need food and a shower." The smell of the frat house lingered. That unwashed, stale pizza and beer smell which made Sei a bit nauseous despite his overwhelming hunger.

"Four cracked ribs and a possible fractured wrist," Forest said from behind Sei, making him let out a long groan. The kids didn't need to know that.

Ki's eyes widened as he took in the golem. Forest actually didn't look like a golem anymore. He'd taken the form of some long dead person he'd found a picture of in one of the books sitting in the waiting room. But Sei knew his kid saw right through the guise. The shift was good. Bonding to Sei had restored the strength of its glamour so it no longer seemed to be coming apart. Even Sei had to peer at the golem from under his lashes, letting the edges trail across his sight before he could see the weird ripple of magic that indicated it was not what it seemed. Ki had always been a bit more in tune to his magic. He also hadn't spent his childhood trying to hide it. None of Sei's kids had. Which meant they all controlled and understood magic like it was the air they breathed. Some days, that wasn't a good thing.

"What is that?" Ki demanded. He looked around frantically. "The wards aren't reacting."

"It's a golem. And tied to me. No, they wouldn't react."

"Dad…"

"It's fine," Sei promised. "He's safe with me."

"Does Uncle Jamie know?"

"Yes, actually, he does. I called him from the office, which is why your sister said she'd make me food. Is there anything edible? I'm starving."

"And smelly," Kaine said as he came up beside his brother. Kaine was… fae. Sometimes Sei would find the human in him, the part that was tied to the human world, but he was fae all the way around. It meant that at ten-years-old he mirrored the twins in growth both physically and mentally. Not because he had to, as Sei suspected his fae form was much older—since crossing the veil did funny things to time—but because he didn't want to be different than his siblings.

"Sorry to offend your olfactory senses," Sei said dryly as he made his way toward the stairs. "I plan to shower first, then find food. Frat stink is something all of you should strive to avoid."

"Jamie made homemade chicken katsu for you. A broccoli slaw salad to go with it," Ki said.

Thank the Earth Goddess for Jamie. Sei's stomach grumbled at the thought of crispy panko fried, miso marinated chicken, and the spicy slaw. He almost turned around and went to the kitchen instead. But he stunk, and he had a golem to keep track of.

"Forest, come," Sei commanded, insisting it follow him up the stairs. He didn't want to leave it alone around his kids, just in case. The bond seemed solid, but he hadn't been able to trace it to its source. And he hadn't severed the original tie because he needed to find its creator.

They made it all the way to the door to Sei's room before another voice stopped them.

"Sei," Jamie called. If he hadn't made a dinner Sei was dying to eat, Sei would have screamed. Cursed. Called him names. All the stuff he had wanted to scream the moment after getting caught in that trap but had convinced himself to hold in. A Rou was poise and polish, power and prestige. Sei fucking hated being a Rou. If he had been able to save his kids from the tie to it, he would have changed their names in a heartbeat. But even when Jamie annoyed Sei, he loved his brother and tried not to give him his foul temper if Sei could help it.

But he needed a shower and food. Stat.

Slowly Sei turned Jamie's way, his whole body throbbing in agony that he was certain a hot shower would soothe. Jamie stood there, his long hair pulled back and arms folded across his chest, shoulders wide and strong. Jamie was a big guy that would make anyone hesitate to get snippy. The lanky blond at his side never seemed intimidated. Guess that was why they'd been married almost a decade.

"You look like shit," Kelly said.

"Smell like it too," Jamie wrinkled his nose. "Sad if even I can smell it." He sniffed. "Frat boy sheik?"

"Ha ha," Sei waved at them. "Do you know how many empty pizza boxes and beer cans are in most dorms? I shudder to think of the roaches and rat feces I am probably covered in. Go away. I need a shower and food."

"I've got golem duty," Kelly volunteered, walking up to Forest and staring at him. "Eerie how lifelike it looks."

"I need to look you over," Jamie demanded.

"Creepy," Sei said. "You're my brother."

"And a doctor," he reminded.

"Nurse Practitioner," Sei clarified, as though that meant anything less. "I've already been checked by medical."

Jamie walked around Sei to open the door to the room. "Then you won't mind if I double check their work."

Sei sighed, too tired to care. "Forest, obey Kelly until I return," he gave the golem a firm command. The creature's gaze fastened on Kelly, watching and waiting. It looked ordinary, though the clothes it wore were a little big as we'd taken things from the lost & found to clothe it. It *was* eerie how lifelike it looked. Not normally Kelly's expertise, since golems were a mix of earth magic and death magic. But he'd be fine. Water could take apart clay easily enough.

Sei didn't bother waiting in his bedroom, instead he made his way to the large bathroom, turned on the water in the shower, and began to strip. Jamie watched with a clinical gaze, assessing. Sei saw him flinch at the bruises, as they began to be revealed in the large section of mirror above the far sink. Sei looked like a big bruise. At least he hadn't lost any teeth, though half his face was mottled with purple and blue.

"Did they do a full scan, check for hairline fractures? A possible concussion?" Jamie wanted to know. Sei stood before him, nude, but uncaring. Jamie didn't look at Sei as anything other than his little brother. Well, maybe as a patient, too. Jamie was a bit obsessed with Sei's health. But Sei had been doing a good job of taking care of himself. Mostly.

"Cracked ribs," Sei said. "Nothing else broken." It wouldn't kill him. Nothing really could.

Jamie was not happy with the discoloration in Sei's left arm. Part landing, part being twisted up in the net, that arm ached. But Sei had broken bones before, and had many a sprain or strain. This felt like bruising, nothing more. The scan of it hadn't shown anything broken, even if it throbbed with a dull ache.

"It's not broken or anything, just bruised. I know the difference," Sei said.

"A golem? Should have sent someone else to take care of it."

"Yeah? Like who? My best people are running around the world saving lives. Should I call them back? A new researcher? A first-year field agent? How many witches do you know who can handle a golem? Have ever seen or met one before?"

"Had you?" Jamie wanted to know as his fingers drifted over Sei's ribs, gently probing for issues.

"No," Sei admitted. "Read about them. It's more Sam's area than mine." The vampires took care of a lot of the darkest bits of magic, and not all of those stories got back to Sei or the Dominion. He was beginning to wonder if that was something he needed to fix sooner rather than later, even if his plate was already full.

"Yet you decided to take it on alone."

"I'm the Pillar of Earth," Sei reminded him.

"And not invincible. I'd also like you to not be the Pillar of Earth."

Sei sighed, the humid warmth of the shower spray, a siren song of desire right that minute. "Still here. And I don't have a death wish. Though I'd like to beat the shit out of the bastard who cast those wards. Can I shower now?"

"Yes. But keep me updated. You feel dizzy, or anything, let me know."

"Sure, sure," Sei said. "Now get out." He headed into the shower, too tired to care about being nice. If he hadn't been so damn hungry, he'd have skipped dinner and gone right to bed. "Thanks for dinner."

"I'll warm it up for you." Jamie left the bathroom. Sei put his face under the spray. It hurt a little, but the warmth also soothed something cold in his gut. Worry?

The shower was a sprawl of stone, wide enough to fit several people, while drowning anyone not paying attention to the multiple showerheads. He preferred to start with the rainfall overhead. And since his body hurt like he'd taken a beating, the gentle fall of heat didn't make him scream in agony. Sei stood under the water, eyes closed, swaying slightly. He could almost hear a song. Not a voice per se, but a humming. Familiar, but still a long distance away. If he let himself drift far enough, linger on the edge of sleep, it almost became real. Sometimes if he let himself dream, he wasn't alone. The memories had faded a lot. More bitter ones kept him from diving too deep.

Life was full of memories. Good, bad, and ugly. He tried to teach his kids that, though they'd had a much easier life than he had. He had never let his mother treat them like she'd treated him. He'd provided for them, while still showing them how to be independent. Which meant the snarky teens would likely only get worse with age. He groaned and tried to turn off his brain a little. He let the wards of the house all connect to him, a flow of earth energy awakening nerves that ached. Healing, though not instant, crawled through him, calming the inner fire and soothing it like a gentle roll of dirt. It wasn't as fast and painless as the garden would have been, but it helped.

He let out a long sigh as the pain in his ribs vanished. One of the few perks of being the Pillar was how well he could heal. He didn't need to roll in the dirt for it to happen, though he found that very enjoyable. In fact, he thought that perhaps after dinner he'd shift into his lynx form, and play for a bit. It was unlikely he'd get to do it alone, as the fae watched him and Kaine would likely join him. But that was okay. Sometimes it was easier for his cat self to let go of all the human trouble rather than let himself stew in it. And he could see the release helping him sleep.

Sei turned the water off, dried himself slowly, examining the remaining bruising in the mirror. His face only held a hint of discoloration, and his chest still had the yellow edges of it, though when he poked at the area he knew had been cracked ribs, it felt fine. He could also breathe again and not cringe. That was a plus. Now he just needed some food and sleep.

He tugged on a pair of sleep pants and T-shirt, making his way downstairs, following the scent of food. In the kitchen, Kelly sat at the table with Forest, though Kelly was browsing his phone and Forest seemed to be staring at Kelly.

"It's creepy," Kelly said without looking up. "But you told him I was in charge so that's his only focus."

"Maybe we can put him on housework," Jamie said as he held out a plate full of amazing food.

Sei took the plate, breathing in the amazing smell of it. He grabbed a fork from the drawer and didn't bother to sit down before shoving a giant slice of chicken in his mouth. He couldn't help it. He'd sort of learned the shovel effect from his kids. They didn't eat with delicate grace. Food went in their pie holes as fast as they could get it there. And he was so hungry, he just didn't care.

He swallowed. "We'd have to be really careful with how the command is worded. Once I know who created him, I'll have to unravel the spells." He didn't mention that he suspected there were mortal souls tied to those spells. The debate over souls versus energy was an ever ongoing one. Religion versus the Dominion. Sei had no real stance, only that he knew there was something there. Was it aware? Or just some energy? He'd seen his father's ghost on many occasions, sometimes in memory like replays, and often it felt intelligent and reactive.

"This was what was causing all that trouble on campus?" Jamie asked as he leaned against the counter.

Sei nodded. "I suspect they were given the golem, though the spellwork might have been theirs. I'll question them tomorrow. The police are supposed to bring them in."

"This is some big magic for a couple kids not in the magic program," Jamie pointed out like Sei hadn't thought of that.

"Not kids," Sei said. Though Jamie had hit fifty, he didn't look older than thirty-five, or maybe Sei was just off as he'd gotten older too. Witches lived, on average, twice the mortal lifespan, so realistically they were all still kids, if they had witchblood at all. "They are all in their twenties."

"You're old, babe," Kelly teased his husband. Jamie mock growled at him. "I still think you're hot. Even if you haven't gone silver."

Jamie was just as blond as he'd always been, though his hair wasn't as long anymore, it was barely shoulder-length. He had that sort of yellow brown shade of blond that looked good with his permanently tanned skin provided by his Native American mother. Sei and Jamie shared a father, but there wasn't much of Dorien Merth in his face, only a hint in the bone structure. Even at fifty-one, Jamie was a handsome man who made people stop and stare.

"You've always had a daddy kink," Sei teased Kelly.

Kelly laughed. "True. He can be my daddy anytime."

"Gross," Ki said as he passed through the kitchen. "Grown-up sex talk."

Sei narrowed his eyes at his kid. "It's different from teenage sex talk?"

Ki shook his head. "You don't do sex talk. Just Uncle Jamie and Uncle Kelly. It's not as weird or gross when it's Sam, Luca, and Con."

"Are they doing sex talk around you guys?" Jamie wanted to know.

"They live and breathe sex," Kura said appearing in the opposite doorway. She bounded to Seiran and kissed his cheek. "Hi, Daddy. You look better."

"Feel better," Sei said between bites. "Might play in the arboretum before bed."

"I'll tell Kaine." She reached out to touch his face, staring at him with more concern than a fourteen-year-old should have. Her dark hair was pulled back into a thick braid, and she was already showing the girl curves that made Sei have fits when she went out without one of her siblings. The way some men riveted on her made him want to turn them inside out with magic. "Sam called. Said he's on his way over. Was mad that you weren't answering your phone. I told him it got broken."

"He going to take over the golem?" Kelly asked.

But that wasn't something Sam normally did. He could take out the golem, burn it up and rip the death magic out of it, but he couldn't unravel the mystery, and Sei needed to find the creator before any of that happened.

"I have no idea," Sei said. He grabbed Sakura's palm and kissed it before taking his empty plate to the sink. "Shouldn't you be in bed? Beauty sleep and all that? It's a school night."

"It's not that late. We have a test tomorrow."

"And studying last minute will help how?" Sei narrowed his eyes at his twins.

"It's not last minute," Ki protested. "We are just reviewing the chapter. We've done all the work."

"We have," Kura agreed. "Kaine could probably ace this too. I just want it fresh in my head." She held her arms out. "Besides we are already ready for bed." And they both were in their pajamas, which was good since it was after ten.

"Where is Kaine?" Sei wanted to know, having not seen his youngest since before he got in the shower.

"With his father," Ki said. "Bryar popped in after you vanished upstairs. Kaine's been in a mood."

"I'll talk to him," Sei promised. Kaine was sort of moody by nature. It was likely a fae thing as they were all sort of quick to jump to extreme ends of emotion. If something was bothering Kaine, Sei would have to call Bryar to work it out. He suspected it was difficult straddling two worlds. Even more so for someone as young as Kaine. Sei tried hard not to demand too much of his youngest. Kaine was a bit scattered on the best of days, but could be hyper-focused if necessary.

Could a magical being have ADHD? Sei would have to call the

child therapist he had the kids see a couple times a year, and ask. Maybe she would have ideas to help Kaine.

The front door opened. Sei felt his wards ripple. It was a bit of welcoming and hesitation. His power said yes, we know these people, and still caution, there is power here. Sam.

"Seiran Rou," Sam growled as he came into the kitchen like he owned the place. The trio had their own place now. In fact, several, as Luca had a skill for making money, and his lovers spent time working at various things that seemed to always do well for them. Sam had often said over the years that he felt Luca and Con had broken the curse he'd lived most of his life under. Sei began to think he needed someone to break his, too.

"Please come in," Sei snarked.

Sam still looked barely legal. A perk of being a vampire. He didn't age. Since Sei was tied to a vampire, he shouldn't have aged either. Though since his vampire had gone to ground some time back, that meant the link was strained and barely existent most days, and Sei had actually grown up. More than just physically, though he had almost two inches in height on Sam now. At five-foot-eight, Seiran was far from the most imposing figure in the room. Sei felt like he didn't look like a kid anymore, and his Asian heritage meant he also didn't look thirty-six, but Sam would be forever young, nineteen, and unfinished. At least Sei felt like his body had a chance to do whatever the fuck it was going to do. Even if that didn't mean he got muscles like Jamie or the lanky height of Sam's lover, Constantine.

"Thanks for your help with the golem thing," Sei muttered, hating having to say those words which he knew would give the vampire power over him.

"Are those frogs on your pajamas?" Sam wanted to know.

"They were a gift from my kids for solstice."

"Frogs?"

"Not all of us dress like we play a bad guy on a TV show," Sei snarked, motioning to Sam's leather jacket.

"I don't *play* a bad guy."

Seiran nodded. "Right. I forgot. Sam Mueller, big and bad, terror of mankind or at least vampire kind. Watch me tremble in fear."

Sam looked stern for a minute. Once upon a time, he had been a sort of doppelganger for Seiran. Though he was Chinese, and Sei was part Japanese, their similarities had been numerous. Both being Asian, slender, and pretty. A history of loving the wrong men had been a trait they shared that Seiran wished they hadn't. Although Sam had two guys who were his constant now. They grounded him in a way that Sei missed having. He couldn't recall if he'd ever felt that same edge of calm that Sam lived in these days, but he had fantasies about it. Being a single dad, even with all the help he got, and head of an important global department of magic, as well as the Pillar of Earth, put a strain on him most people would never understand.

It was why he often retreated into his lynx. He never left the arboretum when shifted. It was a rule. He was too easily lost in the earth, worries simplified to the animal nature, giving him peace he rarely experienced.

The two of them had little in common anymore. Sam's short hair, shaved on the sides and long on top, was maintained at his lover's insistence, and he still dressed in a lot of jeans and leather. He was handsome in a bit of a mobster sort of way, mostly because it turned Luca on for Sam to look like a bad guy.

Sam's scowl turned to a grin. "Anyone tell you you're too old to be in an Asian boy band?"

Sei's hair was a messy mop that didn't quite reach his shoulders. A crazy bit of curl had appeared when he let it grow a bit, but without the added weight of having it long. It had also lightened over the years, taking on a touch of the golden brown of Jamie's blond tones beneath the dark brown Sei had been gifted from his father. He didn't think he was as pretty as he'd been in his younger days. Yeah, Asian boy band material? Not so much.

Seiran nodded. "Yep, can't sing either. I dress mostly for work."

"You sing just fine. Frog jammies are work requirements?"

"Frog jammies are 'I'm going to bed' wear. Aren't you working? Shouldn't you be in a suit? Or is thug sheik on the menu for your guys tonight?"

"Ronnie," Sam groused.

"Sammie," Sei grumbled back. "I already thanked you for helping me bind the golem. Unless you've got a book stashed in those too tight pants of yours about golems, I am planning on taking myself for a bit of a spin around the garden and then to bed."

"You wish you knew what was in these pants."

"Not without substantial eye bleach."

"I'm hot," Sam defended.

"Not my type."

"No. True. You like them tall and blond."

Seiran didn't really like much of anything these days. He wondered if Luca and Con would be bursting through the door too, or if he would just be blessed with the vampire tonight. "If you're not here to give me info about the golem, why are you here?"

Sam finally turned to stare at the golem, as though he'd just noticed it for the first time. "You brought the fucking golem home?" Sam asked incredulous.

"What else am I supposed to do with it?"

"Um, leave your work at work?"

"Right, 'cause you do that all the time?" Seiran said. "Who brought me pixies thinking they'd mix with the fairies?"

"How was I to know pixies and fairies have some sort of intrinsic hatred of each other?"

"Research?"

"That's your job. I'm a problem solver. And my problem was solved by removing the pixies."

Which Seiran had then had the work of finding a new home before his own became a war zone. They now lived in a nice garden maze in the UK somewhere, with lots of signs around it to keep humans away. Pixies didn't like humans much and were carnivorous. Much like gnomes, they couldn't really be around the human population without causing trouble.

"Vampires know exotic pets have to be cleared through Max now," Sam continued. "No pixies, gnomes, griffins, or gargoyles. Funny how much of this shit I used to think was all make believe."

Better off for most humans to believe that. It kept them out of trouble. "Yeah, well, someone found magic to create a golem by sacrificing three lives. I'll be able to question the guys using it tomorrow. But I suspect it was sold to them, possibly one of them bound to it with a minor spell, which was why the glamour was unraveling."

Sam blinked at the golem, studying it. "Nice cover. Boring. Forgettable. The magic is tight."

"He's had my power to refuel him. Which means he's not unraveling anymore. At least until I take the spell apart." He was human looking. Though in reality *he* wasn't correct as golems were genderless. The persona Forest had chosen appeared male. But since there was something in there other than magic and sticks, Seiran felt wrong calling him an it. Like somehow it would erase the lives lost to create the being.

The department media group had taken snapshots of Forest using the image of each of the three who had been murdered to create the golem. The shifting of its glamour to each of them insanely accurate, believable, and disheartening. Well, all but the third who appeared blurry and undefined. For the first two they had names, and addresses, even rambling about things each of them had liked in life. The third was male, dark hair, but it was all they could get out of him before the golem turned combative, which made Seiran shut down the questioning likely before they should have. How much of those souls were trapped inside? He didn't want to think about that. The more he stewed on it, the more he wanted to unravel it.

Did it know who created it? Yes. Could it tell them? No. More magic. Spelled not to divulge things. More spells woven in unfamiliar ways. In fact, even trying to unravel the golem to free the souls bound to it, was a maddening mess of attempting to complete a puzzle in a language they didn't know. Sei had the entirety of the Department of Magic researching. He could force the earth to take it back, but it might not unbind the souls. Not everyone was convinced they were souls. Seiran had seen enough to make him think it was more than simple energy. He didn't want to chance leaving them locked in some sort of stasis for the rest of eternity.

Seiran couldn't leave the thing locked up within the Dominion walls, hoping the golem didn't get out or let someone else in. The tie to his creator had to be severed too, or else they might break through any lesser witch's hold. Which meant Sei had to bring it home with him.

His wards were strong enough to keep anyone out, and the binding he'd wrapped around the golem should keep the golem from being called out by anyone else. It was as safe as he could make it. As long as he kept the golem near him. Which meant he probably wasn't going to get much sleep tonight.

Sam frowned. "This is really bad timing."

Was a golem ever good timing?

"I need you to come with me to see Max," Sam said.

Seiran glanced down. "Pa-Ja-Mas."

"Whatever. Max won't care. You just have to come with me now."

Leaving the house was the last thing Sei wanted to do. If he couldn't play in the garden before bed, at least he'd like to snuggle up with his kids for some dumb movie or even hold them while they fell asleep. Wow, he was feeling old tonight. Sure, still healing, but that couldn't be all of it?

"Can't we do this another night?"

"No," Sam folded his arms across his chest.

"I am not a vampire lackey."

"Actually, you are," Sam said.

"Gabe is gone." It still hurt saying his name. Memories of those last few months too hard for words most days. Sei wanted to remember his boss at the bar instead of the lover he wasn't sure had ever been real. And a decade and a half was a long time to be alone.

"That's the problem, Ronnie. He's back."

CHAPTER 5

The car ride gave Sei a long time to stew. There had been a bit of an instant uprising in the house with his kids, his brother, and Kelly protesting, which had riled up the bond on the golem.

Negative emotions and death magic didn't seem to mix. Good to know. However, it also meant Forest sat next to him in the backseat, Sei in the middle, Sam on the other side of him. The car was driven by one of Maxwell Hart's many hired drivers. Seiran kept his hold and attention firmly on the golem. He would have to spend more time researching it. Was there a way to stop negative emotions from feeding it, or was that simply how golems worked? Perhaps it was another spell he had never encountered. The stack of new magic he was discovering today was bordering on uncomfortable.

His power should have been enough to hold it, no matter what. Didn't earth surpass death? Staring at Sam's reflection in the glass, Sei thought, maybe not.

Sei hadn't changed clothes, instead choosing to shove on a pair of garden Crocs and follow Sam out the door. Since the house was far outside of the city, and Hart haunted downtown, it was a long drive.

"You're too quiet, Ronnie," Sam said staring out the window.

But Seiran wasn't sure what he felt. Numb, mostly? Confused? The storm of emotion he'd received from his family had been intense. For himself, he couldn't really concentrate on a specific feeling. He had dreams from time to time. A stirring of memories, sometimes good, sometimes bad. In truth, he'd given up hope years ago, not only of Gabe's return, but of any semblance of not being alone forever.

Which was a little unfair, because his kids, his brother, and his friends, were his life. And he was never alone, from family to work, to the earth that fueled his power. He didn't date. Not that he felt he couldn't, more that it simply felt strange. The few times he'd tried it had ended in disaster, so he had stopped trying at all. Men flirted with him, he'd had a dozen offers from powerful witch families for an official marriage and more kids. As if he needed that kind of work and a loveless tie to people he didn't like—not the kids, the witch families. In truth, he chose loneliness a lot of days, finding it more soothing than memories of things lost.

"I don't know what to feel," Sei admitted quietly. "How is he?" Did he even care? Yes. And wasn't that terrible? Those last days, the betrayal, and then that final memory of Gabe giving himself back to the earth, letting go so as to not hurt Sei. Conflict of emotions, okay that was a bit of a battle Sei hadn't expected. Too much all at once to figure out when he was tired and drained from a long day.

"He's different. Doesn't even look all the same. Max says it will take time for him to be like he was," Sam said. "Memories scattered, a lifetime of puzzle pieces, I guess."

A millennia of puzzle pieces then, Sei thought, since Gabe had been one of the oldest vampires still alive. "He doesn't remember me?" What a startling thought that was. Gabe having been such a huge part of Sei's life, only to have been such a small one for the vampire, that he'd been forgotten.

"Yes, no? Maybe? He said vampires don't touch witches. Seemed to be remembering his sire…" Sam paused, then added, "and Max."

"Max or Titus?" Sei asked. Maxwell Hart had been Gabe's first love. In retrospect, Sei had learned that when Gabe had gone to ground, but never confronted the vampire about it.

"Titus," Sam said.

The knot in Sei's gut tightened.

"You know Max isn't interested. He's got that shifter fetish down tight. Doesn't even mind the smell. Their blood has the taste of dog. I don't know how it doesn't bother him. The smell alone makes me gag most days." Sam rambled, something he rarely did, but Sei tried to pay attention to his voice instead of the chaos of rising emotion. "Ronnie?"

"What?"

"You don't have to be what you were before," Sam said.

"I'm his Focus."

"Which doesn't have to be sex or romance, or more than just a partnership. A partnership with boundaries and rules."

Sei sucked in a deep breath. He knew that a Focus didn't have to mean romance, or even friendship. Vampires in the old days used to find the most powerful warriors and bind them just to gain power themselves. He'd spent the last decade and a half reading everything he could find on vampires and their lore. Some of it provided by Max, most of it buried deep in the bowels of the Dominion libraries. Witches were not encouraged to bind with vampires. But Gabe had been his first real love. Not his first relationship, or even first sexual partner, not by far, but real love. To think about being tied to him, and that emotion forever lost? Not possible. No matter how much it hurt.

And wasn't that a terrible realization, that despite everything, the betrayal, the years alone, the self-doubt that any of it had been real, Sei still loved him. He didn't even know if Gabe would ever be that person again. And still his heart stuttered at the memory of Gabe's smile, or the way he held him.

He had cried a long time after Gabe had gone to ground. Never in front of his family. They didn't need to see his weakness. Jamie had been uncharitable enough, wanting to destroy everything that had been Gabe's. Sei didn't have the tears anymore. Or at least was unwilling to release them.

"Ronnie?" Sam asked quietly.

"Fuck you," Sei growled.

"You wish."

"Not without serious brain reprogramming." Sei sat very still, staring out the front of the car like it was fascinating. He knew the answer before he asked, but had to ask anyway, "Is there a way to break the Focus bond?"

"Other than true death? No," Sam said. "And could you maybe wait until one of your kids is old enough to step in as Pillar before you jump off something high?"

Sei sighed heavily. "I wouldn't do that." Not that it would kill him anyway. His tie to the earth meant he lived until it was done with him. Since he was still nestled firmly in the strength of the Mother's power, he doubted that would be any time soon.

He couldn't imagine putting that burden on one of his kids. Or the grief of his death. He'd been thankful they were all too young to remember Gabe, and so they hadn't had to think of him as dead, as Sei had. They simply didn't know him at all, or as anything other than rare mentions in old stories. Better that way, it had to be, because it was all Sei could give them of the man who had abandoned him.

"Maybe you should have brought the fairy?" Sam said after another long stretch of silence.

"Kaine is having some issues. I think Bryar is dealing with that."

"Not sure Bryar has the most objective ideas when it comes to child rearing."

He didn't. But Kaine was more fae than human, and Sei could only help with so much. It was a variance of magic as well as a lack of the physical mortality that Sei's other kids had. Kaine created magic with thought, spells and wards were unnecessary. He lived and breathed magic, was created from magic itself. Sei understood the difference. He straddled those worlds himself. His ability as the Pillar of Earth meaning he didn't need a lot more than intent. But that wasn't how the rest of the world worked.

Witches used spells. The fact that Sei and Kaine didn't, made them the quirky ones. Even Kelly who was the Pillar of Water, used spells, incantations, and wards. He had some unstructured magic, but the bulk of his abilities were directed by the symbolism they'd grown up learning.

"Bryar is very black and white," Sei said. Much like fae in general, no matter the power level or branding, they were all a bit cold and very literal. He loved Kaine, but sometimes relating to him, or making him understand, felt like shoving the Taj Mahal through the eye of a needle. Impossible.

"I'm working on Kaine. He is trying. That's all I can ask." Sei almost added that Kaine was just a kid, as he was younger than the twins, but that wasn't true either. Fae weren't born as babies, not in the way humans were, or even witches who had longer lives. Time across the veil was completely different, which meant for all Seiran knew, Kaine could have lived a thousand years already.

They rode in silence a bit longer.

Sam sighed. "That golem is creepy."

"You've dealt with golems before," Sei pointed out. Sam more often than Sei. They drove through downtown now. Streets dark and mostly empty. The late spring weather still dropping chilling air at night. He should have brought a coat. Or maybe dressed in more than pajamas.

"Only to set them on fire. Melt the clay, dilute it with water, breaks the spell." Sam stared at Forest who remained mostly motionless but looking human. The golem didn't react at all to the idea of being destroyed. Seiran was certain he could unravel the spells binding him rather than outright destroying the golem, but not until he located the one who had created it. At least that was something he could focus on.

"Does Max have books on necromancy?"

"Maybe?" Sam shrugged. "He's got that big vault of stuff that the rest of us don't get to see much, including a list of all the vampires in existence. But you can ask."

"Is he more likely to say yes to me, or to Luca?" Sei asked, wondering if Luca, one of Sam's lovers who also happened to be Max's son, might have more access.

"We'll ask and see, yeah?" Sam said. The car pulled into the parking garage of a luxury high rise, which didn't surprise Sei at all. Max never stayed in one place long. He'd been in Minneapolis for a while, and had taken over St. Paul when Gabe had gone to ground. But he traveled enough that he bounced place to place rather than nesting anywhere.

The driver had them buzzed through the security gate and drove them to a guarded elevator. "Intense security," Sei said. It reminded him of a military base rather than a complex of condos.

"This is a vampire only building. Max uses it for meetings and visiting vampires. He pretty much only stays here now when in town. Feels a bit like a prison to me." Sam said. The car slowed to a stop and the driver got out to open the door.

This area of town was more the CEO end of the high-rises. It was a little shocking to find a vampire specific building standing in the middle of it all. Max was a CEO of a couple dozen businesses, some bigwig in the business world. He had money, power, and the attitude to go with them. He'd taken over running a lot of Gabe's businesses, and Sei had been grateful. Sei did not have a business degree nor did he care for all the upkeep, but he did have a growing stream of revenue from all those businesses that far outweighed what he made at the Dominion. Would Gabe be able to take over his businesses again? What about the bar? Sei still worked there some weekends to clear his head of all the bullshit red tape of the magic world.

"There's just so much," Seiran muttered. "Not the best time."

"Never is, Ronnie."

They got out and Sam led Sei to the elevator, taking them up to the penthouse. Sei's gut clenched as they traveled higher, the tiny box making it hard to breathe. Or maybe it was the anxiety over having to see him again after all these years.

Gabe's arm sprouted branches, leaves, and flowers, the earth eating away at it. His grip crumbled with his strength as the muscles dissolved into fine particles of earth.

The memory was vivid and intense enough that Sei staggered. Sam steadied him, but said nothing, not even to snark. He did pull a handkerchief out of his pocket and hand it over. Only then did Sei realize tears were falling again. Dammit.

He wiped at his face and sucked in large gulps of air, trying to prepare as the elevator finally stopped at the penthouse, the doors sliding open to the giant space fit for a king. Max always did live large.

"Rou," Max greeted from his spot on the couch across the room. He had a laptop open in front of him and seemed to be centered on it. If there had been shifters there, they were gone now.

Sam stepped out of the elevator first, the guards staying behind. Seiran followed, with Forest trailing behind like some strange magical duckling.

"Interesting," Max said. "Death puppets are complicated."

Of course, he'd recognize the thing. "Do you have books on necromancy I can borrow?" Sei asked, trying not to panic as his heart sped up. Where was Gabe? Would Sei fall apart the second he saw him? Fuck, he was not ready for any of this.

"I'll have to make a few calls." Max's gaze lingered on the golem. "Strong magic."

"It was unraveling," Sei said. "My magic fuels it now."

"Partially," Max agreed. He, as a vampire, didn't really have magic, but he did seem to understand it better than most. The structure portion of mortal magic seemed to appeal to him, so he'd studied it, found and memorized every book he could find on it. Which was why he had a vast library of things not even the

Dominion knew. Some of the darkest books ever written were hidden away in Maxwell Hart's private library.

"I need to find who created it before unraveling it," Sei informed him. "Until then I have to keep control of it."

"It will be easier to control it if you give it blood," Max said. "Everything is so much easier to control with blood."

Fucking vampires and their obsession with blood. Sei was suddenly very tired. "Where is Gabe? I'd like to go home and get some sleep. Some of us have to work regular mundane jobs."

"You don't actually," Max corrected. "I manage your money. You're one of the richest witches in the world, even if you pretend otherwise." He set the computer aside and stood, stretching like he'd been sitting too long. Max was an attractive man, tall, dark, and dangerous. He came across as wealth and sophistication, but underneath was a barely veiled layer of ruthlessness. Sam basked in it, all vampires sort of did, so Seiran didn't blame him, but it made Sei's anxiety rise. "Would it help to hash out your irritation here?" Max prompted.

"Irritation? At what? Being dragged out of my home at this late hour?" Sei folded his arms across his chest. He'd rather deal with a dozen rabid golems than this vampire bullshit.

"At the fact that he and I were once lovers?" Max said without emotion.

"No." The reminder squeezed Sei's heart like it was clenched in someone's fist. Seiran wasn't at all like Max. If Gabe liked men like Max, what did that mean for their relationship? Had it all been a power play? "Are we done here?"

Max crossed the room and slid back one of those giant doors to reveal a room. For a minute Sei was worried Gabe would be naked in bed or something after being thoroughly fucked by Max. But the room wasn't even a bedroom, more of a sitting area with a few bookshelves and several armchairs. Gabe was sitting in one of them, eyes closed, almost appearing to be asleep.

Sei felt stuck in place, chest tight, anxiety rising, all signs of a panic attack which he hadn't had in ages. He concentrated on counting his breathing, taking deep steadying breaths, in and out. He didn't close his eyes or try to shut down, as that would mean a full-scale panic attack, and embarrassment later. He would hate to show that sort of weakness in front of the vampires. Though it was a near thing.

Gabe didn't look the same. Sei could understand what Sam meant about that now. He was a bit thinner, though still wide through the shoulders. His blond hair longer than Sei ever recalled it being, falling around his ears in long curls, but not quite long enough to reach his shoulders. It was also a bit darker, more a dirty blond than the pale wash Sei's memory clung to. And in Sei's entire time of knowing him, he had never known Gabe to have a beard, but now he had a well-trimmed box beard. With his eyes closed, and blond lashes falling over his cheeks, he looked angelic, harmless, even if Sei knew otherwise.

Not the man he knew, Sei tried to remind himself, even as his body reacted, drawn forward with a need to touch. The jeans and long-sleeved T-shirt weren't normal wear either, as Gabe had always preferred a more business style of attire unless he was at the bar. Polish, that had been the Gabriel Santini that Seiran had known. This was something else, vulnerable? Or just pretending.

"Gavriil," Max called, "your Focus has come for you."

Gabe opened his eyes, blinking and taking a deep breath as though he had been napping. He glanced around the room, seeming to size up everyone for a moment before his gaze fell on Sei. The green, vivid and clear, more so than Seiran could recall it having been even on that final day.

"Seiran," Gabe whispered, "I'm so sorry. I love you so much. I didn't mean... I would never hurt you..." But he had. A thousand times over. Gabe bowed his head. He swallowed hard, put his hands back to the earth, then stared at Seiran when he said, "To the earth I commit myself."

The memories, bittersweet, cut like a knife because there was no recognition in his eyes.

CHAPTER 6

The meditation helped. With his stomach full, the warmth awakening all those long immobile nerves, Gabe could relax and sort out his brain. Max had to finish up some business stuff which had been more noise than Gabe could handle as he'd been processing. He'd been given the closed off room for space.

The memories of Titus, well Max now, were the easiest to sort through. The affection and heartbreak all rising as though he were feeling them for the first time again. They did fade as he worked through the memories. For a while there had been an almost impossible to resist urge to interrupt Max and demand attention. Instead, Gabe tried to find more recent memories. Those were more broken, shattered like glass into fragments so small he knew it would take time to put any of it together.

His sire's image brought up a lot of jagged pieces. From her death to a man who'd tried to kill him… Roman. Right. Even those memories were scattered. He wondered if it would have been easier if he'd written things down beforehand. A journal or memoir of sorts. Max had given him a cell phone. Gabe sort of remembered them, small handheld computer devices. A world of knowledge in his hands, powerful.

Maybe he could record videos to himself for whenever this happened again down the line. Max had assured Gabe that going to ground was a normal part of being a vampire, indicating he did it himself for a week, once a year.

"Think of it as a vacation," Max had stated. "Schedule it, and maintain your power and sanity."

That sounded like a good idea. Obviously, Gabe had not been doing that before since he had been down a decade and a half, or thereabout. He'd wanted to start reading up on all he missed and search out the information on the witch who was his Focus, but Max suggested the quiet. Let the pieces fall into place instead of jamming all the memories at once. Too much would turn him revenant, Max said.

Revenant.

That brought back vague memories. A club, lots of bodies filled with blood, some dying. The taste on his tongue bitter, almost foul. Even the shifters had tasted better than the dying groupies at some club. It felt strange that he'd have done that. Though he knew he had plenty of moments in his life where he fed from whatever he could. Maybe that had been the reason?

A face flashed through his memory again, too fast to make out much more than long dark hair and blue eyes. The more Gabe tried to reach for that particular thought, the faster it vanished, and his head began to hurt. He stopped chasing them after a while, instead following easier trails like of Sam, the vampire with an attitude who had apparently been working for Roman, but now belonged to Max? He would have to ask.

When the door opened and Max called him, Gabe had been half asleep, dozing on the edge of drifting memories, letting them go where they would.

"Gavriil," Max called, "your Focus has come for you."

The name was wrong. He wasn't Gavriil anymore, but he opened his eyes hoping the Focus, witch, or whatever would bring back more memories. He expected to be walloped with them, only there was nothing.

He was younger than Gabe had expected, appearing mid-twenties at most. Had his aging slowed? Was that the Focus bond? Or the fact that he was a witch? Gabe wasn't sure it would be okay to ask. He'd always found silence the safest bet when he wasn't certain of a response.

The man, his Focus, was beautiful, pretty as only Asian men really seemed to be. His facial bone structure delicate, with high cheekbones, and slanted eyes. Slim and lean, more like a runner, he wasn't overly tall, but balanced. Hair a bit of a mess of pale brown hanging near his shoulders, and pushed back out of his face. The eyes were the one thing that seemed to stir some sort of memory in him. That sapphire blue gaze sad, watery, even filled with pain. Gabe had an inclination to comfort him, like it was something he'd done often, but he remained rooted to the chair.

The man sucked in a deep breath and turned away, focusing on Max. "Is he sane?"

"As sane as possible for any vampire," Max replied.

Sam stepped up behind the man and put a hand on his shoulder. "I can stay with you if you need. The guys won't mind."

There was a third man standing behind them, still as a tree, not even breathing. Curious. Gabe stared at it; the lines of magic wrapped around it looking like lasers of rainbow colors. Not a man. Some sort of creature? Magic? Had the witch created it? A person out of organic material?

It had an unusual overlay, that appeared almost tangible. Gabe stared at it, trying to sort through what it meant. In reality, part of it mirrored the makeup of a vampire. Though vampires seemed to have one very solid tie to organic matter, which Gabe could see in specific lines of power. One of them actually seemed to be linked to the man who was Gabe's Focus.

What had Max said his name was? Say-ron. Seiran Rou. Sam

called him Ronnie. A tease that made Gabe think maybe the witch wasn't as strict and irritated as his expression made him out to be.

Gabe blinked and stood up, feeling a bit wobbly. He'd have to learn to not be still too long as it slowed blood flow. A tug of memory in his head said it was something he was familiar with in the past. He hoped the sluggishness wore off soon.

The man didn't move, or speak directly to Gabe. How was he to react? Greet the man? Introduce himself? Pretend he knew him? Gabe looked to Max for guidance, but found himself ignored.

"Once he's back to himself, I'll go over his portfolios with him. It will be easy enough to transfer all his businesses back. Most of it is managed by my people anyway," Max said having returned to staring at his computer screen.

"And how long will that take?" Seiran asked. He had his arms wrapped around himself and was staring at the floor. "Before he remembers anything?"

"Not long I suspect. A few days maybe? Better for him to remember in small batches than all at once. No need to shake the revenant loose," Max answered as though the revenant wouldn't be an issue.

Gabe knew what that was, the soulless need for blood that could take him over. He had vivid memories of that darkness eating him up, slowly taking over. Is that what had happened? Why he'd gone to ground? More questions and no answers. Though turning into that berserker that slept inside all vampires would explain the witch's anger.

"I'm sorry," Gabe said finally, "I will do my best to remember." He didn't like feeling weak or beholden. He hated this fog over his thoughts and memories. The pained expression on Seiran's face made his heart hurt, an intense and weird sensation since he didn't recognize the man at all.

Max waved a hand. "Go. Some of us have work to do," he said. Seiran flinched and turned toward the elevator.

"Those books?" Seiran called back as he hit the button that made the door open.

"I'll make some calls," Max said. His gaze fell to Gabe. "Go."

"What if I hurt him?" Gabe asked, feeling unsteady. Max's tie was strong, holding the dredges of darkness back that Gabe knew at one point he could contain the revenant himself. Would he have that control again? Would distance between them give the darkness rise?

"It won't be the first time," Max said.

"The witch can put him back in the ground, if necessary," Seiran said of himself. "Especially if you even look at my kids wrong. Let's go."

Gabe ground his teeth together at the coldness of that tone. Whatever hurt he'd caused before must have made the witch hate him. And since they had a Focus bond, it meant they were stuck with each other. Great. Well, they could work it out as a balance somehow. As long as Gabe had enough time to regain control of his strength and at least some of his memories. Maybe he could give the witch some space then.

"I would never hurt a child," Gabe said, feeling confident of those words.

"Right," Sam snorted. "How old was Sei when you first took him to bed?"

Had Gabe seduced a very young witch? That didn't feel right.

"I was legal," Seiran said. He had his hand on the edge of the elevator door to keep it open. "Forest, come."

The creature turned and loped into the elevator like an obedient dog. Gabe really didn't want to be that whipped for anyone.

"Do you want me to stay with you?" Sam asked Seiran.

"No. Keep your loud sex life at home. My kids don't need that drama."

Sam laughed, "Sure, Ronnie. You know it's the only action you see in your house that isn't the muscleman and his boy toy. And how gross is that? Your brother?"

"Jamie's attractive," Seiran said.

That statement brought a rise of jealous to Gabe's gut, and a flash of darkness tugging on him. He sucked in a deep breath, feeling the air a cold bite filling his lungs clearly enough to shove the darkness back.

Seiran had apparently not missed it because his gaze was centered on Gabe. "Would you rather stay here with Max?" The question was phrased neutral enough, but the tone was tight.

Gabe thought he might actually prefer to stay, but only because he worried the darkness would rise again. He squared his shoulders and walked toward the door. "I am not myself," he said, feeling that edge of darkness lingering. "Perhaps the other vampire should come?"

"He doesn't need my help," Sam said. "He doesn't even have to break a sweat to put you back in the ground. He could probably even call it therapy."

Gabe stepped into the elevator, finding a spot near the back corner to give them some room. Seiran let the door close, not bothering to say goodbye to either vampire, and pushed the button for the garage. The elevator began to descend.

"I want you to promise to do just that," Gabe said after a moment of silence.

"What?" Seiran asked staring at his own reflection in the shiny chrome of the elevator door instead of at him.

"If I try to hurt anyone. Put me back in the ground." Another minute of silence passed and the elevator stopped, opening to reveal an underground parking garage and a car waiting.

"That's the plan," Seiran said as he stalked to the vehicle.

A man standing beside the car opened the back door and Seiran climbed in, followed by the creature. By the time Gabe dragged himself into the backseat, the creature was sitting on the other side of Seiran, and Seiran was seated in the middle, his back ramrod straight.

The door closed behind Gabe, and Seiran only glanced his way as the man who had held the door for them got into the driver's seat. "Put on your seatbelt," Seiran instructed.

Gabe glanced at the creature, who was wearing a belt, and Seiran, both wearing the belt already. The witch must have been talking to him. He reached back and pulled the belt down, having to brush against Seiran's side to click it into place. It was familiar, the sensation of touching the witch, like he'd done it many times before, but the memories lingered on the edge of his conscious, not close enough to grasp. Gabe stared out the window instead, hoping that the drive would bring back more memories.

The trip took a while and Gabe used the time to study the city they passed, and the long road beyond. The scent of honey and vanilla teased him with an edge of memory, like it was just out of reach. Frustrating, but he didn't reach for it for fear it would flit away. He concentrated on his breathing, a steady in and out that helped him feel almost normal.

By the time the car pulled up to a gate and a giant house beyond, Gabe felt clear enough to keep the revenant down if it happened to rise. "This is nice," he said softly.

The fence giving space to a large and somewhat wildly grown garden. It didn't look unattended, as the grass wasn't overgrown and crazy, but there were trees of a dozen different types, from citrus to nut to pine, all things that only grew in varied climates. But hadn't Max said this witch was a Pillar?

Gabe tried to recall the specifics of what a Pillar was. One of the five elements of power, if he was remembering correctly. The Pillars were chosen by the element, as sort of an apex of magic, or at least that was the basics Gabe could remember.

That meant Seiran was the Pillar of Earth, able to grow things year-round in any climate perhaps? There were flowers and cactuses, and an endless spread of strange plant life. "Interesting garden."

"The fae have gone a little crazy with it," Sei said as the car stopped in the round drive before the stairs leading to the main door. "Kaine, one of my kids, is sort of playing with his affinity to grow things. The earth doesn't mind as long as I keep it contained to the yard. The other two have mostly outgrown their need to experiment."

"Kaine," Gabe said, thinking about that, "Is part fae?"

"Yes," Seiran agreed.

The car stopped and the driver got out to open the door. Gabe unlocked his seatbelt and got out first, waiting for the witch and the creature to follow. The house itself seemed illuminated with lights in the windows, and a glow of power. Pillar magic, perhaps? Or something more. The distance from the city allowed the night sky to be filled with endless stars. Crickets danced around them in a noisy array, unbothered by their presence. He wondered what time of year it was. Not winter, obviously, fall perhaps? The trees weren't changing color, not that he'd be able to use that to gauge time in the witch's space.

"And the other children?" Gabe inquired. "Are they part fae as well?"

"No. All witch. Their mother is in New York right now. She's the director of Foreign Magic Relations for the Dominion."

Gabe wondered if her distance was a temporary thing, or if they were not in any sort of relationship. Though the idea of Seiran in a relationship stirred the jealousy again. He swallowed it down. Max had led him to believe that the witch had been his lover, but enough time had passed that Gabe would not have faulted the man for finding someone else. "Are you married?"

"To their mother?" Seiran laughed. "No. Her wife would gut me. The twins' birth was an arrangement."

"And the fae?" Would the fae marry a witch? They were sort of similar in species, though there was a bit of a class war between witches, whom the fae saw as mortal, and the fae. Gabe startled at the memory, realizing somewhere he had a lot of knowledge of the fae.

"Another arrangement," Seiran said as he stepped up to the door. It opened before he could reach for it, and a big, muscular man stood there, his shoulders broad, blond hair pulled back, expression stern. "I'm fine," Seiran said instantly.

But the man's gaze fell to Gabe, and an unfriendly scowl was directed his way.

"It's fine," Seiran assured him again, stepping through the doorway. "Gabe, come in," he added, and Gabe felt the magic of the house jump to him. It was a bit of a quirky sensation, like ghost hands running over his skin to memorize the feel of him. But he followed the witch inside, the creature trailing after them. The large man closed the door behind them.

"He looks strange," the man said.

Seiran sighed. "Gabe, this is Jamie, my brother. You'll probably remember him eventually."

"Remember me eventually?" Jamie's voice went frigid. "He doesn't remember you? After all the things he did?"

"What did I do?" Gabe asked.

Jamie opened his mouth as though to fill Gabe in, but Seiran held up a hand to stop him. "No. Let him remember on his own. Max says it will keep the revenant from rising."

"If the revenant returns, I'll put that piece of shit back in the ground," Jamie snarled.

"Sounds like you'll have to get in line," Gabe said.

Seiran sucked in a deep breath, then stepped forward to give his brother a hug. "I'm fine. Go to bed. You have to be up early."

"There's blood in the freezer," Jamie said. "You don't have to feed him. There's enough for a week, and I can get more." His glare made it clear that Gabe was not a friend. "I left a new phone for you on your nightstand. Everything is already programmed in. Maybe put the golem in the arboretum? You can ward the area to keep it in there."

"Thanks. I might do that. Everyone is in bed?"

"Of course," Jamie agreed. "I'll make sure everyone is up and off to school tomorrow, so you can get some rest."

"I appreciate it." Seiran let go, and Jamie headed upstairs. "Forest, come," Seiran directed the golem again. Golem. That brought another flash of memory that Gabe couldn't quite sort out. Had he seen one of these before? The weave of it seemed familiar, but not enough to jog any old memories loose.

Seiran headed through the main hall below the stairs and the golem followed. Gabe trailed along. They entered a kitchen, and Seiran paused to point at the giant fridge. "The blood is in the freezer there if you need it."

Gabe thought about that for a minute, even gazing around the room to try to identify the different pieces of technology. His gaze finally landed on the small metal box that looked like a microwave. "Okay?"

"Do you need blood right now?" Seiran's tone had gone tight again, reserved and a bit tired.

"No. I fed on the shifters Max had visiting." The bitter edge of their blood still lingered as an aftertaste. He hoped he didn't have to feed on shifters regularly, they didn't really appeal. Though he'd take the nourishment from wherever he had to.

"Good." Seiran turned and opened a wide double door that led out into an enclosed arboretum. If the outside garden had been a little wild, this insolated glass box was a jungle. And the dancing pops of color weren't from any actual light, but fairies. Another trickle of memories hit, and Gabe felt a bit dizzy. He got flashes of faces, fairies and fae, he'd met in the past. The notation settling in place that he knew the difference, fairies like these were a type of fae, one of dozens. Then there was the garden itself. The space echoed with an overlayed memory of barren ground, and a roll of pain through his gut that felt like the revenant rising.

Gabe took a step back, returning instead to the kitchen, sucking in gulps of air and clutching the counter. Seiran returned a few moments later, minus the golem and stared at Gabe from a few feet away.

"Are you going revenant?" He asked, not daring to get closer.

"No." The darkness wasn't rising, but the memories were overwhelming in that moment, even if he couldn't sort them out enough to understand them. "Too many memories at once, and not enough to clarify."

They stood in silence for a minute or two, until Gabe could breathe again.

"I have all your stuff still," Seiran said after a few minutes. "It's a bit of a mess," he admitted. He turned toward the far wall and opened a door, which showed a stairway leading down. "This is probably a good place for you to hang out during the day, too. Mostly light proof."

Gabe followed slowly, keeping a hand on the wall as they descended into a dark space. The basement below was finished, walls bland, and floors a hard type of tile. Boxes were everywhere. The only windows were covered in thick curtains, and the overhead lights were a scatter of those inset can lights.

Seiran went to a set of boxes, opening the top two and then putting them aside before finding another. "There are some clothes here. I don't know if they will fit anymore." He turned and pointed to the corner of the room. There was a large box bed covered in a dust sheet. "That was your bed. There is still grave dirt in it, not much. We will probably have to add more. I'll send Sam a text to get some. Bathroom is through that door." He pointed off to the side, then wrapped his arms around himself as though he were cold. "Do you need anything else, right now?"

Answers? But he could see the witch was tired, and he had his phone. Maybe he'd do some researching. "No, thank you," Gabe said, weaving his way around the space to keep distance between them. The witch seemed nervous enough without him getting too close. "And I'm sorry."

"For what?" Seiran asked.

"Whatever I did to hurt you."

Seiran sighed. "Doesn't mean much when you don't remember."

Gabe could understand that. "I'm still sorry. You look tired. Maybe you should get some rest?"

"Don't touch my kids, okay?"

"I don't plan to," Gabe promised.

Seiran turned as if to go, then paused, like he wanted to say something else, but decided against it. He shook his head and mounted the stairs, even shutting the door behind him as he vanished up into the main part of the house.

The silence was intense. The weight of the space and the memories it held, strong enough to make Gabe want to sit down and meditate again. Dozens of boxes, probably filled with details of his past. At least the space itself seemed void of memories. New to him, perhaps? He made his way to the first pile of boxes and began opening them, mentally categorizing their contents. The space itself was pretty organized. Clothing on one side, books and documents on another. There were no photo albums or anything really sentimental. Had he been that cold before? How long had the darkness been pulling at him before he'd gone to ground? He'd always thought himself a bit more human than that, even if vampires didn't have a lot of humanity after a couple of centuries passed.

He found a laundry area on the other side of the bathroom and began to sort through the stacks of clothes to remove the musty smell. Everything had been sealed in plastic bags, and seemed in good shape. Lots of business-like attire. Not all that unlike Max. But they had said he had managed businesses before.

His phone pinged, a dancing sound that made him jump. He pulled it out of his pocket and stared at the screen for a minute, making out the words.

Mike: Heard you're back. How much do you remember?

Who was Mike?

Not enough. Gabe replied. *Max said I should remember naturally.*

But Gabe was more than willing to admit how frustrating that was. He needed answers. *Can I ask you some questions?*

Mike: Of course. You are my sire.

And that was a revelation. This Mike was a vampire, and Gabe had made him. Well, this was a place to start at least. He made his way to a chair, clearing off the dust cloth and sitting down. Maybe he would find some clarity.

CHAPTER 7

Seiran had gone to bed, finding Kaine curled up in his space, and rather than waking him, crawled in beside his youngest to sleep. He'd need to press his kid in the morning, or sometime the next day. Find out what was happening with Kaine, and how he could help. If he hadn't been so tired, and the clock reading after two in the morning, he'd have woken Kaine then. He wrapped his arms around his baby, pulled the blankets up, and closed his eyes.

He felt Kaine leave sometime later, but didn't rouse. He also heard Kura come in, felt her kiss him on the cheek, before the house settled into silence again. Only then did he sleep hard. Falling into dreams of watching Gabe unravel again.

That was when someone shook him, and he jolted awake, sitting up in bed and breathing hard. He'd had enough abrupt awakenings over the years to not instantly attack, but finding Gabe in his bedroom, leaning over him, made his heart race and put a spell on his lips. Seiran stopped just before unleashing it.

The windows were shut tight against the light, though fingers of the glow still made it through, illuminating Gabe, and Seiran stared at him. Had he gone revenant? His eyes were green, and he didn't really avoid the bits of light spilling into the room.

"Gabe?" Seiran asked, wondering if he was actually awake. Gabe kept looking toward the door. That was when Seiran heard it. A banging. It was a thud that shuddered the house, the vibration rolling through Seiran's core.

"That golem thing?" Gabe said. "It's trying to get out. Sorry to wake you. But no one else is home, and I was worried when it started throwing itself on the wards."

All of that was a lot to process straight from sleep without any coffee, but Seiran jumped out of bed and headed toward the door. He was surprised to find the hallway filled with sunlight. How had Gabe gotten upstairs? Normally the pull of the sun made him super tired and he'd be in bed by sunrise. Vampires claimed it felt like it burned, though Seiran had never actually seen sunlight make a vampire burst into flames. It appeared to be closer to midday, but the vampire seemed wide awake and unharmed.

"Doesn't the sun burn?" Seiran asked.

"No," Gabe said, appearing thoughtful as if only realizing that vampires didn't normally spend a lot of time in the sun. The banging shuddered through the house again.

Seiran took that for what it was, unimportant at the moment, and raced down the stairs. Gabe was right. The golem was throwing itself at the door, bouncing off the wards, battering itself against the magic. It didn't bleed, but it didn't look human anymore either. Somehow the tie Seiran had to it wasn't strong enough. Why was it trying to get out at all? It should have been at peace among the organic matter of the garden. The fairies wouldn't have messed with it, and in fact, seemed to be missing from the garden, likely disturbed by the golem's unnatural presence.

Had something called it? Was that why it was freaking out?

Gabe stood in the kitchen, keeping his distance from the door. "Shouldn't you unravel it?"

"I need to find who made it before I do that. People died to create that," Seiran defended keeping it whole.

"All death magic requires death, and blood," Gabe said quietly.

"Are you remembering more?"

"A little, in small chunks." He looked away. "If you give it blood, you might have better control of it."

"But?" Seiran could tell he left something unsaid.

A wave of darkness crossed Gabe's eyes. Almost like something lurked inside. Though Seiran knew there was a revenant inside of all vampires, he hadn't before Gabe went to ground. He had studied long enough now to know a lot of their secrets. Him standing in the sunlight surprised him, the revenant not so much.

"I can't help the jealousy that rises at the thought of someone else having your blood," Gabe admitted. He kept his gaze focused on the floor. "I don't know how I will react. Which is not fair or rational, and I'm sorry."

Well, that was a conundrum. "You're saying that I need to give the golem blood to control it, but that if I do so, you might lose control of your revenant?" Seiran clarified.

"Maybe?" Gabe sounded apologetic.

Seiran thought about that for a minute but headed to the door to the arboretum. He threw open the door, almost expecting the golem to charge him through the ward, or stop, but it continued to throw itself into the ward like a mindless battering ram. "Forest, stop," Seiran called, trying to bind it by the name again. That was golem basics, bound with their name and blood.

Bam! Forest didn't even pause. Seiran wasn't sure he recognized the name at all. Okay so maybe it did need blood. He called roots from the earth, asking them, rather than demanding because the earth hated demands, for the roots to wrap around the golem, to stop him. Maybe if Seiran cut his finger? Gave it a few drops? He glanced back at Gabe who stood a few feet away, gaze on the golem.

The roots rose, and tried to create a bond, but the golem ripped right through them. "Fuck," Seiran said. He had two choices now, tempt it with blood, which meant bigger than a pricked finger, or unravel it.

"Should it have this much power away from its creator?" Gabe asked.

No. And that was the problem. With Sei's power wrapped around it, True Named, and distance from the creator, it should have been little more than a clay doll. "I'm going to have to give it blood," Seiran admitted, bracing for Gabe to go nuts.

The darkness flashed over the vampire's face again, and he swallowed hard, but focused on the golem. "I can try to hold it. You'll have to feed it blood as well as etch symbols of ownership in your blood on it."

Seiran gaped. "You know a lot about death magic?"

"I'm a vampire," Gabe said. "We are death magic."

And obviously he was remembering things he'd never before shared with Sei. Maybe he'd been that far gone, forgotten most of it, or Tresler, the former head of the now dead Tri-Mega, had already had control of him.

"Fine," Sei agreed. "Try not to attack me." He made his way to the knife board on the counter and took out one of the small steak knives. Jamie kept them sharp, but it was still going to hurt.

Gabe waited beside the door. He put a hand up, and said, "You'll have to drop the wards so I can get through. I have to be fast."

"Will you be strong enough?" Sei wondered.

"We will find out, won't we?" He waited, braced like he was ready for a sprint.

Seiran raised a hand toward the door. "On the count of three. One… two… three." He relaxed the extra ward meant to lock the golem into the arboretum. It slammed through the door, causing a ripple in the wards of the house, nearly knocking Seiran off his feet.

And that fast, Gabe was on him, wrestling him to the ground. It wasn't easy as Seiran thought it might be for a vampire. The golem was supernaturally strong, fueled by death magic, earth, and whatever the caster had juiced it with. In fact, Gabe barely seemed to be holding it back.

"Spell," Gabe said with a grunt, trying to use his body as an anchor.

"Blood coming," Sei warned as he put the knife to the inside edge of his arm and sliced. It was a sharp pain, fast and stinging. He set the knife aside and squeezed his arm to let the blood pool, then coated his fingers in it. Of course, getting close to the vampire was part of the trouble.

Gabe's eyes went black, but he held onto the golem.

Sei carefully bent to spread blood on the lips of the golem. Well, not lips so much as a gape in the mass of clay and sticks that created it. He had to recoat his hand, pressing for more blood even as he was healing the cut at almost vampire speed, to draw the symbols of ownership. He'd always hated this sort of thing, an enslavement really, rather than a spell. Total control, which shouldn't have bothered him because Forest was a thing, not a person, but it didn't feel that way.

The spells began to wrap around the golem. An invisible tie that made it hard for Sei to breathe for a moment. He could feel souls within it, struggling, trying to escape, and deeper, something dark, almost like a vampire revenant, twisting and flailing to answer a call. Not a golem of the normal sort at all. Not just fueled by will and death, but by actual souls. He might have suspected before, but now he was certain and could even feel the distinct difference of each. Three. There were three souls trapped inside the golem.

Strangely enough the signature of them didn't feel normal. Not human, Seiran realized, as that pulsing memory of revenants brought a startling thought to sink like a stone in his gut. Not human souls, at all. Was that possible?

Seiran tried to follow that call with his magic, even while tying the spell around the golem so tightly it felt like a spiderweb wrapped around an unwitting fly, squeezing tighter and tighter. But the call vanished, cutting off before Sei could reach any recognition of the source, not even a direction.

He snarled in frustration even as the spell completed and the golem stopped moving. The roll of Seiran's magic retook the golem, sliding the appearance of a human back over it. Gabe still held on as though the thing were a wriggling leviathan, instead of stone still as it was now.

"Gabe?" Seiran called softly. The vampire's eyes were closed and he seemed to be breathing hard, while motionless as only a vampire could be. Seiran took a couple slow steps backward, putting the counter between him and the vampire. The Focus bond meant that Gabe probably wouldn't kill him. Maybe even couldn't since Sei was the Pillar of Earth. But that didn't mean Seiran couldn't experience physical pain. He'd survived gunshot wounds to the head, being absorbed back into the earth, and a dozen other attacks over the years. He'd never experienced having his throat torn out, drowning in his own blood, while a revenant fed at him, and he hoped to never have to.

"Gabe?" Seiran called again.

One second Gabe was across the room on the floor, holding the golem. And the next, he was inches away from Seiran, only the giant marble island slowing him down as he reached for blood, his black eyes glazed over with a red edge of madness.

Seiran's heart flipped over, thinking he'd have to put Gabe back in the ground, and likely ruin his kitchen doing so. But the vampire grabbed the knife Seiran had used, and licked the tiny bits of blood from the blade.

It clattered to the floor with a metal clang, and Sei expected Gabe to reach for him next, but he was gripping the counter, eyes closed.

"Maybe... you could go wash off the blood?" Gabe asked in a very tight voice.

Seiran's gaze swept from the vampire to the golem. "There's blood in the freezer for you."

"There is," Gabe agreed quietly, but didn't move from his spot, plastered to the edge of the marble island. Seiran really hoped he didn't damage the stone.

"The golem?" Seiran backed away, toward the stairway that led upward.

"Bound for now. Yours… ours."

"Forest, go sit in that chair until I get back," Seiran commanded, feeling the magic rip through him like a fist of energy rather than a request.

Gabe sucked in air and squatted down beside the counter like the command had made it harder for him to hold back. "Go, clean… please?"

"Okay, going, sorry. Be right back."

"Don't run," Gabe squeezed out, his face below the counter edge now. "Might chase…"

Predatory instinct. Vampires were predators after all. Seiran knew that. The few he interacted with most days were so human-like that he sometimes forgot. But he moved slowly, backing toward the door, counting to keep his heart rate as even as possible until he reached the stairs and headed upward. He would have to get ready for his day anyway. He'd need to get to the office, and put the entire task force on finding who had killed vampires, not humans, to create a golem.

CHAPTER 8

It took Gabe a while to regain control. Hunger expanded in his gut in horrible, rippling pain. He heard the shower turn on upstairs and breathed deep with the hope that the scent of blood would soon fade.

He estimated it probably took a good ten minutes to move from the counter. But he found the freezer with blood in it, wrinkling his nose at the smell. Old blood. And not the witch's.

There was a handwritten note on the microwave with instructions on how to warm it. Gabe followed them to the letter, trying to focus on the rotating cup warming, rather than the sound of Seiran moving upstairs. The need to find him was intense. Like distance was a bad thing. Gabe hoped it was due to the lack of blood, whether that meant in general he needed to eat, or that he craved Seiran's blood, he wasn't sure. The latter he knew would not be welcome.

The tiny droplet that had remained on the knife he'd licked didn't satisfy him so much as intensify the craving. And it couldn't be correct anyway. No one tasted that good. Blood wasn't like regular food. It couldn't be rich and decadent like a piece of chocolate fudge cake drizzled in ganache and topped with the sweetest, juiciest strawberries imaginable.

He didn't even know what that was—those flavors, the texture—as he was sure he'd never eaten it. Yet he could vividly recall every detail of the dish, as though it had been a long time favorite. Perhaps not his favorite, but the witch's.

Blood was usually warm, metallic, and slightly bitter. Though the taste… small as it had been, and the lingering scent of the witch, claimed otherwise. A memory tied to the witch, perhaps? It had felt more real than that. Tasted like things Gabe couldn't possibly remember. Vampires didn't eat regular food. Their systems were too delicate for that. But Gabe could recall how the cake would melt on his tongue, the rich decadence of the chocolate topping, a lingering bite of sweetness with an edge of the bitterness.

Maybe that was why vampires were warned to stay away from witches. Their blood was addicting. The power in it? Or, something more? Perhaps it was the witch himself that was different, appealing to Gabe because they were bound? Even some part of the death magic that animated vampires?

The microwave beeped, and he carefully took the cup out, the ceramic hot enough to burn, but he didn't loosen his grip on it. The pain was welcome, clarifying, grounding. It pushed back the edges of the revenant. He waited, letting the liquid cool a little before taking a sip. It was foul. Old, dead, weak, human blood. He could live this way, he knew he had in the past, but it would take more of these packets, and the lingering edge of the revenant would remain.

His gaze fell on the golem. They weren't all that different. The golem needed blood to be controlled, and Gabe would need blood to solidify his sanity. How long could he wait? Would he become like that animated toy and throw himself at the power soon? Maybe he shouldn't have risen yet. He shouldn't be this unsteady if he'd been ready to return. Had something pulled him back early? He vaguely recalled a tug of something while he'd lingered between worlds. Not the witch. He'd have recognized that. Death magic.

He stared at the lines of magic tying up the golem. Part of the witch now, but so much death magic. Creating that, perhaps? Powerful enough to drag him out of the grave early? That couldn't mean good things.

Then there was that unusual overlay on the golem. Like there were things inside it. Golems were empty vessels of intent, fueled by death. It shouldn't have anything inside. He tried to clarify what he was seeing, the swirling lines of three distinct colors. Not ties to Seiran or even the creator, something else. Souls? Not human ones either as they almost felt like... revenants.

Was something trying to pull revenants out of vampires? Was that why he'd awoken?

The witch hadn't been willing to destroy the golem. Needing to find who created it. Gabe understood that. Death magic was never kind. Though Gabe was not as convinced of a crime as the witch seemed to be.

Vampires used to hunt necromancers. No one much liked the idea of being controlled by some magic puppet master. Gabe could vividly recall a battle or two with a particular monster of mortal making. They were called the Dark Ages for a reason. The wars of magic wielders, and beings provoking a war, that had almost eliminated humanity. Witches and their ilk on one side. Shifters, and a dozen other monsters, on the other side. The vampires hadn't begun on a side. Until their food sources began to die out.

Gabe sipped at the nasty blood, letting it remind him of a battlefield of corpses, reanimated, as a particular nasty witch had sought to destroy the stronghold Gabe had created for himself and a handful of his children. He'd been obsessed, not with power back then, but safety. And there was safety in numbers, distance, and stone walls. At least until the darkness came.

Having come into the world before the insanity of Christianity had taken over global religions, he hadn't worried much about good or evil. People were food, be they lords or peasants. The only real evil was poverty and starvation, and death was often a kindness.

For a while he'd followed the fringes of the movement, an almost hippie-like sense of love and peace, which would crop up over and over throughout history, only to be quashed by whoever the ruling class was, with war and death. He seemed to recall becoming familiar with the organized portion of the religion that grew up around him because it wielded power. And again, his thoughts returned to the ultimate goal, safety for him and his.

The witches had created their own movement in direct opposition to the church. Again, vampires were caught in the middle, accepted by neither, as most of the other supernaturals fought back and died. Pointless destruction. That's what humans did best, be they religious humans or magical ones. Which was why it struck him as weird that he'd be married to a witch, in the metaphysical sense at least.

Survival? Or something more?

The scent of Seiran's blood still lingered. A long wafting of the most decadent of perfumes, leading like a trail upward, not fading as he'd hoped. He sipped the blood until the cup was empty, knowing the taste was not at all what the witch would be.

Maybe he could seduce the witch. The vague memory of past seductions indicated he'd used that to feed. Perhaps even on the attractive man who was tied to him. Anger and betrayal were strong emotions, a delicate line walked with love. Gabe knew he had done something wrong. He didn't know what. Mike hadn't known specifics when he'd asked and there had been nothing in the media he could find. Whatever had happened, they'd kept it private.

He wished he remembered more. The few things he'd found on his phone, before napping under the pull of the rising sun, were scattered, somewhat political, and very censored. The Dominion had erected Seiran Rou as some sort of golden boy of men practicing magic. Gabe suspected a lot of that was editing and spin. The impression he'd gotten from the witch himself, was of a man less patient with the bullshit of people, any people, witches or otherwise.

He was also the type of man who got shit done. Dozens of articles about solved magic crimes testified to that. Which was something else that led Gabe to believe that the by-the-book persona portrayed to the world, was not who Seiran Rou was. It wasn't like they could remove him, so instead they used him.

Having the power of a Pillar, meant he would be in control of that element until that element reclaimed him. Death for a Pillar rarely came in sleep from old age. It also meant that others would hesitate to cross him. And that pleased Gabe for some reason. He hated the idea of anyone tormenting the witch, though he suspected it still happened from time to time.

Their short time together made Gabe believe that Seiran had a backbone of steel, even if he didn't always act like he was the most powerful in the room. How easily could the Pillar of Earth take a vampire like Maxwell Hart and put him in the ground? He could probably unravel a vampire as easily as the golem. But he didn't.

Everyone indicated that Gabe had harmed him. Why not unravel *him*? Or take vengeance on all vampires? The answer, Gabe suspected, was humility. Seiran Rou didn't need to be power hungry because he had more power than anyone else on the planet. He didn't need people to worship him or fear him, the entirety of the Dominion watched his every move. Like they would slap him down if he stepped out of line. Maybe they sent him strongly worded letters regularly. Gabe would have to do more research.

The sad part was, that the more he looked into the witch, the more Gabe hurt. Physically and emotionally. It had begun with a headache, and the constant echo of his old sire's admonishments about witches, mixed with tiny pops of memories, and images, all a chaos of broken puzzle pieces. The emotional bits were harder to explain. His rising worry, and an almost visceral desire to touch had awakened with the bashing of the golem on the wards. Gabe could sense the wards now, his senses tickling with their energy, as though they were a part of him, but separated by a barrier.

It was their tie. The Focus bond, stretched between them, weak, and unfed from years of distance. But not all that unlike the tie to the golem, a bond of firm magic, extending only so far.

Gabe rinsed out the cup while studying the magic wrapped around the golem. The new spell, written in blood and strong green ribbons of earth magic, wouldn't have been visible to most anyone else. The golem sat in the chair, motionless, more like a statue than a person, though it appeared human. The bonds holding the golem was stronger, detailed in blood magic. Gabe could separate out the colors of magic, those of its creation, and those of Seiran's spell; a web of woven lines, colors, and pulsing magic, that felt alive.

He had a sort of visceral longing for those strands to encase him. The Focus bond would be deeper than a handful of pretty ties. It should encase them completely, much like he imagined the witch would feel right now, with water running over his skin.

For a second, Gabe was upstairs, thoughts laced over Seiran's, feeling the heat of the water, almost too hot, as it pounded over their skin in a fierce rhythm. Standing for a long time under the spray, more than to wash physically. Was he washing away the memories? The blood? Or the tears that blended with the water?

Gabe withdrew as though burned by the thought. Back a day, and already tearing the witch apart. Maybe they hadn't been well suited. He'd have to ask Max if there were other options. Perhaps they could maintain distance as a sort of partnership. He didn't want to force himself on the man, even if they were bound.

The golem began to fidget. Odd. He'd been so still before. Gabe could feel the golem tied to him through the witch, faint as it was. The sudden action almost felt like a tug on their connection. The golem tapping its feet and drumming its hands on its thighs seemed abrupt. Gabe stared another moment longer, then he heard the shower turn off upstairs.

Something yanked hard on the tie to the golem. Gabe gasped, reacting by grabbing that tie for himself, and holding it in place. He could vaguely recall spells. Binding things, more vampire related than he thought actual magic. It was the type of things a sire could use on a fledgling vampire to control it. Gabe extended that strength over the golem, trying to keep it from going nuts again. If he had some of the Focus's blood himself, he'd have been stronger, or even if the golem had been a vampire rather than a creature made up of magical death, he might have been able to hold it firmer. But it did stop moving, gaze turning Gabe's way, eyes dark and vacant, like a revenant waited there.

Okay, that wasn't a good sign. Gabe set the empty cup in the sink and slowly moved around the counter. The golem's attention firmly on him, but Gabe didn't feel like he had any better control of it. The witch's magic was threaded through the spell as though Gabe had pulled from a well not his own. Had Seiran noticed? Would he be mad? Maybe that was what Gabe had done before, perhaps not accidentally.

He wondered how far the control went, but wasn't about to start pushing his boundaries. The last thing he needed was a witch on the warpath any more than he needed the golem to go nuts right now.

What had they named the creature again? Names had power. He studied the scattering of symbols, finding the one on its forehead glowing a little with power. Was someone else using its name?

Gabe sorted through memories like wading through high tide until the symbol popped up with recognition. Forest. That was it. "Forest," Gabe said, addressing the golem. "Stand."

The creature stood, though the fidgeting returned, his... *its* gaze remaining on Gabe. Gabe kept his grip on the bonds tight, like holding a brand-new vampire back from its first kill. That had never been easy. Vampires often found themselves back home, slaughtering loved ones because the memories of humanity mixed with those of the revenant. Was this one trying to return to those who had once loved it? Or was it merely being called?

Gabe glanced upward. Maybe they should stay close to the witch. At least until Gabe was strong enough to hold a baby vampire again. Or until he tasted the witch from a vein.

His body reacted to that in a way that almost startled him. And he found himself suddenly standing on the stairs instead of beside the counter. That small amount of blood, and the idea of drinking from the witch made him hard, needing, and almost brought the revenant to the surface to take it.

He sucked in air, gripping the railing, and hearing it crack beneath his strength.

The golem moved behind him, standing at the bottom of the stairwell looking up, still fidgeting, but gaze solely on Gabe. Fuck. Distance for the golem seemed to be bad, meanwhile, Gabe was fighting to keep himself in place. Maybe they both had to stay near the witch.

Gabe swallowed hard and said, "Forest, come," as he headed up the stairs. Maybe the witch would put him back in the ground today. And that might just be okay.

CHAPTER 9

Seiran emerged from his shower to find Gabe and Forest in his room. The golem sitting in a chair near the door, and Gabe staring at the contents of Sei's bookcases.

At least he hadn't emerged naked from the shower. Years with kids taught him that naked around the house meant someone was getting an eyeful. But the robe still made him feel vulnerable near Gabe. He had to work not to grip it tight like his virtue was in question.

He headed to his closet, a giant walk-in thing, which was better organized because Jamie was sort of obsessive about everything in its place these days. Not that Sei's wardrobe had lots of color to work with anymore, or variety. Most everything was work related. He had a few suits, but did so few formal affairs anymore, he didn't know if they would fit.

His mother had talked of having an old school coming out party for his kids, like one of the balls of yesteryear. He had put the kibosh on that fast enough. The point of those things was to make good matches among the witch families. Teenagers didn't need to be married off like cattle, and he'd told his mother if she tried something like that, she'd find herself on his bad side, and cut off from access to her grandchildren.

She was much more wary of him than she'd been when he was a child. But he'd also done a handful of pretty damn near impossible things that had made her realize the true strength of his magic. Tanaka Rou had always been a ball-busting tiger mom, but she treated his kids with a lot more compassion and grace than he'd ever seen as a child. Fear of him? Or love for the babies? He didn't care as long as it produced results.

"Creepy," Sei said to his unexpected visitors as he pulled out clothes for the day and set them on the bathroom counter. "There's a thing called boundaries."

"The golem is calmer close to you," Gabe answered still not looking his way. Sei wondered if he was completely back or his eyes would still be black.

"He should have stayed in the chair. I gave him a direct order."

Gabe said nothing. Seiran returned to the bathroom and closed the door, like it would stop either of them from busting in on him. But he dressed in a hurry, brushed his teeth, and combed his hair back.

He felt a bit self-conscious stepping out of the bathroom. But he'd chosen a pair of pale brown skinny jeans, with a long-sleeved black T-shirt instead of his usual slacks and button up. If he was interviewing the jocks today, maybe it would help if he looked less like some stuffy office worker, and more like one of them. Though as he pulled his hair up into a small pony tail, he stared into the mirror and felt weirdly young looking. Closer to forty than twenty, but he still looked like a kid. Witch genes or the Focus bond? He sighed, and made his way back to his room. His appearance wasn't why people didn't take him seriously, that problem was mostly related to his gender.

Forest still sat in the chair, but he was fidgeting. Tapping his feet, drumming his hands on his thighs, while his eyes looked oddly hollow. Gabe stood across the room, arms folded across his chest like he was hugging himself, but his fists were clenched and eyes closed. Was he still fighting the revenant? Maybe remembering things? Or was being this close to Seiran difficult for him?

"Maybe you should sleep?" Seiran offered. "Since it's daytime?"

"I did sleep for a while," Gabe said. "At dawn. I laid down on the bed you said was mine. Slept for a few hours until I felt the golem."

Gabe had felt the golem first? Or heard it? "You felt it throwing itself at the wards?"

"Before that," Gabe said. "It was a pull." He was silent another minute or so before adding. "I think I felt it before, too. When I woke from the grave. Something really strong and powerful…"

Did that mean Gabe had been pulled back early? Maybe that was why his control and memories were so messed up? Seiran didn't think that was good news for either of them. If he had to put Gabe back in the ground, he would, but knowing that he might spend another decade or even a century alone, that might be too much for him. "Do you think it brought you back too soon?"

Gabe seemed to be focused on breathing, or meditating. "Maybe? I mean, I felt the pull, but could have probably ignored it if I wasn't ready. It's not tied to me. More a brush of strong magic," he hesitated and added, "like when the hairs on the back of your neck rise, and you're not sure why. Something… might be nothing."

Only it hadn't been nothing. Whatever this was had created a golem, and was doing what? Trying to call it back now? "Something called it?" Could Gabe sense the death magic controlling it, could he follow that magic? If so, that might be easier than Seiran trying to drag the answers out of jocks or even the puppet itself. Gabe finally opened his eyes and they were green. Seiran let out a long breath of relief.

"I don't know. Both, maybe? The dreams when the sun is high are often faint." He was quiet a minute, gaze roaming over Seiran, but not in a way that felt overtly sexual. More assessing. "I think I recall, that we sleep better with the grave near?"

"The magic of vampires, if that's what you want to call it, seep into the ground a vampire uses as a grave." Seiran picked up his phone and sent Sam a text about needing grave dirt for Gabe. "You'll sleep better when we get more earth in the box." He tugged on a pair of shoes and debated how the day was going to go. The golem's movements tugged at his magic, like they were small attempts to subvert the bond. That couldn't be possible, right? Not after giving it blood and wrapping it in earth magic. "I have to go to the office."

"You need to keep the golem close. Something is pulling on it. Calling it maybe…" Gabe said quietly. He looked at the golem.

"I'll take the golem with me." Seiran had to question the jocks anyway, maybe putting the golem in the room with them would yield useful information.

"I…" Gabe began but seemed unable to form the thought he needed.

"You had some blood from the freezer?" Seiran asked. It was still hard to look at him. The similarities between the current Gabe and the man Seiran remembered, seemed few. The width of his shoulders, but that was about all. The unruly mess of his blond curls, unlike anything the Gabe of old would ever have worn, was oddly appealing. And Seiran had the urge to run his fingers through those curls, discover if the hair was as soft as it looked, and if he could wrap his hands in the length to tug him close for a kiss. Would his lips be warm and welcoming? His gaze indicated there was something awake there, maybe not human, perhaps not even a full memory of what they'd been, but a glimpse?

The edge of vulnerability intrigued him. In their handful of years of dating, Seiran couldn't recall a time he'd known Gabe to be uncertain. He'd been the strong silent type, which had been part of their downfall. Survival mechanism, or had he simply been that far gone?

Seiran bit back a distressed sound and forced himself to take a few steps away. Maybe going to the office for a few hours would help. Distance couldn't be bad right? Even though Seiran wanted to wrap his arms around Gabe and cry to let out the years of loneliness.

"I did, but..." Gabe paused and sighed deeply. "It's not... I don't know... my control is better when I'm close to you." Gabe paused, letting the thought linger a moment half spoken.

The last thing Seiran wanted was a vampire raging out of control in his house when his kids got home from school. "You're saying you want to stay close in case I need to put you back in the ground?"

Gabe swallowed hard, and nodded.

"It's daylight out."

"I think if I can keep covered in the car, it will be okay. The hallway didn't burn."

"At all?"

"No. And I stood outside your door debating for a while whether or not to wake you." In the full light of the hallway, the many windows would have been pretty bright.

This day was just full of unusual revelations. "My car is at the parking garage at work, so I'll have to call a lift for us. Are you a danger to the driver or anyone else you encounter? I may rule the archives of the Dominion libraries and a couple dozen investigators across the world, but there will still be people around. Witches."

"We aren't supposed to touch witches," Gabe said.

"Except me..."

"You are my Focus."

Which didn't exactly answer the question. Seiran packed his bag. "But you still don't recognize me?"

"No. I'm sorry."

Seiran thought about that for a while as he moved around the room, and put his bag over his shoulder. It still stung a little.

"I..." Gabe began again. He once again hugged himself. "Am drawn to touch you. But I won't," he said hurriedly. "Unless you want me to. I just wanted to let you know, that even if my memory has not returned, I'm still drawn to you."

Seiran let out a long breath as he debated those words. "Do you want to hurt me?"

"No," Gabe promised.

"Okay," Seiran agreed, keeping his distance.

"But I crave your blood," he sounded almost apologetic. "The taste was…"

"Yeah, witch's blood has a kick," Seiran agreed. "And since I'm the Pillar, it sort of means blood on steroids to you guys." He made his way to the door and pulled up the app to request a driver and a specialized car with tinted windows, just in case. He had no idea how he was going to explain the vampire at the office. Though in reality, he shouldn't have to. As Director of MI and the Pillar of Earth, he shouldn't have been dancing on a short leash. If only those things got him the accreditation he deserved.

"That is an understatement," Gabe muttered as he followed. "Forest, come," he commanded, and strangely enough, the golem did as Gabe said. Using Seiran's magic? Or death magic? Seiran wasn't sure he wanted to know.

THE CAR RIDE had been almost eerily silent. Seiran crammed in the middle of the back seat of a specialized SUV with Gabe on one side, and the golem on the other. The golem stopped fidgeting when Sei touched him, almost like the pull on it stopped? Or was muffled?

It left a lot of questions. Was earth not stronger than death? Was there a way to muffle the creator's bond permanently, or until Seiran could figure out who that was? Would another creature of death magic, like a vampire, have better control of it?

If things went Sei's way today, he'd hopefully be able to unravel the golem before heading home this evening. One less problem would help ease his growing anxiety.

Gaining entry to the Dominion building was more annoying than usual. The guard on the front desk, a rotation of witches with strong telekinetic abilities, usually air witches, often gave him crap. He brushed it off as teasing most days. The checking of his badge, his sign-in process, and scrutiny they gave his file. Today, filling out visitor forms nearly had him at his breaking point.

"Enough," Seiran growled at them. "The golem is part of the current investigation, and I'm not filling out fucking forms for it." He'd already created a half dozen for Gabe, since he wasn't normally authorized personnel.

"Policy..." the witch began.

"I'm the Director of Magical Investigations," Seiran reminded her.

"That doesn't excuse you from the rules," the witch snarked back.

This was why so few men still worked for the Dominion. Kelly didn't have an office job. He was the Pillar of Water, and head of a private school for witches. Jamie was a nurse practitioner now, and these things were why. There were less than a handful of men working in the Dominion at all. And to this day, Seiran was still the only one with a high-ranking position. Most witches assumed that was because his mother was still regional director. How they explained away the fact that he was the Pillar of Earth, he didn't know. But with the constant bullshit they were given, it made sense why so few wanted anything to do with official channels and Dominion politics.

Men shouldn't have power over magic. It was *against the natural order of things* the vocal influencers shouted from the rooftops, or at least their media platforms. There were still media outlets that called him infidel and a dozen other terrible things. Everyone waiting with bated breath for him to turn into some sort of raving madman so they could burn him at the stake in a public display of why men shouldn't have magic. Not that they couldn't, but *shouldn't*.

Seiran was tired. Tired of the politics, of being second-guessed, and putting up with people's bullshit when he had a job to do. He let out the earth. Felt the warmth of Her flow over him. The floor at his feet bloomed with moss and flowers, and the reception desk where he rested his hands began to crack as plants erupted from its surface. He knew from his experience that his hair would take on a shade of green, and flowers would weave through it. His eyes would glow with the pulsing power of the earth. A small thing to call Her forward, a little show of how aligned She was with him, how much She approved of him. He wasn't a figurehead stuffed into a role, he was power, Father Earth, as selected by the Goddess herself.

"As the Pillar of Earth, chosen by the Goddess, I am allowed my servants, and none but Her is allowed to question me," Seiran said, stating the Dominion doctrine as though it were a bible quote. He glanced at Gabe and added, "That belongs to me, and to the earth."

The guards stepped back from the desk. Fear and surprise palpable on their faces. It gave Seiran no satisfaction. But it wasn't even the first time he'd had to flex a little power in his own workplace. Each time it would result in a changing of staff, and eventually re-education. He'd get a few weeks, sometimes even a few months of a semi-respect before there was a changing of the guards again. It was as though the Dominion cycled through staff to ensure they didn't gain respect for him. And he'd long since stopped trying to make nice with anyone outside his department.

He was so done with it. Maybe it was time for him to retire, too. Find another job, less full of bullshit and more rewarding. He knew of a handful of field agents that were qualified. He'd have to pull them back from overseas to take up the position, but maybe they'd want that? Something more stable than running around the world chasing magic? The only reason he'd stayed as long as he had was for the stability of his home life. His kids needed him, so he'd endured. Maybe they were old enough to have him away a couple days a week? He'd have to have a family meeting about it before he made any major decisions. And solve the golem problem, which meant dealing with the bullshit a bit longer.

He sighed and stalked past the desk and to the elevator that would take them down to the dark depths of the archives. He had never been moved to the main level with all the other directors. Hadn't let it bother him much since he didn't have to spend more than a meeting or two a week with the bunch. But now, it irritated him.

Maybe that was having Gabe close? Or the golem tugging at his energy? Or maybe he was just getting old. He felt the Goddess begin to recede as he stepped into the box, though behind him a trail of growing things etched his footsteps into the stone. Gabe entered the elevator and took a spot in the back corner. Forest found a spot near the side. The golem's fidgeting had stopped again, though it gazed at Seiran with a sort of disturbing and hungry look. For Seiran's power? Or his blood?

Before Seiran could close the door, Director Han put her hand on the edge and stepped inside. "Good of you to finally join us, Rou," she said as she let the door close and hit the button for the basement level.

"Director Han," Seiran greeted without warmth. She was a high-level fire witch, at least as old as his mother. He often wondered why she hadn't stepped down to give one of her children her spot. Not much within the Dominion was earned anymore. The entire structure was a hierarchical mess. A handful of witch families ruling like royalty, when, in fact, their power was waning. Perhaps none of her children were powerful enough to take the reins from her.

She stared at the golem and Gabe, arms crossed over her chest, and facing them directly, which was strange elevator behavior Seiran knew was meant to make them uncomfortable. But neither reacted. Forest, likely because it wasn't human at all, and Gabe, because his attention was still on Seiran. While the vampire's gaze was intense, it wasn't uncomfortable, more a meditative awareness, as though Gabe was using Seiran as the Focus he was meant to be.

"We've already questioned your witnesses," Han said.

"What?" Seiran growled. "That's not your place."

"Their families didn't want to wait around until you decided to roll in. Some of us were here early."

"And I was in the office until after nine last night. I can hold any of them without charges for up to a week. But I wouldn't expect you to know that since you're not part of MI, and I'd say none of this is your place."

"You're out of line, *Director* Rou," she said, as though he didn't deserve the title. The door to the elevator opened to the nearly empty basement area. "I've left the reports on your desk."

"You let them go?" Seiran was incredulous. "They were in possession of a golem created through death magic." He pointed at the golem in question. "You let them walk without being questioned by my department? And I'm out of line?"

"Death magic isn't a thing, Mr. Rou," Han said, seeming to suddenly forget he was Director. "I would have thought you learned that in college."

Seiran stared at Forest, and even Gabe, who to his eyes, looked like death magic. It was a stark distinction in how the earth perceived them. Maybe it was exclusive to earth?

"I would think, Ms. Han," Seiran said, purposely dropping the director title from her name too, "that if you were of a reasonable power level, you'd be able to perceive what is right in front of you. Death magic in two different forms."

"They are earth magic, Mr. Rou. Death magic is part of earth magic, just as weather is part of wind and water." She turned and headed toward the file room, one of the few areas Seiran spent very little time because everything was computerized now. Some of the older witches didn't much care for technology. "I suggest you work on unraveling that golem before it hurts anyone else. If you're incapable, I'm sure we can find a witch who can take care of it quickly enough." A glow filled her eyes as she stared at the golem. "Fire takes them out fairly easily."

Seiran stepped in front of Forest. "I need those students brought back in." He also needed the golem in one piece.

"They've already been questioned. It's just a toy they found."

"Right, because golems created from murdered vampires are things found at the local park?" Seiran demanded.

Han looked startled, and so did Gabe at that moment, both of them looking at the golem now, who stared with creepy eyes at Seiran.

"Murdered vampires?" Han asked.

"How many witches do you know that are strong enough to murder several vampires to use it in a spell? Bring the students back in, Director Han," Seiran demanded.

"You'll upset their families."

"I thought they weren't from witch families?" Seiran asked. "That dorm is a non-witch dorm." And an all-male dorm. Which meant a handful of things that made sense to Seiran all at once. First, that a witch family had shoved its male offspring into a non-magic dorm, and second, that it was unlikely there would only be one male witch of some power hiding. Most of the powerful families still denied the power that could arise in some of their males. It wasn't that they didn't want the power in their families. More that they believed male witch equaled evil. And nothing Seiran did could dissuade that. It was an oddly false belief, as the history was vague at best, with only a handful of male witches labeled as *bad*. Their label had been unjust as far as Seiran was concerned. They'd risen up against the oligarchy of power, and had been slapped down, villainized and murdered to keep them silent.

Were there evil male witches? Probably. But not at any higher rate than female ones. In fact, in Seiran's tenure as Director, he'd seen more than two dozen female witches tried for malevolent acts that could be called heinous. Not a single male. Some would call that a failure of the Dominion, others called it bias in favor of

Seiran himself. But he didn't believe in killing people for no reason, and left those sorts of monstrous decisions up to the courts. His job was simply to ensure the integrity of the evidence was sound.

He stalked past her and down the hall toward the musty book archives that he'd made his home away from home. He'd call them back in himself, or go see them one by one if he had to. Either way, he was tired of all this bullshit hindering his investigations. "Forest, come," Seiran commanded.

The golem jolted as Seiran's magic wrapped firmly around it again, and followed. Gabe taking up the rear.

"That is the sort of magic that we used to kill male witches for," Director Han said quietly, like she missed the good old days of burning anyone who disagreed with her at the stake.

"The golem? Or me?" Seiran paused to look back and ask. He got the feeling she meant him. "Good day, Director Han. I'd appreciate if you'd stay out of the Investigations Unit in the future, and I will be taking this to the counsel about your overreach." He was done being nice, and now he had a lot of fucking cleanup to do before he even got a chance to follow the trail of a murderer.

CHAPTER 10

"I get the feeling this sort of thing happens often?" Gabe asked quietly as he followed Seiran through a dark length of several corridors.

"Unfortunately," Seiran said.

The show at the main desk above had been impressive, and a bit intense. Gabe had felt Seiran's magic rise, and had tamped down hard on his control to keep from drawing more of the power into himself. If the witches had felt any of the rolling boil of the earth lingering like the abyss of ultimate power that Seiran seemed to teeter on the edge of, they wouldn't have given him shit. As it was, Gabe almost blacked out for a half second, the power that incredible. How it didn't tear the witch up was unfathomable. "Seems like they'd get the point?"

"The Dominion changes up the guards often. And a lot of the Directors are old, set in their ways, like Han." Seiran led them through a double door and the dank, dark areas of the bowels of the building suddenly seemed to brighten. Not due to windows or anything like natural light. In fact, the walls seemed to be made from stone, carved out of a rock tunnel perhaps, rather than built with man-made material. But the lights were bright. Dozens of sunlamp-looking things, and walls of greenery decorated a wide reception area.

Wards wrapped around them. At first it was a bit suffocating, and painful, like Gabe was encased in stone. He stopped for a minute, fearing that pressing forward would destroy him somehow, but after a few seconds passed it seemed to accept him and ease. The accompanying warmth, a sort of welcome edge of magic, enveloped the area. Seiran's magic, perhaps? Or the wards welcoming his magic.

A man sat behind the main desk, obviously some sort of reception area of this lower level. He was adorably young with high cheekbones, whiskey-colored eyes and glowing, teak shaded skin. Was he even old enough to work in a place like this? Maybe Gabe's perception of age was off, and since the man worked for the Dominion, he was probably a witch. Slower aging perhaps? Although Gabe could vaguely recall that not all witches got that perk.

The man stood when he saw Seiran. "Director Rou," he greeted. "Director Han was here. She left files. She said she was taking over the interviews you had?"

"Thank you, Page," Seiran said. "Call the families. Tell them I need them back here now. Their release was not authorized by MI. And if I have to, I'll have them all arrested."

Page nodded. "I'm sorry I couldn't do more."

Seiran sighed. "They don't see you, Page. They only acknowledge me because of my power. I'm sorry you're forced into this role."

"I love my job," Page protested.

"As my secretary?"

"Assistant," Page corrected. "I do more than answer phones. I work for the Pillar of Earth." He sounded reverent with those last few words.

"Right, 'cause that's a big deal," Seiran grumbled as he walked past the desk and into a nearby office that was little more than a wall of windows surrounded by a well of plants.

Gabe nodded his head at the young man, who widened his eyes when he saw Gabe, and the golem.

"Oh, I forgot you had already left by the time I brought the golem in last night." Seiran pointed at Forest. "That's our golem. And that's Gabe, a vampire…"

"A vampire in the archives?"

Gabe offered a hand. "Gabriel Santini," he said, recalling what Max had said his name was.

"I thought the only vampire Director Rou worked with was Mr. Mueller?" Page asked. He shook Gabe's hand carefully, as though afraid to really touch him.

A wallop of jealousy filled Gabe in that moment, and he couldn't stop the rise of it from showing on his face. He knew because Page took a step back, even though the desk separated them.

"Sorry," Gabe said and took a few steps backward himself. "Mueller?" He asked Seiran, turning his gaze away from them both until he could control his reaction again. He hoped his eyes had only gone dark, and not red.

"Sam," Seiran said.

"The guy with the attitude," Gabe said thinking of the first vampire he'd encountered when he'd been pulled out of his grave.

"That's Sam," Seiran agreed. "You're too young to have ever met Gabe," he told Page. "He went to ground almost fifteen years ago."

Page's eyes widened further. "That's a long time. I mean, I've read about how vampires go to ground, but never really thought how weird that must be to lose years."

"Weird," Gabe said, "is an interesting term for it." He felt some of the jealousy ease as he didn't think Sam and Seiran had anything intimate going on. And if they did, it wasn't really Gabe's place to get between them, even if his vampire instincts went a little crazy.

Gabe turned his attention to Seiran. "You told the other Director that vampires were used to create the golem. How can you tell?" Maybe it was the power Gabe was using to try to keep a leash on it that Seiran sensed?

"Their soul energy, if that's what you want to call it," Seiran replied. "It feels vampire. I should have realized it last night when I was questioning it. But I'd been out of touch with the vampires for a while and forgotten the subtle differences."

"Vampires have souls?" Gabe clarified. He knew they had something that animated them, and a consciousness that was free-thinking beyond the bloodlust, but seemed to recall something telling him vampires were soulless.

"Vampires were human," Page said from his place behind the desk. "We all have advanced studies now, after the Vampire War caused so much havoc. The fact that law makes them treat vampires as human is the only thing that keeps us civil. It makes sense that vampires would have souls, even if they would be changed much like their physical forms when they're brought over. I'm sure there are lots of religious debates on it. Like some religions debate whether witches have souls or not."

"The whole soul debate in general is a mess. All sentient beings have a life force. All living things, even plants, have a life force. What doesn't have a life force? Plastic," Seiran said. "We poison the earth with more of it every day."

"Does She complain?" Page wondered out loud. "I mean I always thought maybe She would one day get mad and just wipe us all out."

"She is not happy about it and shows Her displeasure in small ways, that are growing in scale," Seiran admitted. "Even I can only do so much to soothe Her."

"Mother Earth must be amazing," Page said.

"She is, and not always kind. Which I wish the world would remember." Seiran dug through his desk, unlocking drawers and pulling out files. The stack already on the top appeared to be from the unauthorized interviews. He barely glanced through them.

"That's fascinating," Gabe said. "When was this Vampire War?"

"About fourteen years ago," Page said.

Around the time Gabe had gone to ground. Had he been part of it? Perhaps lost in bloodlust over some battle? If the revenant had risen, that could explain a lot of things. He watched Seiran's body language, catching the nuance of tight shoulders, and lips pressed in a line as he flipped through the folders.

"The acknowledgment that vampires are sentient beings and not just demons walking around eating people is what the agreements are founded on," Page added.

"Agreements?"

"With humans and witches," Page said.

"The war was between vampires and humans and witches?" Gabe wondered. It seemed a very dumb thing for the vampires to try to demolish their food source. Why? Control? Were the vampires not allowed to feed?

"The vampires wanted world domination," Seiran said. "Tresler's goal was to enslave the vampires to his will, and subjugate the rest of their food supply to little more than cattle. He underestimated his reach."

Tresler. The name brought a handful of images to mind. Gabe worked to not grab for them, instead letting them come and go, settling where they would. Mundane things, like meetings, or perceived conversations, but a bitterness lingered. Not emotionally, but more as a taste. Like some bitter reminder of a flavor. He caught the image of a bottle that seemed to be filled with blood.

"Did we drink blood from bottles?" He asked before really thinking about it.

Seiran sucked in a painful breath, but his gaze met Gabe's. "It's what he used to gain control of the vampires. Tainting the food supply with his blood. It's not on the market anymore. Vampires have to get their blood the old-fashioned way."

"Hunting for it?" Gabe asked, knowing that couldn't be true.

"Yes, and no," Seiran agreed. "Blood must be given freely. It can be bought from donors, like the packets in the freezer at home, or fresh from the vein if it's consensual."

Gabe caught another flash memory of a club with willing donors who were all dying. The smell of their impending deaths foul. He could recall he'd fed from more than one throat there. It made his stomach clench. Hunger. He shouldn't be hungry already. But even dying blood, fresh from a vein sounded better than something from a packet.

"There were clubs?" Gabe asked quietly, sensing it was a bad topic, but wanting some clarification.

"They are all gone. At least as far as I know. Outlawed," Seiran's tone was clipped and he didn't look up.

"The donors were not willing?" Gabe wondered.

"The donors were often too far gone to realize they were being murdered."

"Some of them were addicts. Not drugs," Page added quickly, "but of being bitten. I guess the allure of vampires is a thing?" His gaze looked over Gabe as though there was some sign saying this is what people liked about vampires. "In the bite, maybe? Not that you're unattractive, Mr. Santini. I just mean… well, I've given blood, to like the Red Cross, before. And it wasn't something I'd say would be addicting."

"There is mind magic in their bite," Seiran said. "To make it hurt less. It is part of what creates the bond to eventually make someone a vampire. Without the bites, and the magic, there would be no vampire."

"Right," Page agreed. "I think I remember reading that. Not sure I'd want my mind taken over like that."

"It doesn't have to be that way," Gabe said. "The bite doesn't have to hurt, even without the bond." He could recall that was the reason vampires seduced their prey. It wasn't like a human salivating over a hamburger. If the hamburger could fight back, maybe. But humans took to pretty words, and romantic interludes, easily enough. "Vampires don't like to create those bonds. It leaves a little of them with each person they feed on."

He could recall the feeling of having too many tied to him, even in small ways. It became a lot of noise. Changing someone to a vampire would shift the drain to a battery to charge the vampire, but it was a lot of work to get there. More vampires under one Sire made the Sire more powerful, but too many bound servants became an issue. Unbound they died quickly, weeks maybe? He seemed to recall a handful of things that happened from a vampire feeding too often on one particular human.

Gabe hugged himself and concentrated on his breathing for a minute as the memories fell into place. Not everything, not even by a quarter, but bits of how vampires functioned, adapted, and survived. Rules, guidelines, and eventually the Tri-Mega had kept control.

"The Tri-Mega?" Gabe asked, suddenly remembering faces, Tresler among others.

"Gone. All of them. There is no real ruling body of vampires anymore. Though Max gets pretty pissy if a vampire steps out of line. Usually sends Sam to take care of it," Seiran said. "Each Master, the head of whatever city, is to control his or her nest. Max handles a lot of overseas stuff too, but I don't think he wants total world domination. People in general seem to irritate him when they ask for too much."

Another memory. Tresler again being broken apart by plants. Hadn't Max said Sam had done that? "Sam took out Tresler?"

"And Galloway before him."

Page laughed. "I knew that guy was a badass."

"Don't say that anywhere he can hear. His head is big enough," Seiran said.

"Sam…" Gabe wished more of those memories would come back, but it was still shattered, the shards too small to piece together.

"He's not been a vampire that long. But he's also a witch, so maybe that's part of it. Forest, come sit in that chair," Seiran directed the golem.

Page paled, hands gripping the counter of his desk, gaze on the golem. Did it frighten him? The existence of it? Or could he sense the power trying to regain control?

The golem moved, crossing the room and dropping into the chair. The fidgeting had stopped at least. Though Gabe still felt a tugging at it, like something was trying to call it, but all of that noise was muffled by the witch's strength.

"Forest?" Page asked.

"The golem's name," Seiran said. "Can you pull all the books on golems and death magic from the archive? I think there are three or so. Though I don't recall anything on vampires being used for this sort of thing. Or of actual souls being trapped inside."

"Sure," Page replied slowly, backing toward another doorway. "Vampire souls? Who would have thought to use them to create a golem?"

"Call the families first," Seiran reminded him. "Get them back in here. I have to find out where they got it from."

"You don't think one of them created it?" Page asked.

"No. I think they got it somewhere. The magic they had in their dorm wasn't the same as what's in the golem. Someone in their family has some powerful skills with wards, but the golem wouldn't have begun to unravel if it belonged to them."

"It doesn't look like it's unraveling now," Page said staring at Forest.

"My magic, and my blood," Seiran said. "I'm hoping to unravel it soon."

"What will happen to the souls then?" Page asked. "I mean if they are vampire?"

"They go wherever vampire souls go when they die."

"That's really sad," Page said.

"It is. But hopefully we can stop it from happening to anyone else. Please get those students back in here."

"Of course, sorry." Page nodded and returned to the desk picking up the receiver for the phone.

He kept his gaze on the golem who was now seated in the corner of Seiran's office. Gabe entered the room, feeling another roll of wards press against him, and then accept him. He closed the door behind him, giving them a bit of quiet as he composed himself. He could also feel Seiran clearer now. The wards wrapped around them were his, and the warmth that gave life to the entire area, from the plants to the buzzing sense of welcome, all belonged to the witch.

It made sense that Seiran would have created this as his home away from home. A sanctuary of earth magic and safety. He doubted anyone could actually enter Seiran's office if he didn't want them to. And Gabe suspected the wards would have slapped him down hard with little flex from their creator.

"You okay?" Seiran asked as he pulled a laptop computer out of his bag and set it on the desk beside the files.

"Yes," Gabe said, feeling it was only half a lie. The sealing of that final ward seemed to stop the constant tug on the golem and he let his shoulders relax. If it had been created from vampires, that made sense, however, he wasn't sure it was something they could control in the long run.

"Murdered vampires?" He added as he examined the golem with that edge of magic which had awakened in him after his first true death. He had never thought of death magic as dark or evil really, as it was what made a vampire. Gabe could recall a handful of times he'd seen it used for purposes that could be called evil, but all magic was that way. "It feels like a vampire," Gabe said quietly. "Hungry and a bit wild."

"You can feel it?"

"Yes. I think through your blood? But it feels like a vampire, so I'm trying to wrap ties around it like I would a new vampire. Keep it from resisting so much." It wasn't all that unlike what Max had done to him, binding him at the core. Though Gabe had not given it blood, not as Max had given him. Perhaps that was why it was a lot of work to hold it?

"Do I need to give it more blood?" Seiran asked.

Gabe moved so fast he wasn't certain how he'd gotten across the room, and had Seiran pinned to the wall of filing cabinets before he came back to himself. His hand was tight on Seiran's throat, but not squeezing, just holding him in place. Their bodies pressed together, Gabe's against Seiran's until they were both immobile. He felt like he was about to snap, but no blood had been drawn.

Seiran waited, Gabe didn't know for what. He expected to be slapped down, drawn back into the earth with little effort by a man so powerful. He actually felt the witch's power, the slow gather of it growing, a pool of energy lapping beneath the surface. But as he touched it, it seemed to dissipate. Spreading outward in a slow curl of strength, warmth, and life that made the plants on top of the cabinet grow. They didn't reach for him, in fact the power seemed to absorb through him, giving him clarity, even while he fought not to let the darkness rise.

Gabe sucked in a deep breath, the scent of Seiran, his blood, his skin, the smell of green things, vanilla, and a hint of honey, filling his lungs. "Sorry," he said, unable to let go. This close, his body pressed to Seiran's, there was a stirring of something in him. A thousand emotions, all tied up and jumbled like a ball of yarn matted in knots, and physically, a reaction of slow awakening desire. It was like muscle memory. His body reacting as it was supposed to, even if his mind hadn't caught up. He and the witch seemed to have had a more intimate relationship in the past.

The warmth of Seiran's pulsing earth power called to something in Gabe's core. It was an ebb and flow of strength. If Gabe worked hard enough, he thought maybe he could use it himself, though he couldn't recall ever having that power.

He stared down into sapphire blue eyes, feeling for the first time as though he recognized them. But that fast the memory was gone. A glimpse of a feeling perhaps. "I think it's the idea of you giving someone else blood," Gabe offered, fighting with himself over the fact that he needed to let go. He wasn't hurting the witch. His grip wasn't strong enough to do damage. But he also had the underlying knowledge that he *could*. Maybe it would be one hell of a battle, him against a witch of Seiran's power. Would he win? His speed and strength before the magic could be cast?

Seiran swallowed. The movement of his throat seeming to give rise to intense desire in Gabe. He found himself tightening that hand a little. Not enough to cut off air, but to feel him breathe.

"You can't kill me," Seiran whispered. "The earth will keep bringing me back until it's done with me. Can you say the same?"

But Gabe didn't want him dead. He just wanted him. In a dozen ways, some of them sexual, some of them bloody. Being a vampire really sucked sometimes. His gaze narrowed down to Seiran's face, while he prayed for more memories. He ran his thumb over Seiran's lower lip and was rewarded with a tiny edge of recognition.

"I don't want you dead," Gabe said, leaning forward to brush his lips over Seiran's. It was the barest taste of a kiss. The warmth of Seiran's mouth feeling like water to a man dying in the desert of thirst. Gabe held there for a moment. The witch frozen against him, unmoving other than to breathe. And it took Gabe another long moment to pull away and release his grip one finger at a time.

By the time he stepped away, they were both shaking. Gabe didn't think it was from fear. But he also wasn't expecting the fist to the jaw that sent him tumbling over the desk and through the glass door, which rained down on him in shards of broken glass and darkness.

CHAPTER 11

Instinct, Seiran told himself. Though the guilt bothered him. He hadn't expected the kiss, the reaction to the kiss, or the fact that he'd pulled strength from Gabe without trying, which caused more damage than Seiran ever could have on his own.

Super human strength wasn't a witch trait. Not without some serious magic backing it up. He could craft spells and wrap magic around himself that would rival a vampire, had done so in many sparring matches with Sam. But that punch had power been beyond any spell he'd ever created.

Seiran couldn't recall ever using Gabe's abilities before. Was that normal? They hadn't been bound long before Gabe's sanity had begun to unravel. Maybe he'd already been so far gone he hadn't realized they could share power. Something else he'd have to inquire of the vampires in his life. He couldn't recall any of the texts mentioning it, but most detailed very little about the Focus bond.

In fact, in history, the Focus bond had seemed to have risen from an upgrade to the feeding bond. A vampire accidentally binding someone they'd been feeding on for a long time. Which shifted the dynamic and gave vampires the ability to move around more in the daylight and among humanity. Perks of being tied to a mortal being, and maybe not the only ones.

Workers arriving to clean up the glass and repair the window created too much noise for Seiran to think. He had a dozen questions at least, and tried to write them down so as not to forget.

The fact that Page was hovering over Gabe, offering an ice pack and kind words, stirred a wave of jealousy to fill Seiran's gut.

Not fair. Gabe wasn't really his, even though they were bound. He hadn't expected Gabe to be able to shift the earth energy so easily. Another thing he'd had no idea a vampire could do without actually being a witch.

The more power Seiran drew, the more the vampire seemed to spread it outwards, channeling it, and rather than using it, it dissipated. It was almost relaxing, a balance of the near cosmic level of strength that Seiran had battled to control for the past decade and a half.

The fact that the power recognized Gabe, hadn't fought him at all, that was unnerving. The earth touched the bond between them and seemed to say *I approve* and turned off the fighting instinct. Seiran had an overwhelming urge to submit.

And wasn't that an unwelcome feeling, but natural? He'd spent so long being strong and independent, that he really hadn't let himself relax. Not that he thought the vampire was safe. Gabe had proven he wasn't years ago, and even if things had changed, the lack of control he exhibited worried Seiran.

The reaction of the golem worried him too. It seemed linked to Gabe, and hadn't he said something about it feeling like a vampire? The files Seiran found were numerous, but none of which his department had looked into. Missing vampires, murdered vampires, vampires in general, got cast off to Max and his people. The Dominion, and especially MI, was too short staffed to keep up with it all. Seiran had been fighting for years to expand the department, trying to push the idea of catching a witch before they were too far gone and had to be terminated. He had always hated being part of the cog in that murder machine.

But when he matched up the pictures of those the golem had showed him yesterday, he found vampire profiles. Missing vampires, rather than human. He'd been right, and a rock sat in his gut over the idea that he'd probably have to hand this whole thing off to Sam, which might mean the end of the golem, but not the magic that created it.

"Enough, Page," Seiran snapped as his assistant continued to hover around Gabe. "He's fine."

All but one of the students were on their way back in. Seiran argued with the family of the last one for a while, threatening his meager legal abilities to have witches detained and jailed for unauthorized use of magic. He hated using that one, as it was very broad, and mostly useless as he couldn't get the police to actually exercise warrants against witches and would have to bring the guy in himself.

"Find those books I asked for," Seiran commanded, needing Page out of his space or away from his vampire for the moment. *His* vampire. Fuck.

"Of course, Director Rou," Page did a little half bow and rushed off to the archives.

Gabe had kept his distance, sitting in the chair beside the reception desk while the maintenance crew cleaned up glass and measured windows. He hadn't spoken to anyone, but had allowed Page to fuss over him a little. His eyes were green, not black, which Seiran hoped to mean that the man had control and wasn't losing himself to the revenant.

He debated just pulling Gabe to the side bathroom and giving him blood. Would that solve this mess? A hungry vampire always created issues. But he shouldn't be hungry. Not after having blood this morning. Vampires, especially the older ones like Gabe, didn't need much blood or all that often. Max had indicated Gabe had fed on shifters, and then the blood from the fridge.

He *shouldn't* be hungry. The idea that he was, really worried Seiran. He could put Gabe back in the ground. But he was also pretty sure it would break something in him. The last strands of hope perhaps.

Seiran grabbed his laptop and files, needing to head upstairs to handle the interviews of the two students who were coming back. Could Gabe wander the main area of the Dominion halls? Would the sunlight be too much? Or the many wards layered across the building over decades? Would they accept Gabe like they did Seiran because of Seiran's power? He had gotten into the bowels of the building just fine, and Seiran's wards had paused, looking him over, before letting him through. Maybe?

He approached Gabe slowly, watching the vampire's body language for any sign of trouble. But he seemed relaxed, though he held the ice pack to his jaw, which was slightly discolored. Healing. But Seiran had hit him really hard.

"I'm sorry," Seiran said. "I didn't really mean to…"

"It was my fault," Gabe replied. "I overstepped."

He had, but that hadn't meant extreme violence was necessary. "I could have pulled away any time," Seiran admitted. The feeling of being pinned to the cabinets, the familiar weight of Gabe pressed against him had awakened a longing in him. He'd been frozen at first, debating on whether or not Gabe was in control, or the beast within him. But either way, it turned him on.

He could hear Sam's snark now, *Who's a kinky bastard now, Ronnie?*

Seiran was too old and world weary to be kinky. But yeah, it had been hard to tamp down on the desire to let Gabe have his way. It wasn't even about forgiveness as much as the fact that Gabe didn't remember him. Did that mean Seiran was just some witch he couldn't wait to eat? And maybe fuck. Okay, those things turned him on too. Seiran let out a long breath and prayed Gabe wasn't smelling his desire.

"Still," Gabe said, "I know better. My control should be better."

"Is it because you haven't had my blood?" Other than the small taste in the kitchen this morning, which seemed like a lifetime ago, though it had only been a few hours.

"Maybe?" Gabe shrugged. "My brain is still catching up on everything. Lots of holes to be filled in."

"What if having my blood fills it all in at once?" Seiran asked. "Maybe we should just get it over with?" He pushed up his sleeve thinking he could handle a bite, even a painful one, which might help ease the desire a little.

Gabe swallowed hard, his eyes flashing to black again. Seiran had to fight to keep from taking a step back. "When I take you," Gabe said slowly. "It won't be anything to *get over with*."

"I didn't offer sex," Seiran said quietly. A partial lie at best. Because he knew it wouldn't take much to be steered in that direction.

"Since you're my Focus, it should be near impossible to manipulate your mind and give you pleasure that way. And without physical desire, or at least dreams to cloud your mind a little, it would hurt. A bite that deep is rarely pleasant. Though the lines between pleasure and pain can be blurred if done right," Gabe said. "When I have you beneath my fangs, it will be pleasure I give you, not pain."

When. Seiran thought maybe he wasn't wrong. It wouldn't be an if, but a when. They were bound after all. Until true death do them part. Would he rather be bound to someone he hated forever? Was at constant war with? Or a place to find warmth and refuge? He sighed, thinking it was all too much for a man as cynical and tainted as he'd become over the years. Trust had always been hard-won. And Gabe had stomped on that trust years ago.

"I need to go upstairs and question witnesses," Seiran said after a minute. The golem sat still as stone in the chair in Seiran's office. The wards of the space seemed to help keep it still. Or maybe that was part of Gabe's power. "I'm not sure you should stay here by yourself? Maybe I should call you a cab and send you back to Max?"

Seiran had already sent Sam a long list of questions, along with the three dead vampire files he could tie to the golem. He hadn't heard back, but suspected Sam was sleeping as he often did in the middle of the day like this. It made him wonder if Gabe should be resting, even if he didn't appear tired or pulled by the weight of the daylight. Would lack of sleep make his control worse? Why did Seiran feel so lost when he'd spent more than the last decade studying vampires?

Gabe stood slowly, as though afraid he'd spook Seiran, and set the ice pack on the desk. "I'd rather remain close to you."

"Why? Is it a blood thing?" Everything with vampires was about blood. That much he'd learned years ago. In fact, a lot of the darker edges of magic that Seiran had been investigating seemed to be about blood. He'd often wondered if it was its own branch of magic. An element unto itself, like earth or water, but hadn't found anyone willing to discuss it with him. At the moment he had to keep himself from remembering the many times he'd fed Gabe in the past, almost all of which had been during sex. Seiran's control was good, but to keep from getting hard if he thought too much about the past? That seemed impossible.

"A little," Gabe agreed. "Though I am drawn to you. Like being close tickles my memory."

"But you don't remember me specifically," Seiran clarified.

Gabe swallowed hard; gaze focused on Seiran's lips. "I remember tiny things."

Had the kiss jogged something loose? It hadn't been much of a kiss really. Not even worth getting upset over. Seiran held his computer and the files to his chest as a shield, reminding himself he didn't need all the answers right now. Not for this at least.

"Right, then, let's go upstairs. Forest, come," Seiran said as he headed for the door. The golem got up and followed along, moving so suddenly from complete stillness that the workers jumped back. They probably hadn't thought it was a living thing, since the golem didn't move or breathe for so long. "Sorry," Seiran apologized to them. "We'll leave you to your work."

Gabe and Forest followed Seiran out of the lower level and back up to the main level. All the warded interrogation rooms were on the main level. But interrogation was used by every department, and often got overlaid with the idea of torture when it came to witches going rogue. Seiran hated the feel of the rooms. The strong cast of nullifying magic dampening the spaces. He could still pull magic, but it broke the null cast, and since a person had to die to create that magic, he tried not to fuck with those rooms unless he absolutely had to.

Director Han was in the hall outside of the main stretch of interrogation rooms talking with another older woman. When she saw Seiran, she turned his way, the disapproval clear on her face. She opened her mouth to speak, but Seiran held up a hand. "Don't even. You know you overstepped. This is my investigation and an MI case."

If a glare could kill, he'd have dropped dead right there. She finally said, "I've assured Ms. Weatherford, that this is just a formality." She motioned to the woman beside her.

Seiran turned his attention to her, and beyond her to the window into the room, where a young man sat. Weatherford would be Kevin Weatherford, age twenty-one, a student majoring in computer science at the UofM. "He's old enough to not need his mother," he paused assessing the woman, "Or grandmother present for questioning." He passed them both without acknowledging them and opened the door to the room. Both women erupted in a squawking protest that he ignored. Gabe and Forest followed him inside the room, but Gabe stayed near the door, his back to it like a guard.

Seiran pulled out a chair and directed Forest to it. At the sound of the name, Kevin looked up, examining the golem. Seiran set his stuff on the table and opened the file with his notes and the previous interview. Kevin was young, not a jock type as Seiran had expected. At least not unless his workouts involved video games. He was thin, and lanky, but didn't come across as physically strong like Sam's boyfriend, Constantine did. Kevin looked like the sort of guy who lived in his parent's basement playing video games all day while complaining no one would date him. Maybe that was why he'd been in one of the non-magic dorms. Shoved out by a family annoyed with his lack of motivation for life.

"It looks better," Kevin said. "Was coming apart for a while."

"It was," Seiran agreed. He pulled another chair over and sat down, giving himself a minute to adjust to the weird absence of power the room provided. He wondered if it would trouble the golem or the vampire, but neither seemed affected by the nullification. "How long had you had the golem before it started to unravel?" Seiran began, trying to gauge how much he'd get from the student before he clammed up.

"A couple weeks," Kevin said. "Will this take long? I'm missing class to be here. Already answered questions today."

"But you were using the golem to go to class for you," Seiran reminded him. As he had accounts from this student's teachers about the golem. Weird behavior from this student in class; inhumane, one teacher had reported. It was one of the things that had led Seiran to the dorm. "Doesn't seem like you care all that much about classes."

Kevin folded his arms across his chest and sat back, looking annoyed, and entitled. Was it sad that Seiran hated witches when he was one?

"Perhaps you're misinformed about why you're here," Seiran began. "You're currently being held for suspicion of death magic, which as you know carries a death sentence. This is not a simple *we ask you questions and you get to go home*, scenario." Seiran could sense the movement from outside the room, a burst of heat and rage, like he was overstepping. But he had no intention of letting this kid walk out. Kevin and his friends had let the golem run free and injure a half dozen people. Even if they didn't make it, they hadn't reported it, even when it began to unravel. That was at minimum a reckless attempt at homicide.

Kevin paled. "I didn't make it," he said hotly. "I've already told them that. I've already answered questions."

"Not for me," Seiran said. "I am the head of Magic Investigations." He raised a brow, wondering if the kid had heard of him at all. His aunt had quite the reputation of being ruthless over the years before she had retired. He didn't think he'd cultivated the same intensity. But part of that was because very few people saw him as really having power among the Dominion. He was, after all, a lowly male when it came to the matriarchy of magic. "I am also the Pillar of Earth. You may call me, Director Rou."

Kevin seemed unimpressed.

Seiran had to hold back his sigh. There was no respect for pillars anymore. He wondered if that was because of him, or the many figureheads that had held the position before him. He pointed at the golem. "Did you know golems can only be created from death magic?"

"Death magic isn't a thing. It's just part of earth. The golem is a bunch of sticks and clay, and a handful of spells. We didn't think it was a big deal," Kevin began talking.

"You've taken some basic magic studies classes then?"

"It's required for all witch families."

"Have you tested?" Seiran wanted to know. He could reach out and feel the power of any witch, even in a nullified room like this, but he made it a habit to not touch suspects.

"No," Kevin said. "I'm a guy."

Seiran waited.

"No power," Kevin finally added.

"Again," Seiran said and pointed to himself, "Pillar of Earth. Being a guy doesn't mean no power."

"My mom says you're just some figurehead they put in office so your mom could get more power."

Well now, that was laid bare. Seiran reached across the table and put his hand on Kevin's arm. It was an instant recognition. Air. Probably level two, which was common among witches in general.

No different than the guards at the main desk had been. As Seiran dug deeper, he heard a pounding on the door, demands for it to be opened. But this was Seiran's case, and his aunt had ensured the rules that limited him were few. MI spent too much time chasing the darkest of magic users to ever be constrained by simple political politeness.

Kevin gasped as Seiran touched his power, studied it. He could be a level three if he worked hard. But the wards hadn't been his, neither was anything of the golem. Not created by him, or even controlled really. Seiran withdrew his hand.

There was an edge of recognition that seemed to come from Gabe. A startled movement, something? Seiran glanced back. Gabe still stood with his back to the door, unmoving despite the racket coming from the other side. "He gave it blood. To try to bind it? I can still smell the edge of it on the golem and him," Gabe said.

That made sense, though how a witch with no training hoped to use their own blood to control something they hadn't created, baffled Seiran. It wouldn't work on the best of days. And even he was struggling to control this thing. Death magic, Seiran was coming to believe, was a different element altogether. Not a facet of earth at all.

"Level two air witch, eh? Too bad your family wouldn't have let you test. You could have been a powerful witch." Now he'd likely spend some time in prison rather than returning to school.

"I'm not a witch," Kevin said, as if that would protect him from using a magically created being for ill gains.

"Do you know what reckless endangerment means, Mr. Weatherford?" Seiran asked. "Do you know what it means for a witch who causes reckless endangerment?" It wasn't a slap on the wrist, even for the powerful witch families. The media followed the Dominion too closely to let anything this public be swept under the rug. If the golem hadn't attacked people, maybe.

"I didn't do anything. I didn't create it."

"Who did?"

"I don't know. We got it from someone. Steve found it online or something."

Steve. Seiran glanced at his notes. The one student whose family refused to return him. This was going to be a fun afternoon. "Why didn't you turn it in right away?"

Kevin looked away, seeming uncomfortable. "We were having some fun is all."

"Having some fun. Sending it to class was fun?" No, that was convenient. What had they done with it before? To have fun with it? Probably when they still had full control and it hadn't begun to unravel. A sick feeling uncurled in his gut. He prayed he was wrong, but his instincts were rarely wrong.

Seiran glanced at the golem who sat blank and unmoving in the chair like it was little more than a statue. It looked like a person because Seiran's magic gave it that strength, but it was a thing. "What did you do with the golem when you first got it?"

Kevin's cheeks flushed pink and he wouldn't look at Seiran. "Nothing big. I mean it can look like anyone, right? As long as we show it a picture, and tell it what to do?"

Except that sort of shift and control, meant the magic would unravel faster. If they'd left it whatever it had been from how it had been gifted to them, they might have gotten away with it longer. Seiran sat back in his chair and stared at Forest, finally saying, "Forest?"

The golem moved suddenly, lifting its gaze to Seiran. Kevin jumped half out of his chair at the movement. "Show me the visage this man commanded of you," Seiran said spreading his magic outward, despite knowing it would disrupt the nullifying field of the room. The golem shifted instantly, appearance changing to that of a girl, probably not much more than one. Teenager at most. Pretty in an unfinished way. And almost completely nude, skirt short like they never were outside of anime, and topless.

They used the golem for sex? That was a new level of kink Seiran hadn't thought possible.

RESURRECTION

Kevin gaped at the girl; his hands clutched on the table. The noise outside grew louder. Gabe kept his arms folded across his chest, acting as a sentinel at the door. Useful.

"What did they ask you to do, Forest?" Seiran inquired of the golem. He knew the many cameras of the room would be catching this all. Good documentation for court. Kevin would be lucky if he didn't get life in prison for this. Death was off the table, since he didn't create the golem. Reckless endangerment would have been for not reporting it. But using it, not only for the classes, but as some sort of deviant sex toy? That was an abuse of a magic object with malignant intent.

The golem got on its knees and splayed itself like it was ready to be taken from behind. It made noises like a porn movie would, but sounded very fake even as it said things like "Fuck me, big boy," and "Oh, yes, you're so thick," in between what appeared to be sucking as well.

"Make it stop," Kevin said huddling back into the corner of the room, while the smell of his arousal was unmistakable. The noise from outside the room had vanished, probably in stunned silence.

"I'm making note that the suspect smells of arousal," Seiran stated for the record.

"I also smell his arousal," Gabe added.

"I'm not..." Kevin protested even as he couldn't tear his eyes away. "It's not... it is just a toy. Not real. It wasn't..."

"Not a toy," Seiran corrected. "That was created from souls. Vampire or otherwise, it still requires new death to create a golem, and an object created from sentient life used for malignant intent, is a life sentence. And there are souls trapped inside, not just some clay vessel empty and ready to do as you command. You raped dead people," Seiran said the quiet part out loud, putting voice to their crimes. It wasn't a toy or a lifeless thing to be manipulated. They had raped it, and "Murdered people."

"Wasn't rape. It's willing," Kevin tried.

"It can't say no, which does not mean it was willing," Seiran said.

He got up. "Forest, stop. Return to the way you were, and rest." The visage of the girl vanished, melting away to the young man from a book Forest had found the day before, and seating himself back in the chair. Seiran felt bad for making it replicate what had happened. The golem probably didn't care, but the souls tied to it might.

He gathered up his laptop and paperwork, more intent on solving this case than he had been before. Logically, everyone knew there were kinks like this. Probably entire online communities committed to this sort of thing, but it wasn't anything Seiran wanted to know about. He'd stop it where he could. His own past of assault reared up, making him nauseous. Therapy could only do so much to quell the trigger of memories. He wasn't that kid anymore. Not helpless. Or he pretended as much, shutting down his emotions. He had a job to do. If there was anything Seiran had mastered in his life, it was survival. The earth might not let him die, but there were plenty of ways a soul could fade until not even the body could return. And he'd seen enough horrors for a thousand lifetimes.

"Who was the girl?" Seiran asked Kevin as he got ready to leave the room and head for the next suspect. "Some celebrity or something?" He hadn't recognized her, but that didn't mean she wasn't famous or something. His kids were more into pop culture than he was. Either way, the charges were the same. He'd press because he didn't like the way the girl looked underage. Bad enough they were raping the dead, even worse that they were perpetuating pedophilia to do it. If it had been his daughter, he'd have fought for a rule change, putting the death penalty on the table. If he didn't kill the kid first.

The earth might not like that, and even take him back, but it would be worth a true death. Seiran had a powerful distaste for child abusers of any kind.

"Steve's sister," Kevin said so softly Seiran barely heard it.

CHAPTER 12

The show was no less disturbing the second time around. And the two women from the first hall silenced the new woman waiting outside the second room.

Gabe acted as guard, using his size, and his natural vampire presence to keep them out. Seiran had gone very silent in the first room when the deviance had been revealed. It was a closing of the link between them. Not cut off, but a firm wall in place, which made Gabe shut down harder on the revenant.

His connection to the witch needed to be renewed. That much he understood now. Whether that was through blood or some actual metaphysical tie, he didn't know. But Seiran closing him off brought a renewed struggle for control. He shouldn't have been this unsettled after going to ground for so long. Maybe he *had* been pulled early. It would explain why his memories were coming back in a tiny trickle and the revenant kept fighting for release.

At least the golem wasn't drawing on him much now. The strength of Seiran's power seemed to have a firm grip on the creature while in this warded area.

The space was unusual. Gabe could feel the absence of magic, other than what Seiran projected, as white noise. Almost a muting of the world around them. It was interesting to see how much of actual *life* was magic. Or at the very least, tied to magic. Himself included.

The second boy caved just as fast as the first, claiming he hadn't raped the golem, and it wasn't really meant to be one of the boy's underage sisters. Something about 'teaching that bitch her place' and 'it was just a game.'

The rage that filled Seiran, becoming a tangible thing as the room seemed to heat, made Gabe tighten his arms. He was already hugging himself, with arms folded like he was a bodyguard, near the door. But the level of anger, feeling almost like fire, reminded Gabe that earth, while most thought was limited to growing things, also included fire, water, and death. Much more than just life. He couldn't recall if he'd ever seen that expansion of power from an earth witch before. But his scattered memory told him he avoided witches. Before this one at least.

This witch was his. He could feel the thrum of that in his bones. Even when the memories refused to clarify. The need to protect him, somehow stop this pain that was making him close off, hurt. It was easy to turn pain to rage, easier than basking in what hurt, and Gabe suspected that was what Seiran was doing.

By the time they left the room, the hallway outside was silent. Only Director Han waited, her face drawn in a pinched frown. "I will have guards sent to fetch the last boy," she told Seiran.

"Don't bother," Seiran said. "My team will bring him in."

"His family needs to know… about his sister. What if he…?"

Seiran barely glanced her way. "Maybe you should have let me question them?"

"These boys come from prominent witch families who donate a lot to maintaining the balance of the Dominion," Han protested.

"Meaning they donate to you? Or offered you money to sweep this under the rug? I believe that's an ethics violation, Director Han."

"I accepted nothing from them."

Seiran nodded. "I'm sure you won't be bothered when I have the Ethics Committee review your bank records." Page lingered near the end of the hallway, an armful of books as a shield while he kept out of the long spread of nullified cells. "Page, please get Director Ariana on the phone for me. I'll discuss ethics with her on route to my last suspect."

"We thought the boys were just using it to take tests for them," Han said quietly.

"A golem is created from new death," Seiran reminded her. "I know taboo magic wasn't taught a half century ago, but it's a required yearly update for those employed here. You can't just scrape together a bunch of clay and *will* it to live. Something has to die to animate it. It's how animation works, it's part of necromancy," he waved at Gabe, "vampirism, all of it."

"The earth has power over life and death," Director Han said.

"Yes," Seiran agreed. "And She grants limited access. The rest of us have to take from one thing and move it to the next to create life. Energy, life, and power are not a vacuum, they need a balance. Living beings died to create that thing. There are souls still trapped inside of it."

"Vampires…"

"Are considered sentient life," Seiran interrupted before she could get more insulting. "And you didn't know it was vampires that created it until I came in and told you." He headed toward Page, Gabe following at a silent distance, keeping the golem in front of him. It wasn't pulling on the bonds for the moment. But that could be the warded area they were in. If necessary, he could jump on the thing and tear it apart. Enough damage and it would take a while to regenerate. Maybe enough time for the witch to unravel it.

Seiran took the stack of books from Page, the young man pale beneath his dark skin.

"I heard about…" Page said, his cheeks flushed pink. "I'm sorry. I know you… well, I hate that you had to experience a reminder."

Reminder of what? Gabe wondered.

"Feel worse for the souls inside the golem who had to live through it." Seiran said. They headed for the front door. The sun was setting, the cast of colors stretching across the windows. It felt a bit unsettling to stare at the fading light. The sun itself already lost in clouds and the horizon, leaving only the wash of colors to indicate the time. Gabe knew he should feel the tug of light in some way. And he supposed he did, a little. The fading edges of fog seemed to be evaporating from his brain.

He thought he'd felt a little sluggish all day, suspected it was the distance from his Focus, the lack of shared blood, but that was only a small portion of it. The sun didn't burn, but it did make him slow. That was good to realize. He could work around it. Maybe he should rest during the daylight hours, even if he wasn't tired.

"It's terrible," Page said. "Who would do that sort of thing?"

"Not everyone sees vampires as people." Seiran had his phone out.

"But they still have souls. They still feel pain," Page pointed out. "To use it that way…"

Seiran's gaze fell on Gabe. There was almost a question in his eyes, like was it true? Did vampires feel emotions the same way regular people did? The answer was yes, and no. Time could dull emotions. But often vampires went to the other extreme, feeling too much, seeking out the fringes of things, love and hate, just to feel. Gabe recalled feeling that way for a while. Could picture a handful of times in his life he'd been considered reckless, just to feel something.

"We do," Gabe said. "Pain and pleasure, hate and love, and a thousand other things. Can we release the souls soon?" He felt bad for those stuck within it, though as the sun set, he also found it easier to wrap his power around it, cradling and comforting it as he would a brand-new vampire. The tugging on it had faded when they went into the warded area of the building, but now in the entry, it finally seemed naturally quiet.

"I hope so," Seiran said. There was an SUV idling outside the main entry. The back door opened and it was the vampire Sam who leaned out. "About time," Seiran griped.

"Shut up, Ronnie. Some of us have to sleep and enjoy waking up with our guys."

Seiran flinched, but headed toward the SUV. "I'll send you notes, Page. Go home. I'll see you tomorrow. Don't worry about calling the Director, I'll phone her myself from the car."

Page lingered near the door, his gaze sad. "I'm sorry, Director Rou."

"For what?" Seiran asked.

Page waved his hand in an all-encompassing gesture. "Everything?"

"It's fine, Page. See you in the morning. I'm hoping to actually get more than four hours of sleep tonight." Seiran looked at the golem. "Forest, get in the vehicle."

Gabe followed since he had no plans to be separated from Seiran. Not until more of his memories returned and he had a better grasp of his control. At least the setting sun eased some of the constant struggle of the revenant. It almost seemed to lay back and rest. Ready to rise fast enough if he let it, but no longer fighting to take control. Normal? Or a consequence of being newly aboveground. Would the other vampire know?

The back of the SUV was roomy. A middle section of seats in which Sam sat, and the back where the golem was. Gabe took the seat beside the golem, and Seiran sat next to Sam, sliding the door shut. Seiran rattled off an address. "Meeting a handful of guards there, to pick up the last boy," Seiran said.

"I get to scare some witch kid? I'm down with that," Sam said.

Seiran handed a file folder over to Sam, who immediately opened it. Were the vampires supposed to have access to Dominion files? The car moved and Gabe studied Seiran as they headed toward the address.

Seiran placed a quick call to the Director of Ethics, mentioning the case he was working on, the severity of the offenses, and how he had been undermined by Director Han to the possible detriment of a child. He ended the short call, which seemed to be a voicemail with, "I hope we are in time to keep her from being abused."

The tightness of his voice at that phrase made Gabe's stomach hurt. Had someone abused the witch? Had it been him? He'd never thought himself possible of that sort of thing. Even in his earliest days as a vampire, he could recall stalking and seducing people, but all were adults in full use of their faculties. It was a vague memory of his childhood, as faded as it was, that made him dislike the young being used that way. Had he been? He couldn't recall, and suspected there would be none alive to ask.

"This is sick shit," Sam said after several minutes of reviewing the files. "I mean beyond your crappy handwriting. These kids are messed up."

"Agreed," Seiran said. "Did you know any of the vampires that we identified?"

"Only from their missing persons profiles. At least we know they are dead. Makes me wonder, as we have almost three dozen others who have been reported missing."

Seiran looked at Sam. "Do you think there are more golems?"

"No idea, Ronnie. That's strong magic. And a lot of golems if so. Who would need a golem army? And why three vampires in one golem? Are vampire souls less powerful than human ones?" He closed the file. They rode in silence for a bit. "Sorry you had to experience that today. I know you have people who handle the sexual crimes area."

"It's fine," Seiran said.

"It's not. But I know no one knew. I mean… well, fuck," Sam said. "Sick stuff."

"I hope the girl is okay," Seiran said, his gaze intent out the side window.

"I've got other vampires in route to meet us," Sam added. He held up his phone, showing a group text. "In case this kid gives us trouble."

"He didn't create it. At least I don't think so. Just used it."

"To rape his sister? Yeah, I know it wasn't really her, but gross."

The bond between Gabe and Seiran closed further, leaving Gabe gasping a little. Too much distance, his brain said. A floundering edge of darkness began to tunnel his vision, and Gabe struggled to breathe. He wasn't sure any of them would be able to escape if his revenant got loose in the car.

"I'm sorry," Gabe said softly. "The bond between us when closed like this, makes it harder to control the revenant." He hated admitting it, worried that they'd put him back in the ground, even though he was doing his best. He didn't think he should be this unsteady. But he couldn't remember any of the specific times he'd gone to ground and returned, if they felt this way and he'd forgotten, or this was unusual.

Seiran looked back at him, and Gabe felt the wall slowly begin to release. It was like fingers uncurling from a tight fist, opening at a snail pace. Finally, Gabe could breathe. "Thank you," he said after a moment. The darkness pressing on his sight faded and the revenant seemed to ease back into the bowels of his conscience.

"Haven't renewed the bond?" Sam asked glancing Gabe's way.

"Renewed the bond? I thought it never goes away?" Seiran asked.

"No, but it gets stretched and weak."

Seiran seemed to stew in that for a minute as Sam continued to read. "What do I have to do to renew it? Give him blood?"

"Well, yeah, Ronnie. He's a vampire." Sam looked back at Gabe. "Holding together okay so far, right?"

"Is it normal to be so unsteady after awakening?" Gabe asked. "I can't remember other times specific enough to recall."

"Yes, and no?" Sam said. "I mean it's always a little touch and go right after a bit in the ground. Never down more than a week anymore myself. But I schedule it like Max says to, and have less trouble. Once I feed from one of my guys, it's a lot better."

"But neither of them is your Focus," Seiran said.

"Not officially. No vows or anything. We don't think that I can make Luca a Focus since he's a dhampir. His power sort of runs parallel to mine. It's like trying to bond to a vampire I didn't make. We've discussed the option with Con. But both the witches and the vampires don't much like bonds between vampires and witches."

"Our relationship is an anomaly?" Gabe asked about himself and Seiran.

"Rare," Sam agreed. "But since you're one of the bigger powers left in the vampire world, or were, everyone mostly left you alone."

Gabe didn't feel like a big power. He wished his memory came back in more than fits and stutters. There were too many blanks for his comfort.

The car pulled up to a giant house not unlike Seiran's home. Though this looked bigger on the outside. One of those sprawling mansions with a dozen wings spread out like fingertips.

"Guess we're not going for subtle," Sam muttered, glaring at the flashlights of cops, black vehicles surrounded by thug-looking vampires, and a line of witches with badges on lanyards around their necks, all in a standoff.

The SUV stopped and Seiran didn't wait for the driver to get out and open the door. He was first out, with Sam quick behind him.

"This is a vampire case," one of the vampires said.

"A witch family," one of the witches said, though her gaze fell on Seiran and it wasn't one of the many Gabe had seen in the last few hours filled with disdain. Her expression showed respect. "Director Rou."

"Emmaline, thanks for coming. Did you review the videos?"

"Yes. Horrible."

"Could we have done this quieter?" Sam asked. "Seems like standing out here making noise is giving our perp a chance to run?"

"He's not here," one of the vampires said. "Family is. Said the kid was out back in his pool house. They have a fucking pool house in Minnesota," the vampire was shaking his head. "But he's not there."

"His family just let him leave?" Seiran asked. "Did anyone fill them in? Check on the girl?"

Emmaline nodded. "I gave them the low-lights. Keeping it minimal and hopefully the worst of it out of the press. Sounds like he never returned home after originally being questioned? We've got the family coming in for interrogation, and I'll have people sweeping the entire property for evidence."

"He didn't create it," Seiran said. "Used it, but didn't make it. I need to know where he got it from."

"The house is empty right now. All staff and family are being transported to the Dominion office. I can take you back to look through his area, but we have a lot of ground to cover. We already have investigators ready to question everyone as soon as they arrive."

Seiran sighed, sounding tired. "Fine." He glanced at the vampires.

"I've got them," Sam said. "Going to have them walk the grounds. See if we can find any of the missing vampires."

Gabe followed as Seiran walked with the witch group toward the house. If there had been wards, they were gone now. Not even a residual lingering of energy. Were there witches who didn't ward their homes?

"Who's your escort?" Emmaline asked.

"Oh," Seiran turned Gabe's way. "This is Gabe Santini. Gabe this is Emmaline Jacques, head of my investigation team here in the USA. I'm glad you were in town."

"Heard about the golem sighting and made our way back. Figured if it didn't go to the vampires, it would be something big. You're sure this thing is made from vampire souls?" She stared at Forest.

"Yes," Seiran said.

"Seems overkill?"

"Unnecessary for sure," Seiran agreed. "No idea why they put souls in it at all? A mistake in the spell maybe?"

"Is there a spell for a transfer of souls?" She asked.

"Not that I'm aware of."

"Very likely an unskilled witch then? A mistake." She seemed to pause at that, her tone hitching a little.

"Still a death sentence," Seiran said softly, as though knowing her question without her saying it.

That seemed extreme if someone had accidentally created the golem, although Gabe supposed it depended on intent. Had they meant to make it? Or awakened to a power they didn't know how to control? Or had something completely mundane turned dark? Didn't any of that matter to the Dominion?

They traveled a handful of hallways and out a back door to a courtyard and a pool beyond. The house sitting on a concrete slab felt very cold, and dark. But there were police and what appeared to be agents of the Dominion moving around the space, cataloging things with photos and little numbered tabs.

"Did you find anything?" Seiran asked.

"Evidence of his presence. We're taking his electronics, searching phone records, getting DNA from the property to see if we can match it up. Treating the whole property like a crime scene so we don't miss anything."

The door to the pool house was open. It was furnished grandly, but little more than a wide-open studio space. It stank of sex, which made Gabe wrinkle his nose. Especially knowing how the day had progressed. Did that mean there was another golem this kid was abusing?

"Stinks in here," Seiran remarked. "Sex, and death?"

Did Gabe smell the death? He breathed deeply, trying to pull out the nuances of the scents, and found it there beneath the overpowering stink of dried spend. "I smell it," he said.

"Death?" Emmaline asked. "We didn't find any bodies in here. No blood spatters. We've already brought black lights in to search."

Gabe turned, following the smell, not deeper into the house, but out and around. He was shocked by the level at which he could track it. Not blood, as that was usually easy to find, but death. It was a dark, musty scent of rot. Not even new death.

Golems didn't have a smell, not normally. Another memory clunking into place. They didn't usually rot. Which meant they had no reason to smell like anything other than the earth of which they were created.

He got the vague impression that zombies smelled. How he knew that or if he had encountered some actual zombies in his life, eluded him. But he followed the scent in a weaving path through a giant, well-manicured yard around tool sheds, and finally into a wooded area.

Seiran's senses were wide open to him now, as if he was trying to sense what Gabe was following. Though the connection was still weak. Gabe worked to keep the lines open as everyone followed him.

Gabe paused at one of the locked tool sheds, and even though he needed to keep going, there was something inside. The strong smell of blood.

Seiran reached out with magic and the lock snapped without being touched. The door swung open. Not full of tools at all, but tables, and stains. More like the space that would be used to gut an animal after a kill.

Emmaline was on the phone calling more investigators, and Sam appeared a few seconds later. "I smell blood."

Old blood. Yeah, a lot had died here. But this wasn't all. Gabe turned and focused on the feeling of rot, and the animation that often came with it. He left the group at the first shed, though there were a line of them, and headed into the woods. Seiran followed.

"Zombies?" Seiran asked quietly as they walked, Gabe mostly

unseeing anything really around them as he was laser-focused on the smell.

"Do you smell it?" Gabe asked.

"Yes, but I didn't know what exactly it was. Old death? We've found old bodies before and they just smell like earth. The rot scent fades pretty fast. You think these are fresher?" He sniffed the air, seeming to find the scent again, and frowned. "It's like death, and rot, but with perfume? Not the sickly-sweet smell of rotting meat, but actual flowers?"

"Only zombies smell like that."

"Not vampires?" Seiran asked.

"No. Vampires don't rot. Even when we go to ground, we are absorbed back into it if we are down long enough. This is something else."

"Zombies aren't a thing," Emmaline said, having left people behind to begin cataloging the sheds as she followed Gabe. "It's a horror movie special effect."

"It's a thing," Gabe assured her. He had a sudden memory of a handful of times in his past he had encountered zombies. Not movies. The real thing. And they felt very familiar. Fuck. "Death magic."

"I am really beginning to think death magic is its own thing," Seiran said.

"It is," Gabe said. "As an earth witch you could unravel the ties that make a vampire, but you can't create a vampire. Death magic is required for animation."

"You're remembering more?"

"Bits and pieces."

The area they came across was a bit of a break in the trees, mostly bland and seeming to be little more than dirt. It wasn't mounds or anything that looked like graves. In fact, the ground didn't appear disturbed at all, but Gabe's revenant was pulling hard at him, wanting out to fight whatever danger they stood in.

Gabe stopped in the center of the small clearing and let his power reach into the ground. Not magic like the witches, but a vampire's strength. He could sense other vampires. Gone to ground here, perhaps? Why?

"There are vampires here," Gabe said. He looked at Seiran. "Can you feel them in the earth?"

"Gone to ground?" Seiran appeared confused, but Gabe could feel when he opened himself up to what the earth was telling him. Gone to ground wasn't right. Left more than a few days the vampire body would reform, eventually returning to their graves. Or wherever most of their grave dirt was.

This ground had been disturbed, and only the barest hints of blackness in the soil gave tell to what lay beneath. Touching them, the bits of darkness, was almost like stirring the revenants. Not possible. Seiran hissed after a moment and the ground began to bubble.

The witches stepped back all gasping at the sight as Seiran's power forced the bodies of vampires to the surface. Not one, or even a dozen, but so many it was impossible to find ground without them. Some had tree roots grown through, and many were actually rotted, taken by true death. A few stared at them with wide, seeing eyes, while staked and bound, limbs missing, covered in lacerations and burns, like they'd been tortured and then somehow bound beneath the earth to keep them silent.

"Holy fuck," Sam said as he appeared behind the group. "What the fuck is this?"

"Your missing vampires." Seiran said.

And then some, thought Gabe at the body count. "Does this mean there are more golems?"

CHAPTER 13

A vampire serial killer was not the news Seiran had been hoping to end his evening with. The amount of law enforcement, Dominion investigators, and vampires that descended on the spot was astronomical. They would need something larger than the normal morgue office to house all the bodies. Seiran suspected they needed more space than the combined Twin Cities morgues could offer.

"What is the point of all this?" He wondered out loud as the group worked its way across the scene. Vampires in the modern day kept their heads down and out of trouble. The Vampire War, even as brief as it had been, only lasting a few months, had been enough to set the entire world against them. Only delicate negotiation had helped soothe some of the frayed trust. Negotiation and time. Was this some sort of revenge? Why so many vampires? And how? Vampires weren't exactly easy to kill, or hold. "Does anyone know the family's history? Is there a beef against vampires?"

"I'll look into it," one of the group Emmaline had brought in, said. Seiran was pretty sure she was on the investigative team, but hadn't personally trained her as he had Emmaline.

Max appearing on the fringes of the group startled him, and the cops who were guarding the area, although they recognized him fast enough and let him through. It was never good when the big dog of vampires showed up.

"Hart," Seiran greeted him.

"How many were saved?" He asked without preamble. "I have a warehouse open for the bodies. We can go through each, identify and notify next of kin and the members of their nests."

"Two are still somewhat there," Sam said. "Might be revenant, so we're being careful."

Gabe had done something with those two that had calmed them enough to be taken to the hospital. They still had to be bound with vampire grade cuffs before transport and treatment. A half dozen vampires had escorted the ambulance to ensure the safety of the EMT and the hospital staff. But the vampires weren't in any shape to answer questions. The torture they had survived brought a lot of uncomfortable realizations. Like the fact that being a vampire and almost impossible to kill, might not be a good thing.

"Broken," Gabe said. "The tie to what makes them human, snapped."

Max studied him, then turned to Seiran. "I've been told the culprit hasn't been caught?"

Seiran felt his cheeks heat. It wasn't really his place to be embarrassed. He hadn't let the guy go. He still didn't believe the missing kid, Steven Brody, had created the golem. The magic of the golem wasn't maniacal or even haphazard. It seemed to have been created by someone who knew how to do it. Or sort of knew how to do it, and had the power to do so. The rest of this mess was anything but a skilled practitioner. It was more a child breaking toys while it played, messy, and erratic, but nonetheless horrifying.

Why have this killing field then? It reminded him of the discovery years ago on the grounds of his father's old mansion in California. The house was now a halfway house and training ground for young male witches, which Jamie and Kelly monitored, and his cousin actually ran the house, but at one time it had been the hub for the Ascendance, a body of male witches practicing forbidden magic to gain more power. He had found bodies, dozens of them, buried to create a ring of dark magic. This wasn't any sort of ring or structure that Seiran could tell.

"Does this look like Ascendance magic?" Seiran asked Max. Years ago, Max had been the head of the organization, but when Seiran had inherited his father's legacy, he'd joined the Ascendance to the Dominion and ended the destructive cycle of dark magic they were using. Or that had been what Seiran thought had happened. Maybe this family had Ascendance members within it that hadn't liked the change.

Max surveyed the field. "Yes, and no? Seems like a lot of wasted energy, of magic? For what? Have they been creating golems this whole time?"

"I don't think so," Seiran said. The life animation didn't feel the same as the rest of the death. He had to admit he was using his tie to Gabe to get a better grasp of it. While the power tickled his senses as the Pillar of Earth, it didn't feel like *his* magic. Could he create a golem from new death? Maybe. He didn't think it would be easy. Not with souls bound in it, as he'd never even heard of that happening before. But maybe a lot of intense spells and practice. Was that what this was?

"Not the same magic," Gabe said absently. He kept close to Seiran, though seemed tense, with his arms crossed. Ever since he'd mentioned on the drive over that Seiran closing the ties between them was making him struggle, Seiran had tried to keep the link open. "This death is almost as if they were trying to do something." He gazed at the golem. "Maybe even trying to make a golem and failed? Choosing vampires because they try to go unnoticed?"

The golem stared out into the killing field with empty eyes.

"Were you here?" Gabe asked. The words felt more like a command than a request, like a vampire sire might make of a fledgling. "Can you show us where you came from? The bodies from which your souls were freed?"

Seiran startled when the golem actually moved. In fact, the entire group of enforcement stopped moving when the golem began to trek across the area, weaving through bodies in different stages of being documented, then packed up and transported. Seiran could feel the tie from the golem to Gabe, and wondered how it was different than his own. It wasn't the gentle thing of the blood bond he'd created before they left the house that day, but almost a net, or thinly stretched webbing that spanned the distance between them. As though Gabe could grab a hold of that web and yank it back in a titanium grip. Was that how it worked between vampires and their fledglings?

The golem finally stopped at one set of charred remains, recovered, but too far damaged to be recognized. The vampires had indicated it was dead, no reanimation available even though the head was still attached. Vampires couldn't heal everything. Seiran swallowed back bile at the horror that they might survive damage like this corpse had suffered. How long had they lived through the torture?

The sheet thrown over it, and a lot of the other worst victims didn't help fade the memory of seeing them come out of the ground. The fact that Seiran had asked for the earth's help in revealing them all, so the team wouldn't have to flounder and use dogs, had meant he'd been in the middle of all that death until the ground stopped rumbling.

Like the worst zombie movie ever realized, with skulls and limbs jutting out in places as the ground slowly spit them out. The dirt a bit reluctant to let them go. *Fuel,* it told Seiran in subtle pictures, reminding him, as though he could ever forget, that the ground ate through organic matter. Didn't matter how they died or what they'd been before they died. Death was an equalizer in a lot of ways.

This badly damaged body was on the far edge of the field, near where the trees restarted. She had even been buried on top of other bodies. Like they'd run out of room. She. Because that's what the golem changed into. The soul seeming to find a few seconds of purchase over the golem's magic.

Forest's appearance shifted, turning to the girl Seiran recognized from the files of the three missing vampires. Blonde hair, young, looking no more than a barely finished eighteen. Not much older than his kids, Seiran remembered thinking when he looked at her file. Though she could have been centuries old, since vampires didn't age. Missing from a nest in Madison Wisconsin, not far from the Twin Cities, but still not a short ride. Had this tortured corpse been her? She looked back at them from the living features created by the golem's visage and seemed surprised to see them all.

"I'm dead?" She asked, as she began to sob, even dropping to her knees and wrapping herself up into a ball. "It's over. It's finally over." She cried while everyone looked on at the mounting horrors of the day. Whatever spell or geas that kept the souls from directing them before had been broken, at least when it came to the killing field. Jana Rosette's body was here, burned, sliced up, limbs missing, and part of a killing field with far too many bodies.

TWO OF THE three vampires who had created the golem were in the field. Only two. Gabe had issued a command for the golem to show them all where the bodies were, and it had led them to the second, but then when it tried to walk beyond the field it stopped. Almost as if it were unable to pass a border or a ward or something. Seiran couldn't find any such ward, nor did the earth around them indicate a marker that could create one.

Seiran's group sat the golem down and recorded what it remembered of the last days of each vampire's life. The torture too much for him to hear, he'd walked away to take in the evening air, and breathe something other than the stench of death, rot, and burned flesh. This was why he was Director now instead of an investigator. Eight years of field work, and hundreds of horrors, though none as bad as this. Was he getting old?

Gabe remained at his side, shielding his back while he watched the golem mimic some of what was done. The sounds alone, of begging, crying, screaming, and a shrill sound like an animal dying, wouldn't go unheard even in Seiran's nightmares.

He wondered if Gabe was angry, or thought he was weak because Seiran wasn't watching. The show earlier in the day had brought back too many memories from his youth that he'd long thought buried. He'd have to restart therapy. Had thought for a while that he'd been free of all that mess. It seemed a different life. But wounds like that never really healed. They scabbed over and sometimes even became scar tissue, waiting for the right snag to rip them open again.

"You don't have to stay with me," Seiran whispered to Gabe. "Not even because I'm your Focus. Max can probably help your control."

The vampires stayed close to the center of the group, observing, not to protect the witches, but likely to bear witness and ensure justice would be served in the end. Max had become the king of the recovery effort, directing everyone for efficiency that Seiran knew both the Dominion and the Police rarely showed. But these were his people, even if none of them had been his fledglings. And Max did *scary super vampire* really well.

"I'd rather stay with you. Unless my presence bothers you," Gabe said so softly Seiran barely caught it. "I have a vague memory..."

"Of?"

"Someone hurt you?"

"Lots of people hurt me," Seiran said.

"Including me?"

Seiran let out a long breath as he tried to sort through what to say. "Yes, but not in the same way. You hurt me by leaving. By not telling me you were struggling. By waiting too long to face what was happening to you, that you did some very not okay things, but none of them directly to me." He let that sit for a minute, then added, "Me, you mostly abandoned." Though Seiran knew it hadn't been Gabe's choice. He'd spent years going over in his mind what had happened and how things might have changed.

They were silent a bit longer, before Gabe finally said, "I think I was pulled this time too."

That comment hit Seiran like a fist in the gut. Who? And how? Did that mean Gabe would have to leave again? He tried to breathe and suddenly found his airway tightening. It had been years, almost a decade since his last panic attack, and this was not the place. He tamped down hard, told himself that he wasn't dying, even if he couldn't breathe. The earth wasn't ready to take him. But his vision narrowed, darkness closing in on the sides. It would be really embarrassing to pass out on the edges of a crime scene.

Strong arms wrapped around him from behind, pulling him into a fierce embrace. He knew from the scent that it was Gabe, but couldn't regain enough control of higher function to respond.

"I'm going to try to soothe some of this panic. Don't punch me, okay?" Gabe whispered in his ear. The wall between them was open, as open as it could be from years of disuse and distance, but the waves of darkness began to recede, and suddenly Seiran caught a breath, sucking in gasping lungfuls of air with Gabe pressed against him, his face in the crook of Seiran's neck. "That's right, breathe."

Would he leave again? Why did that tear Seiran up? He'd only been back a day or so. Gabe didn't even remember him. It shouldn't hurt like this.

"I was down a long time," Gabe said quietly.

"But maybe not long enough," Seiran said, his heart still pounding.

"We'll deal with that as it comes. Now, do you need to be here?"

"I'm the Director of Magic Investigations."

"Which I take to mean you're more a manager than an active investigator. Am I wrong?" He wasn't wrong. Seiran had taken the role so he could be home more with his kids. "Your people seem competent. And if they aren't, Max has things in hand."

"What if there are more?"

"Bodies? Your power already crawled through the grounds of this property and found nothing else, right? I felt that."

Were they supposed to be linked like this? Sense each other's powers, maybe even borrowing them? They hadn't gone that deep before, but maybe that had been because Seiran hadn't been willing to be that open, or Gabe had been hiding as well. Would he remember any of their time together? Or would that all be lost in the blackness of the revenant he'd become?

Seiran's phone rang, silencing his thoughts, because it was Kaine's ringtone. He pulled out his cell but didn't free himself from Gabe's arms. He hoped no one judged him for accepting an embrace while standing on the brink of all this horror.

"Hey peanut, whatcha need?" Seiran answered the phone.

"Will you be home soon?" Kaine asked, his voice soft and careful.

"Do you need me to be?" It was a stupid question because he wouldn't have called otherwise. "I just have to let my people know I'm leaving. They have all this in hand."

"Okay," Kaine's voice was still small. Seiran sometimes forgot that Kaine was very young. Maybe not in fae terms, but in human terms he still had a lot of growing to do. The fae didn't automatically know all the secrets of the universe either. And Kaine was only half fae, the other half mortal, whether that be human or witch, didn't seem to matter more than that he needed to be held sometimes. Seiran was pretty sure they all forgot that from time to time when Kaine seemed so grown up.

"I'll be home in less than an hour. Is that okay? Is Jamie home? Can you snuggle with him for a bit?"

"He's here. We're all gonna watch a movie." Even though it was late and a school night. Jamie must have understood that something was happening, even if Kaine wouldn't share it with him.

"Okay, I'll be home soon. I love you." Seiran said. When he'd been younger those words were hard to say. Expressing emotion meant being vulnerable and letting that person know they had power. But he adored his kids and tried to tell them often that they were loved, and were everything to him. He never wanted them to feel unwanted or a burden, like he had growing up.

"I love you too," Kaine said, sounding a little lighter. Seiran hung up, worry still lingering in his gut. Not just for the case, but now for his kid.

Gabe slowly let him go, and it was a little sad to feel the warmth and weight of him vanish. "Let's talk to those in charge, so you can go see your kid. Sounds like he needs you."

Vampire hearing was profound even on the worst day. But Gabe was right. Seiran was wasted in this space. Everything had to be documented and cataloged, evidence filed. His job was to delegate, review, and step in when necessary, but there was really nothing for him to do right this minute as his people had it all in hand. Everything from identifying bodies, to recording comments about the magic energy left on the remains, his people, the police, and the vampires, all seemed to be working in tandem to get it done. More Max and Emmaline's direction than his.

Gabe turned them toward the field and found a handful of vampires with their backs to them, as though acting as a barrier between them and the field. None of them looked their way, but quickly dispersed as they approached. A guard perhaps. Since Sam was nearby, he thought maybe Sam had sent them to ensure Seiran and Gabe had a bit of privacy. Sometimes he could be human that way, when he wasn't working himself into a frenzy trying to be an asshole.

Seiran found his way to Max and Sam, as his own investigators had finished with the golem and Forest was sitting at Max's feet, silent, and completely immobile. Seiran wondered if he could release those two until they found the third. The bonds were complicated, interwoven, knotted. He could sever them all, but not one at a time. He felt bad about keeping them here at all, but they were still missing one body. Did that mean there was another killing field somewhere?

"Can your magic release them one at a time?" Seiran whispered to Gabe. He knew the other vampires would hear, but he didn't need everyone in his business. "I don't want to release the last one until we find his body."

"It should be possible," Max interrupted. "If you'll allow me to take the golem with me this evening?"

"Can you control it?" Seiran asked.

Max nodded. "The souls within are still vampire. I will simply give it blood and rebind it to me. The visage won't be as perfect as yours, but it will have to do. I have more questions for the other two. Vampires shouldn't have been so easily lost."

Seiran stared at the golem. "Okay. Forest, obey Max. He's going to help you." Not that Seiran thought the golem really understood what that meant, other than the direct command to obey. "I'll let Emmaline know. Make sure she's got all the video evidence she needs from it before they are released."

Max nodded, his expression blank. Normally he portrayed bored indifference, but this seemed something else.

"You okay?" Seiran asked, though he wasn't sure what possessed him to. Max was not a vampire who shared feelings with anyone.

"Is anyone?" Max replied. "There should not be this many vampires missing or dead. Where are their sires? How were they taken so easily? Why vampires?"

"No," Seiran agreed. "But they aren't all from here, right? Wouldn't Mike have said something if this many of his were missing?" Technically they'd been Gabe's. Would Gabe have to reclaim them from Mike? Or would Mike remain in control?

"Not from here. None of them are," Sam answered. He had a checklist on his phone. "But all from the surrounding states. Makes you wonder what he was using as a lure."

Max's gaze fell on Sam, expression assessing. "You think the witch hunted them?"

"Lured them in probably. For what, we don't know. But this isn't all that different from what happened in Romania three years back."

Seiran hadn't heard about that, but the vampires rarely shared. "Were they creating golems?"

"No, zombies. Vampire zombies," Sam said. "Found fire is really useful with that sort of thing. Just about the only thing that can kill a vampire zombie is fire, other than severing the magic that rebirthed them to begin with. I was only there for cleanup. Didn't meet the actual witch that time. The nest there had killed the entire coven."

Vampire zombies. That sounded really bad. "But all of these are just dead," Seiran said as he stared across the mass grave. It might take days to move them all.

"Yeah, they either really fucked up and couldn't make it happen, or it wasn't their goal. Maybe their goal was to create the golem," Sam said.

"If death magic isn't their strength, it's almost impossible," Max added. "Even most vampires have very little death magic at their fingertips." He looked at Gabe. "One of the last of the truly powerful is among us, only newly resurrected."

Gabe was a master of death magic? That was news to Seiran.

"It was why Tresler wanted him so badly. What better way to put the fear of vampires in humanity, than to raise legions of zombie soldiers? I don't believe it worked the way he had hoped it would," Max added.

Gabe remained silent at Seiran's back. Probably thinking, as

Seiran wasn't certain what he remembered. "He says he thinks he was pulled early," Seiran said quietly, not really wanting to think about that.

"It's possible," Max agreed. "Or he could have felt the use of the death magic, as great as it must have been to create the golem, and been brought back to deal with it. It would not be his first golem."

"Gabe can create golems?" Sam asked, incredulous. "I thought his big skills were seducing barely legal witches and managing bars."

"I'm not sure he ever created one, but unraveled plenty. And I recall a zombie war a couple hundred years ago that he put down with a decisive and swift victory. It was one of the things that made the Tri-Mega fear him."

"I don't remember any of that," Gabe said. "I vaguely remember zombies. Lots of zombies. The smell is a bit unforgettable."

"Perhaps you should renew the bonds with your witch and see if it clarifies your memory," Max suggested. "I will handle the golem for the evening, and the rest of the body removal. I have a lot of nests to contact. Bad news to deliver."

"Thank you," Seiran said. "And, I'm sorry."

"Not your fault. Though I will be pressing for more investigations into some of the higher ranked witch families. This is unacceptable in any form. That they were my people gives me the reason to push a lot of buttons. I will not let it happen again. No matter what I have to do."

"Good luck," Seiran said. "I've been trying to do that for years. We're short staffed, and the Dominion is reluctant to give me more money to build up the department."

"Afraid of the skeletons in their closet," Max nodded. "But I am not a male witch to be discounted. The fact that you still let them underestimate you, is infuriating."

"Sorry. I'll remember to be more of a dick," he promised. "I'll even take lessons from Sam."

"Fuck off, Ronnie," Sam said.

"You first, Sammie." At least Seiran felt lighter as he made his way to his people to let them know he was headed home. He had a baby who needed him and this was well under control. Sometimes it paid to be the manager, even if most of the time, it just pissed him off.

CHAPTER 14

The trip back to the Dominion to retrieve Seiran's minivan, was done in silence. Gabe was grateful that Seiran did not close the bond, even as worn and faded as it was. The tie felt a bit like it was wrapped in cotton and covered in fog. But it kept him clearheaded, and had rewarded him with a slow trickle of memories.

A bonfire. A very young witch. Sam had been right; Gabe had seduced a barely legal young man. The glimpses were stuttered, and limited to snapshots rather than full replays of events, emotions, or even memories of conversations. The tears came back several times. Gabe had been good at making the witch cry. A thought that made the knot in his stomach tighten.

But his scattered memories made him realize, for all the shit Seiran Rou experienced, the witch was insanely good at surviving. No matter what anyone threw at him. Hopefully they could mend their bond and Gabe would have more details. The snippets he got weren't enough to clarify the thousands of questions he had. Their time together short, but seemingly complicated.

With the close of the day—the full darkness overhead passing by as they drove—and even though he felt calmer, the hunger grew. He shuddered at the thought of drinking from more bags. But he'd do it. He hated to think he'd be a danger to the children he had yet to meet. How old were they anyway? The one on the phone hadn't sounded very young, at least that he could tell. And since he'd been in the ground almost a decade and a half, they had to be under that, right?

The gates to the house finally appeared. Large looming things that really kept people out because they were so high a drone would be needed to see over them without triggering the security cameras or wards Gabe knew were all over the property.

"Drones?" Gabe asked suddenly, remembering the vague image.

"Yeah?"

"I remember drones were a thing becoming popular."

"In the military back then, yeah. They used them during the Vampire Wars to scan for lower heat signatures at night. Now just about anyone can have a drone. They don't all do fancy stuff like that, but Ki has one. He mostly takes pictures of birds with it," Seiran said. He sounded tired, but was attentive at the wheel, steering them up the big circular drive and parking near the front door.

Jamie was there on the steps waiting, and so was another man that pinged something in Gabe's memory. "Mike," he said as the name popped up like it belonged. Dark hair, wide shoulders, and a tan skin tone that had him looking a bit Middle Eastern.

"You remember him?" Seiran asked, putting the car in park, but leaving the keys in.

"Um, no, but yes?" He had no idea how to explain.

"Sounds complicated," was all Seiran said as he got out. Gabe followed his lead.

"Hey, Boss!" Mike said. "Wow, haven't seen you looking this rugged since Ireland about a hundred-fifty-years ago. Not a bad look though." Mike held out his hand, which Gabe took in a handshake. There was a flood of images then. A wave so strong it nearly sent Gabe to his knees. Lots of Mike and a dozen different names he'd called himself over the years. As well as a sense of kinship that locked into place.

"Sorry," Gabe said, trying not to succumb to the desire to lay on the ground and let the memories fall where they may. It didn't hurt, not really. More that it was too much. Information overload. A thousand ants in his brain all trying to find their way back home at once while traveling in different directions.

Mike didn't let him go, instead tightening his grip which half helped Gabe stay upright. "Just breathe through it," Mike said clapping him on the back with his free hand. "That first big rush is a real bitch." He pulled a handkerchief out of his back pocket and handed it over. "Nose is bleeding. That's normal too."

"Mike is going to take him to feed," Jamie announced to Seiran.

Gabe felt a wall build against him almost instantly, like Seiran was gearing up to be hurt. Fuck.

"Is that a good idea?" Seiran asked. "He's sort of hanging on by a thread."

"I've got him in hand," Mike said. "As one of his betas, I'm strong enough, if necessary. I think he's just struggling with not having fresh blood, and too many memories out of place. It happens after a long bit in the ground."

"What was the longest you were ever down?" Jamie asked him. He didn't seem to have the same dislike for Mike that he had for Gabe, but then Gabe suspected Mike hadn't done something terrible to Seiran.

"A decade," Mike said. "After that excursion in what is now Egypt. Those fuckers really liked messing with death magic for a while. Pulled some crazy shit in the name of their gods, or whatever. Thankfully, the embalming crap was saved for the rich and powerful, so they just ignored the rest of us mostly dead looking things. Can't imagine what coming back from an embalming would do to a vampire."

"Ancient Egypt?" Jamie asked. "Like the *Mummy*?"

"Don't get me started on mummies. Not at all like the movie.

Much more terrifying when books of the dead are involved. Luckily, we destroyed the last of those."

"Are you pulling my leg?" Jamie asked.

Mike laughed. "You'll never know."

The nose bleed began to slow, though now Gabe felt a little light-headed. "Is it safe for me to leave when we haven't renewed our bond?" He asked Mike.

"Yes. The bond will never be completely severed. It's just a bit withered right now. Probably best that you not feed on your Focus right away anyway. Too much at once. We don't want your brain to explode."

"Feels like it already has." He had a throbbing headache all of a sudden.

"That's the need to eat. Let's get you fed."

Gabe couldn't help but look at Seiran as Mike led him toward a truck. His witch looked devastated. "Maybe I shouldn't go."

"You should. He needs to take care of his kid, and you need to find some sanity. Yeah?" Mike opened the passenger door of the pickup truck and motioned for Gabe to get in.

"Do I have a choice?" Gabe wondered as he got in and pulled the seatbelt on.

"Until you're the normal Gabe, nope."

"How will we know I'm normal?" Gabe asked as Mike got in the driver's side.

"When you remember regular shit, like the fact that man is the love of your life. And you are one of the most powerful vampires left in the world."

Gabe cast his narrowed gaze on the man. "I don't feel like I'm some big and bad."

"You weren't. Not bad, not really. More indifferent." Mike turned on the truck and waved to the group, before driving them out. Gabe felt the bond slowly stretch, already thin and weak, it felt like it would snap at any moment. Or maybe that was him. He clung to the door. "There wasn't much that interested you until you met that witch."

'It doesn't sound like meeting him was a good thing."

'On the contrary. It was probably one of the best things that happened for all of us." Mike sucked in a long breath. He steered them back toward the city. "You needed to go to ground long before you met him, but refused. We all suspected it was because you weren't planning on coming back. Then Seiran..."

"Was I me? The normal sort of me, at all when we..." Had he been broken? Would he remember all the details of his time with Seiran? A handful of broken memories weren't going to help him mend ties, or even become a partnership if that was all they could have. He would need to know as much as possible.

"Yes. And no." Mike shrugged. "Sounds weird, but you were different after you met him. First, you never went for pretty men before him. It was always the big and burly type. Your choices of women were a lot more lenient than the man who caught your eye."

"I'm bisexual?" The word sounded like a memory, but didn't feel quite right.

"Maybe? Lots of labels these days for nuances. Not sure it matters much. You were attracted to whatever, and never had trouble getting attention. Seiran Rou was an unusual distraction."

"Young." Gabe said.

"Yes. But you wouldn't touch him until he was legal by law, even though he chased you."

That was an interesting revelation. "Yeah? But a witch?"

"I think he was it for you. Once you'd had him. Blood, body, whatever poetic crap you want, he was it. You began crafting your life around him, even though he was skittish and refused to commit those first few years. He grew up abused in a dozen ways. I didn't realize how many witch families rule through abuse until I met him. At least their male children. The other one, the water witch? And Jamie, Rou's brother, run a sort of underground network to get witches out of bad situations. Not just the boys. There's a line of vampires who help with that."

Gabe thought about that. Seiran had said he'd been abused a lot in his life, though not from Gabe in a physical sort of way. It was little relief to know he hadn't used his fists, though he suspected abandonment probably stung pretty deep too. "Still? At the Dominion office, many treated him with disdain. But he's the Pillar of Earth, and insanely powerful. It makes no sense."

"Right? We call that Darwinism at work. But Rou is wasted at the Dominion. He's tried for years to change them. Succeeded in small ways. Males can be tested now for magic, even get education in some of the better schools. But very few witch families allow their males to test, or attend classes. And almost none get jobs dealing with magic within the Dominion. Any who try outside of it are shunned." Mike drove them into downtown and an area that brought rise to a handful of vague memories. Gabe let them come and go as they might, not trying to grab on for fear of losing them. "In fact, Dominion membership is down. Witches are opting out, keeping under the radar per se. Not attending witch classes, although I don't think that's a good idea, and often turning down offers to work for the Dominion. But Seiran still tries to change them."

"Why does he still try?"

"His kids. Doesn't want them facing the same things he did. Isn't that what most people want? Well, rational people anyway. There will always be assholes. And technically, they're your kids, too."

Gabe blinked, "What?"

"It was an agreement, between his very powerful mother and yourself, that Seiran would provide a Rou heir. You negotiated it to gain his freedom, but he was coerced. He'll never say that he didn't want kids, not out loud where they can hear. He loves them, would give up everything for them, but had never intended to be a father. You were supposed to be there to help. Their mother is actually Jamie's half-sister, though she and Rou are not related by blood.

But her spouse drove a wedge between them, so she's not involved with the kids much. Kaine's conception was a bit more complicated, but no less coercion. This time by the fae. Dominion bullshit pissed them off, and Seiran bore the brunt of that too."

"I went to ground before they were born?" Gabe tried to process the fact that he'd been part of that coercion, and was supposed to be a father. Abandoned. Not just Seiran, Gabe realized, but the children. No wonder they were all mad.

"The twins were born before. A few months, I think. Those last months you were bad. Never seen you like that before. Tresler's influence, maybe? You were very scattered."

"I feel very scattered now," Gabe admitted. They turned into a parking lot, that looked mostly full, and a bar that brought up a wild dash of memories. He hissed in pain and pressed the cloth back to his nose as he felt more blood trickle. "Bloody Bar and Grill?"

"Your bar. We closed it for a private party tonight."

"Not sure I'm up for a party."

"Your nest is all here. And with them, volunteers, *cibos*, those your flock feed on, who are willing to feed you. You need real fresh blood. Even after your witch allows you to drink from him again, you'll need to find a handful of willing donors. There is no more bottled blood. And while the bagged stuff can work in a pinch, it will not keep back the revenant."

"Seiran strikes me as the jealous type."

Mike laughed. "Yes, but only because you never did explain vampirism to him. He's been learning from Sam. That punk is all attitude." Mike parked and turned off the truck. "You'll want to find donors who don't irritate your Focus."

"What about sex?"

"Blood and sex are nice together. Hell, it's part of what being a vampire is. But it's like regular folks and food foreplay. Not required, just an extra spice. You can enjoy your Focus that way, but your regular food sources don't have to be sexual. And really, who's got the time for all that? I have almost a dozen regulars I cycle through. I help fund their college education, and they are good."

"Pay for blood."

"*Cibos* are a regular thing. Common. There's an entire application and interview process. Max has it streamlined on the network he built for us. I'll have to make sure you download the app."

"There's an app? For vampires?"

Mike got out; his grin huge. "Of course. Welcome to the modern world, buddy. How do you think it makes it so easy for stuff like this?" He waved at the building. "Let's go meet your people."

They headed to the door and Mike greeted a woman who opened it. She appeared almost as a Viking, tall with hair in a thick braid, sides shaved, ice-blue eyes. "Hey, Zoe," Mike said, stepping past her into the space of the bar.

Gabe made his way in too, the scent of alcohol and food strong in the air, as well as blood. The room was lousy with vampires, and a couple dozen humans. Maybe witches? He couldn't really tell without getting closer.

Zoe closed the door behind him and locked it. "Heard you're a bit out of sorts," she said with a thick accent. Not Viking then, not unless Vikings were very British. And how he knew that was another puzzle piece falling into place.

"Yes," Gabe agreed.

"Let's get you a seat and we'll go slow. Do you remember how this works?"

"No," Gabe said.

"Each time you touch one of your get, it should trigger a renewal of the sire bond. Which should bring rise to memories. Too much at once…," she shrugged.

"I sired all of you?"

"And many more. Only Max has more fledglings than you. And that's likely only because he took Tresler's get after Mueller killed him. Those that survived his destruction anyway." She directed him to a booth with plush seats laid into carved mahogany wood. The outside of the building hadn't looked quite this posh, but the inside appeared better than well-kept. Hardwood floors that gleamed as though they were cleaned and polished often, walls a pale blue, with whimsical art scattered around the room. The bar appeared to be something carved out of wood and topped with marble. All very high end, and almost none of it triggered memories. New perhaps?

"I've heard Mueller's powerful."

"Your first get in almost a century, so sure."

Wait, he had created Sam? "Sam?"

"Yep. That little monster. The original bond was created by another, whom you killed, and not many vampires can take over that sort of bond to raise a vampire." She shrugged. "I'm sure it will all come back. Mike says you're getting the oldest stuff first? Maybe we'll start with the oldest and work our way forward?"

"Okay," Gabe said somewhat hesitantly.

"Each will offer you one of their servants. A nip from the wrist, usually. Nothing more intimate unless you negotiate with the *cibo*'s vampire. Then a touch to renew the bond. It should ease the memories to have a bit of blood first." She looked around the room. Many of the *cibo's* were eating, and drinking, though it didn't smell like alcohol was on tap tonight. "All of these are well-bonded to their vampires. Most have been with them for years."

"I'm not really hunting?" Gabe clarified. Perhaps he could explain that to Seiran and gain forgiveness. Though the idea that he would have to ask for forgiveness chafed. This all seemed to be part of what it meant to be a vampire. Maybe that was his fault too, as he hadn't seemed to have educated the witch on how vampires worked. On purpose? Or had he been that lost? He wondered if he would know by the end of the evening.

"Only a little. You may find some among this group you wish to make your permanent *cibos*. Those you'll have to make an appeal to, negotiate with their masters, seduce, if you will. But stalking the night as a shadow to feed? Very few do that anymore.

Though I know Sam still does. He enjoys terrorizing people who hurt others. He'll actually spend the wee hours of the morning stalking downtown, looking for car thieves or some other random crime, to feed on them and scare them into not doing that shit again." She laughed. "Crime rate in the cities has gone down substantially. Politicians and media attribute it to cops, and law."

"But it's Sam stalking the night?"

"Seems to be. Anyway, let me send Waverly over. He's got a handful of *cibos* you'll like, and he's almost as old as you." She pointed out a mountain of a man who sat near the bar with a handful of pretty college-age girls. His gut clenched at the idea of drinking from them. Too young, his head said. Not Seiran, his gut chimed in.

"Will I have to drink from all the cibos?"

"No. Choose one from each fledgling. You won't need more than a sip. In a few hours you'll be near bursting with blood and memories, hopefully." She gave him a friendly smile but didn't attempt to touch him. "I'll be by later with my picks." She pointed to another booth filled with men who looked a little older, probably late twenties, early thirties, all seeming to be chatting about something on their phones as they were sharing pictures. "I like my food a bit more seasoned than some of these."

Gabe nodded. "I think I do too."

She headed across the room as Waverly approached alone. He was a bear of a man, easily six foot four, and huge through the shoulders, a ginger tint to his hair, and a well-maintained, but long beard decorated his face, and actually seemed to soften the small bead of his dark eyes. "Boss," Waverly said, sitting down across from Gabe.

The girls hovered near their table, all seeming a bit nervous. If this was how the evening was going to go, it would be brutal. Gabe didn't care for unwilling food, or worse, scared food. It was a solid realization that had him sitting up straighter as he examined them.

"I'm supposed to pick from them? Do you have anything not so skittish?"

Waverly laughed, a booming, almost affectionate sound that did nothing to ease Gabe's headache, but did make him feel like he'd heard it before, many times. "I wondered about that. Thought maybe you liked skittish now. Though last time I met that witch of yours he was mostly steel instead of willow. But I brought Angelica too." He waved his big meaty paw toward the bar and a woman stood. She was no scared kid, but a woman probably closer to forty than twenty, the vague beginning of lines near her eyes indicated she smiled a lot. And she wasn't the thin twig the others were, instead curved and proud in tight jeans and a low-cut top. Her dark hair was pulled back into a ponytail, brown eyes confident.

She crossed the room without the hesitation or fear the other girls had shown and sat down in Waverly's lap. He wrapped a firm arm around her and delivered a kiss, before saying, "He doesn't like the chickens."

"Who does?" She asked. Angelica held out her hand toward Gabe. The entire arm a bare stretch of flesh that shouldn't have been all that interesting. But the blue trace of veins beneath, and thick smell of blood had Gabe clutching the table, his stomach trying to claw its way up into his throat. "It's okay to be a bit rough," she assured him. "I'm not as young as I look. Or fragile."

"She'll be changed in the next year or so," Waverly added. "Had her almost a half century now?" His gaze met hers, as though he was confirming the dates. It didn't seem possible that she could be that old.

Gabe's teeth seemed to throb. Oddly enough, his cock didn't react. Not like it had to Seiran when they'd been in the kitchen. Though he could smell her blood and felt himself begin to salivate. He blinked, his vision narrowing a little. But he took her hand, and luckily did not get a rush of memories from her. Either they hadn't met before, or had very little contact.

And he hesitated, breathing in the scent of her blood, warm and fresh, not the decadent chocolate cake with fresh strawberries. More like spice and mulled wine. He pressed his lips to one vein, feeling it beneath the skin like a heartbeat. He knew in that instant a dozen things he'd forgotten. Like how to bite with precision, and heal a wound. He didn't realize he'd actually punctured flesh until the hot bite of her blood flooded over his tongue. Not as good as his witch, but so much better than a bag.

Seasoned, Zoe had said. Yes. He very much preferred seasoned. He heard the small sounds coming from her, Waverly kissing her, their gaze locked, as he shifted the pain to pleasure for her. Gabe worried he'd drink too deeply, but Waverly reached out a hand, and laid it over the back of Gabe's.

The memories were a sudden jolt like being struck with lightning. Gabe could do little more than hold on.

CHAPTER 15

Seiran worked to shove back the well of emotion battering him. He didn't have the right to feel betrayed. He knew Gabe would need to eat, and not just blood from bags or him. He'd done enough reading, and asked plenty of questions over the years, to know the many things Gabe hadn't shared back then. And bottled blood, which was no longer a thing, meant that vampires would need regular donors. The stuff from the bags, even as tested and monitored as it was, lacked a lot of the living nutrients and magic essence needed to sustain a vampire.

But logic, as sound as it was, couldn't alleviate emotion, which was anything but logical. The anxiety over Gabe having to go back to ground intensified too. What if he hadn't been ready? What if he went nuts and hurt one of the kids? What if Seiran ended up alone again? He supposed that was the least of all evils if he was being honest.

Gabe hadn't been back long enough for him to get attached. Except that standing in that field, surrounded by horrors, and wrapped in strong, comforting arms? Nothing could compare with that. Maybe that was a memory he could hold on to for a while.

Seiran mounted the stairs in a rush, passing Jamie without

comment. He had a feeling this separation—Mike showing up as he did to take Gabe—the very *second* they arrived, was Jamie's fault. He couldn't help but be mad, even if Jamie was probably right. But he had more important things to deal with than his own struggles right now. His baby needed him.

Inside the entry, Kaine waited, looking small, like he rarely did, closer to his actual human age than his siblings, but the unmistakable fire of his hair and giant blue anime-looking eyes made Seiran just want to wrap him up in hugs forever. Technically, in the human realm, he was ten. And at that moment, he looked it, unfinished, young and afraid. Little more than a child, and not trying to mimic those around him with glamour and fae magic. Seiran grabbed his baby and squeezed, holding on tight. "What's wrong?"

Kaine collapsed into Seiran's arms, his face snuffling into Sei's neck where it met his shoulder, hot tears finding their way to his skin.

"Oh, baby," Seiran said, "Talk to me." He carried Kaine through the house and out to the arboretum, where everything was still and silent. The only lights were decorative, rather than the rolling glow of the fae. The twins had a strong affinity to the earth, but this was Kaine's play zone, as the other two had mostly outgrown the space. Toward the back there were a handful of beehives, full of fat honeybees that lived and loved the space year-round. But even their buzzing was quiet and distant this late at night.

Seiran sat them on a stone bench near the little water fountain Kelly had added a decade back. The sound a delicate gurgle of rolling water, soothing as they sat among the blooms. He let Kaine cry. Didn't try to pry out whatever might be wrong, simply held him, rocked him, and whispered soft comforting things.

"I'm here," Seiran promised. He would never abandon his kids. The earth would have to reclaim him first. The fae weren't as kind, didn't really think of themselves in the parental sort of way. He didn't fault Bryar for that. Bryar tried more than most of the fae would, spent time with Kaine, tried to teach him things, and offer comfort. He copied a lot of things Seiran did, trying to provide for a child who wasn't really wholly part of either world. They all sort of forgot sometimes, with the intense power that Kaine showed most days, that he was still part human, even if that part was witch.

Seiran hummed and sang a little. He didn't do lullabies, had never really learned them, even in the children's youngest days. They'd always been fonder of popular music. He sang through a couple Christina Perri songs he knew, the crooning easier than most of the more upbeat stuff the kids enjoyed. It wasn't about the words anyway.

When the tears slowed and Kaine breathed deeply against him, he gently asked, "Do you want to talk about it?"

Kaine clung a while longer, time passing, but no one bothered them. Seiran hoped the other two were in bed at least. "It's not fair," Kaine whispered in a half-broken breath.

"No," Seiran agreed. Nothing was fair. He didn't know what at this particular moment, but found few things were. "Can you tell me about it?"

"The babies died."

"Okay, which babies? Fae babies?" He didn't think so as fae children were rare, at least among Kaine's class of fae, which had been part of his agreement with them. The fae valued power. Magic created the fae, so Seiran's power combined with a fae was certain to create a powerful child. And it had, but not one that really fit in either world. They thought they had all the answers, but Kaine was too human for them.

"Bunnies," Kaine corrected.

"Okay. We had bunnies?" There weren't any wild animals in the arboretum. Just the bees and occasionally the fae. And on the new moon they all shifted to play, the twins as foxes, Seiran as his lynx, even Jamie as the big bear he was, though he often swam with Kelly. Kaine bounced around in forms, able to have many without any sort of trouble. He seemed almost weightless most days, flying high without fetter. Seiran hoped his baby wouldn't one day float away never to be seen again.

"Outside," Kaine agreed.

"We had baby bunnies outside and they died?"

"Yes."

"It happens sometimes."

"A bird got the mommie."

Ah, the circle of life. Beautiful and horrific all at once.

"I looked it up on the internet. Ki helped. Kura too. We tried to save the babies. Feed them…"

"And they didn't make it." Seiran hugged him tighter. Had they told him, he might have been able to get the bunnies to one of the nature societies for help. But he'd ask his older two about it later. For all he knew they'd contacted someone, and tried to care for them while waiting for a reply.

"No," Kaine snuffled. "Everything here dies. I hate it." His tiny fingers dug into Seiran, hurting, but Seiran said nothing. Kaine didn't always remember he was stronger than normal humans. And nothing he could do would permanently hurt Seiran. Seiran tried to let him feel, no matter what it was, and work it out. It was one of the few ways to really help Kaine understand the differences between the worlds.

Kaine wasn't bound by a mortal form. Having been born of magic, rather than mortal birth of a being, he pinged around, trying to feel and learn, but still free to try things most would never even dream of. It was a bit godlike, which Seiran always found disconcerting. Though since his tie to the earth gave him a lot of similar traits, he tried not to get too worked up about it. But training Kaine at a very young age, that other people were more fragile than him, had been difficult. Seiran thought they'd done a good job, but maybe it still needed to be reenforced.

"I'm sorry," Seiran said. He kissed Kaine's hair and rubbed his back, continuing to rock him gently. The human world wasn't really any less cruel than the world across the veil. But Kaine didn't need less hope. "Would you rather stay with Bryar?"

"No," Kaine said fiercely. He pulled back to put his little hands on Seiran's face. "You can't die."

"I'm not going to die," Seiran said. Not any time soon at least. The earth made it uncomfortably clear that She was fond of having him as Her advocate. She wanted him to do more, but seemed to understand he was one being, and limited by the brutality of the world at large. Humanity was working hard at killing the earth and therefore themselves. The Goddess would send more disasters, and Seiran's warnings were only heard by so many. They were all on a runaway train.

"If I go... and come back, sometimes the time is different."

"Yes," Seiran agreed. The first time it had happened, weeks passing without seeing his kid, he'd panicked. And he had not been kind to Bryar, who informed him that not all things ran linear like the mortal realm, or as slowly. "It's why when you're here, it's important that you spend time with us."

"I'm not like Ki and Kura."

"No," Seiran said, "But not all that different, either. You're still mine. And I love you. You understand that, right? You will always have a place with me. I will always love you, no matter what."

"Even if it's my fault the bunnies died?"

Ah, the missing puzzle piece. "Why do you think that?"

"I tried using my power to help them."

But Kaine didn't have power over living things, or at least things with souls or esoteric energy like souls. His abilities ran similar to Seiran's, almost a pillar level control of magic. Which make plants grow, but the only real control on the living it had was to take them back to be used as fodder for rebirth. He could imagine what terrible accident must have happened. The earth snatching the babies from them, or even the babies decomposing in an instant. Heartbreaking, and devastating, but an accident.

"And you didn't mean to hurt them," Seiran said.

"No," Kaine promised.

"Did your uncle talk to you about why that happened?" Because if Jamie was good for anything, it was explaining science and magic in terms anyone could understand.

"Yes," Kaine said.

"And you understand? We don't have that power. Not you, not me, we can't bring the dead back to life. Energy given has to be taken from somewhere else, it's a balance." The bunnies had to have been very near dead if the earth had accepted them easily. It didn't normally steal life just because someone willed it to. Though on the rare occasion it could be merciful. The earth was often swift and cruel, that was true enough, but not even Seiran could demand it kill someone and expect compliance. They called him the Green Man because they reasoned he was married to the earth. A partnership, not a dictatorship, and certainly more a matriarchy than a patriarchy. If he started killing people at random, without Her consent, She'd take him back without a moment's notice. Fuel was one thing, unnecessary fodder another. "Had they already passed? The babies?"

"The littlest one wouldn't move anymore," Kaine admitted softly. "Uncle Jamie wanted us to go inside. Wash our hands."

Because Seiran's many years of OCD cleaning had ingrained itself in his family. And Jamie had known those bunnies weren't going to make it.

"They weren't dirty," Kaine whispered. "No more than I usually am."

"You're a bit of a pigpen," Seiran teased, still rocking Kaine lightly. "If rolling in the dirt were a hobby…"

"It feels good," Kaine admitted.

"It does sometimes," Seiran said. He looked around at the huge space. The arboretum itself larger than the house, extended to give them all room to run, but warded, because beyond these walls, outside and into the woods, Seiran still had trouble not letting the earth take complete control of him. She was more than willing to steal his free will, and make him Her puppet, whether that meant the rest of his life as little more than a lynx, or being used to demand change through mortal violence, he'd never wanted to know. They played inside to keep him sane. "Do you want to run with me for a bit. Looks like we have the space to ourselves."

Kaine climbed down out of Seiran's arms, dropping to the ground and stripping like he was in a hurry. Though technically, Kaine didn't have to. He wasn't bound by those rules. It was just a habit he'd picked up from his family. Seiran calmly folded the discarded things, then began to remove and fold his, setting them on the bench.

Before he could get his shoes off, Kaine was changed. Not a fox or lynx, but a cat with a dusky tan color, white through the face and paws, and some dark bits on the back. This form was tiny, maybe eight pounds, and what Seiran now knew to be called a sand cat. It also seemed to be the form Kaine defaulted to most often when not influenced by his siblings. A choice? Or simply the easiest one for him? Seiran didn't demand answers. Kaine might not even know himself. Maybe in a few years Seiran would try to pry.

The door to the house opened and Jamie appeared, not actually entering the atrium, but setting an old-fashioned alarm clock on the steps beside the door. Then he left as silently as he came, closing the door behind him, and leaving them to their comfort.

Seiran finished stripping and let the change roll through him. It was easier near the new moon, the gravitational pull less on the earth, but he could do it whenever. Most witches couldn't change at all, and the few who did, it was only around the new moon. He remembered his first few times changing outside of the new moon, how much he'd struggled, and it had been slow and painful. Now it wasn't any different than all the rest.

The first few seconds were always a bit disorienting. The earth became loud, almost a siren call, irresistible. It was a lot like a screaming *come to me, child* song that repeated over and over in his head. If the door outside hadn't been locked and warded, he wouldn't have stayed. But even as a lynx, he knew the wards were there. Strong, and they would sting if he got too close to the barriers.

He hopped over a slew of decorative rocks to find the loose area of soil that was always left open, and often refilled with fresh topsoil. He flopped over and rolled around; the dirt cool and welcoming on his fur.

A tiny missile pelted him in the stomach, little claws and sharp teeth nipping. Seiran reacted by tackling, rolling and then cleaning. Dirty baby. Kaine struggled to get away, indignant because he wanted to be dirty. He skittered away, jumping sideways, a ball of floof with a tail puffed up. He was tiny compared to Seiran's lynx, which was more of a Canadian type of lynx, mostly gray with giant paws, though not much more than twenty-five pounds. Kaine was tiny, his head smaller than Seiran's paw. Which meant Seiran was always careful and aware of his baby.

They chased around for a while, Kaine landing on Seiran's back a few times. Seiran picking him up by the scruff a time or two, to carry him out of a particularly high tree. It was a constant battle of play, bath, play, snuggle, and play.

Kaine woke the bees. He danced around in the flutter of wings like he was king of something. The bees seeming a bit disoriented, but deciding to go to work anyway, and finding nearby buds to feed. Seiran sent out a bit of magic, the tingle spreading from his paws into the earth, waking worms and roots, springing more flowers to bloom.

Kaine leapt at him, trying to grab him by the throat like he was fierce and deadly, but Seiran let him hold on. The baby teeth unable to do much more than cling to fur. He began to groom Kaine's fluffy tail. He didn't have one of his own, his was more of a stub, and was somewhat grateful because they always got covered in dirt.

Kaine wriggled against him until he could curl up against Seiran, until their hearts beat together. Seiran wrapped himself

RESURRECTION

around his cub, cleaning, keeping him warm. And wondering where that sudden annoying beeping sound was coming from.

He tried to ignore it. His baby was sleepy. They could both use a nap. But it didn't stop. Seiran snarled in the direction of the noise. Near the door. Not to the outside, but the mortal dwelling. Not willing to leave his baby unprotected, he picked Kaine up by the scruff and headed to investigate. He needed to at least stop the noise.

Near the step leading up to the house a little metal thing danced and beeped, buzzing and shaking, with painful noise. Seiran set Kaine down and batted at the box. It flopped over, but continued to writhe and scream. He started grumbling at it while Kaine curled around him half dozing.

The door opened and a human man stood there. He didn't move for a moment after the door was closed, not even after Seiran smacked the noisy thing a couple more times, unable to shut it up. He finally looked up at the man with hope that human hands could turn it off.

Oh, right... he could be human. He'd forgotten for a bit there. The change rolled over him, and he barely noticed Jamie walk past him, retrieve their clothes from the bench, and set them down beside him. Only then did Jamie turn off the damn alarm clock.

Seiran's skin and nerves were still raw. Kaine remained a cat, nestled in Seiran's arms, barely rousing even when Seiran dressed.

"Bunnies?" Seiran asked, his voice still a veritable growl from the change.

"Were already mostly gone," Jamie said. "Told them to leave the babies, and called it in this morning. The rescue center is backlogged, and said maybe tomorrow? The kids," Jamie shrugged. "The internet makes everyone feel like superheroes sometimes. But they were already mostly gone. Kaine released them. Thought that if they weren't tied to their weak, mortal forms, they could thrive and dance like he does. Life is sometimes cruel."

"Ki and Kura?" Seiran asked. He understood the release of souls from a living form well enough. Had done it innumerable times for those who'd been sentenced to capital punishment by the Dominion. They refused to change their rules, so he'd shown up to as many as he could to ease the passing of each witch. It was a simple severing of the metaphysical cord that bound mortal flesh to the essence of a person. He tried to explain to all of his kids how it worked, so when he couldn't shield them from life's horrors down the road, they would understand the experience.

"Cried a little, but okay. They get it. I'd have buried the bunnies if I could have gotten the kids inside. Tried to explain to Kaine, but he insisted he could save them. But plants and bunnies aren't the same thing. Bunnies might not have big souls like people, but they still have something that needed to be bound to their mortal form. Maybe it's different across the veil?"

It was. But Seiran only nodded. The fae world wasn't built on the same rules as the mortal one. And trying to define all the nuances was best left for philosophers.

"The twins are sleeping. I checked on them again when I heard the alarm." He picked up the clock and they both entered the kitchen. The clock went back in its place on a shelf beside the door. It was a way to bring him back, one of the few that worked every time. A set allotment of time he could play, but beyond that, it was hard to return. Even if he wanted to be with his kids.

Seiran had to fight through the fog of the lynx resettling inside his head and wondered if that was how Gabe felt. It was almost midnight. He sighed. Who needed sleep?

His baby obviously. Seiran didn't try to move Kaine from the crook of his arm, curled up like the cutest little baby kitten anyone had ever seen. On the counter was a normal spread of bowls and ingredients. An array of options to help Seiran soothe his mind and reorient himself in his human side.

"I'm off tomorrow," Jamie said as he headed to the counter. "Link will be back from California midday."

"What is your kid's favorite?" Seiran asked, seeming to have lost that memory. Though he could sort of recall Lincoln's face. It had been Solstice when he'd seen Jamie and Kelly's little boy, as he was off in witch training camp. Link's powers of water and earth had started very early. A rare mix of the two that had everyone worried. Everyone except Seiran, Kelly, and Jamie. Link was a good kid. Smart and sweet, and only a year younger than Kaine.

"He loves brownies," Jamie said.

"Blondies," Kelly corrected appearing from the stairway leading upward. "The cookie ones with the peanut butter chips in them."

"You should be sleeping," Jamie grumbled at him.

"Not if we're baking for my kid. He loves that triple fudge cake you do too." Kelly said and smiled as he peered down at Kaine. "What a sweet baby."

"He's had a rough day," Seiran said as he rubbed Kaine's little belly and scratched under his chin, being rewarded with a tiny kitten smile.

"Do you want me to take him, or measure ingredients?" Kelly volunteered.

"Ingredients?" Seiran asked, as he didn't want to give up his baby so soon. He planned to hold on to all of them as long as he could.

CHAPTER 16

Seiran tucked Kaine into bed, and snuck down to the kitchen to shave off a second piece of cake. He'd already had a jumbo slice. But stress set his sweet tooth on fire. And he'd filled the house with the scent of baked goods, prepped and ready for the next day, so the temptation was irresistible. The kids would love it, even if they all tried to limit how much sugar they ate.

He'd have to be sure to hit the gym soon, or at least do a hardcore sparring match with Sam to work off some of the calories. Seiran told himself that it didn't much matter anyway if he put on a few pounds, no one saw him naked anyway. Well, other than his brother to check for bruising and broken bones. And that was too weird to spend much energy worrying about.

But Seiran ate the slice with slow reflection, savoring the fudgy cake and the bittersweet ganache. Kelly's last-minute thought to adding cherries to the cake batter had been divine. It had only been the pie filling stuff, not even anything he'd made from scratch, but it added so much fluffy moisture to the cake, and a bite of tart and sweet cherry, that Seiran was certain to be baking this again.

Everyone else had gone to bed. He had insisted, taking his time to clean the kitchen and put everything away. Even packing up lunches for the kids for school tomorrow. They'd be thrilled to find blondies in their bento boxes. He still put little affirmation notes in them every day. It probably wasn't cool to get notes from your dad when you were in high school, but they hadn't complained.

Seiran was tired. He knew he couldn't sleep, and didn't bother trying. His mind clouded with anxiety over Gabe. He hadn't meant to shut the bond down. It had been an instant reaction to the idea of Gabe feeding on other people. Jealousy, fear of renewed pain, and way too many memories made it impossible to unclench that fist. If Gabe went nuts, would it be his fault? Would someone even call him? Could he tell through their tie as faded and weak as it was?

He hadn't felt any changes to the bond. Not any sort of tugging from Gabe, or awakening of it that might indicate he was more himself. Seiran swallowed a laugh. Himself. Who was Gabe? He didn't think he knew. And that was the heartbreaking part.

He angrily stabbed another bite of cake. It was an exercise in mindfulness for him to pick out the flavors and define the texture. It helped soothe his anger, but not his frustration. Should he be worried? Should Gabe be back? What if he went crazy, and Mike had to put him down? How much damage could Gabe do? Seiran wondered if he should have gone with. Wasn't that part of his responsibility as a vampire Focus? Only now did he realize how young he'd been to make that decision. Realistically, he had sort of forced the decision on Gabe. A life-or-death situation. Though Gabe hadn't really been in danger of dying, had he? Vampires were far from physically fragile.

Seiran growled at himself. Dwelling on the past had never given him anything but pain. He cut the last bites of cake up smaller, counting bites, and trying to find clarity in the racing of his mind. He wasn't a kid anymore. He should be able to handle anything. Like being a grown-up meant he somehow had all the answers. What a joke.

The front door opened. Seiran tensed, knowing there was only one person it could be. He'd have to remember to have Jamie oil that door since the hinges squeaked. It could be Sam, he supposed. And that was likely how Gabe had gotten the key. Had probably even been dropped off at the front door by Sam, who was still Gabe's fledgling, even if Gabe had severed their tie before he'd gone to ground.

Seiran felt the bond tighten, Gabe close. He forced himself to let his hold on it relax; it was a bit like a flower blooming. A slow opening of something delicate, still weak, but slowly filling.

He braced his hands on the counter, trying to not imagine terrible things and offer judgment when it wasn't his place. Sam had reminded him that they didn't have to be anything anymore. Nothing more than a partnership. He could manage that, right? The kids didn't need to see Gabe as a parental figure. They had plenty of that without a vampire ex-lover added to the mix. Seiran didn't need a partner. Had spent almost a decade and a half making his way without one. He had friends he trusted to have his back if necessary, he worked hard to be a good father, and a good witch. Those were some of the few things in his power. Being a good lover? He wasn't sure that was ever in the cards for him. His wild days in his youth, the many incidences in the past, and losing the man he thought he had truly loved. They left an impression.

Not broken, he reminded himself. Resolved, resilient, and able to handle just about anything. Except maybe losing that love a second time?

The sound of footsteps drew closer. Seiran's heart sped up. He worried Gabe would look like he'd been seducing and feeding people all night. That was what vampires did, right? How would he react? A jealous rage? Tears? Stunned silence?

Gabe had always been good at keeping his feelings and memories locked down. It had always been one of the things that annoyed Seiran most in their relationship. Seiran was the out of control one that felt too much. But maybe it was more that he was the only one of them willing to share it.

Not anymore. He kept his own memories and emotions locked away as best he could. An invisible barrier between them that didn't close the bond, but kept the tide of his internal chaos to himself.

When Gabe stepped into the kitchen, he didn't look debauched at all. He didn't really look any different than when he'd left. Though his skin had a bit of a tan tone to it, and his eyes were a vibrant green when Gabe's gaze fell on Seiran. Like life had been added to him. Seiran had thought he'd looked good before, but now, that last edge of waxy paleness gone, he was breathtaking.

Had that been the draw? Maybe it was just a physical thing, Seiran thought. Attracted to a beautiful man. But there had been plenty of offers over the years, beautiful men a plenty. And even trying to convince himself it hadn't really been love, Seiran knew it was, and still tried to recall what it felt like all these years later.

Was it supposed to be raw? Almost sharp? A need to touch and be touched, while fearing both at the same time?

"Shouldn't you be sleeping?" Gabe asked quietly.

"Probably," Seiran admitted.

"Your baby is okay?" Gabe remained standing in the doorway keeping his distance, but looking casual, leaning against the wall, hands in his pockets.

"Yes," Seiran said. "He's a kid, and sometimes the world is hard."

Gabe chuckled lightly. "Understatement of the year."

The sound brought memories to the surface for Seiran, even making his body react, as he'd heard that laugh before. Had it really been so long ago? It wasn't fair that Gabe was so beautiful still. Seiran remembered his younger days and the handsome man in a suit, perfectly trimmed hair, and clean shaven. Poise and polish had been Gabe back then, rock solid. Almost too good to be true, but as in life, that was never reality. This version of him was a bit wilder. Less contained to a role of the perfect businessman, and Seiran wondered which was the truth? Neither? Both? Would he evolve each time he had to go to ground? And would that be the short trip each year like Sam, or something worse like a lifetime of long stretches of loneliness for Seiran?

"You don't look like you were partying," Seiran said.

"Not really that kind of party. But I smell like the bar. Even if it's just food and alcohol. Sounds like I'll have to do this sort of thing periodically as my people come in to visit over the next few months? Might take up to a year for everyone to stop by. It was good to reconnect though."

"Your flock was there? I know Mike has quite a lot of them in town now."

"About two dozen?" Gabe said, seeming to think about it. "Not even a drop in the bucket of those who are actually mine. But that would be way too many to fit in even a stadium. Not sure how many are still in this world. Not when you count those I created, and those they created." He fell silent for a minute, staring into the distance as though lost in thought. "Good though. Mike picked those who sort of space large chunks of time."

"Do you remember more?" Seiran wondered if he was there at all in Gabe's memories, or ever would be.

"A lot, yes. Not all, but it's coming back." Gabe moved away from the door, crossing the room in movements that felt more like a tiger than a man drunk on blood would look. "You're familiar with the reconnection ceremony?"

"Read about it a long time ago. You take blood from their *cibos*?" Seiran couldn't help the hitch in his voice. "Maybe negotiate for some of them to become your *cibos*."

"I think we'll save that part for you. The negotiation and choosing *cibos*," Gabe said. He stopped at the other side of the counter, keeping the space between them, but his gaze intense.

"I'm not sure how that would work."

Gabe shrugged. "We have time. That smells good."

"I love cake," Seiran said lamely. "Chocolate the most."

"Maybe that's why the small taste of you I had," he glanced at his phone, "yesterday now, tasted like chocolate cake?"

Seiran thought about that. Did blood taste different to vampires? He'd read some poetic stuff like that, but thought it all conjecture to sound flowery and less brutal. Sam never mentioned it, but his eating habits weren't something Seiran ever tried to pry into.

"I haven't had cake in a couple weeks…" He tried to recall the last sweet he'd eaten before Gabe had that leftover drop from the knife. "Mostly been eating fresh fruit and real cream. The kids have a half dozen wild berry bushes on the property. They all go crazy this time of year. Blueberries and raspberries mostly."

"But you tasted of chocolate and strawberries," Gabe said mildly.

"I think you're imagining things. Does everyone's blood taste like something?" Were all the *cibos* so alluring that way?

"Yes. Not all good. Some blood is sour, or bitter, some sweet. Some spicy. Some a mix. Doesn't seem to be related to the food they eat as much as their personality."

"I am not a chocolate covered strawberry."

"Not moist and sweet?" Gabe asked, sounding amused.

Seiran licked his lips and wondered why his body responded to those words. Thoughts and images filling his head with so many sexual innuendos. It had probably been too long since he'd had sex, even by his own hand. And Gabe was hot. No way around that. "More tart and bitter."

Gabe nodded, "A bit of bite on the chocolate end, less sweet and more decadent, fudgy and rich."

This was not going in the direction Seiran had hoped. He didn't want to feel drawn to reconnect. Desire and longing. Though that was a lie too, since he'd felt the pull the minute he'd set eyes on the vampire again. Time hadn't severed the Focus bond or his emotional ones. No matter how much he might wish it would have.

"I should go shower," Gabe said, turning toward the door to the basement.

"We should probably get the sharing the blood thing over with,"

Seiran said quietly, feeling some giant knife tearing into his guts with a thousand worries.

"*Over with...*" Gabe muttered. "Well, come down then. Let me get the bar smell off. I had forgotten how much it can linger."

"I like the bar," Seiran said. "Even if it stinks sometimes. Food sometimes smells, but it's always good."

"Do we serve that cake at the bar?" Gabe nodded to the last dredges on Seiran's plate.

"No. This is something new. With cherries. Didn't know if I'd like it, but it's just enough to keep the cake from being too over the top with chocolate. The bar keeps things easy. Basics like brownies with ice cream."

"Not much of a bar anymore though, right?" Gabe said. "More a posh drinking spot, known for good food. Smoking no longer allowed."

"Yeah, that started ages ago, before you went to ground really. I tried to fix up the menu and suddenly it became a place to eat."

"And Mike ran with the concept. Three locations now? Bloody Bar and Grill? A menu with bite."

"It was kind of a funny logo idea, but people like it. We sell T-shirts and stuff. Sometimes even host weddings. Each location has a rolling menu based on the area it's in." Seiran knew they all did well, but it felt strange to be discussing food. He got up and rinsed the plate before putting it in the dishwasher. "Cupcakes decorated like a vampire bite..." It sounded cheesy, but was a big requested item.

"The cherries would be a good touch to that, a bit of red tartness inside?" Gabe said, a brow raised as he stood near the door to the basement. He opened the door, "Coming?"

Seiran sucked in air, trying to calm his anxiety and racing mind. They didn't have to be anything. Sharing blood would be important to keeping Gabe sane, but they didn't have to be what they were. If they'd really been anything at all. Did he want that? He didn't know what the fuck he wanted in that moment.

"Maybe we can get this over with?'" Gabe teased.

CHAPTER 17

He headed down the stairs, and Seiran trailed behind slowly, closing and locking the door behind him. He didn't need his kids running around in Gabe's space. Not that they ever visited the basement when they had an entire wing to themselves. His mother's over-the-top choice for the house had seemed stupid at the time, but years later, filled with teenagers and almost teenagers, there was never enough space.

"It wasn't like a sex party or anything," Seiran said as they entered into the living space below. There were still boxes everywhere, though a few things appeared to have been opened and rifled through. The bed was made instead of covered in a dust cloth. The room cluttered, but not as lifeless as the storage space it had been.

"No," Gabe said with a light laugh. "It's more like meeting all your buddies out for drinks."

"Except the drink is people," Seiran said from his spot near the stairs. He didn't think he'd be able to negotiate for someone to feed Gabe. Wasn't sex and blood the same thing to a vampire? He thought he was grown-up enough to handle it, but had to admit to himself that some things were just ingrained. Gabe wasn't really his, hadn't ever been. What right did he have to demand?

Gabe paused to look back at him. "Sex does not equal blood. Or vice versa. I suspect that was my doing? That you think that way?"

"I am under the understanding that being bitten hurts without it?"

Gabe nodded, looking thoughtful. "My fault. I'll work on that." He took off his shirt, and it was so much like a striptease, even though Seiran knew it wasn't meant to be, that his mouth watered. The body wasn't all that different. He didn't have the same super defined muscle that Seiran could remember, but none of the tone had really been lost. Gabe looked healthy, but without endless abs and the superhero arms that Seiran knew had been fantasies generated by media stereotypes rather than memories. There was a familiar scar on his chest, beneath one pectoral muscle. Seiran knew it was from being stabbed with a spear, but not all the details of it.

He couldn't peel his gaze away as Gabe kicked off his shoes, and his hands went to the button of his pants, unhooking them, and shoving them down to reveal royal blue undies that encased an incredible ass, and outlined his cock, which was partially hard. He was far too pretty. Seiran hugged himself, trying to tell himself it was okay to react, his body did what it did. He didn't have to actually play out any fantasies, even if his cock was hard as a rock and begging to be touched. And what an unusual feeling to have after so long. He'd rarely found anyone at all appealing. But right this minute, his body was on fire.

It had to be exhaustion. Yeah, that was it. It had been a long day. Lots of terrible things. He was tired. Inhibitions lowered due to weariness. Sure.

Gabe headed into the bathroom and turned on the water, but he didn't shut the door. After a moment steam began to fill the room, fogging up the mirror. Seiran tried to look away when Gabe shed the last bit of clothes, but that ass was amazing. Stuff of legends and memories he hadn't been sure were real.

"You can join me," Gabe offered as he stepped under the spray of water in the giant walk-in shower. It wasn't as big of a bathroom as the one Seiran had, but still a stone inlay of wide-open space to bask in the heat of the multiple shower heads.

"Maybe we should do this another time?" Seiran said softly, though didn't move from his spot clinging to the wall beside the stairs. It gave him a view of too much, and he should have walked away, but his head swam with a thousand scenarios. "You really didn't sex up any of the *cibos*?"

"No," Gabe said. He washed under the spray another minute, before rinsing off. He shut off the water and reached for a towel. "Since they weren't mine, that would have been rude. And not all *cibos* are into that. Some just want college money."

Seiran did not watch him painstakingly dry every inch of his body. He didn't. Well, he did, and barely breathed the entire time. Where was the air? Did this room feel claustrophobic all of a sudden?

Gabe wrapped the towel around his waist and looked up. Green gaze finding Seiran, and it wasn't a condemning stare, or even a teasing one, instead it was filled with heat. Seiran pressed himself to the wall to keep from trembling. He shouldn't still feel this way after all these years. The pain, being abandoned, those last few days, weeks even, of Gabe unraveling, cruel comments, and the complete shutdown of everything they had been.

Gabe crossed the room, not adding clothes or anything as he made his way to Seiran. Not stalking exactly, but Seiran still felt a vague sense of unease. Wariness. *I am vampire, be afraid.*

He didn't stop until he stood close enough to touch, so close in fact, that Seiran could feel the warmth and moisture from the shower lingering on his skin. The scent of him clean and fresh.

Gabe touched Seiran's face, his palm warm, fingertips soft as they seemed to trace his cheek and the side of his lips. "Over with, you said?" Gabe asked.

"I mean, it seems important that we…" Seiran trailed off, not sure what to do. Those green eyes, intense, and bringing back so many memories. He wasn't sure whether to run away or throw himself into Gabe's arms. "I'm not a kid anymore," he said.

"No," Gabe agreed. "I'm grateful for that." He leaned in close, his lips only inches from Seiran's, the warmth of his body heating Seiran. "Remember that first kiss?" Gabe asked. "When you asked me, who kisses like that?"

Seiran sucked in a deep breath, but smelled and tasted only Gabe. Did he remember? Maybe it hadn't all been a lie or an act.

"You remember?"

"Do you?" Gabe wanted to know. His hand went to Seiran's throat, his thumb still caressing Seiran's lower lip, though they were so close, all Seiran could see was Gabe's eyes, his head tilted a little as though ready to kiss him. He didn't think he'd say no in that moment. Despite the danger. Gabe could hurt him. In a thousand ways. The hand on his throat indicated that with subtle strength.

"Yes," Seiran admitted. "No one kissed like you did."

"Do," Gabe corrected and captured Seiran's lips with his own.

It was a few seconds of floundering. Seiran unsure what to do, sink into the warmth or fight. But Gabe pressed him into the wall, the heat of his body, relaxing as well as stimulating. And Seiran let himself fall into the kiss. Devouring is a word he'd thought for a long time described Gabe's kisses. And that was true enough. But the dance of exploration, Gabe's tongue in his mouth, exploring, wasn't brutal, though it wasn't delicate either. It was a duel of their tongues, and reminded Seiran of things he'd long forgotten.

It felt like coming home after a long trip abroad to stop some crazy witch magic. He hadn't done one of those trips in years. The feeling, intense and familiar; he couldn't hold it back.

Gabe broke the kiss, his fingertips running down Seiran's cheek. Had he been crying? Fuck, he hadn't meant to look weak. But Gabe didn't pull away. In fact, his grip on Seiran's throat tightened a little. Seiran sucked in air, instinct rather than need. Gabe wasn't really stopping his airflow, more keeping him in place. And that hold felt like iron, immoveable. He should have been afraid.

Gabe kissed one cheek, and then the other, gently lapping away the tears. "I have a handful of memories of you crying."

He remembered. Seiran trembled.

"I don't like seeing you cry," Gabe said. He breathed out a long sigh, and turned his face into Seiran's shoulder. Seiran wondered if Gabe would bite already, and tensed. "Are you afraid?" The hand on his throat tightened again, this time cutting off Seiran's air a bit.

He swallowed hard, his body reacting not in a bad way, but aching for more. Man, he was messed up. "Not afraid of anything," Seiran said quietly.

"No?" Gabe placed a tiny kiss on the side of Seiran's jaw and worked his way down, decorating Seiran's neck with soft kisses. "You smell divine. The revenant says we could feed on you for a long time. Glut ourselves with your blood and magic."

But if the revenant was in control, he wouldn't be this contained. Seiran sucked in a narrow breath and called a bit of power. Nothing harmful, just a reminder, as he shifted the world around him to create a growing wave of ivy that sprouted from the bits of organic material in his clothes, and the cotton terry of Gabe's towel. The vines wrapped around Gabe in small hugging bands, harmless right now, but Seiran could change that at any time.

"Kinky," Gabe said with a light laugh, not easing his hold at all. His eyes flashed black for a second, and then the vines began to fade, falling away as Seiran's power was dispersed.

Seiran gasped because that shouldn't have been possible. Gabe should not have been able to control Seiran's power.

"You're my Focus," Gabe reminded him. "That means what is yours is mine, and what is mine is yours." He loosened his grip a little but didn't pull away. He was completely nude now, towel gone, and Seiran's shirt half destroyed, so it was skin to skin, or at least chest to chest. Seiran's heart rate ratcheted up, a bit of fear rolling beneath his skin. What if Gabe could control his power? What if he went out of control again? Who would stop him then? The power of a master vampire and the Pillar of Earth at his fingertips, he'd be unstoppable.

"You are afraid," Gabe nodded lightly. "It's good to fear vampires a bit. The darkness inside is never completely gone. It always hungers."

Seiran felt the slight skim of teeth along his throat. Nothing that broke the skin, just the barest of touch. And he wanted it bad. To be bitten, taken even, and reminded of what they'd been before everything had gone to shit.

"I'm not afraid of you," Seiran whispered.

"No," Gabe said. "It's you that you fear. Losing control, becoming the monster the witches think all males with power will become. Hurting your kids, or the world, even when the world rejects you." Gabe's body pressed him into the wall, and Seiran bit his lip to keep from begging for more. The heat of Gabe's cock pressing into his hip telling him there was a bed a few feet away, they could…

"You don't know me at all," Seiran said.

"Hmm," Gabe murmured, and kissed Seiran again, diving deep until Seiran was panting, the small bits of air from Gabe's hold and the kiss leaving him gasping, spots of darkness popping around his gaze. Exciting and terrifying all at once. He was so hard it hurt to be wearing pants, even though they were made with some stretch. Not enough give.

Seiran interlaced his fingers through Gabe's hair, the length unfamiliar, but soft, even with the still dampness of it. It gave him something to hold on to as he returned Gabe's kiss, his body begging for a thousand things he wasn't ready to voice.

Gabe lifted him, hand leaving his throat and going to his hips, pressing them together. Seiran couldn't help but wrap his legs around Gabe, the need to get closer, to be touched, loved, an irresistible desire. Gabe turned and carried them to the bed, lips joined, bodies pressed so tight together that they fell on top of the mattress in a tangle of limbs. Gabe's weight pressing down on him, feeling so good and wrong all at once.

This wasn't supposed to happen. He wasn't supposed to give in so easily. But as Gabe unbuttoned Seiran's jeans and shoved the fabric down, everything away, baring him, and then pressing heated flesh to heated flesh, Seiran could only cling to the shocks of need. His legs were still tangled in his clothes, even as Gabe took both their cocks in one hand and stroked them together, grip just this side of pain, the kiss not ending. Seiran trembled, waiting for the pleasure to erupt into an orgasm. Waiting for Gabe to sink his body inside Seiran's and the bite of pain from being fucked and bitten. Too long, Seiran thought, since he'd had that sort of pleasure. He could handle it just this once, right?

Gabe's weight holding him down felt like a thousand forgotten dreams coming back. Seiran's brain stuttered with worries that this was just sex, that Gabe didn't really remember him, that it was just some fling. But his body screamed, yes, more, take everything.

Gabe broke the kiss to trace a line down Seiran's jaw with his tongue. Would the bite come soon? Seiran couldn't stop thinking about it, wanting it. His body thrumming with a dozen needs all at once. Gabe reached down and shoved the last bits of fabric off Seiran's legs, freeing them. Seiran wrapped them back around Gabe's waist, needing him closer. His ass clenched in need, wanting him inside, begging to be filled—the heat between them something he didn't know how it could possibly be natural—but he couldn't refuse. It was like clinging to the last raft on a storm swaying ocean. Have it or die.

"Please," Seiran whispered. He wanted Gabe's hand back at his throat. He wanted to be flipped over and taken hard, reminded of the weight of Gabe on his back, the feeling of Gabe's cock splitting him open, the bite of his fangs on his throat. Seiran wasn't a kid anymore. It was okay to want. He was bonded to Gabe forever. Not something they could break. Why not indulge? Why not enjoy? He trembled with need.

"Please," he begged again, opening himself, his mind, his body, the bond, everything, just to be touched again. Loved again.

Gabe wrapped him up in strong arms, kissing again, even as he lifted Seiran and carried him further onto the bed, reaching for the pillows and the drawer beside the bed. A tube of lube dropped down beside them, and Seiran stuttered for breath, wanting so much and lost in the glide of skin on skin while Gabe kissed him, ran firm hands over him. He worried briefly if Gabe would hate the changes the years had brought.

"Beautiful," Gabe muttered, and flipped Seiran over, pressing himself to Seiran's back, then rising to kiss a short line over his shoulders. "This is what you want?" Gabe asked, his cock sliding between Seiran's thighs, hot and branding, making Seiran's body clench with need. The tip of Gabe teased Seiran's balls with rocking kisses as Gabe held Seiran up.

"Yes," Seiran agreed. He wanted so much. But hated the idea that Gabe was only doing what *he* wanted. He wasn't some toy to be played with and put aside.

Gabe laughed and sank teeth into Seiran's shoulder. He didn't break skin, but it was close and Seiran nearly came at the edge of pain dotting the intense roll of pleasure. Gabe picked up the lube and opened it.

"How old is that?" Seiran wondered even as the sound of the slick made his body clench with need again. He gripped the sheets; glad Gabe's arms were strong enough to keep him upright. He thought he'd feel a bit mortified to find himself face down, ass in the air begging for it, even if that's what he really wanted to do in that moment.

Gabe turned the tube over. "Fairly new, I'd say. Since the expiration is in two years." He reached back with the slick, running his fingers over the crease in Seiran's ass first, spreading the slick in small circles around his hole, teasing.

"Fuck," Seiran snarled. "Don't need the teasing." He wanted Gabe in him. Now.

Gabe pressed a finger in, not gentle or slow, but a firm digit inside, spreading the slick and finding Seiran's prostate. Seiran's body clenched around Gabe's finger, trying to keep him inside, needing so much, and knowing it had been a long time. Gabe's fingers wouldn't fill him. Not like Seiran wanted them too. He needed that hot branding dick in him bad. Even if it hurt a little at first. That was okay. He liked that first edge of burning discomfort. The pleasure much more intense then. It had been so long, he even wondered if that was right. Toys could only replicate so much.

"Toys?" Gabe muttered, seeming to catch the thought. "We'll have to play sometime." He removed his finger and pulled Seiran back so Gabe could have a firm grip on his hips. Gabe's cock slid over Seiran's hole a few times, teasing as Gabe moved his hips and forced Seiran to stay still with a brutal grip.

"Stop teasing me," Seiran growled. He reached back to grab Gabe's hair and tug.

"I thought you liked teasing?" Gabe said as his cock pressed into Seiran.

"Fuck." Seiran froze, trying to relax as the girth of the intrusion bore down on him. Maybe he should have been prepped a bit more. That did hurt, but not in a bad way. The stretch intense, burning, and so fucking good. He tried to keep from clenching around Gabe's dick, but couldn't help it. He'd clench and then unclench, body sucking Gabe deeper, until finally, he felt spread wide, filled completely. Gabe's balls pressed to Seiran's taint.

Gabe held them there. Seiran's body gripping him in surges as the pleasure rolled through him, begging for more. Gabe kissed the side of his face, and neck, seeming to be waiting for something, even as Seiran kept his grip tight in Gabe's hair, and pressed his ass back into Gabe as though needing more.

Something released in Seiran's body, and Gabe slid in a tiny bit more. The clenching and gripping inside less tight and more a dance of erotic need. "There we go," Gabe said as he slid his hips back, sliding out while Seiran's body tried to keep him inside. "So responsive."

"Don't…" Seiran begged him not to stop.

Gabe pushed back in a few times, a slow test of the friction. Too slow for Seiran's wants. He wriggled his hips trying to get more, but Gabe held him firm. Then Gabe adjusted his hold, shoving a pillow beneath Seiran, and rising to a kneel for a better angle. Seiran had to release his grip on Gabe's hair. Gabe's teeth playfully clipped Seiran's shoulder again as he said, "Ready?"

Seiran was more than ready, for anything, he didn't even know what he was agreeing to. Whatever. He made a noise that he hoped was affirmative, and Gabe slammed into him. It wasn't soft or kind, or sweet, or romantic. What Gabe gave him then was the pounding he'd craved. Brutal, fast, far faster than he could have moved if he'd been human, and deep, the angle changing with a tiny roll of his hips as he shoved inside.

Seiran lost all other thought, memory, and emotion. His body singing in triumph even as it fought to accommodate the intensity of the pounding. He sucked in large gulps of air, wave after wave of pleasure building. Gabe holding him firmly in place, splitting him in two with every thrust, and building the friction of intensity throughout his body.

Gabe wrapped his arm around Seiran's waist, bringing them closer, even while still spearing him hard, and pressing him into the bed. Gabe returned a hand to Seiran's throat. Kissing the side of Seiran's face. "You like this," Gabe whispered. He squeezed his hand the smallest bit, limiting how much air Seiran could draw.

Stars exploded inside Seiran's head. His body following suit as he came hard, a rush of heat like lava pouring down his spine to awaken every nerve in his body. His body clenched and spasmed around Gabe, feeling the heat of Gabe's spend fill him. Seiran's vision narrowed into dark tunnels and pops of light, lack of air and too much sensation assaulting him all at once. He almost passed out, but his racing heart, and Gabe letting go of his throat, brought him back from the edge.

He felt covered in sweat and come, filled to the brink with the hot spend of everything he'd missed for far too long. Held in Gabe's arms, it didn't matter that Gabe's weight held him down, or the arm wrapped around him bit into his stomach. He turned his head to the side to lay it on the pillow and gulp air. His body pulsing, oversensitive, but still wanting more, even while Gabe was still inside.

"You didn't bite me," Seiran whispered, feeling a bit sad. He'd wanted that just as much as the sex. A bit of affirmation that they went together, the blood and the pleasure.

"Later," Gabe said, rolling them to the side, keeping himself pressed into Seiran for another minute as though savoring it. "They don't need to go together."

But Seiran liked them together, he realized. Sex and the bite. Had that been him instead of Gabe? He sighed as the flood of his overactive mind stuttered back to life.

He felt Gabe smile into his shoulder. "It's like that, is it?" He pulled out, leaving Seiran feeling gaping and empty, air cooling his skin. He didn't like it. He liked it even less when Gabe got up and went to the bathroom. For a few seconds the terrible feeling of being alone again filled him. Abandoned. Used up and left. Worthless.

But Gabe stepped out of the bathroom with a washcloth in hand, and returned to wipe down Seiran's ass, and cock. He tossed the soiled pillow off the bed, before curling around Seiran, and pulling the blanket over both of them.

"You overthink a lot," Gabe said as he spooned himself around Seiran.

He did. Always had.

"I'm not going anywhere," Gabe said. He reached out and hit a button on the remote that plunged the room into darkness. Only a thin ribbon of light came from the bathroom. "I may not remember everything, but I love you, Seiran Rou. A decade and a half, or even a century isn't going to change that."

Seiran couldn't help but collapse in Gabe's arms and cry. Not bad tears, but cleansing ones. He fell asleep praying that when he woke, it wouldn't all be a dream instead of reality.

CHAPTER 18

Arriving home, Gabe was drunk on blood and knowledge. All while his brain still throbbed with holes great enough to look like Swiss cheese. He felt a bit overconfident, and alive in his skin. He'd also been burning with need for a particular witch. The second he'd stepped in the door and smelled the decadence of chocolate cake and Seiran, his libido throbbed, demanding pursuit.

It was a bit of an unusual feeling. The aching physical need to reclaim what belonged to him, and the emotional connection that sank into place demanding to be strengthened. Even while his brain circled through broken images that barely gave him a glimpse at the full picture of his past.

Seiran's comment about getting it over with, like letting Gabe touch him was something to endure, pricked his ego. The memories of Seiran were scattered, broken, flickers of bits and pieces, even while Gabe's heart ached like a knife had torn through him. Seiran was his. Gabe had sat in a booth at the bar contemplating the emotion for a while, half dozing from being overfull with blood, and swirling memories. At first, he thought it had been possession, a need to reclaim something his revenant considered theirs, but it was more than that. The well of emotion running deep even with only vague remains of his memory in place.

The tears. Fuck, he hated those tears. But they were his fault this time. With most of his hunger satiated, his body demanded touch and a reconnection with the man he loved. There was no other explanation for the intensity of the emotions. It hurt to breathe for a while. The thought of losing what he'd found, that he'd been the reason everything was messed up, nearly breaking him. He sat hunched over the table, struggling to power through the tide of rolling memories, emotions, and self-destruction he'd wrought.

Still so scattered. It drove him fucking mad. The holes like gaping wounds of his past, unable and unwilling to heal because that would be acknowledging his failure.

Even the vague memories of Titus were disjointed. And not nearly as vivid or emotionally powerful as the ones he had of Seiran. Love and infatuation were two very different things. He'd died twice for Titus. The first time as a mortal, and the second as vampire to his first forced grounding. And he'd felt pain and loss each time, heartbroken, lonely, but it didn't breach the surface of the well of emotions tied to the witch.

Sam had been the last to visit, not offering a *cibo* to Gabe, as Gabe had already had Luca's blood when first arisen. The stirring of broken memories slotting back into place had made Gabe dizzy, hands digging into the table, even as Sam sat there quietly.

"You hurt him again, and I will fuck you up," Sam offered, looking bored.

"I thought I was supposed to be some sort of super vamp that all the baby vamps were afraid of?" Gabe had asked him.

Sam snorted. "Sure. Maybe? The fuck I care. Treat the witch good, or else."

They sat in silence a bit longer as Gabe sorted memories, his forehead pressed to the wood tabletop. "I love him?" Gabe asked after a while.

"You did," Sam agreed. "Was that legit?"

Gabe thought so. That ache to have Seiran close didn't feel like the Focus bond. The desire to see him smile, know he was happy, those were intense. Almost as intense as the pain of knowing he'd really fucked up. And on top of that major screwup, he'd been forced to ground for over a decade when Seiran had needed him most. "I cheated…"

"Not sexually," Sam offered. "I questioned folks after you went to ground. Sounds like you couldn't get it up. Whatever Tresler did to unravel your control, made you hungry. You were gorging on blood. Not that regular blood from addicted and dying humans does much for us."

The reminder brought back a bitter taste in Gabe's mouth. Like he could remember the hint of death on his tongue. Bad blood. He'd never been a fan, though knew it had been necessary from time to time over the long years of his life.

"Not *cibos*," Gabe said.

"Seiran's the jealous type. I don't think it was a good idea for you to be feeding only from him and the bottled shit. Probably a good idea to set up an arrangement like Max has. Maybe let the witch choose?"

"You think he will?"

"I think Seiran is practical. If you make clear to him, you're not having sex with blood donors, he'll get it."

Sex and blood. They went well together. A perk of being a vampire, but not a requirement. Though the thought brought back visceral memories of Gabe in bed with Seiran. Sex and blood. Yeah, their relationship had been very defined that way. "He was young…"

"Was. Past tense verb. I know you vampires think of life in different terms. All humans nothing but babies, but he's not a kid anymore. Don't treat him like one."

"You're a vampire too," Gabe pointed out.

Sam shrugged. "I also don't use that seduction bullshit."

"Right. No seducing your lovers and feeding on them?"

"Only Luca. Con isn't into that, and that's okay. I eat well enough. We have an arrangement. And I have other *cibos,* as well as hunting. You'll need to make one with Rou."

"Does he hate me?" Gabe wondered. The memories were so disjointed. In fact, the bits at the end, had giant holes. He remembered his arm aching, organic material sprouting from it. A flex of power from the witch that could force the earth to take him back. He'd done something, though couldn't remember what. He even had a vague glimpse of twin infants. But only a snapshot. The rest was lost to the memory of tears, and finally cold resolve when the witch walked out.

"No," Sam said after a few minutes. "He probably should. But love is that way. Forgiving even when it shouldn't be. You abandoned him when he needed you most. Even if you couldn't help it, it doesn't hurt less."

Gabe wondered about the anger in Sam's tone. More like Sam had been abandoned. But maybe both? Gabe got the impression that he'd brought Sam over, and knew he was fairly young, but still only had bits and pieces. "I abandoned you?" Gabe asked after a few silent minutes of debating. Pull out the thorn or let it continue to dig in?

Sam stiffened and nodded. "Severed our tie."

A young vampire cut off from their sire always turned revenant. Gabe couldn't imagine himself doing that. And Sam sitting there, not only alive, but in control? That was amazing.

"I'm sorry," Gabe said.

"My superpowers appeared then, so whatever. I suspect you'll be saying sorry a lot in the future."

"Probably," Gabe agreed. "Do words help at all?"

"No," Sam said flatly.

Gabe sighed, "I will do my best to be better. It's all I can really offer."

"Best you tell us if something is happening this time. The

revenant taking control or you just wanna be done with this world. No more of the lone wolf bullshit."

"Okay."

Sam stared at him awhile longer like he was debating the truth of that, but didn't press further. He had offered to escort Gabe home. Home, Gabe wasn't sure he had one. It was supposed to be with the witch, but he would have to mend those fences if he could with a half broken memory.

They rode in the car in silence, Gabe lost in thought. There was still a lot missing. Mike said it would take a while to regain it all. His life long enough that the history books couldn't keep up. Gabe didn't feel that old. And many of the memories felt more like a movie replay than something he'd experienced. A lack of emotion tied to some of them, kept them surreal. But Seiran, he hadn't been sure about that emotion until he'd stepped in the kitchen to find him awake.

The need to reassure him had been intense, making Gabe work hard to keep himself from crossing the room and wrapping his arms around Seiran, demanding to know everything he'd forgotten. And Seiran's gaze had delivered heat and interest, enough to know that he still physically desired Gabe, even if the man was obviously very tired. The shadow of exhaustion etched on his face and his slumped posture.

Gabe could work with that, interest and a lowered guard. And the sex had been amazing. Seiran begging beneath him, so responsive, tight, and warm. The connection between them at the tip of his fingers, close, but they weren't ready yet.

Gabe had wanted to bite and drink deep. He'd nearly come undone at the idea of devouring the sweet flavor of Seiran's blood along with the singing intensity of their sex. But he'd withheld.

Blood and sex could go together. And those two together with his Focus? He suspected he might just unravel again. Would the revenant rejoice? Or break free?

No need to scare the witch.

Seiran, Gabe thought. Sei. He'd fallen asleep in Gabe's arms. The stress and tension finally seeping out of him and leaving him to what seemed to be restful sleep. They would need to share blood soon. It would strengthen their withered bond and help his control. But all at once would have been too much, maybe for both of them.

Seiran's phone rang a half dozen times, coming from across the room where it had fallen. The volume low, but enough to make Gabe tense fearing it would wake Seiran. But he seemed to be sleeping deeply. Gabe even dozed for a while, a few hours perhaps. Flitting from nightmare to nightmare, some in which he killed Seiran, others that he began slaughtering at random. All leaving him on edge, fearing the revenant would break free if he actually slept deeply.

He was woken again by the sound of knocking. It was light, and it took him a moment to orient himself, where he was, and the man in his arms.

He worried getting up would wake Seiran, but he was fast asleep, nestled deep within the blankets. Gabe extracted himself carefully, grabbing his dirty shirt off the top of the basket in case there was a kid at the door. He paused at the top of the stairs, breathing in the scent of the older muscular man.

Jamie. The memories walloped him with another nosebleed.

Gabe sighed, and lifted the shirt to brush away the blood as he opened the door a crack. If Jamie wasn't alone near the back of the kitchen everyone would be getting an eyeful of naked vampire, but he was.

Jamie's gaze was cold, going to the shirt and the blood on it now rather than Gabe's nudity.

"It's mine," Gabe said quietly, lowering the shirt to show the blood coming from his nose. "Memories of you returning with a vengeance. You should be pleased."

"That memories of me hurt you? Sadly, not enough. Is Seiran okay?"

"He's the Pillar of Earth. Do you really think anything I could do could hurt him? It is my understanding that he can't die until the earth allows him to. She'll keep bringing him back." There was a sudden image in his head of Seiran being shot, right through the forehead. He even felt as though the bullet had entered his own skull, burning into his brain and then turning everything dark. Thankfully it only lasted a few seconds, though his nose began to bleed harder. Gabe pinched it and tilted his head back. "Fucking memories."

"Not all pain is physical."

"That's for fucking sure," Gabe agreed. "Seiran is fine. He's asleep. Doesn't seem to get much of that these days." The comment was a bit accusatory. Jamie caught the tone and bristled as though gearing up to attack. Then a younger blond man appeared.

"Kelly," Gabe said. He was going to need to eat again soon if he didn't stop the nosebleed, or at least all the overwhelming memories that were triggering it.

Kelly put a hand on Jamie's arm and stepped between them. "Feeling more yourself?" Kelly asked cheerfully.

"Somewhat," Gabe agreed. "Do the kids need Sei right now?" There was light coming from the arboretum, and distantly the windows, though the curtains were drawn. Morning, but Gabe wasn't sure what time in the morning. Early? "He needs some sleep."

"We've got the kids. Taking them off to school," Kelly said. "Picking our kid up, but we'll be out for a few hours." He tugged Jamie away from the door. "You've got a bit of time alone. I trust you found the lube I left in the drawer? Figured it was best to be prepared."

"I did. Thanks."

Jamie began to protest, but Kelly shoved him toward the door out of the kitchen. "They are consenting adults, and you don't get to choose for them," Kelly told him. He looked back at Gabe and winked, before shoving the big man out of the kitchen despite the bluster.

Gabe closed and relocked the basement door before heading back down. Seiran hadn't moved. Gabe cleaned up, rinsing away the blood as best he could until it finally stopped. He stared at his reflection a while, wondering if he should shave, maybe cut his hair. It was a bit wild. Did Seiran like it? That was more important than Gabe thought it should be. But he could wear his hair any which way. Over the years he'd learned to use it to blend in where he could. Changing it wasn't a big deal. Letting Seiran choose would be a small thing, perhaps a step in the direction of forgiveness.

But with it was a sense that he hadn't been himself in a long time. Existing, rather than being. Did he have a preference about his hair? He wasn't certain, but liked the feel of it, long in his fingers, and the scruff of the beard. Maybe burying himself in some sort of model of perfection wasn't the best way to keep sane. Would Seiran still love him if Gabe was no longer that man?

He wondered at that. He'd come apart in the end. Not himself, perhaps the revenant taking control, but not openly slaughtering people. He couldn't remember. Not really. Everything was broken to tiny bits of memory like slivers of glass. Andrew Roman. Not his real name, not by a long shot. But a long-time enemy.

There had been an explosion. Gabe had only the barest memories of it. He'd been in the ground. Seiran brought him back? Gabe wasn't sure that was possible, even for a witch of Seiran's power. He suspected that the more pieces that fell back into place, the more he would hurt. Physically and emotionally.

Abandoned. That was a pretty bad thing. But it sounded like more than that. If the revenant had been in control, it could have been really bad. The possibilities ran from full out slaughter of everyone and everything, to rage filled rambling. Somehow Gabe didn't think it was only the latter.

Seiran's phone buzzed again. Gabe made his way back to dig it out of Seiran's clothes, finding the screen locked but a notification of a lot of missed messages. Should he wake Seiran? Since the family had left for the day and all of them seemed all right, he wondered what was so important, but didn't know how to unlock the phone.

Passcode. Seiran's birthday maybe? He tried to recall that, but couldn't. He got a dozen other memories, small bits about food, medication, and a cat.

Not a housecat. A lynx. Seiran?

Powerful witches could change shape, though it was rare. Gabe seemed to also vaguely recall that it was illegal. Could anything really be illegal for the scion of earth, which was essentially what a pillar was.

Gabe's gaze landed on the sleeping man, the light from the bathroom not illuminating much, but enough to study him as he slept. Beautiful, much as Gabe had thought the second he'd laid eyes on him. Both in the past at some late-night party, and recently when he'd been reawakened.

The unfinished youth was gone from his features, which pleased Gabe. As if given the chance, he'd have waited until Seiran was older before approaching him. That middle stage of life more appealing, the man, rather than the child, his goal.

What if he had waited? Would those years have been less fraught with trouble and pain? Would he have found someone else? Gabe sucked in a difficult breath at that thought. Someone else having Seiran, loving him.

Seiran had over a decade to find someone else, but hadn't. Lack of interest? Gabe had thought love a fleeting thing. Another human emotion that rose and retreated like the tide. He also recalled going to that party looking for a meal, but not really caring. He'd been on the edge of the abyss even then. Needing to go to ground, but fearing that when he did, he would not return. It was the way of old vampires. Eventually, unless something big distracted from the monotony of existence, they all went under to never return.

Why hadn't he? He recalled a vast number of his get. Some very powerful and old. His sire bonds would have fallen to them.

Though he feared they might have been too great a burden. It shouldn't have prevented him from doing what needed to be done, which had been letting himself either pass or renew. The revenant would be fighting less if he'd had a full renewal. But it didn't feel as wild as the vague bits he could remember intermingled with his past with Seiran.

Gabe left the bathroom light on, and crawled back into bed, wrapping himself around Seiran. He set the phone on the nightstand and spent a bit of time watching Seiran breathe. It was familiar, but different than what he remembered. His short hair, paler than he recalled, though full and light, with the barest hint of curl. Seiran's skin tanner than the almost alabaster Gabe remembered it had been, as though now he got a lot of sun. His body lean, not soft, but not some sort of bodybuilder like his brother obviously still was.

Half-brother. Right. Gabe recalled they shared a father, but not a mother. And a thought leading to Seiran's mother gave him horrific memories. Was that terrible woman still involved in their lives? She'd coerced Seiran into having children, even if it had to be an arrangement. Legacies and names to be continued. Gabe recalled a debate with her. The threat to lock Seiran away forever using all the power of the Dominion. Torture for an earth witch, separated from the earth, unable to use his power. Gabe had been part of the coercion. He wondered if he'd been in a clearer mind if he would have just stolen Seiran away, hidden him somewhere until the witches got bored searching for him. Or brought fire and brimstone to the table and showed them his true power?

He sighed. Some big strong vampire he had been. Afraid of some witches.

Seiran's phone buzzed again, and Seiran stirred in his arms.

Gabe tensed.

Seiran stretched, but didn't seem alarmed by Gabe wrapped around him. "I should get up. See kids off to school," he grumbled.

"They already left," Gabe said quietly. "Kelly and Jamie took them to school."

Seiran laid there a bit longer, eyes half lidded, looking tired. Finally, he said, "This doesn't feel real."

"What doesn't? You and me?"

"Yes."

"Do you hate me?" Gabe asked.

"That would be cruel since you confessed love a few hours ago," Seiran said.

But that wasn't an answer either. "The emotion is there, but memories still shattered," Gabe admitted.

"You love me, but don't know why?" Seiran sighed. "Super. And awkward."

"I'm sorry," Gabe said. He ran his fingers along Seiran's arm, bared and free of the blanket, tracing the feeling of his skin. Familiar and not.

Seiran shivered, but didn't pull away.

"You can tell me to stop," Gabe said. "I'm just… trying to remember."

"I'm not the same."

"No." Gabe actually found himself fascinated at how the touch stirred memories, and still felt like a discovery. "Can what I did, in the past, be forgiven?" He finally asked hating the idea of dancing around the issue. "I don't remember a lot. But am not willing to use it as an excuse."

"Maybe?" Seiran sounded uncertain.

"Okay."

"We need to have boundaries."

"Okay." Gabe let his fingers roam, gaze following. He thought he could spend days rediscovering the man in his arms. "I don't remember you having this muscle tone?" Gabe traced the definition of Seiran's biceps.

"MI has physical requirements for field agents that I insisted be added years ago. Not fair of me to make everyone else meet them and ignore them myself. Sometimes we chase people, or run for our lives."

"You run for your life?"

Seiran smiled. "No. But again, others do. How can I lead them if not by example?"

Gabe thought back to that first night he'd awoken. Seiran had seemed weary and been bruised, though all that was gone now. "You were injured."

"Yeah. Not superman as much as some people would like to think I am."

The memory of a flood and roots flailing from the ground like the arms of a giant octopus startled Gabe. He got the sense of death, temporary, but still there. Bits that refueled his rebirth and power. He was a creature of death after all. "Not far from the truth either."

Seiran sighed. "It's not really a superpower."

"Escaping death?"

"I still die. She drags me back. It's not fun."

"You'd rather leave your kids?"

"No," Seiran said firmly. "They aren't ready for that."

But something in his tone told Gabe that Seiran had been ready for a while. That thought hit Gabe like a knife to the heart. Because of him? Or something more?

He hadn't realized he'd gone silent until Seiran said, "You can't shut down on me."

"Sorry. I was lost in thought."

Seiran sat up, pulling out of Gabe's arms and frowning at the blankets, as though annoyed to find himself naked beneath them. "Should have known nothing would change."

"I'm not sure what you mean by that," Gabe said.

"This," Seiran waved at Gabe as though he were the problem.

"Me?"

"Yes, you. This whole brooding vampire bullshit. The whole 'I need no one' crap."

"I wouldn't be here if I didn't need you," Gabe said. "You're my Focus."

"Right." Seiran threw the blankets back and got out of bed. He gathered up his fallen clothes in a rush, and looked around a minute before finding his phone. Then he headed for the stairs.

Gabe leapt up to follow, feeling like he'd stepped in something big, but had no idea what.

Seiran paused at the top of the stairs, seeming to listen to the house for signs of movement, before opening the door. He darted out, heading around the corner and up the stairs. Gabe stepped out into the kitchen, the dredges of light had turned into a stunning bright wash of whiteness, as he hadn't realized the kitchen was mostly white with stainless steel.

It was draining standing in that edge of sunlight. He hadn't felt it that intensely the day before. But he followed Seiran up the stairs and down the hall to Seiran's room, admiring the witch's backside on the way.

"Stop following me," Seiran said as he opened the door to his room. He stepped inside and threw the clothes into a basket near the bathroom door and the phone on his bed.

"Tell me what I did wrong?"

Seiran glanced back his way, gaze trying to meet his, but pausing a few times to wander lower, before snapping back up again. "Could you put some clothes on?"

"Distracting?" Gabe asked.

"You know I find you attractive. That was never a problem," Seiran snarled as he disappeared into the bathroom and Gabe heard the shower turn on.

"Spell out for me, what was the problem? Pretend I don't remember." Gabe heard cursing. Steam filled the shower and as Gabe followed him into the bathroom, he thought about how he'd like to be in the shower with Seiran, taking his time to relearn the man's body as well as soothe his frustrations.

"If this memory loss thing is bullshit, we're done," Seiran said.

"I wish it were," Gabe said. He leaned against the cold tile near the edge of the entrance to the shower. He had never thought someone could angrily shower until that moment. But Seiran's jerky movements and fast shampoo job made him think the witch was not only angry but in a hurry. Was it crazy to look at him and salivate over how sexy he was? And at the same time fear that anger being directed at him?

"Stop staring at me," Seiran growled.

Gabe turned around and folded his arms across his chest, giving Seiran his back. "Okay."

CHAPTER 19

Seiran's ass ached in reminder that he'd folded like a deck of cards. Fuck Gabe for being handsome. Not even handsome, but beautiful like only a work of art should be. He stood there, completely nude and seeming not to care. It made Seiran angry. Mostly at himself for caving to his desire. Well desire, and a few pretty words.

"Talk to me," Gabe said. "Tell me what I did."

"That's a joke, coming from you," Seiran said. He was tired of forever being the one to share, speak up, and not getting the same courtesy back.

"It seems like the best way for us to work together is to talk to each other."

"Since when?" Seiran demanded. He rinsed the soap out of his hair, and hoped he'd gotten clean enough without a thorough scrubbing. If he was going to be around vampires today, questioning when and where they'd last seen their now deceased friends, he prayed he wouldn't go into the room smelling like sex. It seemed, at the very least, cold in light of the mass death they'd just discovered.

"What do you mean by that?"

Seiran turned off the shower and grabbed a towel, drying off as he made his way to the walk-in closet. "You're the king of not telling anyone anything. It's your *modus operandi*. The whole reason no one knew you were fucking struggling until it was too late, was because you wouldn't talk to anyone. Not me, not Mike. No one." Seiran grabbed a pair of jeans and a T-shirt with a Disney blue alien, upside-down, that said "I Tried." He would need a bit of cheer today when facing a warehouse full of bodies and their grief-filled flocks.

Had his people gotten through questioning the family? He would have to read through their reports when he had a moment, and hoped he wouldn't have to question them himself. His people were good, most of the time. Face to face with some of the Dominion's political elite? That might be a lot to ask of them, but he tried to begin his day hopeful.

He yanked on his clothes and ran a comb through his hair, finding it just barely long enough to pull back into a ponytail. The front escaped a little, falling around his face, making his cheekbones look sharp and delicate, which he found annoying. But he wasn't out to impress anyone today. Not while cataloging bodies and searching for magic evidence as he suspected the day would go.

He hadn't realized Gabe was still there until he turned around and found him lingering in the doorway to the bathroom, expression clouded.

Seiran sighed. "Look, I get it. You're back from the grave and your brain is sort of like mashed potatoes. Maybe I should drop you off at Max's for a few days? You can find some smelly shapeshifters to feed on while I work?"

Gabe wrinkled his nose. "Not a fan of shapeshifters and we haven't renewed the blood bond. I need to stay close to you. The revenant is more unsettled than it should be."

Seiran folded his arms across his chest and wished for a thousand things that had never been within his grasp, including a supernatural sense of patience. "Because you were pulled early. A decade and a half in the ground wasn't long enough. Funny how you chose to start something while standing on the edge of insanity. Makes me question your judgment."

"*You* pursued *me*," Gabe said. "I don't remember everything, but I remember that."

"And you kept me at arm's length long enough to keep yourself from facing execution. I just wanted to get laid, not be bound forever to your obviously selfish whims." Seiran left the bathroom and dug out a pair of shoes. He'd be on his feet all day and needed something comfortable. He wondered how many vampires would be lingering at the location Max had created for the bodies. He could do with dealing with less vampires today.

Gabe stood in silence, which drove Seiran's rage to the brink thinking he was being shut out again. He turned around to add another heated comment, but found Gabe lost in confusion, blood trickling over his upper lip as his nose bled. Seiran paused.

"I'm sorry," Gabe said as he pinched his nose. "Too many memories at once bring on the nosebleed. It's a bit dizzying. Trying to put the pieces back where they belong. I'm not trying to be silent. Trying to make sense of things feels like a complicated math problem that I once knew I could solve, but can't quite put the x and y in the right place."

Losing blood after feeding last night seemed like a bad idea. Seiran grabbed a towel out of the drawer near the sink and handed it over. Gabe pressed it to his nose.

"Wouldn't it be easier if you slept during the day?" Seiran asked quietly. "Give yourself some time to recharge?"

A wild look passed over Gabe's face, not like the revenant was taking control, but full-on fear. He was afraid that if he went to sleep, he wouldn't wake up? Or that the revenant would grab hold?

"Gabe?" What was he afraid of?

"I slept a little," Gabe said quietly. "With you."

"And it was bad?"

"Disjointed and filled with nightmares. Not really restful. And I don't think it was because you were there. I think it's because the revenant isn't settled," Gabe said fast, like he was trying hard not to add insult to injury.

"Would having my blood settle the revenant?"

Gabe thought on that for a minute. "I don't think so." He looked away and sucked in a breath deep enough that Seiran could almost feel the need to follow suit. "Something is tugging at it. As though whatever yanked me from the ground…"

Seiran couldn't help his flinch at the idea that Gabe hadn't been ready to come back. How long would he have been gone? A century? More? Would Seiran had kept his sanity? Would putting him back help either of them?

"Like the power is still out there. I can touch it, almost." Gabe's gaze found Seiran's again. "I'm sorry it's a bit vague. I'm trying to put words to feelings that don't really have defined classifications." He turned toward the door. "If you'll give me a minute to clean up."

"Will you be safe around people? In a room full of dead vampires? I need to look over all of them. My people probably have already, but…"

"You're a superwitch," Gabe teased, "you might catch something the average witch doesn't."

"Maybe," Seiran agreed.

"Happens a lot?"

"Sadly, yes."

"Perhaps you need to find better witches?"

"I think they need more training. Most come to me with very little knowledge of the darker bits of magic. Many don't believe those things really happen, or that power even exists. Not until they confront it face to face. A lot of them don't last longer than a year. The dark side of magic becomes too much for them."

Gabe gave him an assessing look. "You deal with magic crime. I would think that meant mostly darker magic."

"Yes. However, the Dominion exists in direct opposition to the Christian Church. It comes at a cost of *bad* witches die, and anything the Church condemns is bad. They only teach kids how to be good little witches. On paper at least."

Gabe thought about that, startled by a memory that he seemed certain of, but couldn't recall having ever voiced. "Christ was a witch."

"Probably," agreed Seiran. "Likely necromancer of some kind, raising the dead and all that. Don't tell the church that, they will insist you get burned at the stake for it."

"And if someone is born with power like necromancy?" At least Gabe seemed to catch on fast enough, even if his memory was Swiss cheese.

"Locked away, shunned, taught to hide it. If they survive the awakening of their power at all. That's where most of the issues I deal with come from. Witches trying to find control in a world that fights to keep them invisible until they are slaughtered for PR purposes." It was one of the biggest reasons he feared for Kaine. The twins earth magic was strong, and would put them at pillar level should he die in their lifetime, but Kaine's power, a mix of fae and witch, would scare the world at large. Seiran created the house as a sanctuary for them to learn and grow in safety. Wards covering every inch of the property created by himself, and layers added by his friends. Everything from fire to water and wind. But he still feared for Kaine every day. Had he gone to school, or decided to cross the veil again?

"Go get dressed. I have to check in with my people." And his kids.

Seiran waited for Gabe to leave the room before checking his phone. Kaine had gone with Kelly and Jamie to pick up Link. It sounded like they had a day planned out to welcome him home. Since Link and Kaine were close in age, they had gotten along well. At least before Link had gone off to camp. Would that have changed?

Something else to worry about.

Seiran had messages from Sam and Mike, asking how Gabe was

doing. A short message from the office with a link to files as they were processing bodies. Page had sent him a short text:

P: *Not feeling well today. Might be in late.*

Seiran had never been an asshole about people having to be in the office as long as they were doing their job. And Page could do his job from home just fine. He sent a message back as he made his way downstairs to find something to eat before heading in.

S: *Take the day off. I'll be cataloging bodies all day anyway.*

I'm sorry, was the reply he got back.

S: *No need to be. Feel better soon.*

Seiran had a message from Max that alarmed him. Not a text. He wasn't sure that Max cared a lot for the nuances of modern technology like text messaging. Usually he sent Sam, but today he'd left a voicemail.

"The souls are still in the golem. I have been unable to unravel the way they are bound. I suspect it is part of the golem having more than one soul tied to it? Sam will be available for questions at your retrieval of the golem."

Seiran heard the vague cursing of Sam in the background of the voicemail like he was unhappy to be put on call for the day. But the message ended there. It was almost nine, which likely meant that Sam was asleep. Max too, as most vampires found the sun draining. Seiran sent a message to Luca instead, *Is the golem with you guys?*

He found a container in the fridge that had his name on it and pulled it out, pleased to find Jamie had packed him a bento box for lunch, and a container of egg sandwiches for breakfast. He took the top off the second container and popped it in the microwave while he waited to see if he'd get a reply.

Gabe reappeared in the kitchen, clean and dressed, wearing just jeans and a T-shirt with a leather jacket over the top. Seiran hadn't recalled packing up those clothes, but it had been so long. At least the air-tight storage had kept them in mostly one piece.

Seiran's phone pinged with a text. *Yes. You can have it in exchange for a slice of cake.*

How had Luca known Seiran made cake? *You're blackmailing me for cake?*

Yes.

How do you know I have cake?

Kelly posted about it online. Pictures of a divine chocolate Rou creation. Has a couple thousand likes already.

Of course, he had. Kelly had a large social media following, not because he was the Pillar of Water, but because he was sort of a hot swimmer who happened to get a few bronze medals in a couple of summer Olympics. Seiran suspected he only placed bronze each time because Kelly feared people would claim his water magic gave him an advantage. And he probably wasn't wrong. Shortly after his last placement, the games had put restrictions on witches in competition. Thankfully Kelly and the handful of other witches had not been stripped of medals, merely excluded as seemed to be their lot in life.

Seiran frowned at the phone, then wrote, *I feel like I'm better off keeping the cake. You can have the golem.*

Please come get it. It's very creepy, was Luca's reply.

Seiran swallowed a laugh, and took out the cake to cut a big hunk off for Luca and Con. How many times over the years had he had people ask him to bake? Tell him to give up the Dominion and do what he loved? But then who would do his job? Who would look after those inexperienced and unprepared witches facing things like they had last night? Not all monsters were things that stalked the night.

Seiran ate fast, filling a travel mug with coffee. "You need blood?" He asked Gabe, pointing at the freezer.

"No. I ate well last night." He couldn't hide the distaste on his face as he glanced at the freezer.

"Does it really taste that bad?"

Gabe thought about that for a minute. "It's a bit like comparing a bowl of flavorless oatmeal to your cake. Nourishment, sure. But not anything anyone will jump at the chance to have. And minimal. Not enough nutrients to really help."

Seiran found that amusing. Old blood was bland oatmeal, gross. "Gotta stop at Sam's and get the golem. Max said he can't release the souls. Does that sound normal?"

"None of this is normal," Gabe said. "Three souls in one golem is overkill. Golems don't need souls at all, more likely they'd be put there to keep them from departing this plane. But why?"

"I was thinking the vampire souls were weaker, maybe? And that's why they used three? You think they wanted to keep the souls here?" Seiran grabbed his keys, put his used dishes in the dishwasher and headed for the garage.

"Vampire souls are no weaker than witch ones. I have no idea why anyone would want the vampire souls contained. Usually once the soul is released so is the revenant, so maybe they are trying to control the revenant?"

"Is that possible?"

"For an outside source? Probably not. It's like trying to put a leash on a wendigo and call it a dog."

"You remember more about this whole death magic thing?" Seiran wondered. "Never met a real wendigo. They are legit?"

"Bits and pieces. It feels like something I know. A muscle memory? Perhaps I can release the souls where Max could not? Wendigos are mostly extinct, I think. Not necessarily a bad thing since they are one of the deadliest creatures on the planet."

Seiran took a minute to process that, wendigos and Max releasing souls, as well as magic Gabe seemed to have. A vampire thing? Or something he'd always had and hidden? He didn't want that fight right now. "Well, we're on our way to pick up Forest now, so I guess you can take a look?"

Gabe nodded. The car being in the garage, meant Gabe didn't have to face direct sunlight. And the heavy tinted, barely legal dark coating, which was meant to help keep Seiran's family life private, seemed to help keep the worst of the sun off of them. He had the radio on low for updates on the news. The vampire graveyard was only mentioned in vague passing. As if the media hadn't been given a lot of information. And it sounded like that was Max's doing since they indicated a 'leader of the local vampire community,' which usually meant Max or Sam. Mike only took lead if he had to. Seiran suspected he didn't care for the spotlight much.

"I will try to share more," Gabe said, staring out the window. He frowned as they entered the one-way mess of downtown streets where Sam's loft was. The trio lived in the warehouse district, which was where all the cool non-humans lived now. But Seiran knew that Luca actually owned and managed half the buildings. The creation of a supernatural hotspot and tourist area, had been his idea.

"I've heard that from you before," Seiran said absently. Hard to take stock in words when they meant so little.

"I'm sorry."

Seiran shrugged. "Can't expect a dog to change his spots, right?"

Gabe didn't reply.

Seiran guided the car to a lot near the loft. It was one of the only enclosed parking garages that wasn't residents only. Everything else in the area was street parking, paid lots near the river, or resident owned parking garages. Being the only non-residential lot in the area, meant parking for any length of time was insanely overpriced. He pulled the ticket, wondering if he could get Sam and Luca to pony up the thirty-dollar fee for his fifteen-minute trip. Could he bill the fee to work since the golem was technically a work issue? He hoped so. Sending three kids to college wasn't going to be cheap.

Max said Seiran was rich, but he never touched any of that money. The accounts, overwhelming in scope and volume, that Gabe had created before he'd unraveled, had never felt like Seiran's. He let them do their thing, and left Max to handle whatever was necessary. Seiran had even refused the attached checking account that Max had tried to give him, indicating he could use it for whatever. He survived on his MI salary just fine. Balancing a very limited budget every month, while working hard to provide the best he could for his kids. He had accepted the house from his mother, paid in full. Still had to pay taxes on it every year, which was more than most people's rent, but his kids never went hungry, or wanted for much. He tried not to spoil them, but admitted to indulging them likely more than he should have.

Seiran found a spot near the elevator stashed between the garage and the main building, and parked. Added the ticket to his pocket and got out, Gabe following. The garage was fairly dark, set to a mild vampire safe level, which meant dim lighting.

"You okay?" Seiran asked as he headed to the elevator and pushed the button.

"Smells like vampires and shapeshifters in here."

"That's the area we are in. Makes sense." The doors opened and they stepped in. Seiran had to enter a special code to get up to the residential floors, as the top two were all that were inhabited. The doors opened to a dark narrow hall in the building across from the parking garage. He made his way to Sam's door. No windows or big banks of sunlight here. Seiran knew the outside of the building looked like a wall of windows, most of them being the new sun-proof glass, and maybe blocked off to create more interior, light-safe rooms.

He knocked on the door, and waited. Heard movement from inside, but was surprised when Sam opened the door, fully dressed, but looking tired. "Shouldn't you be sleeping?" Seiran asked with a raised brow.

"I'm your bitch today, so the boss says," Sam did not look happy about that.

"I only need Forest. You can go back to bed."

"Did you bring cake?" Luca appeared from behind Sam dressed in nothing but a pair of too tiny bikini undies in bright purple. He looked every bit the boyband rock star Sam had accused Seiran of being. Pretty, and not overly muscled, but defined enough to be a model in just about any market.

Seiran held out the container. "Your blackmail, sir."

"He's mine," Sam growled.

Seiran squinted. "No debate, Sammie. Golem?"

Luca stepped past Sam to take the cake and kiss Seiran on the cheek. "Thanks, love. Can't wait for a taste of the divine."

Sam looked about ready to kill.

"Are you trying to get me killed, or rev your boyfriend up for something?" Seiran asked. Gabe wisely stayed behind Seiran, silent, and staring down the hallway rather than into Sam's space. Vampires could get very territorial. Something Seiran had forgotten. Was Gabe struggling with that? Now that he had some memories of Seiran?

"Happy," Luca teased, doing a little roll with his hips, "for cake."

"Forest, come," Sam snarled as he shoved Seiran out into the hallway. A second later, Forest appeared, looking like himself, or at least like the golem Seiran had sent off with the vampires. No release of the souls, and the magic keeping it human in appearance still seemed to be working, even over the distance. Sam closed the door behind the golem, leaving Luca alone to his cake fetish.

"Share some with Con," Seiran called, hoping he heard through the thick door. He turned to Sam, wondering if the grump was from being awake or something else. "Fill me in?"

Sam stalked to the elevator, Forest dogging his steps and Seiran and Gabe trailing behind. "They aren't decomposing," Sam said.

"Huh?" Seiran asked, trying to figure out what that meant as he walked.

They got in the elevator. Sam hit the down button and folded his arms across his chest. "The vampire bodies. The ones that don't feel like anything? They should be more broken down than they are. We've got some missing for months and still looking fresh. Well, mostly fresh. Like they were put in the ground and then their souls pulled later?"

But that wasn't possible. Vampires decomposed just like regular humans did once they were true dead. Gone to ground was a different process, their souls would still have been present, the magic of a vampire allowing their bodies to turn to dust and reform, but they didn't decompose. Not decomposing at all sounded like something else. Seiran frowned, trying to think of a reason for the bodies to still be protected by vampire magic when they were soulless.

"There are more golems," Gabe said as the elevator brought them back to the parking level. "The souls pulled from the bodies, but not released to true death is keeping the bodies from decomposing. Means there is nothing left in them but the revenant."

"There are more golems," Seiran repeated feeling the bottom drop out of his sanity. Like an army worth of golems.

"Or vampire zombies on call," Gabe added.

"Fuck my life."

CHAPTER 20

Gabe wandered between the rows of bodies, keeping out of everyone's way, and trying to place what he was feeling. Not only from the bodies of the vampires themselves. That was sort of a weird emptiness. Death, but not. It felt vaguely familiar? But whatever memory that came from hadn't found its slot in his mind.

Some had the revenant close, almost a bit of a dark shadow peering out from between the lines of magic wrapped organic matter. A few were nothing left but organic material breaking down, and some still glowed with magic. It didn't seem time or torture specific, but Gabe mentally categorized the things he saw hoping to share them with Seiran later.

The golem was still and silent. Whatever had been tugging on it the day before was gone, leaving it almost like it was floating in the sea of Seiran's power. Gabe found the listlessness of it a bit disconcerting, like it could explode into action at any second and was biding its time.

The fact that he couldn't release the souls either, not without a complete breakdown of the body, was unusual. That too, had been muscle memory. As if he'd done it a thousand times. Yet this golem was tangled, the ties almost like barbs to cut whomever tried to unravel them. And he debated on destroying it outright. Would it harm the souls within? Or finally give them rest?

Then there was Seiran, who took charge of the room the second he walked in. Didn't matter that it was a mix of high-level vampires, police, and MI investigators, they all took notice, and gave him command.

It was different than last night, when everyone had been fixated on removing the bodies, helping those that seemed to be savable. It was almost as if they recognized this level of magic was Seiran's forte, and got the fuck out of his way so he could fix this mess. If there were witches who thought him suspect, they were not there. The police, the MI investigators, and the vampires all deferred to him without any resistance.

Gabe was surprised by the bit of pride he felt for the respect showed to Seiran. Not that he had any say in the creation of it, but that these people recognized his worth, and treated him like the intelligent and powerful man he was. Why didn't the rest of the Dominion recognize that? By design? Gabe was beginning to believe they did it to try to hold him back. The Director the other day seemed well aware of his power, even while she tried to take control of something that wasn't her department. She had to have witnessed the entire display at the front desk. Why shove him aside? Other than to make him feel like he was worthless, and powerless. Yet he persevered.

Here he was king. Pointing out small bits of magic he detected, or finding small bits of fiber or other physical things that the police and investigators might miss. Like some sort of supernatural bloodhound, he tracked through each, seeming to sense more than the entire room of people combined.

The bodies were numbered based on when they'd gone missing. The two that they knew to be part of the creation of the golem sectioned off to one side. They had not found the third. Which left the question, where was that body? Was there another graveyard?

Nearly a dozen true dead. Decapitated, substantially rotted, and difficult to identify. They'd been gone a while. Those were the oldest of the bunch. But there were a lot more that didn't seem to be rotting. Or at least suspended in a middle stage of decomposition, as though it had begun, but was achingly slow?

And so many vampires with that odd echo of emptiness. As though something was tied to them, only not. Sam had been wrong. They *were* decomposing, at a rate so slow it would take them a century or more to find true death. That, in and of itself, was torture. Soul not present, but not released. It was a strange combination that was both confusing and horrifying.

Gabe could sense it most from the oldest bodies. Like the animation that created the vampire was fighting the drag of death. Did that mean the souls could be returned to fix the vampires? Or that only releasing the souls from golems would grant them true death? The questions were dizzying. He knew he couldn't feel those normal ties that would allow a sire to raise a vampire. He could recall having to pull a few vampires from the earth over the years, or untangle them from their revenant. These were little more than magic encased corpses, empty. Like bottles waiting to be filled with the oozing darkness of the revenant. Creepy.

Gabe stood nearby as Seiran examined those who had been used to create Forest. The golem lingered near the wall, looking very still, though human in appearance. Seiran had commanded the golem to stay put and it hadn't moved. Gabe didn't feel anything pulling on it either. That made him think that whomever was doing this, knew they'd found the killing field and was perhaps trying to hide? Was it the missing kid? Steve, or whatever his name was? Gabe listened to the many voices around him, trying to process all the information while keeping a close eye on Seiran.

Sam had found a spot in the corner away from everyone else and curled up to nap. He had grumbled after they arrived about 'unvampirely hours' and 'fucking witch bullshit' which had Seiran casting him off to improve his mood. Sam's *fuck you, Ronnie* hadn't stopped the vampire from finding a place away from the crowd.

The time passed quickly, and Gabe felt the sun high in the sky, peaking then beginning to fall. He tried to clarify what he felt in ways he thought might be helpful to the investigation. But as everything else in his head since he'd awoken, it was a muddle.

"These bodies are a lot more heavily damaged than the rest," Seiran said. Gabe thought it was more to himself than anyone else. These two, the ones used to create the golem, had also been missing longer than the others who hadn't found true death. A couple months, while some were only a few weeks old. Spaced out as far as Gabe could tell. One or two missing a week, from all over the upper Midwest. Meaning someone had specifically gone out of their way to try to make it seem as though the disappearances were random.

Vampires went missing all the time. Taken down by other vampires, or disgruntled humans with race issues. It was one of the reasons vampires kept to their flocks, and checked in regularly with their sire or the master of their territory. The badly damaged bodies hadn't been reported missing until weeks after they were suspected to have been taken. Lax masters. Gabe wondered if Max kept track of that, or anyone did now that the Tri-Mega was dead. Bad master vampires could lead to more than just dead vampires. It could lead to another war. Gabe had seen plenty of those in his lifetime.

A handful of the investigators, witches Gabe thought, had to leave to throw up. They rushed off, looking a bit green and did not return. Seiran paid them no attention, instead documenting minute details with the medical examiner. None of the vampires would be cut up or autopsied as was the standard for a murder. Max had refused on behalf of all the vampires citing the monstrosities already suffered to them.

Gabe had received a voicemail from Max indicating he was to ensure the humans followed the rules, whether they be ordinary mortals, or witch ones. He'd also left off with, "I expect you to put them back in the ground as soon as possible. The *right* way this time."

What had that meant? Wouldn't Seiran be the better one to ease the vampires to the next life? Free them? It was another piece in the puzzle of Gabe's memory. He hadn't asked Seiran about it.

Gabe looked out over the sea of bodies, finding it a weird murmur of disquiet. Not like a graveyard, which he'd always found peaceful. He even remembered a handful of battlefields, long fallen to the silence of death, and blood-strewn hillsides, all feeling a little less empty than this. Those places had an energy, whether it had been the rages of a former battle still echoing or the howls of the dead screaming for justice. This was hollow.

His gaze fell on Seiran who kept returning to the two golem vampires. Something about them made him frown, so Gabe frowned too, trying to read Seiran's emotions without digging too deep. He could tell that Seiran felt something—magically speaking—that was different about them, but couldn't place it. It frustrated him. And he kept checking to see if he missed something. Gabe looked over them again too. Wondering if he could discover the missing piece.

The two vampires attributed to the golem, were badly mutilated. Cut up, burned, parts missing. According to the information they'd gotten from the golem last night, the torture had been extensive. The others, not as much. Some damage here and there. But not like these, which were almost physically unrecognizable as people, or vampires if they weren't considered people. Would a vampire survive that amount of damage? The simple answer was yes, but also maybe? It depended on the age and strength of a vampire.

Gabe couldn't tell who sired them. And that wasn't unusual. It simply meant that whomever they belonged to, wasn't some large power that Gabe had met before. Even with his broken memory he suspected he would know the signature of most of the powerful left in the world. Like he'd met or bargained with them in his life, and maybe he had.

Underneath his senses, that odd ripple of aching emptiness trickled. He had the strange notion that he could reach out a hand and pull them to their feet, what was left of their feet, and make them dance. Not their souls, as they weren't there at all, the vague glow of them still entwined in the golem. But the bodies.

"They feel like the newly dead still," Gabe thought out loud, but only so Seiran could hear.

"What does that mean?" Seiran asked.

"When a body is first put in the ground, or even still in the morgue these days as it takes so long to bury people in this century, they have that weird sensation of emptiness. Like the soul has just left and it's a vessel ready to be occupied by something else. Lots of legends of demons taking over a corpse that was left aboveground too long." He glanced around as though trying to catch a glimpse of that darkness rising.

Seiran's expression was assessing. "Was someone trying to summon a demon?"

Gabe didn't know. It was simply a sensation he'd felt before. "I wish I had better answers for you."

"Maybe they failed and were stuck with a golem? But the golem has souls in it and demons need a body without a soul?"

"Met a lot of demons?" Gabe wondered.

"One." Seiran put his hand over his heart as it began to race with merely the suggestion of the demon. Gabe heard the sped-up pace even though he was three feet away.

"I'm sorry. Didn't mean to frighten you."

Seiran wrapped his arms around himself, closing his eyes for a moment, and counting. Breathing slowly in and out. Calming himself, Gabe realized.

"First time I ever thought for sure, if I died, I would not be coming back. Worried about leaving my kids behind."

"I'm sorry," Gabe said again. He had scattered memories

popping up that seemed to be labeled *demon*. Though the lack of emotion attached to it, seemed to mean it hadn't scared him, or he hadn't been closely involved?

"Summoners are terrifying things," Seiran said after a moment.

"They can be, without training. Maybe this golem was the first?" Gabe whispered, keeping his voice low as he mostly wanted his thoughts and attention directed at Seiran. He wasn't even sure he should be there, since the space had been restricted to police and MI witches. The handful of vampires remaining were medical personnel, and a few of the masters these missing belonged to. Gabe had greeted them briefly and left them to their somber identification. He also hoped to get Seiran's mind off the past.

"Could that be why it's so messy?" Seiran asked, looking from the golem to the bodies.

"Maybe," Gabe said.

"Necromancy? Or some messed up spell?" Seiran looked up, his expression thoughtful. "When I found the golem, it was tied to a complicated ward that drew energy from me. I thought the ward a bit haphazard at first, though artful. I think the tie to the golem was actually the haphazard part."

The missing student, who was from a witch family, hadn't ever tested. His family claimed he had no magic. But that was often the way with male witches. Gabe thought that interesting since there were two male Pillars of magic right now. But how would they test for death magic? Ask the witch to raise a corpse? That would probably be easiest. And likely rewarded with a public execution.

"Necromancy," Gabe said instantly. The residual energy of death magic echoed through the room. Not a spell. Spells were defined things with sharp edges and firm boundaries. Unless the caster was a total screwup which usually got themselves killed. But no, this had a taste of something very familiar. The caress of death rather than the anvil of time. "Newly awakened perhaps?" His gaze fell on the golem. "The first sort of an accident, but got better over time?"

"But why the torture?"

That was the part that didn't add up. A necromancer wouldn't need the vampires hurt to raise them, or even draw the souls out. A strong necromancer could do insane things to a vampire. Gabe had vivid, but disjointed memories, of some very epic battles against necromancers. Not always on opposite sides, but enough that the vampires seemed to see those born with death magic as enemies. Kill or be killed had been the motto for certain types of magic wielders over the years. Two types being the most dangerous to vampires. Necromancers and summoners. One dealt with death, the other with life. Polar opposites, and equally dangerous.

"What about the history of the family? Records of unusual magic?" Gabe asked.

"They don't write that stuff down," Seiran said. "Most of those families spends gads of money rewriting history to hide just this sort of thing."

"But no relatives cast out, or suspicious? Anything?"

Seiran pulled up his phone and scrolled through files. It was a lot of information, and Gabe didn't try to read over his shoulder. The files were set up with a snapshot overview on the first page, then long detailed supplemental documents attached. Seiran cruised through them like he'd read them a thousand times, and probably had. "It's a big family. Lots of offshoots too." He frowned. "Even Page is technically part of the family. Though it seems like his branch of it has been cut off from the main line for a while." His frown turned to pinched lips. "Apparently for one of his grandparents marrying someone of the wrong color."

Gabe sighed, feeling bad for the kid. "Page has power. I could sense that from our short meeting."

"He's never tested, but I did sense something in him. When I was interviewing for an assistant, after going through about two dozen witches who treated me like I was *their* assistant, I picked him even though he had no experience. He has to meet all the Dominion class requirements now that he works for me. Defense training, magic 101, de-escalation; he does a lot more than answer the phone and file. He has helped with a ton of my research. Knows the archives better than me."

"He's worked for you for a while?"

"Two years," Seiran said. "Long enough for me to treat him like family. He's picked up the kids from school before. Even had Solstice with us last year. As far as I know, it's only him and his mom."

"Would he know anything about this relative?"

"I think they are like third cousins or something. I'll send him a message. I think the stuff we saw from the golem yesterday got to him." Seiran sighed. "I really hope he doesn't quit."

"I think it got to everyone," Gabe said.

"Even you?"

"Even me. Never been a fan of rape and torture. Not even in the days of pillaging and raiding. War crimes were always war crimes, even if they weren't recognized that way by history. Many drown in the bloodlust. I didn't. At least not after I became a vampire. Too easy to let the monster out and destroy everything."

Seiran's gaze was assessing. Like he wasn't sure to believe it or not.

"Not all vampires are brutal assholes," Gabe said. Though he had to admit, he'd met a fair share. It sort of came with the whole having to survive on blood thing. Blood made everything seem more savage.

"That makes it sound like you were a bloodthirsty asshole when you were alive."

Gabe's memories of that time were vivid, but skewed, broken up by facts and things he now knew were reported wrong in history. He *had been* a bloodthirsty asshole, though at the time he hadn't thought so. He'd been on a quest for knowledge and world domination, proving to everyone that he could. Until he met his end. "I was."

"Were you someone famous?" Seiran wondered.

"Aren't we all in history?"

Seiran narrowed his eyes and Gabe held up his hands in defeat. "We don't share our names from before the change. It's like deadnaming a transperson. That person is gone. We are reborn."

"You weren't Gavriil?"

"That is my reborn name. It's evolved to Gabriel over the centuries."

"Titus... Max had another name too?"

Gabe nodded, seeing for a moment all the way back to those final days of mortal life. His lover had already been taken from him for the first time. He hadn't realized he'd get another chance after crossing over, but it hadn't been a choice he'd made either way. "After we are changed it can actually take a few years to remember our mortal lives. Most sires don't encourage the memory. Sometimes it triggers the revenant to want to go back and feed on those we loved in life."

"Twisted," Seiran said.

"Yes."

"Sam didn't forget."

"Sam is a witch. He had also been bonded to two vampires prior to his change."

"Don't call him that to his face. He hates it."

"He has a lover who is a witch," Gabe pointed out.

"Con hates the Dominion. They'd kill him if they could. It was you who kept them from taking him when they put down his sister."

"Me?" Gabe tried to recall that and came up blank. He remembered the tall lanky man who kept his distance from the vampires when Gabe had first reawakened, but nothing from the past. "Guess that memory isn't back."

"Maybe you have to touch him? Meet him up close?"

"Maybe," Gabe agreed.

Seiran's phone buzzed back from Page. He frowned at it. It was a response to his question about how well Page knew his cousin. The reply only said, *I'm sorry.*

Apologize for knowing him? Or not knowing him? It seemed weird.

Seiran made his way to a private corner away from the group and dialed his phone. Gabe could hear it just fine, both sides of the conversation, but didn't think any of the other vampires, including Sam, were close enough to catch it. Though in a space this quiet, sound echoed a little. Gabe put his back to Seiran, hoping to shield some of the sound.

"Page," Seiran said.

"I'm sorry," Page said rather than a greeting. He actually sounded like he was crying. "I'm so sorry."

"I know this is bad," Seiran started slowly, seeming to catch something in the young man's tone, "A terrible thing."

"I didn't know..." Page said, sucking in air and voice trembling. "I wouldn't have..."

Seiran paused, and Gabe tensed as he caught a nuance in the tone. Guilt? Had Page been part of this?

"Page, I'd like to talk to you," Seiran said quietly. He turned away from everyone, pacing further from the group. Gabe followed, keeping a slow pace that made it look like they were talking rather than trying to cover up a conversation. Fuck. What did Page do?

Page was sobbing now, babbling apologies, sniffling and muffled. Gabe listened intently. "I didn't know..."

"Did Steve make you do this?" Seiran asked quietly, catching on fast, though he said Page had been working for him for two years. He probably knew his assistant fairly well.

"I wouldn't have, if I had known what they were doing... even to... free them. I thought it was only a few. Didn't know about..."

"Page," Seiran said gently, more like he was speaking to one of his children rather than his young assistant. "We'll fix this. Are you at home? Can I meet with you? You can tell me how this happened?"

"I'm not evil," Page gasped, his sobbing garbling what he said. Sam was awake now, staring in their direction. Gabe worried that meant he'd go after the kid. How did he hear when he was halfway across the room and Seiran was whispering? Maybe being a witch made his hearing more sensitive even than a regular vampire?

"I don't think you are," Seiran said. "Can you tell me what happened?"

"They were being hurt," Page whispered, sucking in large gulps of air and Gabe could hear him struggle to keep from totally falling apart. "Suffering."

"And you thought putting them in the golem would free them?" Seiran asked. Was Page a necromancer? The transfer of souls was usually a bit more complicated than that. But he was very young. Gabe wondered if he had had any training at all.

"Less pain," Page said. "He promised to stop hurting them."

Seiran nodded like Page could see it. "You didn't know what he would do with the golem."

"He said he just wanted it to help with chores and stuff. I thought it would be better than torture."

"And what about the rest?" Seiran prodded gently. Sam was headed their way now, though no one else was.

"I didn't know."

"Did you make more golems?" Seiran asked quietly.

"No. I promise. I'm not even sure how I made Forest. It was a mess. I…" Page cut off, sucking in air like he was hyperventilating.

"I need you to breathe for me, Page. Breathe and count with me. I'm going to lead, okay? And once you're calm, I need you to tell me where you are."

"They'll kill me. The Dominion. I don't want to burn. I didn't mean to hurt anyone."

"I know that, honey," Seiran soothed, his tone soft. "You know I won't let anyone hurt you. Breathe with me." Seiran mimicked taking long, deep breaths, talking Page through a panic attack. The kid had a right to be afraid. Accident or not, one time or not, the Dominion would kill him. It was what they did to witches who had power they didn't think they could control. That was what Seiran had been trying to tell Gabe. And what Gabe's broken memories were reminding him of in small chunks. Seiran had nearly been locked away in a concrete room to try to keep him from realizing his power. Coerced to create children that the Dominion could possibly use. Gabe had been a pawn in that game too.

Sam stood nearby, arms folded across his chest, facing away from Seiran, looking out to the sea of bodies, expression blank. Gone was the snark, and with it the last bits that looked human. Everything he presented was a cold and emotionless killer. Would Sam kill Page first? Was that why Max had sent him?

CHAPTER 21

Seiran did his best to calm Page, even while trying not to panic himself. Page, his assistant, who wouldn't hurt a fly, had created the golem. The fear that filled him couldn't be expressed without alerting everyone. And Sam stood there, looking ready to kill.

Yet the whole thing felt familiar. Not unlike Kaine's story about the bunnies. Freeing them from mortal pain. Was that what Page had done?

He said he hadn't created more golems. Should Seiran believe him? And what did all this mean? The deaths? The torture? Steve trying to create a golem but unable? Why so many dead vampires? And how? One barely legal witch kid shouldn't have been able to do something this massive. Not without help. That thought burned in Seiran's gut.

Not without help.

Sure, he had his buddies mess with the golem, but their signature wasn't anywhere over the massive grave of bodies. Not fibers or even a residue of their presence. The mounting evidence Seiran had collected, magic bits and fibers, would hopefully help them trace the murders back. Would it all go to one kid? Seiran didn't think so. His family perhaps? A large coven of several families maybe, with this sort of death toll. No one person killed this many without getting caught. But a coven? Easy enough.

This kid had somehow convinced Page to create a golem for him. By torturing vampires until Page could no longer stand watching the pain? How could he have held three vampires hostage, and kept them bound well enough to torture them? There wasn't a power or spell that could bind the revenant of a vampire once it had broken free. It was why they were forced to ground or were outright killed to keep them from raging. Beheading was thought to be the only thing that worked on a vampire gone rogue if they couldn't be put back in the ground.

Seiran couldn't imagine a revenant not rising from torture. Pain, rage, and fear meant loss of control. A revenant was a vampire's berserker rage; the stuff of nightmares. It bordered on the edge of demonic, though was less a hellborn creature, and more an animal of instinct.

Who had created the dorm room ward? There were too many unanswered questions. No one was strong enough to do this on their own. Not even Seiran thought he could bind a couple dozen vampires and torture them until he got someone else to comply. One golem with three vampire souls stuck inside seemed to be his limit. Maybe that was because death magic wasn't his strength?

Why had Page been involved at all? If the family cast out his family decades ago, why use him? Because he had power? Because they were tracking that line, looking for power?

Gabe stood nearby, seeming to catch everything, but not looking as murderous as Sam. If Seiran hadn't been so focused on Page, he might have been able to sort through some of Gabe's thoughts, as Seiran felt a handful of them pushed his way. Like Gabe had insight to share, but didn't want to vocalize it. Seiran had to calm Page first.

"Where are you? At home?"

"No," Page whispered. "I need to stop all of this." He sounded tired, like he'd been battling guilt for a while, crying long enough to have lost the energy to fight the tide of emotion.

"Page, honey," Seiran said. "Please don't do anything." He knew that tone. Had heard it a handful of times in his life. Usually, it was when he faced down a witch who would be slated for execution on sight. Or who was awaiting the stake. Resignation. The utter lack of hope. Sometimes he lost those witches to death by cop, others he couldn't stop their execution, even if he freed their souls to move on before the pain began.

His heart sank at the idea of losing Page. Two years he'd seen Page every day, treated him like family, had him over to his house for movie nights. Seiran had rarely treated Page like an employee. Maybe that was Seiran's first mistake. Had he been blinded to what Page was? No. Seiran didn't think Page would have done any of this without some sort of extreme circumstance.

"I don't want to burn," Page whispered. "I just didn't want them to hurt anymore. I didn't know he would…"

"I know, sweetie, please. Tell me where you are. Let me help."

"You're one of them," Page whispered. "I know you don't want to be. You've always treated me well. Seen me," he said, his voice filled with tears. "I'm so sorry."

And that hurt like a knife in the gut. Seiran had hated being tied to the murderous end of the Dominion. No matter how hard he fought, he rarely saved anyone once the Dominion had branded them rogue. It was the first time he thought that maybe they'd done it on purpose. Shoved him into a role where execution was a constant reminder to him not to rebel, and to prove to him how powerless he really was. Meanwhile, he couldn't die. Not unless the earth had forsaken him. It was like slow torture, he realized. Death by a thousand cuts. No wonder he felt soul weary.

He sucked in a deep breath and tried to sound calm. "I do see you, Page. And I won't let them hurt you."

"You can't stop them. You've tried," Page said with a shaky voice. "I've seen you cry in your office when the rest of the world thinks the Dominion is triumphant. I proofread your reports. I know how they change your files. Taking things you worded so they know it was an accident or an extreme situation, and rewording it to add malcontent to justify the death sentence. I've seen too much. Watched them use you to track down those to kill. I don't want to be next."

All of that was true, and it made Seiran's anger rise to squash his panic. He'd been used a long time to help murder other witches. Less than a handful ever really deserving of the death they brought. He thought if he stayed, kept pushing for change, that someday it would help. Seiran also admitted he'd been afraid. Not that they would kill him. The earth's affection for him meant they were powerless to physically harm him. But that didn't mean his family was safe. Could he protect them from something like this? If it had been Kaine in Page's shoes? Would he? The answer was a firm yes. They had planned out entire contingency plans with the idea that *someday* the Dominion would come for them. Not a question of *if*, but of *when*.

"I won't let them hurt you, Page," Seiran said again, feeling a well of resolve rise within him. If that meant they'd try to take him down, so be it. "I just need you to be safe until I get to you."

Sam was on the phone now. Seiran suspected he was talking to Max, but couldn't focus on two things at once. Not when he had a life to save.

"It's too late. I shouldn't have…"

"You thought freeing them would help. I understand."

"It wasn't the first time," Page whispered so softly that Sei barely heard.

"That you released a soul? Or made a golem?"

"I've raised things before. On accident. First time it happened I was seven."

Seiran clenched his fist. "Page…"

"Family tried to teach me to bury it. I'm evil. They told me that since I was little."

"Having this power isn't evil. You didn't ask for it."

"No. But I shouldn't have used it."

"It's like asking us not to breathe, Page. Impossible."

"I read about the golem, but never made one before Forest. They killed my dad, you know. It's listed as suicide, but my mom told me that was a lie. She said if the family knew how powerful I am now, they would do it to me too."

"Your mom helped you hide your power to protect you? She sounds pretty great."

"She is," Page sniffled. "Tried so hard to teach me. But it isn't the same as her magic. And it was an accident when I raised Mattie."

The family had known. Fuck. Seiran was so enraged that Page hadn't been trained. Kelly and Jamie had four halfway houses set up for young witches. Those who didn't have the financial ability to afford training, or whose families tried to pretend they didn't have power. It made Seiran angry that Page had been missed. "Mattie?"

"Our cat. She had a heart attack one day, was only ten or something."

"It happens that way sometimes. I'm sorry."

"I cried for days. Barely slept. Kept having dreams of her being there. And then one night, she was."

"Oh, Page."

"Mom was horrified. Had to go to the family to help put her back." Page sucked in a stuttering breath. "I asked them to show me. To help me."

"They refused?" Seiran guessed.

"Burned her. Was the only thing they could do to keep her from rising. But she was there, *hurting, aware...*" He sounded heartbroken, and Seiran could only imagine the horror of watching that.

"Page, I'm so sorry."

"I've done the best I can to learn on my own. Keep it from happening again. I'm sorry," Page whispered. "I taught myself as best I could. Learning to release them so they wouldn't end up like Mattie."

Burned to ash to release the soul. Seiran could only imagine how terrifying it was to learn that on his own.

"I'm not evil, even if they say I am."

"I know you're not, honey. Let me help." Seiran said. "Please let me help." He headed for his car, Gabe hot on his heels and Sam close by.

"I'm sorry. Please don't hate me," Page whispered again and hung up.

"Fuck!" Seiran screamed into the air outside the warehouse. Gabe didn't hesitate to follow him as he raced toward the car even though the sun was still high, but Sam did.

"No," he told Sam.

"He murdered vampires," Sam said as he paused under an overhang.

Releasing the souls from their body was a bit like murder, but not how Sam meant it. "Not because he wanted to."

"You don't know that. It's not like you're the best judge of character." Sam waved his hands at Gabe.

"Leave me out of this," Gabe said. He looked at Seiran. "Do you know where he is? Can you find him?"

"Can you drive?" Seiran asked. He tapped his phone and sent an emergency alert out to his family. Anyone in his circle really. That meant Jamie and Kelly, the kids, the witch houses, and even his mother. Level red. It meant nothing shy of the apocalypse. He'd apologize later if he overreacted, but keeping them safe was key. If the day went the way he was suspecting it would go, everyone was going to be after him soon. And them, because they were a way to get to him.

"Do you remember how? I know your license needs to be renewed and all that, but can you drive if I cast a spell to find him?"

Gabe nodded. "I can."

"Max isn't going to let this go," Sam said.

"And Page isn't the root of the problem. He's just a pawn on the board," Seiran snarled at him. Like he'd allowed himself to be. Like they all had. Seiran burned with rage over all of this. The family, the Dominion, and his own failure to recognize a young witch needing help. What did that say for him as a father? What was he missing in his own kids? "I'm not going to let him die because it's convenient for everyone else."

"Ronnie…" Sam growled back even as Seiran made his way to the car, leaving Sam under the overhang. "We won't be far behind."

"Hopefully far enough. Tell Max there is more to this. Keep an eye on the golem."

"The Dominion will kill him before Max will have the chance, and this is a vampire issue," Sam yelled. "The witches knew. This has been going on for months. There's no way to hide this. We won't let this get wrapped up with political red tape."

"I didn't know."

"There's a lot you never seem to know. How much are they keeping from you? How much are they using you? When will you finally say enough is enough?"

Seiran paused, his heart pounding, and tears fell hot on his cheeks, though they were angry tears rather than sad ones. He hated that sometimes he couldn't rein in the emotions. "I think right now, to be honest."

Sam's gaze met his. "Ronnie, don't get yourself killed. This could spark another vampire war."

"So be it," Seiran said, "stay safe." He rushed into the parking garage, toward his car. He was tired of being a pawn himself. For the Dominion, the vampires, everyone. He was getting too old, which he equated to being tired of everyone's bullshit.

"You have a way to find him?" Gabe asked again as he took the keys from Seiran and opened the door to the driver's side.

"A spell yes, inspired by one of the kid's video games actually."

"Okay, what do we do?"

"You drive. I'm going to cast, and fly a bit. Try not to open our bonds too much."

"Fly?" Gabe asked.

"We call it Odin's Eye."

"Like the stories of Muninn and Huginn?"

"Exactly, borrowing the sight of a bird. Tracing magic signatures. It's a bit complicated to explain, though easy enough in practice. It will be erratic to describe where we are going, so try not to kill us?" Seiran ducked into the passenger seat, strapping on the belt, and setting his bag at his feet.

He got affirmatives back from Jamie, Kelly, and in tandem each of the kids. Luca and Con's reply popped up too. The houses began checking in. They would have to do head counts before locking the doors and setting the wards to maximum.

Was it sad that they'd planned for this? For something big? Seiran set his phone in his bag and prayed for a minute for the strength to protect everyone.

It was an impossible dream, but one he'd been fighting for his whole life.

"Birds aren't air?" Gabe asked.

"Birds are life on earth, which all falls to my domain." Technically everything on the planet was his domain as long as the Goddess allowed him the strength. Earth, fire, wind, water, spirit, death, and life. As long as the world continued to turn, She could grant all to him. He might have an affinity for the earth, but She considered him her scion.

"A lot of people underestimate you," Gabe said as he started the van and headed toward the exit.

"They do," Seiran agreed. "But not for much longer. I'm sorry you had to be awake for this. I think everything is about to become a shitstorm."

"Rather be a part of it than in the ground not able to help."

"Thanks," Seiran whispered, happy to not be alone after years of aching loneliness. He began whispering, his hands glowing with power. A bit of a poetic chant more as a focus for himself than actual words for a spell. He hadn't needed words in over a decade.

But the thought behind the words clarified, sending his mind and vision skyward, to borrow wings and search the horizon.

He'd made a habit, over the years, of memorizing the energy or magic of the people closest to him. The first time the twins changed, shifting to their foxes, they'd been young. Even younger than he'd been for his first change. And Sakura had slipped away from them, vanishing into the woods surrounding the house. It had taken him three days to find her as he kept losing himself to his lynx, and after that he'd begun memorizing the way the earth saw each of them. All as unique as snowflakes in a delicate dance of power woven with life.

They made the rule that no one changed outside of the arboretum anymore, and Seiran could track his family, his closest friends, and even his assistant by recognizing the magic or life of the being. He didn't need to change to his lynx form to do it. He'd taught Jamie the spell, and the twins had mastered it without much effort. Kaine didn't need the spell at all to find anyone. His fae power superseding mortal constraints. Yet another reason for Seiran to rise, and break free of the Dominion chains. He needed to make sure no one could look at Kaine and plan to kill him just for existing. But first he would begin with Page.

The raven flew higher, arcing around in a circle until Seiran spotted the wave of familiar lines and colors. This glowing gaze of magic wasn't as defined as real sight. He'd not be able to make out street names and addresses, only direction and distance, but at least it was somewhere to start.

CHAPTER 22

Gabe had to admit it was a lot more distracting than he thought it would be, sitting in the car next to a spell that pulsed like snapped live electrical wire burning into his vision. It made it hard for him to navigate the car out of the dark lot because the light was so bright. But once out into the light of the day, the brightness balanced enough for him to see the road and the buildings. He had to squint, his sensitive vampire sight making the intensity of it all a little painful. But Seiran needed him.

"Which way?"

"Left," Seiran said, his voice deep and echoing, and Gabe caught a glimpse through the bond of flying, like a bird drifting high up over the area, it caught a glow of energy like a beacon, and was headed that way. He had to lock down his edge of the bond to keep himself from following the flight. That was some crazy power. Even with their bond not renewed, he had to work to stay in the here and now rather than a magic-filled sky.

Gabe pulled the car out onto the street and headed left, navigating free of the city, because the vision he'd caught was of trees and a less populated area. He had no idea what the spell was, but it felt godlike. Large enough to find anyone anywhere, but still contained in a small enough space that no one else could detect it. Brilliant.

Could Seiran's power flit to any animal or living being? Definitely godlike. How much did he suppress every day to try to fit in and comply?

Gabe followed the directions as Seiran muttered them, and had to work hard from letting himself fall into the gaze that Seiran was seeing. It was almost an overlay on reality. Two places at once. Gabe drove fast, but carefully, thankful he remembered the basics of driving as more of a muscle memory than reinstatement of vague rules.

Outside of the city, northwest instead of the southeast in which Seiran's house was, where Gabe wasn't as familiar with the streets, but worked hard to weave around traffic and finally turn onto a quieter road.

"Close," Seiran said, voice rough, and the glow he held fading a bit.

"Can you find anyone this way?" Gabe wondered.

"No. Only those I've memorized their life force. My kids and family mostly. A few of my investigators, and Page."

"Me?"

"No," Seiran admitted. "But I plan to remedy that if you're staying."

"I'm not going anywhere," Gabe said as he found a way down a side road that was little more than ruts for tires. They were getting into the woods now. He didn't think it was part of the state forests, but wasn't sure it was private land either. Maybe a hunting spot?

He drove a while, weaving until he wasn't sure he could drive much further, but then there were other cars. Flashing lights and a dozen cars parked in a clearing. That couldn't be good.

Seiran swore and Gabe felt the spell snap away, the light vanishing, as well as the intensity of power. Director Han stood on the edge of a clearing with a handful of other women her age, all wearing Dominion badges. None of this looked friendly, in fact everyone was armed, and Gabe could sense the magic pulsing of energy from the witches. They were prepared for violence, not taking someone in for questioning or even a peaceful arrest.

Why were none of Seiran's people there? Even if they'd been busy with the other site, the investigation team should have been at the forefront, but none of the badges were the bright lime green Gabe had seen at the warehouse marking all of the investigators. Gabe's stomach lurched.

"Does this feel like a set up to you? Why are none of your people here?" Gabe wondered if Page had set them up.

"He wouldn't," Seiran said, catching Gabe's thought.

"But you didn't know he had this power, what else could he be hiding? And how would they have known?"

"Someone else called them? I have a lot of people." Seiran said.

"Would Sam have called them?"

"Sam doesn't work for the Dominion. He works for Max. The only reason the vampires work with the Dominion at all is because of me."

"You have a lot of allies for a man the Dominion keeps trying to shove in a basement like he doesn't exist," Gabe remarked.

Seiran sucked in a deep breath. "I do."

"They don't look like they want to negotiate."

"The Dominion doesn't negotiate. They just kill."

Gabe let that comment filter through him. "You don't strike me as the kind of guy who kills for the sake of killing."

"I'm not. I don't actually kill them."

But he'd never been able to stand in the Dominion's way before. Except... A vague memory came into place. "Sam?"

"That was more you than me," Seiran admitted. "Sam did a lot of shit, but once a vampire, he was out of the Dominion's hands. I don't think making Page a vampire is going to be a way out here. Plus, Sam was already mostly dead when you brought him over."

"And tied to Roman," Gabe recalled. "And necromancers aren't supposed to be changed."

"No?" Seiran asked. "Why can't necromancers change?"

"They don't usually rise," Gabe said. Something else tugged at his memory. A familiar but vague idea of vampires and necromancers mixing. "If he is a necromancer at all, and his comments about the souls makes me think he's not. We will have to find another way to save your assistant. Or let them kill him."

"He said he raised his cat," Seiran pointed out.

"Living enough that her soul was there, that's not necromancy. She'd have just been a rotting corpse without the soul. Putting her back in the ground wouldn't have needed fire."

Seiran seemed to think about that for a minute. "You don't think he did this on purpose? He's not our killer?"

"No. I'd have sensed it. Whatever pulled me from the grave early wasn't Page. It was bigger than Page." Gabe felt that in his gut. An awareness that the constant tugging on his revenant was a demand from somewhere. A witch perhaps, more likely several. But he knew he'd have recognized that tug from Page if it had been him.

Seiran was silent as Gabe directed the car near the edge of the grouping. How many cops and witches were needed to take down one witch? This seemed like overkill, even for a baby necromancer. Gabe suspected that Page's powers, as strong as he might be, were still undeveloped, and minimal. Could he be powerful enough to raise an army of the undead? Maybe in a few decades with a lot of training.

And with that came another strange bunch of memories as if Gabe had received training. Death magic was something all vampires accessed in different terms. Raising armies of zombies and golems weren't usually in their scope. Yet he could almost feel the pull of those things. Like he'd done them before. But that couldn't be right. Necromancers didn't rise. Once the grave claimed them, it never let them go. Why did he feel like that was only mostly the truth?

"There is only one way to save him," Seiran said.

"Unleash the kraken?" Gabe asked in a half joke as he parked the car.

"You have no idea how close to reality that is." Seiran was out the second it stopped and Gabe rushed to follow. There was a pit of rage built up inside of Seiran, he could feel it rising, bits added to the top with each event making everything tinted with an edge of red. It was almost like a red out. Gabe knew the vampire berserker rage well, though he couldn't recall experiencing it himself in centuries. The revenant completely lost to bloodlust; it was a boogeyman of vampire lore.

But Seiran wasn't a vampire. Would being tied to one be enough? Could the revenant gain access to the witch? And how much trouble would they all be in if that happened to the Pillar of Earth?

Gabe found it strange, how instead of it being something that suddenly appeared, that anger seemed to have been pooling for a long time. Walled off behind wards and shields, buried as though that would stop it from someday spilling over. How many injustices had it taken to reach the breaking point? The wards around it felt like a dam about to burst, the pressure on the other side far beyond what Gabe could imagine anyone holding. But he recognized it, as though part of it belonged to him. How was that possible? He'd been in the ground over a decade.

"Seiran?" Gabe started to ask, but Seiran was laser-focused on the group in the clearing. They were staring at him too, hands going to weapons, and witches with a spell on their lips. There was no sign of them taking Page alive. This was orchestrated murder in the making.

"Stay close to me," Seiran instructed as he stalked toward the witches. "What are you doing here?" He demanded of them.

"Taking down a rogue witch," Director Han said. "His family told us of his deviance. No wonder you kept him locked away in your department. Hiding him. Your position will be under review, Mr. Rou."

"That's Director Rou," Seiran corrected. "And he's not rogue. He was coerced into creating the golem."

"Doesn't matter," the woman next to Han said. "All of your kind are evil. We will wipe their blight from the earth."

"Not on my watch," Seiran said. "Not anymore."

Gabe felt the shield form around him first, an invisible barrier that pulsed with so much energy it almost hurt, like standing too close to a flame. Seiran's form changed, becoming that Green Man persona again, his hair longer, woven with ivy and flowers, things blooming around his feet as he walked unfettered toward the group who now backed up as though terrified. Had none of them seen this side of him before? Or was it the molten rage that seemed to send a shimmering flicker of light along the edge of the magic?

The ground welled up, heating and cooling instantly, forming almost volcanic rock formations as he stalked forward. Sprouts of green and pops of color forming in the rocks soon after. It was breathtaking, beautiful, and terrifying all at once. Gabe kept his shields up, the bond weak between them the only thing keeping him from rolling in the power like a cat immersed in catnip.

Seiran held out his hands, and there were guns pointed their way, as well has a handful of spells that Gabe could feel hit the walls of the barrier, spattering harmlessly like bugs on a windshield. The magic around them built, a living thing of wild energy and such naked intensity so filled with earth, that Gabe longed to bask in it. Like dirt fresh from his grave it was renewing, and clarifying all at once.

The spells and bullets hit the shield, deflecting or being completely absorbed. Each wave of magic adding to the barrier and the power like Seiran ate it all. Or at least transformed it into something he could use. And unlike the rest of the witches, he didn't need spells. He put out his hands, made a shoving motion, and the crowd was walloped with a surge of air so strong it threw them all backward and even tipped some of the cars on their sides like he was a superhero rather than a witch.

There were curses hurled, screaming, more bullets and spells. Everyone backed away, huddling together and fixated on Seiran for the threat he was. Gabe hoped that meant Page was safe for the moment.

Their withered bond blazed with electricity and Gabe could almost touch Seiran's power like it was his. If they renewed the bond, he could become a conduit much like Seiran was. Would he be another link to earth? Or more an anchor for Seiran's power?

Seiran slowly backed them away from the group and into the line of trees like he could sense where Page was, and he probably could. His eyes glowed with that eerie spinning gaze of magic, not unlike seeing the actual earth turn from space, a thing of life, color, and power. Was he seeing everything? Or was this part of the spell? Gabe worked really hard not to distract Seiran as he hoped they would both somehow survive today.

The trees wove together beyond the circle of those gathered, growing and twisting together in a natural wall. Like old legends of castles surrounded by forests of thorns and impassable brambles, the barrier formed in seconds. A dome of earth magic as Gabe had never seen in his life.

Gabe stayed close to Seiran. The power burning hot, making Gabe sweat. He clung to their bond like it was the only thing keeping him from burning up in the wake of this incredible power. He understood at that moment, what Seiran had meant about not being afraid of Gabe. This was godlike power, not only one single spell, but the strength in one being, unleashed.

"You'll burn for this Rou," Han was shouting.

Bullets hit their shield and turned to flowers and butterflies. Gabe had to work not to pause and admire the beauty of it. They approached the wall. Would they scale it? Gabe didn't like the look of those thorns, more like swords or stakes than regular thorns. Many a foot long or more. As they approached the wall, the trees opened a pathway, narrow, but clear of barbs.

Gabe grabbed a handful of the back of Seiran's shirt to keep from being left on the wrong side of the barrier. It was disorienting as they walked through, the power a roll of color and billows of energy that had Gabe hunched and clinging to Seiran like a lifeboat.

When they emerged on the other side of what had to be at least ten feet of natural barrier, and several dozen yards distance into the thickest part of the woods, they found Page and another man. As soon as they passed through the barrier, it closed behind them, and the rolling shield of magic around them vanished, leaving them in the clearing with the men, separated from the world by a dome of woven oaks so dense Gabe was certain it would take a massive number of explosions to tear through them.

From the inside, the dome seemed huge, towering into the sky, and encasing a distance of at least a half a mile in all directions. Far in the distance away from Seiran and Gabe, behind Page, was a cabin, appearing well maintained from the outside, but lines of dark woven magic were etched into the core of it. Gabe yanked his gaze away from the engraved spells, and to the men on the ground.

Page's face was streaked with tears, and holding a gun. The other man was slumped over several feet away. Page seemed unfazed by the barrier or Seiran's power on display. The man on the ground lay still as death, and when Gabe listened hard for a heartbeat, he couldn't hear one. Was the man dead? Had Page killed him?

"I'm sorry," Page said again, raising the gun, not to point at them, but to his own head.

"Don't..." Seiran said reaching for him.

Gabe was already moving when the gun fired, and Gabe's heart sank as he was certain he wouldn't be fast enough. The shot rang through the echo chamber of woven magic in a booming thunder of destruction.

CHAPTER 23

Seiran gasped in horror when Page raised the gun to end his own life. All in the space of less than a breath, Gabe was there, taking the gun from Page, and control of the situation, though not fast enough to stop a bullet from being fired.

The shot ricocheted off the wards of trees and magic, pinging around a few milliseconds, spitting shards of wood and rippling the barrier. The sound hurt, loud and booming. Pain flared white hot, burning into Seiran's side. Had he been hit? His hearing echoed for a minute, pain in his head, as well as blossoming in his chest.

Beneath the mounting emotions, a tsunami of energy and the rising pain, he teetered. Was he still standing? He put his hand to his side, over the pain, the lower edge of his chest, and a rush of heat and liquid poured over his hand. Fuck, he hated being shot.

It was hard to breathe through the mounting rage, but he struggled to rein it in and focus. The Goddess had a lot to be angry about, and She was more than happy to let Seiran use that as fuel, tying Her rage to each mounting injustice of his life. This bullet, while trying to save a life, was another pebble added to an overfull bucket.

The entire area was silent. The echo of the shot fading into nothing. The center of a storm, the magic growing and swirling around them. Seiran had to blink hard to see through the roll of power. His chest ached like there was too much weight on it. The bullet hadn't gone that deep, had it? Piercing something vital? He blinked back stars and waves of darkness, though couldn't tell if they were from the power or the wound.

Page was on the ground. Gabe holding him down, gun kicked away, but Page wasn't resisting at all.

"I'm sorry. I'm so sorry." Page cried. It tugged at Seiran's memory, the dozens of times in his life he'd found himself broken, lost, and without hope. Why did he keep getting back up?

"Seiran?" Gabe called; voice tight.

Seiran stood very still, his heart racing, his mind filled with endless ideas of revenge and natural disasters he could use, power pulsing in every cell. He had never let it overflow like this. Had never given Her the chance to completely take him. He had always thought She would force him to shift and he'd forever wander as a lynx, lost to the simplicity of his animal half, not that She would use him to end the world. He fought to hold back while She beckoned him to let Her have control. She wanted to use him. Instill Her will into him and tear everything apart. And if he was hurt enough to let Her have it…

"It would mean the end of humanity," Gabe said softly. Seiran felt the words in his mind more than heard them. "This rage is not yours."

But it was. A molten lava of burning anger as familiar as the air he breathed. A lifetime of being slapped down, shoved aside, abused, and left abandoned, had fostered this rage. The Goddess was merely an echo of what was already inside. Seiran could feel storms building across the globe, a surge of power mounting in the core of the earth as it readied itself for a massive global shift of tectonic plates. The destruction of all of it on the tip of his fingers. He wouldn't have to do much, simply let go of his control. She would step in and complete the necessary change.

Change. Seiran had wanted change for so long, but been unwilling to be the force behind that chaos. Not anymore.

He swayed, dizzy, lots of blood lost. His arm was numb, head swirling with magic and pulsing life as the Goddess rushed to heal him while demanding his obedience. He wouldn't die. Never did, even when he'd wanted to a thousand times. It added to his pain and rage. Not being allowed to rest, or to end the grief of being forever alone. He wouldn't die, but he might pass out.

Gabe appeared there in front of him, reaching out blood covered fingers. Seiran blinked, disoriented by the pull of the endless swells of power and Gabe in front of him, bleeding.

"Not me," Gabe whispered. "I'm not hurt. You are."

Seiran glanced down to find himself bleeding, a hole neatly through the right side of his chest. The burn of a collapsed and pierced lung distant beneath all the power, but as it filled with blood his brain tried to tell him he had to do something or he would die. All alone again, to suffer and sink in the darkness, then dragged back to repeat it all over like some miserable *Groundhog Day* redo.

"You're not alone," Gabe whispered, his hands on Seiran's face, kissing the tip of his nose. "You have the kids, your brother, your friends, and me."

But he was going to leave again, wasn't he? Gabe had been pulled from the ground too early, which meant he'd go revenant and people would die if they didn't put him back. Seiran didn't think he could handle that, not again. He'd been grieving for over a decade, tired and lonely, heartbroken by fate's turn, and trying to put on a happy face for those around him.

All that pain added fuel to the rage. The Goddess taking hold and fanning the flames to a raging inferno. It would have been so easy to give in, and let himself dive into hate. He stood as Her scion, but also the last barrier between Her and world destruction.

Funny, he didn't *feel* that important in the grand scheme of things. One lone man, happy to be hidden away from the world with his family, and wishing for the man he'd loved back, even if sometimes that hurt.

"Sei..." Gabe whispered, his arms strong as they surrounded Seiran, keeping him upright. "I'm not leaving. Look at me, okay?"

Seiran had to work to raise his head and meet Gabe's gaze. It was blazing green with power and magic. Beautiful.

"You are beautiful," Gabe said pressing his forehead to Seiran. "And incredibly strong."

"I didn't mean to..." Page sobbed from his place on the grass. "I would never hurt him."

"I need you to hear me. Sei?"

"You don't even remember me," Seiran said absently.

"I do remember," Gabe whispered. "More every day. Have you written me off completely? Was I such a monster to you?"

That stung. Gabe a monster? No. Absent. Yes. Matthew had been a monster. A monster both Seiran and Sam had survived. Sam had become a bit of a monster himself, ruthless at times, but also a squishy marshmallow inside. As a vampire he got to let the monster out often. Was it as freeing as Seiran suspected it would be? But wasn't that what Seiran was too? A monster? Letting innocent witches die?

"You are mine. Everything to me, even if the Goddess forsook you, you'd still be mine. With or without all my memories, your trauma, and our combined power, you are mine. Can you focus on that?"

Even if he was evil? But that was a thought burned into him from a lifetime of brainwashing. What was evil? He'd caught glimpses of it over the years. It began with madness and corruption of power. He was on the edge of that now, right?

Would he ever just slaughter people for the hell of it? Probably not, at least not while he still retained control. If he gave the power to the Goddess, broke down that final barrier, would he be evil or simply a tool She used?

"If you let Her rage, what will we have left to save? What about your kids? And Page? The Goddess would destroy them too."

Seiran's mind swirled with too much thought. The Earth wanted everything gone so She could restart. Humanity was a blight, an error She wouldn't make again. Destroying it was necessary, even if that meant in the end Her own scion would be forever lost. She pictured a world without people like some utopia of endless grasslands, stretching deserts, global forests, and sparkling blue oceans. And all that might have been reality, if he was willing to let Her have control. He was drowning in the tide of Her desire to destroy it all. Not his rage, though he had plenty to spare.

Did he really want to lay down and die? Give up all of humanity just for rest? He sighed, the weight of it all too heavy for one man. He'd never asked for any of it. Seiran wasn't some superhero despite the insane amount of power he could wield. He was meant to be a guardian, a voice of reason for the Goddess, brought to humanity. Most days he felt like a villain, helplessly shoved into a role that everyone hated him for. Was there a way out other than death?

Page lay on his side in the grass, crying an ugly sobbing sound of desperation. He was unhurt, and unbound, he could easily grab the gun. End himself, or try again with Seiran, but that wasn't his nature. Seiran had chosen Page because of the young witch's gentle heart and passion for learning. He would have recognized if his servant was touched by threads of darkness that took over minds with corrupted magic.

"Page isn't a bad person," Seiran felt himself whisper. It sounded distant, like there was too much noise in his head.

"No," Gabe agreed. "Your kids aren't either. You? Kelly, Jamie? Con, Luca? Even Sam. Do they all deserve the end of the world? Do you feel the chaos in your mind? The edge we dangle on? Can you feel it like I can? And our bond isn't even renewed."

The Goddess didn't care about Seiran's family. Or him. Not really. She was in pain, and he understood that. But Seiran would never hurt his kids. Never let anything separate them. He'd survived countless traumas which stained him to this day. He'd fought to keep those horrors from touching his kids. Was that all moot?

The world was flawed, sure. Humanity was a blight, but who was he to end it for them all? And why should he have to give up everything again? Rip everything from his children? Including their chance to save the world, or hide from it. Whatever their choice, he'd stand by them.

He'd given up the man he loved. He'd given up his choice of careers. He'd given up freedom to tie himself to the witches who hated him, protecting the twins. He'd bound himself to the fae forever to keep them from waging war on humanity. He'd even made promises to the vampires, and bound himself to one who had left him alone for far too long. All for what? To end here because the Goddess was angry?

Everyone demanded, no one gave back. And Seiran was done with all of it. Being a pawn. Being left alone and discounted. He was tired of hiding who and what he was, just to make people comfortable.

He'd always hated and admired Sam for being exactly who he wanted to be. Sam took no one's shit. Stalked the night and even beat people up to blow off steam. People treated him with wariness. Not simply because he was a vampire. But because he was *Sam*. Maybe for once in his life, Seiran needed to be more like Sam and care less about what everyone else thought.

Seiran could end the world. One and done. Mass destruction ushering them into a new age of dystopia if anyone survived at all. Everyone treated him like he was putting on some show, spinning the media to seem more powerful. When he was the ultimate end of all things.

Why didn't he let Her rage? Why had he allowed them to continue to disdain him, slowly letting Her die, so they could live? His death meant nothing to them. But his death meant nothing to

Her either. Hadn't he thought for years he'd been ready to die? At the cost of the entire world? His kids? His friends?

No. He wasn't ready to leave this world. And while he was a conduit, he also had free will. Another flaw in the design of mortality. But Seiran would take what strength he could.

He sucked in a hard breath, his lungs aching with heat as though the rage were a temperature instead of an emotion. Gabe stood in front of him, his clothing smoldering, skin pink, standing in a well of power so great that if it kept going, it would burn them both up. Seiran's gaze met Gabe's, and he couldn't voice the words, a plea for help to roll back the oncoming tsunami. There was so much, and Seiran felt like he either let it happen, or let himself burn up in Her rage. He could stand in the doorway, but didn't know if he could close it anymore.

Without him a new pillar would be chosen, if humanity survived at all. Jamie, maybe? Could he survive this onslaught hidden behind the wards? Maybe he could soothe Her rage better than Seiran had? Jamie had always been good at talking people down, part medical training, part who he was. What if it went to one of his kids? They weren't ready. Seiran knew they weren't. She'd rip control from them immediately. He'd been battling Her song since the moment he took the role as pillar. A siren's song that never relented, leading to the same death and destruction as in stories of old. And he wouldn't wish that on anyone.

He stared at Gabe, begging for help and unable to move for fear that he lose his grip on the last shred of his sanity. But he also feared the fire burning them up, and knew in the back of his mind that vampires were highly flammable. Would it kill Gabe to be near him? Would Seiran survive Gabe's true death? Even after more than a decade of separation, he couldn't help but realize how much he loved Gabe. Missed him with every breath, even while fearing what they'd had was all a lie.

"It wasn't," Gabe promised, hugging Seiran tightly in his arms. "Let me show you. Let me help."

Gabe wrapped around him, like a cool wind rising to ease the heat. His lips brushed Seiran's, fingers curling into Seiran's hair. And this too was familiar. Filled with memories of their days years ago, and how Gabe would hold him. Beneath that was an icy touch of something dark, and almost welcoming. The fingers of the grave, Seiran realized.

"I am Death," Gabe whispered, as he kissed softly over Seiran's cheeks and lips, decorating Seiran's face in delicate touches to cool the fire.

"I'm death of the world," Seiran said, feeling it in the core of him. It was more of what She wanted, than what he wanted. He didn't know if he was strong enough to keep Her from taking control.

"But you don't have to be. You were meant to be life."

Seiran laughed a little, the sound painful and bloody, hurting as he felt like his lung was coming apart on the inside. It probably was, half drowning in his own blood, and Seiran's right side felt numb. He didn't feel like life.

He couldn't raise his arm to touch Gabe's face like he wanted to. The pain intensified. The dome would fall if he died again, as temporary as She allowed his deaths to be. It also meant they'd take Page. Probably kill him before Seiran could return from the place between worlds.

"Help me," Seiran begged, not certain what he was asking for. Gabe couldn't shove back the tide of death any more than Seiran could.

"We must renew the bond," Gabe said, his arms like a vise around Seiran, the only thing keeping Seiran on his feet. The power and pain, a matching tide of darkness rising to take Seiran. He wasn't sure there would be a world at all to return to if he died this time.

"Yes," Seiran agreed. He'd give Gabe the power if he could, even if it meant Seiran ended up alone again. As long as his kids were safe, and the world still whole. He had something to come back to, even if it meant forever walking away from the Dominion, and witches in general. He was done being a cog in that wheel.

Gabe kissed him again, lips on his cool and sweet, like a drink of water after too long in the desert. Seiran sank into the touch, closing his eyes. Gabe kissed a line down Seiran's neck to place a gentle kiss over the pulsing vein there.

"I hate that you're already losing blood," Gabe muttered, lips against Seiran's skin like a caress.

"When I die, you'll have to take Page to safety. The barrier will fall." The top edges in the center were already withering. Seiran either had to release his control of Her power to try to save himself, or let all of it fade as he was dragged back to the world between. The mortal body was so fragile.

"You're not going to die," Gabe promised. His fangs pierced Seiran's throat. A sharp spike of pain for a hot second before it shifted to power, while Gabe drank deeply.

Seiran's heart stuttered. Too much blood loss. The injury and now a vampire feeding, sounded like a good way to speed up his death. But Gabe's long gulps of blood felt like it was coating their bond, which absorbed it, expanding, sponge-like. It brought rise to more power, a cool and soothing glide, not unlike water. Though Seiran recognized it for what it was, the true touch of death. Not that ripped from the worlds darkness he'd experienced too many times. But a gentle cradle of soothing peace.

When Sam had first gone to ground, he'd been terrified. Seiran had been with him, watched his fear, and also thought to be afraid. Death meant an end to things for most everyone. Not for vampires, and not for Seiran, but he'd feared it just the same. Now Sam looked forward to his week of rest like it was a vacation.

You should try it, Ronnie, Sam often told him. *Best sleep I ever get.*

The delicate touch of the cool fingers of death were soothing. Even as the darkness rose up over his vision, leaving him with little more than a vague tunnel of light. He felt boneless in Gabe's arms. Even while the fire in his chest still burned with pain. Waves of magic pooled outward, beginning with their bond, and spreading into the distance, dampening the fire. He could feel Gabe in his head, speaking, but couldn't make out the words.

The Goddess's power met that cool breeze and seemed to calm. Like lava hitting the shore on a beach, stinging at first, then sizzling as it cooled to solid rock. His chest burned, and Gabe pressed his hand hard against the wound, seeming to spread the cool waves over the heat, drawing out some of the sharpness.

"If I die," Seiran slurred, "Get Page to my house. Jamie will protect him."

"You're not dying," Gabe's whispered in his ear, face pressed to Seiran's cheek. Seiran felt like a limp doll in his arms, weak, though calming, the rage not gone, but edges soothed. "We are immortal."

"What are you doing?" Seiran wondered as he tried to remain conscious. The cool power spread the heat and fire outward, a tide of rolling gentle pulses quenching the flames. He sucked in a deep breath, surprised to find his lungs full, both of them with cool and refreshing air.

"The world underestimates you," Gabe said, his lips finding Seiran's again for the briefest kiss, a brush of lips more than a taste. "And me."

"I don't…" Seiran began, trying to sort through the swells of cooling heat to find something solid to hold on to other than Gabe. He was there, everywhere, in Seiran's mind, pressed against his body, holding him up in a thousand ways. It felt like a dream, or a distant memory.

"And I'm sorry for that," Gabe said. "My fault. It should have always been this way. You and me, united in the bond, inseparable. Your power mine, and mine yours."

The layers of magic continued to flow between them until Seiran felt full, sleepy, and calm, the last of the rage trickling away. He breathed deeply, feeling safe for the first time he could remember in over a decade, and warm. Bits of memories took root in his mind. Moments with Gabe in the past. The good times rather than the bad. The way he'd kept close and worked hard not to push. Seiran had been hesitant to begin their relationship back then. Sex had been one thing; relationships were where the abuse began. He'd been so broken.

Had been. Ha. As though that had changed. The trauma didn't fade, only how he dealt with it changed. Bury it? Bask in it? Or learn from it? Wasn't that what Gabe had been pushing for all those years ago? Seiran didn't linger over those memories, the arguments, or his constant battle to find himself. He wasn't that kid anymore.

"No," Gabe agreed. The memories shifted to the past few days, of Seiran holding Kaine, protecting Page, and even investigating with everyone around him jumping at his command. "You are so fucking beautiful. Strong. Independent. But you don't have to hold up the world by yourself anymore. Let me help."

"If you leave me again, I will kill you myself," Seiran said, his head swirling.

"Threat received," Gabe said, sounding amused. "You'll have to deal with me going to ground semi-regularly. But it won't be years at a time."

That he could live with. Seiran sighed, relaxing into the arms that surrounded him, and letting the bond open completely. It felt saturated in power now, both the heat of life, Seiran's power, and the cool essence of death, Gabe's power. He could have basked in the sensation, a feeling of completeness he couldn't recall ever experiencing.

Balance, he realized. For so long he'd been holding back the Goddess's power on his own, not realizing that it should have balance.

"I feel light-headed," Seiran muttered.

"It's the bond settling," Gabe agreed. "And a bit of blood loss. Your body trying to catch up."

Seiran looked upward at the withering barrier above. He was going to pass out. The combination of the bond, healing, and the cooling of the rage sucked the energy out of him. That wasn't good.

Not dying was good, but the barrier failing when there were witches waiting to kill them outside?

He muttered a handful of words, pressing the power not into this world, but the veil between. A request, not a demand. He prayed someone on the other side heard. Would Bryar be listening?

"I'm going to pass out soon," Seiran muttered.

"Okay," Gabe agreed, not letting go.

Seiran could bask in this feeling forever—safe and loved—like a dream. "Barrier will fall," were the last words he got out before that final tunnel of light vanished and he fell into oblivion.

CHAPTER 24

Seiran went limp in Gabe's arms. At least his heartbeat was strong. Their bond pulsed and grew in strength with each beat. Every nerve and cell of Gabe's body was on fire. He was going to need a lot more practice if he had to regularly diffuse the power of the earth elemental Herself. Seiran might call her a Goddess, but Gabe had met plenty of Her kind before. Powerful, yes. But also, very shortsighted and destructive.

The barrier overhead was failing fast, dark lines of rot and disintegration beginning to thread its way down the sides like fingers of death. They didn't have much time before it crumbled and whatever madness the witches had planned rained down on them.

Gabe tried to grasp at the power of the barrier, but couldn't hold it. Too much for him without some substantial training. It felt a bit like trying to hold back the ocean with a fishing net, and Gabe's power sliding right through the holes. Without some tie to Seiran, or a ward renewed regularly by blood and magic, it was a temporary thing. And he knew that outside waited death for all of them.

He carefully lowered Seiran to the ground. If the barrier

crashed and the witches came in shooting, he'd need to try to keep Seiran from being hit again. It was his fault Seiran had been hit to begin with. Gabe had moved without thinking. He should have blocked the shot all together, and taken the bullet himself, rather than let it go wild. He hadn't expected the trees to act like some sort of impenetrable force for the bullet to bounce off of.

Blood still trickled from Seiran's side, although it had slowed, and the wound was healing, no longer a gaping hole, his breathing clear of blood. The bullet had passed through him, Gabe could sense that much. But losing blood from the wound and then Gabe having to drink from him was a lot. He'd be out for a while, even with Gabe's bond working hard to heal him.

Gabe's head throbbed. Memories like a mallet on his skull. The rich and decadent flavor of Seiran still zinged on his tongue, the power circling through Gabe's system, dizzying. It was a lot all at once, and he'd have to sit for a while to let the pieces drop back into place. But that would have to wait until they weren't about to be mobbed and murdered.

"I didn't mean to hurt him," Page was still sobbing, curled around himself on the ground.

"I need you to get behind me," Gabe said quietly. "That barrier is going to fall and they are going to come at us with an army." His gaze fell on the still man lying in the grass. No sign of life in him, but a ripple of darkness told Gabe the death was new enough. He also didn't appear to be wounded at all, no blood on the grass, or scent lingering other than Seiran's.

"Did you?" Gabe wondered if Page had shot him.

"He was already gone when I got here," Page whispered. He crawled closer, avoiding the gun like it would burn him.

Why come here at all? Lured to a body? A trap? A reason to kill him without evidence? Would he even get a trial? No wonder Seiran had been enraged.

Gabe's gaze fell back to the cabin and the lines of power etched into it. Dark magic if there was a color to magic. Spells and wards not laid by personal power, as much as death magic. That felt very familiar, though Gabe didn't recognize the lines. He, much like Seiran, had never really needed spells to direct his power.

"You've been here before?"

"The family's cabin. I never came here growing up. Just that one time when I raised Mattie. It was where they burned her."

"But Steve asked you to come here?" Gabe deduced.

"Sent me texts. Said he had proof it was all me, and would take it to the Dominion." Page bowed down over his knees, hunched in a ball, like making himself smaller would make him disappear. "It's all my fault. He was hurting the vampires."

"He's the one who made you create the golem?" Gabe asked.

Page's face crumbled again. "Yes. I'm so sorry."

"Be sorry later," Gabe said, watching the barrier continue to crumble. "We need to find a way to survive right this second."

"They'll kill us anyway. It's what they do."

Fuck. Gabe put Seiran behind him along with Page, trying to think of a way to create his own barrier as the walls fell. Darkness pulsed from the ground, familiar, cold and soothing. Like death. He glanced behind them at a small cabin a good twenty or thirty yards away. A hunting cabin maybe? He could feel bones beneath them, long still. Lots of death around them actually. Spades of it etched into the magic, the ground, and even the air. It felt like a place a coven met regularly, burning their elements into the area to combine their power. But most covens didn't have death witches. At least Gabe didn't think so.

Seiran could connect with the earth elemental, but Gabe could feel the familiar cool gaze of an old friend. Death as powerful as earth, a polar opposite of life. It was why Seiran and Gabe balanced so well. Had he known that at the time? A vague memory tugged at Gabe's brain, that yes, he had recognized the draw of life.

His sire had ensured he had a healthy fear of witches in his first few years of rebirth. She hadn't really known then, what he could do. Only that the blood of witches could make a vampire more powerful. She didn't want him to have that kind of power. But when the magic of the dead began to awaken in his bones, morphing with intensity as it lay in forced dormancy, he'd realized his true potential. He also understood why it terrified her so much, as it did most of the world now. Once again, he could feel that old tingle of magic building within, as though too long unused and ready to rain down fire and brimstone.

All vampires had some death magic, part of their reanimation, mostly. But Gabe had never been much like the rest of his brethren.

"Is this some kind of old graveyard?" Gabe asked. Too many bones to be natural. The stain of blood so vast it would take centuries to fade.

Page shook his head. "No. I don't know? I feel something? I thought it was just my blood, Steve had been demanding it for a while. Claiming he needed it to control the golem. I gave him vials. But it's bigger than that."

It was. And Page was a baby witch who was only beginning to grasp what he was. Would be a shame to lose that power so soon. "He probably did need your blood at first to control the golem. Doesn't sound like he was a necromancer or a summoner."

"I don't think so. I don't know what that second one is. His family has earth powers. Not as strong as the Rous, but powerful. The previous Pillar of Earth was one of theirs."

"You are a summoner, Page. One who manipulates souls and spirits. One who can call demons to this world."

Page gasped. "I would never... I didn't mean to... I thought I was..."

"It's a part of necromancy. But a necromancer can't put a soul in a body. Most magic can sever the tie between a mortal shell and the immortal soul, be it human or vampire. But putting them in the golem? That is not a necromancer skill."

Animating a golem didn't usually take a soul. Though death was required to charge it. Golems were animated by intent, fueled by death magic. One specific goal for it to focus on at almost demonic strength. Gabe remembered that now and wondered if there were still any texts about it.

"*I* am a necromancer," Gabe said as he put his hands to the ground, digging his fingers into the soil to reach the cool touch of his power through the earth. Much more than animal bones, though those were plentiful. This felt similar to the killing field they'd found of vampire bodies, only older, the bodies partially reclaimed in some spots, and none nearly as fresh, other than Steve. Interesting.

Page shivered. "What are you doing? I feel it…"

"Waking the dead," Gabe said. He rolled the magic up, the buckets of it still dripping and sloshing through him like waves hitting a shore, and layered it over the ground. The spirits of these beings were gone. Unlike the vampires, they were completely empty. But humans didn't have revenants to hold the monster inside. They moved on quickly, which left what remained as easy puppets. It wouldn't be much, bones weren't very frightening, but maybe enough to terrify the witches and buy them time?

Gabe shoved his will into the ground, spreading out the magic, using Seiran's blood as a boost, and the ground began to move. Not from earth magic, but the crawling of dead things from their graves. It ached within Gabe, like a muscle too long clenched and gone unused. Had he suppressed it that long?

This power was not welcomed in the modern world. He recalled that clearly now. When was the last time he'd stretched those icy fingers to touch the bones of mortal existence? The rush of it ran through him in an energizing thrill as the remains began to pop from the ground, latching together with the last remains of mortal energy to become almost zombies, or mostly whole skeletons. Not possible in scientific terms as there was little tissue to hold them together. His magic didn't care. They knit themselves together, digging their way out of the ground and rising up to surround them.

Page curled up in a ball behind Gabe, shivering and repeating, "Holy fuck."

The last to rise was Steve. His body jerking upward as though pulled by strings rather than human muscle and bone, which he still had. A broken neck. Gabe could tell that now from the odd angle of his head. The soul long gone meant he'd been dead likely more than a few days.

Gabe looked at Page. He could have killed him, though Page was a smaller man than Steve had been. But stealth was a good equalizer. It would mean that they had both misread Page, though Gabe was rarely wrong about anyone. At least as long as his brain wasn't clouded by magic or the revenant.

He recalled Tresler's bond beginning to tie him up in magic built through small doses of his blood. The tainted bottled blood had taken years to build up a bond. It had been like slugs slowly growing through his system. And now that he remembered, he really wanted a hot shower. Or some type of dialysis of his blood to clear out any residue of that monster.

The dead continued to rise. Way too many for some random cabin in the woods. Dead only a few months old? A few years at most. The sheer number was insane. Not even a few dozen, but over a hundred at least. The further he let his power reach, the more bodies he found. Animals closest to the cabin, but as he pressed further, more and more humans, even a few witches. He could separate those by the way they swayed in his magic. Not as still as humans, as witches, even after death, could turn into feral, flesh eating things. He'd have to keep an eye on them. Another necromancer would have to pull them free from his grasp to really shift them, but he had no idea if there were necromancers in this coven or not.

"Why are there so many?" Page whispered and the ground continued to spit them out. They formed a barrier of skeletons, and rotting corpses, encircling them in all directions as the trees Seiran had woven into a magic ward, disintegrated.

"Someone has been murdering a lot." The ground was charged with it. Blood, death, violence, perhaps torture, obvious as some of the dead were missing parts, limbs, the back of a skull, even half a ribcage in one nearby case Gabe could see. Holy fuck, was right.

Had they begun here? Murdered animals first to add to their power, then stepped up to humans and witches? Perhaps that hadn't been enough so they'd begun experimenting on vampires? It was dizzying. The power wasted, the sheer number of corpses. Not the work of one barely legal witch, of that much Gabe knew.

He poured his strength into the growing surge of dead, shielding them even as they continued to rise and spread out further, as the tree barrier fell, baring them all to the violence that awaited them beyond it. Gabe couldn't see the witches or the police, but he could hear them all now. The chanting, and the murmur of voices from the police. No warnings issued to stop or even a chance of being taken in alive.

And wasn't that infuriating? There they stood, face to face with a legion of the dead who'd been slaughtered by what Gabe was certain was a fairly sizable coven, and their only goal was killing Page? Maybe Seiran and himself as well? By design, or pure stupidity?

The revenant rose to the surface of his conscious. Not taking over, but adding a red haze to his sight. It was a bit of a welcome feeling, that zinging power and absolute *give no fucks* mentality the revenant provided. He had learned to balance this power centuries ago, teetering on the edge of the darkness taking over.

Until he'd been forced to swallow it and exist in a world that found him terrifying.

Maybe it was time to remind them why they'd been afraid. It seemed like they'd been fucking with Seiran for long enough. The possessive monster in his gut told Gabe that Seiran was his, and even the revenant recognized that. Good. He was done with all of this bullshit.

A raven landed on Steve's shoulder, staring down at Gabe who was still crouched low, giving no one with a gun a target. The magic would have to get through his barrier of death, and death was an old friend of Gabe's.

The raven leapt down, landing near Gabe and trotting over, changing as it went, into Sam. That was something Gabe didn't remember.

"Don't stare at my naked ass. There's obviously some shit you didn't tell us," Sam said waving a hand at the dead amassed around them. "How bad is Ronnie hurt?"

"Bleeding, but healing." His heartbeat was strong and Gabe felt every pulse of it through their bond. "The Goddess is shoved back for now."

"Yeah, I guessed that from the level five hurricanes that popped up all over the globe and then suddenly vanished. Fucking witch bullshit." He looked at Page. "Don't suppose this is the baby witch causing this mess?"

"He's a summoner," Gabe said. "Better with souls than with the dead. Created the golem, but it sounds like the family was blackmailing him for blood to work spells with."

Sam sighed. "More bullshit we didn't know. The witches want you all dead."

"I'm not afraid of witches," Gabe said. He could call this army to move, and even begin to awake more if needed. The power stretched, unlimited, his bond to Seiran fueling him with energy from the rotating of the earth. "This is a lot of dead for some random family hunting cabin," Gabe pointed out. "Seem a little suspicious? Do you see the lines of magic etched into the cabin?" Behind them the cabin could no longer be seen through the stretch of the dead.

"I saw it from above. Hate this witch bullshit," Sam snarled. "A lot of fucking dead. But we only have a few options here. Either you go all lord of the darkness and command the zombie army to attack their ass, or we negotiate."

"Is there anyone to negotiate with? Any sanity left among the Dominion?"

Sam's gaze fell to Page. "We could give them the witch."

"Not an option. If they want Page, they'll want Seiran too. This whole thing feels like a set up. Or at the very least, an opportunity to smack him down."

"It probably is. They've tried to oust Rou from the board every year for as long as he's been on the board. A thousand written warnings, all bullshit. If it weren't for him being a true scion to the earth, and his ties to the vampires and the fae? They might have already removed him." Sam glanced back toward where Gabe could hear the witches and police gathered. It sounded like more activity. "Tanaka's here."

An instant bit of rage surfaced in Gabe, strong enough he had to work hard to keep himself from leaping over the group and eviscerating her.

"Woah, big guy, rein in the demon. She's on our side."

"She's not," Gabe corrected. "I remember…"

"Yeah, shitty mother. Pretty good grandmother though. Has cut ties to the rest of their horrific family and spent the last decade doing everything she can to protect all her grandkids. Even Kaine."

"Yet she won't protect Seiran? His kids need him." Fuck, that was a brutal wave of memory falling into place. The manipulation, the way she'd abused Seiran, beaten him down. Gabe hated that he hadn't been able to stop it. Negotiating for the twins had bought them time, and Gabe had been planning to take them all away, even if that meant rising again as he once had.

"She will, and is. She's here to negotiate."

No. Gabe wasn't playing that game again. "Tell them to clear a path. That is the only choice. Clear a path or I will clear one myself."

"Let her through, just her," Sam said. "Let her see for herself that it is you who wields the power, not the baby witch over there."

They all thought this was Page? Gabe really had held this in too long. He stretched out his magic, using the dead to see beyond the circle and the swell of cops beyond, perched behind police cars, weapons drawn. As if a gun could sever the tie between Seiran and the earth, or Gabe and Seiran. The witches were doing spells, though none seemed to be taking hold. Something about the land was breaking the magic. Interesting.

Gabe sent out a ripple of energy toward a group of witches who were trying to create a spell through joint effort. He felt their spell shatter like glass, broken by death, like most everything of mortal creation was.

Huh. Fascinating.

He found Tanaka standing not far from the farthest outer layer of his wall of the dead. She didn't appear afraid, only resolved. He'd kill her if he had to, even if that meant facing Seiran's wrath. Sometimes family was toxic no matter how much a person loved them. And Gabe knew Seiran loved his mom, even though Seiran knew how terrible the things she'd done were.

"Tanaka Rou," Gabe called, using the dead to carry his voice. "You alone, are allowed to pass."

Silence fell over the crowd beyond the barrier. And Tanaka hesitated as the first row of skeletons moved to let her pass. She'd have to walk the gauntlet, passing row by row of the dead until she reached them, the shambling bodies filling in behind her. If Gabe felt one ounce of her was willing to sacrifice her son, he'd show her how horrible a death could be at the hands of zombies.

She stepped forward. A wild array of gasps and shouts came from the group beyond. Concern for her, or just outrage? Gabe didn't much care anymore.

When Tanaka passed through the final barrier, Gabe studied her. Noted how tired she looked. Sam had returned to his raven form, and was observing in silence with dark and intense eyes.

"Is my son still alive?" Tanaka asked.

"He is," Gabe agreed. "And I plan for him to stay that way."

She blinked at him, gaze studying Page for a moment, and

seeming to take in Seiran's prone form, but deep breathing. "This is your power?"

"I am death," Gabe said. "Yet I killed none of those around me. Care to explain how there are so many bodies?"

Tanaka looked around at the group, taking in the different states of decomposition and decay, and then finding Steve. "There have been rumors."

"About a coven slaughtering hundreds?"

"There are always rumors," Tanaka said. "Would you let Seiran's investigators in? To document?"

"Would it make a difference? Isn't it the standard of the Dominion to kill things it can't control? That would include Page, Seiran, and myself, right?"

"Normally," Tanaka said.

"But I am not subject to your rule. I am not a witch."

"You are a necromancer."

"Which your people claim don't exist because you fear us so much. Meanwhile, the true terror is the Pillar you've all decided wasn't worth the time. He just saved your asses from world annihilation by the earth elemental."

"I did feel that. Every earth witch on the planet felt Her… discomfort."

Discomfort. What a fucking joke. Gabe shook his head, done with all this. He stood, and lifted Seiran into his arms. If they had guns aimed, they'd better hope it was a bazooka. Not much else could put him back in the ground. Not even the witch in front of him. She was strong, but not nearly the supernatural power Seiran had.

"We're done," Gabe said. "With the Dominion, and all this bullshit."

"Is that what Seiran wants?"

"Seiran never wanted any of this. He wanted a quiet life. Now he just wants to keep his family safe. This," Gabe waved at their surroundings, "was what you wanted for him. Power. Status. Though no one fucking sees him for what he is."

"You don't either. You've been gone too long. You can't possibly know what is best for him."

Gabe snorted. "Fuck you, Tanaka. Some Dominion coven murdered hundreds of humans and vampires, and we are the problem? Push this and it becomes war between us and the witches."

"You speak for yourself, or for the vampires? I don't think Hart would appreciate that."

"If you think Hart has more vampires under his control than I do, you're mistaken. War between witches and vampires, Tanaka. Or let us go in peace. Find out who created this," Gabe pointed to the mass of bodies. "Because it wasn't us."

"I don't have that power."

"Then what use are you?" He snapped. "What are you even fucking doing here?"

She opened her hand and a rock fell to the ground, crystal looking, and Gabe worried it was some kind of spell or something, feared he'd let her in only for her to trick them all. But the rock flashed with a tiny flicker of magic, and out rolled a small brown cat. The cat darted toward Gabe, too small to cause damage, but it grew as it moved, turning from cat to child in a shift more flawless than Sam's had been to the raven.

A little boy who looked ten or so, with a mop of bright red curls, and Seiran's sapphire eyes stared up at Gabe. He was fully dressed and not at all human. Gabe blinked down at the boy, who he had heard of, but hadn't met. "Kaine?"

"You have to follow," Kaine said in a whisper. "Stay close, else you'll get lost." He smiled at Page. "You too, Page. Papa would want you safe." Kaine reached Gabe's side and touched Seiran's face.

"Follow where?" Gabe wondered. But Kaine held out a hand, and a rip in the fabric of reality appeared. A flickering of what Gabe pulled from Seiran's mind, rather than his own. The veil between worlds. "I'm not sure that's a good idea." People went through the veil and never came back. Even Gabe knew that.

"You have to," Kaine said. "I'll hold Page's hand, and touch Papa's leg. Don't stop touching me, no matter what you see inside. Okay?"

This was a really bad idea. Gabe waited for Tanaka to protest or something. But she'd brought Kaine to them. For this reason? She put her hands to the ground and the earth flowed upward, swallowing up all traces of Seiran's blood. Gabe should have thought of that. If he'd left traces of Seiran the witches could have used it to hex him.

"Can you tie that one to me?" Tanaka asked, pointing to Steve. "I'd like to question him."

"Question, or hide evidence?"

"Question. The dead can only answer true."

Gabe was surprised. Since the darker magics seemed to have been purged from the Dominion, he didn't think Tanaka would know much of it.

"My husband was the child of a legend of dark magic," Tanaka said.

"Ruffman," Gabe recalled. Though he didn't think he'd ever met the man. He'd heard rumors of his magic decades ago. And he'd been murdered by the Dominion, set up as some warning to all other witches. That was when Gabe had really buried his power. Fear, apparently. At least he was beyond that worry now. As long as their reach was, Gabe didn't think they really had the power to destroy he and his.

She nodded, "Seiran's grandfather."

"Technically, Seiran could have some of this magic." That made sense too. Why the earth was so strong within him, and death and destruction followed. The scope of his power as a pillar had been beyond all others before him since day one.

"Yes," Tanaka agreed. "He's been very good about detecting the dark magics."

"And the Dominion wants him dead for it?"

"I'm running out of ways to protect him," she admitted.

Gabe sighed. "Then I guess it's time to show the Dominion they have something to fear." He looked at Steve, who looked fresh and almost alive if it weren't for the tilt of his neck. Gabe wove his magic through the corpse, charging it enough that it would stay animated without having to be close to him. "Obey Tanaka Rou," he instructed the zombie. "If someone causes you harm, return to me," he added. If someone tried to unravel the tie, it would fight to find him, able to track him across the world if necessary.

She stared at the zombie and it stared back, waiting for her orders.

"The rest should fall as soon as I cross the barrier." Gabe didn't think he could hold the shambling dead together from beyond the veil. Not without weaving each and every one of them into something more substantial. Though with the amount of power he'd spilled into the ground from Seiran's overflow, anything could happen.

"Understood," Tanaka agreed. "Go. Protect my son as you agreed to decades ago."

Sam bounced around near the portal, but didn't enter.

"Sorry, Sammie," Kaine said. "Meet us at home?" Sam bobbed away, watching as Gabe tightened his grip on Seiran. Gabe felt Kaine touch Seiran's leg. Page reached out a hesitant hand to Kaine, and they all moved forward. Gabe sucked in a deep breath and prayed that they would find their way to the other side. He had never crossed the veil before, though he could recall that Seiran had, and often found himself lost there.

"Don't let go," Gabe said to both Kaine and Page as he followed them all through the rippling tear between worlds.

CHAPTER 25

The trickling tug of magic woke Seiran. He instantly worried that he had died again, though his chest still ached and he seemed to be floating. He sucked in air and arms tensed around him.

"Don't move too much," Gabe said.

Seiran blinked, the world around him swirling with intense magic, undefined, but strong enough to make it hard to breathe. They'd crossed the veil?

"It's okay, Papa."

Seiran turned his head to find Kaine guiding them. His baby was not a baby at all here, and it made him sad. Kaine looked a lot like Bryar, handsome and strong, hair more like the back of a ladybug red, than any color found in the human realm for hair. Kaine gripped Seiran's leg, and Page held on to Kaine's other hand. Gabe carried Seiran. What had he missed?

When he looked up, Seiran found Gabe struggling. It was the easiest way to describe it. The edge of the revenant lingered, Gabe's eyes tinged in red, his shoulders tight. "Don't close the bond or pull away," Gabe said quietly.

And Seiran understood. Gabe was not a creature of the fae

realm. Seiran didn't know if vampires ever crossed the veil. He knew most humans would be lost forever if they did. But Kaine guided them with purpose, the world undefined and ever shifting around them. Seiran relaxed into Gabe's hold, trying not to focus too much on their surroundings. He didn't need to give them purpose and chance getting them lost. His own control and understanding of the fae realm limited at best.

"Almost there," Kaine said.

Nothing looked different at all, but Seiran felt Gabe warring with himself. The revenant wanted out, and the pull of magic in this other world seemed to have more power to set it free. Seiran suspected that was a bad thing. He sucked in a deep breath and let himself relax, even closing his eyes to open himself as much as possible to Gabe. He'd spent years finding clarity in this place, even when things were undefined along the edges of the world. The fae only let others see so much, and he'd not once been allowed into their living spaces, though he'd seen them from afar. Not castles or magic abodes like the story books at all, though some of the newer fae found ways to mimic mortal comforts.

This wavering wall of magic, not unlike a tunnel, that they walked, was the fringes meant for travel. Sometimes unsavory things lingered, waiting for hapless humans to stumble inside, and they would feast. Kaine's power surrounded them, a bubble of warmth and clarity, which gave them a path seeming to be made from stone, but only projecting a few feet in front of them.

And then there was a door. "Page, can you open it?" Kaine asked.

Page reached forward and turned the handle. It opened to darkness, but Kaine tugged them forward anyway. Gabe taking the lead, and the entire group passing through.

When they emerged on the other side, it was to the arboretum and the ring of mushrooms that lived untouched in the far corner. Seiran breathed a sigh of relief as they all passed through, and the door closed behind them, sealing off the other world.

"Careful of the mushrooms," Kaine warned them. Gabe stepped over the ring. The tension in his shoulders vanished, red haze finally fading from his eyes, and he seemed suddenly exhausted. Page still clung to Kaine's hand, though Kaine had released Sei's leg. The door to the house opened and Jamie stood there, looking worried.

"How bad is he? Is he still bleeding?" Jamie waved at them to enter the house. "Let me look." The island counter was cleared and Seiran groaned.

"I'm fine," he grumbled.

"You were shot. Sam said you were still bleeding."

Gabe crossed to the wide island and set Seiran down. "I can't tell if he's still bleeding or if this is the blood from the first wound? Time is really off over there."

Jamie shoved Seiran's shirt up.

"Boundaries much?" Seiran griped.

"Shut up and let me look," Jamie demanded. He probed at the wound, Gabe lingering nearby. Kaine looked like his child self again, small and uncertain.

Seiran reached for him. "I'm okay, baby."

Kaine's eyes glittered with tears. "It's my fault."

"What? What is your fault? This is not your doing." Seiran waved at the pink scar from the bullet. He was no longer bleeding, but he did feel weak. He'd need food and some rest.

"You gave too much to me. It's why you can't hold back the Green Goddess very well anymore."

Had Bryar told him that? Seiran swallowed back his frustration. It wasn't fair to put that burden on Kaine. He hadn't had any say in how he was created, and it had been Seiran's mistake. "Baby," Seiran said, running his fingers through Kaine's hair. "You are exactly as you should be."

"But you're not as strong."

"I can't imagine how insanely powerful he would be if he were stronger," Gabe said.

Kaine's watery gaze met his. "He'd be able to keep Her from taking over better. He could leave the garden."

Something in Gabe's expression changed, like he understood. "I'm here to help now. Maybe we can work on that?"

Kaine took a quivering breath and nodded. Seiran tugged him close and kissed his scalp. "You done poking me?" Sei demanded of his brother. "Maybe I could have some food and get filled in on what the heck just happened." He moderated his swearing for his kid. And two seconds later his other two appeared, racing across the kitchen to wrap their arms around him. Gabe had to take a step back. At least he didn't look like he was fighting the revenant anymore.

Across the veil is bad for vampires, Seiran heard. Was that Gabe in his head? Gabe nodded and gave them all space. Seiran's kids wanting hugs and assurances.

"Your boyfriend raised an army of the dead," Jamie said, not looking happy.

Boyfriend. It was such a weird term. Gabe was more than that, but the lost years made it feel both too much and too little. "Wait, army of the dead?"

"He's a necromancer," Kelly said as he entered into the kitchen. "And hot damn the footage. It's all over the news." He held up his tablet and showed a video of skeletons animated and acting like a barrier.

Seiran sat up slowly and reached for the tablet. "What?"

"They should have come apart when I crossed the veil," Gabe said. "I only bound Steve to Tanaka so she could question it. The others shouldn't still be whole."

The video footage said otherwise. Seiran caught a glimpse of his investigators at the scene, though there were obviously arguments going on between the witches and the human investigators. Seiran hit the volume button to listen to the reporter.

"Authorities are at odds with the Dominion right now due to the number of bodies," the reporter said. "While the Dominion claims this is some sort of trick of a witch gone rogue, several of these bodies have been identified as missing persons." The video panned to a handful of the animated who still looked somewhat human. Decaying, but not far enough to hide who they had been. "Vampire leader Maxwell Hart has insisted on a full investigation, adding that he has a mass grave of vampires similar in scope. And Senior Director Rou has indicated her full support of an investigation."

The camera changed to Seiran's mom standing in the center of a group of reporters and next to human police officers. It was dark outside, lights from cameras bright and washing some of the color out of her face. Or maybe she was that upset. "This is the second incident involving the Brody family and their property. I am declaring that a full investigation will be held into this family and their acts," Tanaka said.

"What about the barriers that have gone up around the country over the Rou house and some of their affiliates?" Someone shouted from the crowd. "Didn't the Pillar of Earth do this?"

"Earth has the power to release those to death, not make the dead rise," Tanaka stated. "I'm saddened that this is not common knowledge. This is obviously a failure of the Dominion, both in training and in monitoring our members."

"But since the Pillar is your son, aren't you just protecting him?" Someone else demanded.

There was movement in the crowd, cops moving aside and reporters pushed back a little as a group of vampires appeared. Max, Sam, and even Mike, all stepping into the center. The reporters shouted questions until it became a blur of noise that didn't stop until Max raised a hand to silence them all.

"We are taking over this investigation," Max stated. The protest began immediately. He held up a hand again, instant silence. "Since we cannot be certain of the Dominion's integrity in this instance, we will be taking over the investigation. These dead were raised by one of our own to protect himself, and the Pillar from being unjustly murdered."

The trickle of noise began again. Max glared at them until silence fell again. He could do scary really well. He pointed off to the side where Steve stood, a zombie looking almost alive, if it weren't for the odd tilt of his head.

"I'm not sure the kids should see this," Seiran said. But they were glued to the screen as much as he was.

"Steven Brody, who killed you?" Max demanded of the zombie.

"My mother," the zombie said in winded slow speech.

"Holy fuck," Kelly muttered.

"Kids," Seiran growled at him.

"Sorry," Kelly said, his eyes huge.

There was a muttering that maybe the vampires could make the zombie say what they wanted it to. But the noise fell again as Sam stepped forward. "We are questioning all the dead. Categorizing them, and will be notifying next of kin. Any and all action against any vampire, will be considered an act of war."

There was a gasp that ran along the crowd, but Max was already moving away, leaving the reporters to Sam. "Once we question the dead, they will be laid to rest at their family's behest." Sam looked around. "Due to the sheer number, this is going to take a while."

"Do you think Seiran Rou had something to do with this?" Someone demanded.

"I think the Dominion is trying to use this event to harm the Pillar of Earth. We, the vampires, are allied with Rou, have accepted him as he has been accepted by the earth. Need I remind you of the events of yesterday? Global catastrophe on the verge of mortal destruction, ended abruptly by Rou himself. The Goddess was angry, and ready to end all of humanity, and he soothed Her rage. Would you rather be in this world, with him or without him? Would there be a world left without him?"

"Rousing endorsement from the vampire," Jamie said.

There was more chatter from the crowd, but vampires moved in to section the dead off and begin questioning them. Seiran was a little shocked at the size of the group, both the vampires, and the dead who stood around like little more than extras from the set of a zombie movie.

"Zombies are real," he muttered, his gaze falling on Gabe who sat in a chair nearby, looking really tired. Sei handed the tablet back to Kelly. He had some catching up to do. But maybe after a real nap? He had to get out of these bloody clothes. "Yesterday?"

"The trip through the veil took a bit," Kaine said. "Couldn't move too fast, or I would have lost you."

"You're still holding them together?" Seiran asked Gabe. Maybe that's why he looked so tired.

"No. At least I don't think so. Maybe I shoved too much into them when I raised them? We had solidified our bond, and your power was still coursing through me. Perhaps that is part of it? I hadn't used that power in so long that it felt…"

Seiran could understand. Sometimes if he went too long without really stretching his power things went a bit sideways. "Necromancer?"

Gabe nodded. "Not a skill well received in this world."

Seiran was briefly annoyed that he'd never been told, but there was too much else to worry about right this second. "Page?"

His assistant was huddled in the corner of the room, like he didn't want anyone to realize he was there.

"I'm so sorry," Page said again.

Seiran sighed. "Yeah, I get it. But sorry isn't fixing anything, right? How about we work on that?"

Page's eyes got really wide. "How?"

"We'll start with the golem. See if you can unravel it maybe?" Sei looked around. "Where is the golem?"

"I think Sam has it," Jamie said.

"I'll call him," Seiran shoved himself off the counter, but when he tried to stand, he found himself wobbly. The kids and Jamie caught him before he could hit the floor. "Maybe I should eat something."

"Someone shouldn't have taken blood from you when you were already bleeding," Jamie complained.

Seiran waved a hand. "Whatever. He helped contain the Goddess. She wanted everything dead. I think the better option is me woozy instead of total world destruction."

"I'll get you some food," Kelly offered. "Jamie made an egg bake that just needs a little warming."

"Can I shower? I smell like blood and death," Seiran asked.

"Cake and strawberries," Gabe mumbled.

Seiran stared at him. "Are you hungry?"

"No," he said, "tired. Used a lot of energy."

That was an understatement. He'd raised an army of the dead after helping Seiran shove the earth back into a box.

"Sam brought grave dirt. The box beneath the bed downstairs is refilled," Kelly said. "Maybe you can rest while Sei cleans up and eats?"

Gabe looked hesitant. Was the revenant still on the surface?

"Is it safe?" Gabe asked. "Will the Dominion come here?"

"Doesn't matter," Jamie said. "We are surrounded by a wall of earth magic. Years of built-up wards, and a fae army stalking the edges of the property. They could try to bomb us into oblivion, I guess." Jamie shrugged. "But we've been prepared for this for a while."

"Prepared for the Dominion to turn on you?" Gabe seemed dumbfounded.

"Yes," Seiran agreed. "Sam's not the only cynical bastard in our group." Seiran had protested the measures when Sam first mentioned them a decade ago. But he hadn't lasted long in opposition. He knew someday they would come for him. Just as they'd come for his father and his grandfather before him. "Do you need to keep me close?" Seiran asked Gabe. Was he still fighting the revenant? Would the grave dirt under his bed be enough, or would he have to return to slumbering in the ground?

"Need, no. But I'd like to stay close. I rest better with you nearby. If you think we have time for rest."

"We'll make time," Kelly said as he warmed up a huge slice of egg bake in the microwave. Seiran's stomach grumbled as the scent of it hit his nose.

"Holy crap I'm hungry," he said.

"Eat. Then shower and sleep," Jamie said. His gaze fell on Gabe. "You can sleep downstairs."

"Are you guys okay with that?" Seiran asked his kids. Kaine was already half asleep curled up in the corner by Page.

"We'll take Kaine up with us," Ki said. "Link is already sleeping upstairs."

"Yeah, he was out hours ago. Said he was super happy to be home before the world ended," Kura added.

"End of the world," Seiran said. "I'll have you know, I stopped that from happening."

"We know. Thanks, daddy," Kura kissed Seiran on the cheek and left him to Jamie. She and Ki crossed the room, where Ki scooped up Kaine. "Come on Page, let's get you ready for sleep too."

Page got to his feet, looking like little more than a zombie himself, tired, strung out, but also unwilling to take any sort of initiative on his own. Seiran was glad there were no weapons in the house other than the knives right here in the kitchen. He didn't need Page thinking that suicide was a way out again. No matter how worried any of them were about the Dominion coming for them.

The kids headed upstairs, and Seiran was relieved that they were safe. He would make sure they all stayed safe. Even Page. Seiran reached out and spelled all the cutlery to not inflict self-harm.

Jamie squinted at him. "Really? You're already running on empty and you couldn't just say, *hey Jamie, fix this?*"

"You'd need a spell," Seiran protested. "I don't."

"Show off," Jamie said as he picked Seiran up and sat him in a chair at the table beside Gabe. "Eat. Then it's off to the shower and bed for you."

"Even with the Dominion about to rain down holy hell?"

"Even with. We have the Pillar of Earth, the Pillar of Water, and a fucking god of death magic in this house right now. Not to mention the fae child, the three super baby witches, oh and your best bud's lovers are upstairs zonked out, so he'll be here soon enough, which means crazy siphon power too. I think we're good."

"The Dominion have numbers," Gabe said.

"But not power. They've spent decades destroying the powerful before they can live long enough to actually control it. That works in our favor, not theirs."

"Are we really starting a war with the Dominion?" Seiran wondered. It felt surreal. He'd spent half his life bowing to their will to keep his family safe while he built up wards and alliances to protect them just in case. He had always hoped it would never be necessary, meanwhile still waiting for the hammer to drop. And now that it had, he felt strangely unsettled.

"Depends on them," Jamie said. "But the vampires aren't going to let this go, and the number of bodies means the humans are involved too. That's a lot to try to overcome with some spin doctoring."

It was, but it seemed the press was already trying to make Seiran out to be the bad guy. "I guess it's war then."

CHAPTER 26

Gabe had expected more protesting, rather than letting him return to his space downstairs with Seiran. But Seiran had eaten, and then used Gabe's downstairs bathroom to shower. Jamie had dropped off a pile of clothes, which Gabe left on the counter, giving Seiran some space. Gabe lingered near the bathroom, not trying to be creepy, but worried that Sei would fall or pass out in the shower.

His aligning memories were a bit jumbled as he worked to make sense of them, but it didn't feel like there were gaps anymore. He sent Mike a few questions while keeping an eye on Seiran. This whole mess with the Dominion felt like something he would have prepared for, and he had a weird feeling that he had? Or at least started to. It was something he'd learned to do over his long lifetime, prepare for just about anything.

He had a lot of questions. Most of them centered on his distrust for the Dominion. It sounded like Tanaka was promising that the Dominion would cooperate. Gabe didn't know if he believed she had that kind of power.

We had a meeting before I went to ground, Gabe texted Mike. *Did anything come of it?*

Mike sent back a link instead of a reply. The first was to an article about a non-profit organization, with a vague overview of details about what it did. Though it seemed related to studying magic. Gabe frowned at it, scrolling through the page and trying to read between the lines.

There was a logo for the organization that looked familiar, and when Gabe navigated his phone back to the main screen, he saw an icon there. An app for the organization? He clicked it, and it suddenly said "Scanning for facial recognition."

Would that work with all the changes to his appearance? Maybe he would need to shave and cut his hair? It seemed to chug for a minute or two before finally confirming his name and opening to a long list of information.

Welcome, Senior Advisor Santini, would you like a tour? The app said in a female voice. But he didn't have time to sort through the app right this minute, as Seiran was swaying. Gabe took a step toward Seiran as he emerged from the bathroom.

He was dressed in a pair of pajamas with *DuckTales* print all over them. Hair hanging loose around his face and looking exhausted. Gabe raised a brow.

Seiran gave him a tired sigh. "No hard conversations right now, okay?"

"Sure," Gabe agreed. "I'm going to jump in the shower. Let's get you into bed though, before you pass out."

"I'm fine," Sei said as he teetered toward the bed and half fell in it. Gabe followed and lifted him the last little bit, tugging the blankets over him. "I heal fast. Especially inside the house surrounded by earth."

"Will the wards drain you?" Gabe wondered if there was another way to keep them all safe rather than relying on Seiran alone.

"The wards have been layered and fed for over a decade. They can last years without renewal." Seiran curled up under the blankets, closing his eyes as soon as his head hit the pillow.

Gabe turned out the light, since he didn't need it even in the dark of the basement, and headed to the bathroom to shower. He smelled of earth and faintly of death magic. Though he suspected the latter would not fade completely unless he went another long spell without using his power. He stripped and stepped under a warm spray of water feeling alive—tired, but alive.

He let the water wash over him and closed his eyes to relax into the heat as it soothed his muscles and eased his mind. He would not be burying his power again any time soon. No matter how the people of this modern world feared it. Having that magic swirling inside him was settling, clarifying, and made him feel strong.

He tried not to reflect on the past too much. The lingering memory of Tresler's forced bond, a violation that bothered Gabe more than he thought it should. His mind had not been his own. How he'd held back the revenant as long as he had, Gabe still wondered. Fear of hurting Seiran? Pulling away, and abandoning him, had likely saved them both from Gabe's rising self-destruction. But he had no plans to use that as an excuse. Nor did he think he was suddenly forgiven. With time, perhaps he could be.

If Seiran had left Gabe in the ground the first time, the bond would likely have been broken by time. But Gabe wasn't sure that Tresler would have ever been discovered. At least not before he'd caused a lot of damage. Sam wouldn't have been saved either, even if the guy bitched about being a vampire all the time. Gabe knew he was happy where he was, stalking the night, and spending his days with his guys.

Gabe decided he would leave the past in the past. It had always worked before in his long years. Moving forward, trying to learn and adapt had always been the best survival option. He would take each day as it came and try to make himself more open and communicative. His long years alone meant he was used to shutting himself away.

Seiran hated that. He wanted a partnership, and Gabe decided it was the least he could do to share more. He also realized it was going to take a lot of doing to actually be forgiven. Action rather than platitudes. That was what Seiran had been saying.

Gabe stepped out of the shower, dried off, and ran a comb through his hair. He dug through his clothes, finding not pajamas like Seiran had, but boxers and sleep pants, which he suspected was better than nothing when he was in a house full of children.

He tugged on the clothes and turned off the light in the bathroom, plunging the space into darkness. He wondered about Kaine, and how the child in the mortal world became some sort of Prince of the fae across the veil. An agreement with Bryar, Sei had said. He'd have to ask more specifics about that one. Gabe had also felt the truth Sei had been unwilling to confirm when Kaine blamed himself for Sei's lack of control over his own power. Gabe had thought that had been his fault, going to ground had cut their bond down to almost nothing. But Seiran's emotions, careful as his words had been, indicated that he had in fact, given a lot of power, more than necessary perhaps, to Kaine's creation. Interesting.

Gabe climbed into bed beside Seiran, who was already fast asleep, and wrapped himself around Sei. That felt right. He wasn't the same man Gabe had known all those years before. Sei had always been cynical and a bit needy. His trauma triggering a lot of personal issues. And while Seiran hadn't buried the trauma, as much as learning to adapt to it, he seemed to function better in difficult situations, not shutting down as he once had. But Sei's instincts of self-preservation had always been good. He also focused more on his kids than himself, doing things to protect them, which benefited them all in the end. Gabe would have to make sure that didn't become a crutch that held Seiran back.

He stretched out his senses, wondering if he could still feel the dead, and was surprised to find he could. A long tie to them reminded him of days many centuries past, in which he used armies of these to guard him and his while they slept each day. The Dark Ages had been dark for a reason. Filled with wars, battles of all species, ending in bloodshed and bodies enough to guard him forever.

Necromancer? Gabe texted to Mike. *Had forgotten that little bit.*

Seems you forgot a lot. But you buried that a long time. Mike responded. *How's your memory now?*

Gabe thought about it for a while. Everything was there. An intensity that almost felt like memories of a memory in some cases. The oldest of them faint enough he wondered if they were real.

Mostly there. How goes the questioning? Zombies didn't by nature speak much. Once they were beyond a certain point of decomposition, they couldn't magically find a voice and the mind was so far gone, there was nothing left to pull from them other than the rattling bones of a skeleton. Those not lost to the earth's renewing strength, like Steve, would still have enough brain matter to speak full sentences. But Gabe couldn't recall many who had been fresh enough to question.

Recording dental impressions. Have Steven Brody and two other somewhat juicy corpses singing tunes.

It sounded gruesome, like they were torturing the dead, though Gabe was pretty certain it wasn't necessary.

Some of the oldest have begun to shatter. We've sorted them as close as possible to age of death and are documenting as fast as we can.

Gabe wondered if he should be there to help. He didn't think he had the motivation to pull himself away from the sleeping witch in his arms, but if he had to, he would.

Do you need me there?

No. Mike replied. *Stay with Rou. The Dominion is up to shady shit. Let us handle this end.*

Gabe frowned at his phone. He'd never been one to stand on the sidelines when a battle was looming. He knew Mike was stronger than most assumed he was. But one of Mike's skills was his charisma. It was one of the reasons Gabe had changed him and kept him close over the years. Everyone liked Mike, and the vampire came across as approachable and engaging. Though Gabe knew he was one of the more powerful of his get.

Call if you need me, Gabe sent back, knowing it would not have to be a phone call, but a tug on the line of his magic. Dozens of his get were in the area. More than he'd met at the bar. Called by Mike to this situation? Or already here and waiting?

Rest. We got this. Been preparing for over a decade.

Gabe sighed. Too many questions, but he was tired. At least he'd get a nap.

Seiran's phone sat on the nightstand. Sam had sent him a comment about being busy and to fuck off, which had made Seiran smile before he'd stepped into the shower. An odd friendship they had. At one time enemies and rivals, they actually almost seemed closer now than Seiran was to any of the others, including his own brother. Even if their banter wound up in a war of cynical teasing. It was a trust level, Gabe thought. Both abused and learning to survive in different ways. But Gabe suspected the two had more in common than not.

He put his phone beside Seiran's and tugged the blanket over them both. Maybe they both could rest a while? They could begin to tackle the problems of the world tomorrow.

He did fall asleep, though the dreams were a bit of an unsettled mess from the past. He vividly dreamt about the fog of hunger and rage that had taken control before he'd went to ground. The feel of Tresler trying to control him, Gabe's revenant fighting back the only way he knew how, through blood and terror. The backbone of a vampire, really. It was a darker side he had tried not to show Seiran all those years ago. Would Seiran have run if he'd known? Maybe. He would have been smart to run away rather than be locked into their bond. Vampires were volatile at best.

Gabe also dreamt of the corpses. Steve who seemed to sit in a chair, still as stone, staring straight ahead at the golem. In the same room? Gabe didn't try to make his mind follow any of them. It gravitated toward the dead because they were his. And he could see the troubled mess of the golem through the eyes of the dead.

Page's attempt to free them from torture, bound them to another kind of torture. Had they found the body for the last unclaimed soul inside it? Gabe studied the lines of the ties for a while, knowing he could unravel the whole thing, but releasing just one would be impossible. All or none. Gabe followed the ties a dozen times, trying to find a way. If they didn't find that body in the second killing field, did that mean there were even more dead? How long had the witches been slaughtering without consequence?

Gabe sighed and let his attention wander from the golem. It wasn't a problem he could solve right this minute.

They were still loading everyone into another giant room in that warehouse Max had set up. The space the vampires had been in, while being cataloged and defined, but not feeling fully dead. There was a partition put up between the groups. But the vampire side was dark. The bodies sealed in body bags, all tagged and marked. Max's crew must have been hard at work.

Gabe wondered briefly how he had enough people to work through the backlog of corpses. It wasn't something any Joe Schmoe could do. Searching for trace evidence, fingerprinting, getting dental impressions, all while dealing with violently tortured and maimed dead. That wasn't for the faint of heart. Yet the efficiency in which vampire investigators moved, led Gabe to believe this wasn't their first rodeo cataloging crimes like this.

He'd have to ask Max about it. Max… Titus… Gabe's memory floated briefly to their time as humans before the change. The short attempt after their change had been disastrous. Neither man who they had been as humans. Max had never given up the idea of world domination, while Gabe had lost complete interest in it. It was why Gabe and Seiran fit so well together. Both had insane amounts of power, but neither really cared for that ultimate level of control. In fact, to Gabe, it was a burden. As if he needed to deal with an entire world of problems. Perhaps that was an issue now as well. If he hadn't taken a step back, and the world still feared him, would Seiran be safer?

Gabe let out a long sigh, relaxing deeper into sleep. He actually dreamed for a while. Floating in weird bits of colored memory from the walk through the veil, which had tried to pull the revenant out of him, to strange wanderings through dark forests and moonless nights. Seiran's dreams, Gabe realized. The calm of the earth resettling. Gabe soothed the rising waves of rolling power with ease. It was like creating a steady blip on a heart monitor. Spikes too large caused trouble, and too small meant death. Seiran slept deeper as Gabe set a rhythm to the magic.

His long years had given him lots of practice. The dead had always been a mess of rising and falling surges. Plagues and wars adding to the ever-rippling flow of his power. It was how he'd lived as long as he had, able to manipulate the waves to his benefit.

He wandered through a handful more of dreams tied to his past before finding himself drawn back to the dead. Like something had again pulled on him, a startling half awareness that had him reaching for the corpses with worry.

It was curious that everything felt so still, almost in suspended animation. Though some of the skeletons fell, as if the magic holding them together would suddenly vanish and they did indeed shatter. The vampires were prepared, as each set of bones stood above a body bag. They fell and landed in a bag, which was labeled and ready for them to be moved. Gabe's power not eternal in this case, even though the Focus bond had extended it.

Not many of the old dead remained standing. The few fresh enough to have any living memory left were seated like Steve was, but still as only death could make them. Sam oversaw the group, which was almost all vampires. A handful of Seiran's MI investigators lingered. Gabe recognized Emmaline, who sat with Tanaka as the two went over paperwork.

Over all, everything was quiet. Too quiet.

Where had that tug come from?

Gabe waited, lingering on the edge of sleep, awareness on the dead, as though waiting for it to pull again. Did someone in these families have death magic? He knew with enough spells and maybe a pact or two with demons, any witch could animate a corpse. Getting it to truly obey was another thing altogether. That took blood and regular sacrifices. Even Page, with his magic so fresh and untrained, would not have been able to hold the dead long. The golem had begun to unravel because blood died. Even in the human body, blood cells died and were used to refeed the body or they were shed. Spells weren't all that different, needing regular renewal.

Gabe kept his awareness half locked to the dead, linked firmly to Steve. Murdered by his own mother, Steve's soul was gone, but within him lingered a dark edge that could be called. Gabe finessed the feeling, trying to recall all the details. It had been so long. The murdered always had a touch of the darkness within them. It could be fed to become almost revenant like, though in humans, and apparently witches, it was weak enough that he would really have to feed them power to get them to move.

Steve was fresh enough that sitting within the mind as it began to decay, empty of all living force, the darkness seemed to rise like the crawl of mold over a water-filled room. Not a pleasant feeling, but Gabe vowed he would ensure Steve went to ground soon. The earth would reclaim him as it should, giving the body true death.

Gabe waited there a long time. Half listening to conversations around him, but not paying attention to any. It was a garble of noise. Loud enough that he almost missed the second tug. Not on the dead, but on the golem.

Forest had been as still as Steve in the chair, not breathing or moving at all, and then he was shifting in his seat, like he was uncomfortable. But that wasn't something golems could be. Gabe studied the magic tying it together. Page's work was a mess. With training, Gabe suspected Page could be an incredible power. Would the Dominion let him live that long?

Forest turned his gaze to Steve. Like the golem could see Gabe resting in the strength of the dead, watching and waiting. But that shouldn't be possible.

The intensity of the gaze heated, and Gabe thought he actually felt warm for a minute. Uncomfortably warm. A spell lighting up like a match flare, brief and hot, and insanely fast. Gabe was still trying to figure out what happened as flames flickered around his senses.

Sam was the first to react, turning, alarmed, reaching out.

It was then that Gabe realized Steve was on fire, and through him, the spell directing back at Gabe, setting him on fire as well.

Gabe screamed, and jerked away, leaving the distant spread of bodies, and leaping from the bed even as the flames burned into his flesh, and began to dig into his soul. He tried to break the bond with Steve, setting the dead free, which would drop them all, but he couldn't break the cord. Not with fire shooting through it to incinerate him.

He floundered, his skin burning up, clothes acting like kindling, intensifying the fire. Panic and pain clouding his senses. The bed was on fire. The room was beginning to burn. Gabe reached out helplessly as he feared that he'd bring death to them all, the warded house burning down with them all trapped inside. That was not the kind of death he was meant to be.

CHAPTER 27

Seiran woke from a dream startled by Gabe's discomfort, a threshold of worry and awareness that Sei couldn't exactly define. But he lingered on the edge of sleep, trying to process if he should actually wake up, or it was something passing.

Then the fire started.

It was heat first, Gabe turning hot around him, and then the flames erupting. Gabe leapt up, and Seiran rolled off the other side as flames lit the bed, and Gabe on fire.

Seiran panicked. He felt Gabe's disorientation, pain and fear, as he floundered away while burning. Vampires and fire were not a good combo, and these flames were not some spontaneous combustion. Gabe dropped to roll on the floor, but it didn't seem to interrupt the fire.

Magic. A spell rather than something of natural origin, it's why it kept burning even while Gabe should have been able to put them out with ease.

Seiran felt the power of it dancing over his skin, reaching for him through the bond he had to Gabe. Seiran did the first thing he could think of and shoved the spell back at the caster. Like a mirror, reflecting back with all the force he could pull in those few seconds of insanity. Any other witch would have needed complicated spells to build up that sort of power. But Seiran bounced it back with a wallop that actually doused the flames on the bed and sent Gabe tumbling backward, partially extinguishing his fire.

The fire alarm was going off in an annoying wail. Seiran felt the last ties of the spell shatter, the casters either injured or trying to escape the backlash. He grabbed a blanket, racing to Gabe's side to douse the flames. He kept his magic pushing at the spell, like a wall propelling at the witches who dared to reach through the distance and hurt them. It was like being in two places at once.

He saw others bursting into flames. Not one, but many, scattered around symbols drawn that Seiran didn't recognize. An organized assault by the Dominion? Or someone else? They screamed and floundered, burning slower than Gabe had, but it would hurt plenty.

Seiran patted at Gabe, thinking thoughts of a cool breeze or icy lake, though he'd need access to a source, or to pull direct power from the Goddess to use either of those.

Then Kelly was there, dousing the flames with cooling water. Soaking them all, and washing the basement floor in a layer of icy spill that would be a bitch to clean up later. But the fire was finally out.

Gabe heaved pained breaths, his skin blackened and flaking away, his blood boiling and burning like lava through his body. Seiran felt the bond between them begin to close, Gabe trying to shut him off from the pain.

"Don't," Seiran demanded.

It will cause you pain, Gabe said through their link.

Pain was a mild statement for the feeling, excruciating, a better term. How was it possible to be that damaged and still feel so much? Or be conscious?

"I am earth. I can help you heal this." It hurt to look at him, blackened and nightmarish, reminding Seiran of the vampire bodies they had found. Had this spell come from the same group?

He had to work to steady his emotions. Now was not the time for panic. The flames were out, and this was unlikely to kill Gabe, but that didn't mean it wasn't going to be brutal.

Jamie took the blanket from Seiran, carefully wrapping Gabe up. "Let's get him to the arboretum." There was no way that touching him wasn't going to hurt. And Gabe seemed to half pass out a second as Jamie lifted him.

Fear and grief rose in Seiran's gut. He knew the damage was too great for Gabe to heal without going to ground. But Sei wanted to scream at the injustice of it. He'd just gotten Gabe back and they were trying to work through shit. Now Gabe would be back in the ground for who knew how long.

They all headed upstairs, passing the kids who were all waiting in the kitchen, awake with wide eyes and scared. The door to the basement had been broken, likely Jamie coming through after hearing the alarms. Everything else seemed untouched.

"Is the fire out?" Kaine asked with huge, terrified eyes.

"It is. It's okay, go back to bed," Seiran told him. It was like three in the morning. They should all be asleep.

"Can we help?" Ki asked.

Seiran reached out to squeeze his kids' hands as he moved to open the door to the arboretum. "Bed. But thank you."

Jamie carried Gabe to a large open patch of dirt in the garden. They all liked to roll in the fresh spread when they played in their shifted forms. It was wide enough for a couple bodies, as even Jamie enjoyed a good roll in the dirt when he turned bear. It was also the only ground that was untouched by plant life of some kind.

The fae swirled around them in a crazy smash of color as Jamie carefully lowered Gabe down and peeled the blanket away. Gabe swallowed and tried to speak. His eyes open, seeming mostly coherent, though Seiran could barely breath through the shared pain.

"Don't. It's okay," Seiran assured him. "Let the ground take you. Rest. Heal." Seiran got a storm of emotions from Gabe. Mostly the white-hot rage that someone had sent a spell their way. Tried to destroy the zombie of Steve, for what? To silence the dead? Destroy evidence? Or an attack specifically to weaken Seiran? Gabe sent all of that in a blaze of hot emotions. "It's fine. I've got this," Seiran promised. "Not a kid anymore, remember?"

He leaned down, careful not to touch Gabe's skin. The blanket had rubbed the blackened bits off, exposing damaged nerves and muscles. Seiran swallowed hard, hoping he was keeping the worst of his fears to himself. "It's okay. Rest. I love you. And I will still be here when you get back." Seiran shoved the conviction of his words into their bond, letting Gabe feel the truth of them. Yes, Seiran would miss him, but it was okay.

Don't want to go, Gabe whispered through the bond, but he was almost completely lost in pain. His eyes turning a mix of red and black, warning of the revenant.

"You can either let go and heal, or keep fighting it and risk freeing your revenant." Seiran hovered his fingers above Gabe's face, not willing to touch him and chance hurting him further. "I love you. But not all is forgiven, so I expect you back soon."

Gabe looked undecided, but Seiran pulled a rolling wave of earth power letting it soothe a cooling wash over Gabe. Gabe sighed, giving up the fight, and began to sink into the ground, the earth swallowing him up in a way that was specific to vampires. It wasn't like zombies in reverse, with vampires digging their way in rather than out, but more like the quicksand of old movies. The ground shifting and becoming soft, fine, and almost like water. Seiran had often thought the kinetic type of sand that the kids used to play with was the closest he could recall to the way the earth reacted to vampires. It could be solid, smooth, and unyielding, but soft and delicate as it cradled them deep.

Seiran watched, until Gabe was completely overtaken. He could feel the grip of the grave as an icy touch to soothe the pain. Gabe's storming emotions vanished in a familiar quash of their bond. Not closing exactly, but becoming less defined. The strength of the earth magic took Gabe fast, breaking down the damaged body and releasing the mixed edges of soul and revenant to drift, dream, and heal untethered by mortal coil.

Would decades pass again? Seiran sucked in a hard breath, his chest tight, and fed the rage.

He'd been complacent too long. Following the rules and keeping his head down. Trying to protect his family and himself from the wrath of those who would never offer him any quarter. Gabe's return had given him hope, not only of finally not being alone anymore, but of finding a way free from all the chains they'd shackled him with. He'd had a few moments of hope, thinking he could escape the Dominion and find another course for his life, Gabe's calm strength and incredible power a wall to hide behind.

But that had been stupid. Seiran didn't need to hide. He was the scion of Earth, the Green Man, Father Earth, Pillar of magic, a mortal god in his own right. And once again the man he loved had been stolen from him while he was expected to sit back and obey.

Not anymore. Stick a fork in him, he was done.

He turned all the grief to rage, feeling it awaken inside, not unlike the revenant he'd recognized from Gabe's eyes in the end. It was a bit like pouring out the cool calm lightness he'd been gifted since Gabe had been back, and taking in all the heat and darkness. Maybe this was what made Sam feel so powerful when he teetered on a red out. A *couldn't give a fuck* attitude that nestled deep in his soul. Burn it all down. Fuck the consequences.

If Seiran didn't have a direction for the rage, it might have turned quickly to world destruction. But Gabe was in the ground. His kids were a dozen feet away. And this rage had a source.

Seiran recalled the last bits of what Gabe had been dreaming before the fire started. The warehouse with all the bodies, Steve and the golem. Something had been pulling on the golem. Casting a spell through it? That was not normally possible. Though a lot of things about that golem had been off. The souls, the struggle to control it, and even Page's recounting of how he'd made it.

Seiran got to his feet and summoned Bryar, which was a tug on their eternal tie. The fae might have chosen Bryar as their sacrifice to gain an alliance, but Seiran trusted him more than any other fae. Not only because they shared a child made of magic, but because Bryar had been born from blood magic spells, and forever craved battle. There wasn't really a better fae to have at his back if he was going to rage against the machine.

Today would be a good day to indulge. No more waiting, no more games, no more sitting on his thumbs and hoping everyone did the right thing.

"Sei?" Jamie said, reaching for him.

Seiran sidestepped him. "Get the kids to bed, please." He let the Goddess rise again. She demanded control and to use his strength to destroy. But Seiran's grip on the power was better. As though Gabe's return, even as short as it was, had strengthened something in him. Could he stand another decade with Her constant demands without Gabe at his side? He prayed he wouldn't have to, but first he had to deal with some witches.

Bryar appeared. Popping from a small glowing bug into the human-sized man. Not much about Bryar looked human in this form. He was too pretty, too perfect, and very ethereal. The misconception of elves, Seiran knew, had come from fae like Bryar. He was also dressed for war. Covered in armor that looked more like a beetle shell than anything human, hair pulled up, and a sword bigger than Seiran strapped to his back. He could have stepped out of an anime or video game and looked like he fit right in.

"We fight?" Bryar asked.

Seiran nodded. "You have to get me there first. But yes, we fight. We kill," Seiran said. He needed to get to the warehouse. No long trips through the veil. "Can you sense Sam? I need to go to where he is right now."

"Sei…" Jamie tried to protest. But Kelly was shuffling him and all the kids inside.

Sei felt another barrier ward go up. Water wrapping a cool

hand around the property, and rain began to fall. Kelly was preparing for more fire. Good because if Seiran had been a fire witch instead of earth, the entire world would already be burning.

Bryar cocked his head to the side. "Fast travel through the veil makes you sick," he said.

"Yeah, well I'm hoping to upchuck on some witches. And then dissect them with plants right after. Let's go." Seiran pointed at Jamie and the kids again, mouthing through the glass door, "Bed, all of you." He took Bryar's outstretched hand and was instantly pulled through all time and space.

With a pop and a disorientating roll, he landed in the warehouse, stumbling to keep his feet as he arrived to utter chaos. It was a battle of zombies, golems, and vampires, some still undead, others true dead. What the fuck?

He swallowed back bile and readied himself to jump into the fray, only he wasn't sure who was on their side and who wasn't.

"About time, Ronnie!" Sam snarled as he smashed a fist into a golem, sending it flying across the room. Not the golem they'd been watching, but one of many new golems.

At least a dozen of them, maybe more, though Forest sat in a chair in the corner and didn't move other than to stare with creepy eyes outward. Steve was slumped in a chair across from Forest, burned, and seeming lifeless. Had the last of Gabe's magic faded when he went to ground?

"We're fighting the golems?" Bryar clarified. "Or is this a kill them all scenario? Please let it be the second."

"Golems!" Sam said.

"That's not as fun," Bryar grumbled as he leapt across the room to hack the head off a golem. While the thing separated, and even looked like sticks and clay, it instantly reformed. "Well, that's better. I love a challenge." He whacked it again, hacking it apart and exclaiming with glee as it reformed. "You do throw the best parties, vampire."

"Why are there still zombies?" Seiran asked as he called roots from the earth to smack the golems away.

"I sort of accidentally borrowed that power…" Sam said, not sounding sorry at all.

"Really? Cause the other shit isn't enough? Fire, earth, water, wind, and now death magic? Are you going for god status?"

"Finally, you admit I'm a god," Sam snarked leaping across the room to pull a golem off a vampire investigator.

"Really, Sammie?" Seiran let his earth powers flow free, the ground turning green and blooming around him. Branches and roots reaching upward like the tendrils of a giant sea monster to wrap around his prey. He reached for the golems and the zombies, trying to define what was still actually living, and what was just an animated being.

With enough wrapping them, the golems had to pause, though they still fought and struggled. Something, or someone was controlling them. At least these felt more like the spells Seiran was used to. Maybe he could unravel the magic binding them to their goal? Usually, golems continued to reform until completing their objective, which was what in this case? Total destruction to all of them?

Seiran reached the nearest golem and found it empty. No souls, just animated sticks. A very weak golem, though as always, the blood magic tying it to this world was strong. But there was also no visible name mark on them, which is normally how a golem was bound. What the fuck?

"Sam, why do these not have a name mark? Is that possible?"

"I think it's just somewhere we can't see right away? And I'm not examining golem buttholes for it." He punched another golem, sending it skittering backward for a few feet, but it bounced right back like a fucking yo-yo.

"Huh," Seiran rolled his earth power through it, searching for the center tie, or *name* as it might have been crafted in the spell. He even pushed out a pulse with his omniscient sight, looking for ripples of magic. And there it was, a mark on this one near the back of its arm.

Seiran touched the mark and unraveled the tie, severing the blood bond. The golem shattered, falling into a heap of sticks and clay.

"Really, Ronnie? Just poof? I thought you wanted to tear some shit up." Sam leapt at another golem, not punching but wrapping himself around it to hold it down. "Find the mark then, show-off. Unravel this fucker before I gotta call up more zombies. This is not a power I find appealing."

"No?" Sei asked, wondering, but he raced to Sam's side, searching for that pulse and finding it on a leg this time. Another unraveled. "Why not just use fire?"

"'Cause we already have burned vampires, and I'm the only one fireproof in the room." Sam brushed the clay off and stared at the mess Bryar was making. "Good choice for child bearing, Rou. He's just another nutjob."

Bryar was surrounded by golem parts, all mixed up and trying to reform, but he kept hacking them into smaller pieces, laughing maniacally like a villain the entire time.

"He's having a good time," Sei offered. "You don't like my parties?" Sei focused on another golem, a writhing leg of foot wide roots ensnaring the creature. "Why are the vampires also zombies?"

"Well, the vampire zombies were an accident," Sam said. "Some of the vampires helping out were on fire. Then the golems poured in and I just thought *rise* and whoops…"

Sam's power was a little wonky on the best of days, even though he did work regularly on training.

"They popped out of the body bags." Sam threw his hands in the air imitating a familiar kid's movie Sei knew he'd watched a dozen times with their kids. "Like daisies."

Sei snorted, and dissolved another golem.

The vampire zombies tore at the golems. Like the horror movies of zombies attacking to tear people up, these zombies did exactly that, a red glow illuminating from their eyes, those that had eyes at least.

The golems were fighting back much the same way, tearing limbs and trying to rip each other apart. It was a bit gruesome, but at least it kept the undead vampires and the handful of witch and human investigators safe. Seiran realized his mother, and a smattering of his investigators were holed up in a corner trying to offer triage to those injured while still having a couple of people guarding against attack.

When one of the golems reached for Tanaka, he feared he'd not get there in time, but the ground in front of her erupted with a giant wall of tangled vines. Not his magic, but hers. He smiled to himself, snagged the golem in a weave of living vines, found the mark and unraveled it.

"How are you finding the mark?" Sam demanded.

"Odin's Eye. The mark glows."

"Hmm," Sam sounded disgruntled, but they had spent some time mastering the spell. Sam had wanted to be able to find Luca and Con if necessary, and Seiran suspected he could find Max that way too. "Do we need any of these whole for questioning?"

"No." Seiran said. "They are soulless. I already bounced back the fire spell. We'll have plenty of burned witches to track, if they survived that inferno."

"Good." Sam stretched out his hand and Sei felt the hammer of power. The room shifted to a weird black and white wash for a half second, revealing the marks on all the golems, and staining them with glowing color so even as the light went back to normal, the mark still shined.

"Now who's the show-off?" Seiran grumbled. Sam's power was more like a sledgehammer than a butter knife. But Sei used it to his advantage, bouncing around the room and unraveling any golem he could reach. It was easier now that he knew what it was. The touch of earth to the mark could send them back to the Goddess, a bit like asking the earth to dissolve the blood used to tie them to this world. Sam was at his back keeping them off him, and even holding some down, until Sei could unravel them.

There had to be a couple dozen golems. All from the killing fields they found? Was that the pull Gabe had felt? Someone trying to control an army of golems? None of them had souls like Forest did. All just toys of some greater magic that Sei would now recognize if he ever met it again. The signature of it strong enough to burn into his memory. Another thing he could track.

Sei landed in Bryar's mess of body parts last, sweeping a wave of magic outward. The reforming golems shattered, clay blasting into pieces, with a messy spray of poop brown. Bryar looked disappointed when none of them got back up.

"Sorry," Sei offered, breathing hard, and dripping with chunks of clay. It looked like they stood in the center of a blood bath, though it was clay rather than blood. Bodies and bones everywhere. The zombies stopped, all turning eerie gazes Sam's way.

"Whoa… creepy," Sam said.

"Put them to rest," Sei said.

Sam blinked at him. "How do I do that?"

And Gabe was in the ground. Was there anyone else to ask? "Didn't you say you dealt with zombies before?"

"Just to set them on fire."

And that didn't seem like the best option since the nests these vampires belonged to wanted them back. "Sammie…"

"Are you wearing *DuckTales* pajamas?" Sam asked incredulous. "To a battle between zombies and vampires?"

"That cartoon is a legend, you know. Do you know how much history it teaches?" Sei said searching the room for survivors and those still in need of help. Maybe Max would know how to get the vampires to stand down? Or Mike? "Who you gonna call?" he said more to himself than anyone else.

"Zombie busters?" Sam asked.

"I could cut them up," Bryar offered. He was splattered in clay and zombie goop, but looked as excited as a child digging into their first birthday cake.

Seiran sighed. He was tied to a bunch of psychos. Though he could not have been more grateful for having any of them at his back.

CHAPTER 28

Max arrived with a heap of vampires, EMTs, and apparently a couple witches. The witches being male, which surprised Sei a little. But Sam seemed to recognize them. Two of them stepped in to help Sam put the zombies down. Necromancers? Sei thought more regular witches, as they used spells to direct the magic, pointing out lines of the spell to Sam.

Sei tried to pay attention to the spell, feeling like he should learn how to use Gabe's power, but he was insanely tired. The exhaustion actually added to his grief and depression over having Gabe go back to ground, and anxiety about protecting his kids.

Would nothing he did ever be enough? He ended up sinking down in a corner, wishing for sleep. Tanaka appeared briefly. "The kids okay?" She asked.

"Yes, safe at home," Sei agreed. "The fire spell hit Gabe." Sei swallowed hard, trying not to picture the damage that had been done. "He had to go back to ground." He wasn't going to cry, and he'd tried to hold onto the rage. But it wasn't really in him anymore to hold onto it. "I reflected the spell back. There are going to be a lot of burned witches."

His mother seemed to take that easily enough, turning to the group of investigators and issuing commands. Including a call to all hospitals and police about severely burned witches arriving for care. If they survived. Sei wondered if he'd killed them. It did bother him a little, even though they'd tried to kill him.

Emmaline appeared with a bottle of water and some wet wipes. "Maybe wipe your hands and face before drinking?"

"Sage advice, my friend," Sei said as he cleaned up and then popped the cap. He guzzled the entire thing before finally feeling like he wasn't toasted inside. "How many hurt?"

"Four vampires. They've already been transported to their grave sites. Hart is hoping they have a full recovery."

"There were no humans or witches close enough to be injured?"

"Not by the fire. A few got hurt when the golems attacked, but the golems seemed to fixate on the vampires, and destroying the evidence." Emmaline looked out over the mess. Bones scattered everywhere, some burned, and the vampires laying down on their body bags looking like broken dolls.

"How much evidence was destroyed?"

"Most of it was saved, at least the records we took. We may have lost some of the remains, and a lot of them are scattered, which means a longer process getting them back to their families, but I documented everything digitally. Saved in four places, not uploaded to the Dominion servers yet."

"Don't upload it," Max said, appearing a few feet away. He had probably heard the conversation from across the room. "It's likely why they attacked. They thought the evidence wasn't saved."

"You think the Dominion did this?" Emmaline asked.

"I don't doubt it," Max said. His gaze found Sei. "How bad was Gabe hurt?"

"He went to ground," Sei said, his voice tight.

Max nodded. "He'll be back."

"In less than a decade?" Seiran couldn't help but feel bitter.

"Likely, yes." He turned toward the door like he heard something Sei couldn't. Tanaka was there as people in uniform with guns shoved their way inside. Not police, as they were already there trying to make sense of the mess. This was an elite squad of witches sent out for enforcement, usually to drag witches to the stake. Their uniform actually mirrored some of the old military uniforms of almost a century ago. He'd always hated the brown and green colors, like somehow, they represented the earth, when they were all political power. This squad had been nicknamed the Death Squad. Sort of a boogeyman of the witch world, though they were all women.

"Fuck," Sei said as they crossed the room, splitting into two groups, heading toward Sam and Sei, looking ready to kill.

Emmaline's eyes widened. "This isn't…"

The group reached Sam first, and tried to use some sort of magic binding on him, which he instantly dispelled with the nullification ability he'd leeched from Matthew long ago. They were already fighting before the group could get halfway across the room to Seiran.

"Enough!" Max shouted, and the entire room went still. "What is the meaning of this?"

"We don't answer to you, vampire," one of the kill squad said.

"But you answer to me," Tanaka stated.

"Not anymore," the same witch replied. "Those witches are wanted for the murder of more than a dozen witches, and you let them, so you are being removed as Senior Director. If you're not up on the stake as well, I'd be surprised."

Emmaline stepped forward. "I think you're mistaken on who murdered who." She waved a hand at the room around them. "We have dozens, if not hundreds of bodies, human and vampire we've been tracking. All leading back to a similar magical signature. A group of witches working together to create death magics. Which means a coven killed all of these people. I have substantial evidence and signature markers of the magic."

"And two dozen witches are dead by a fire magic spell," the witch said. "Cast by Mueller and Rou."

"I reflected a spell that had been directed at me," Seiran said. "My lover was badly burned."

"And several of our vampires," Sam said.

"I did not cast that spell." Seiran said. But he knew that didn't matter. They'd been looking for years for a way to kill him. Now Sam too? And removing his mother from her role as Senior Director? This all sounded planned. Though he doubted they bargained on having two dozen witches dead to do it.

The witches were headed his way again and Max scowled, but the room was suddenly full of vampires and human police.

"We are done," Max stated as the kill squad was surrounded by vampires, the police looking ready for shit too. "No more kowtowing to the Dominion. I have vampires dead and tortured by witches to create golems." He pointed at Forest who was the only golem left in the room. He still sat in the chair, though he looked more like sticks and clay than a person, but occasionally flash-shifted to one of the visages of the vampires whose souls were trapped inside.

"You don't have power here," the witch said again.

"I think you're mistaken," Max said. More vampires appeared, pouring through the doorways even though it was daytime. "I think it is you who do not have power here."

The vampires reached the first group of kill squad witches and grabbed them, despite protests, and clapped them in nullifying cuffs. Seiran blinked at the insanity of it. Dozens of vampires, accompanied by the human police, arresting witches?

"By whose power do you dare?" The witch demanded. "These monsters murdered Director Han and leading members of three other families."

"By Executive Order of the President," Max said.

And that's when the military entered. The soldiers raining down on the place like it was a war zone. Guns at ready, and all of them wearing nullifying amulets. They had come for witches.

Seiran gaped at it all. Never in a million years would he have thought the government would rise against the Dominion. And certainly not in his defense.

"The Dominion is being declared a terrorist organization," Max continued. "Charged with multiple abuses of power, including murder by magic, embezzling, and extortion. The President and all of Congress has reviewed the overwhelming evidence that contains decades worth of misdeeds."

How was that possible? The Dominion worked really hard to control the information released to the public. Even editing Seiran's reports and reclassifying a lot of what he'd cataloged over the years. He looked at his mother, who stood silent, and unsurprised by any of this. Not the kill squad orders, or even Max's rebuttal of them. Had she done this? Been feeding information to the government?

She glanced his way and gave him a tiny reassuring smile.

Holy fuck, she had!

"I have a list of witches who are declared as belonging to us," Max continued. "Including the Rous, and Mueller."

"And Jamie, Kelly, Con, and Page," Seiran whispered.

Max nodded. "The list that belong to us, is large and growing. Witches have been defecting for years, tired of the manipulation and murder of their kind for power." The kill squad witches were bound and gagged with charms to keep them silent. "We actually have ways to jail witches without murdering them." Max's gaze found Sam. "Please have all of their IDs checked. I suspect a lot of these are on our Crimes Against Humanity list."

Sam cursed, but nodded. "Fucking bullshit witch shit." He took a tablet from one of the other vampires and logged into something.

"What is even happening?" Seiran asked. His mother stepped in close to squeeze his shoulder. "Shouldn't you arrest me too?"

He had helped. His investigations over the years often ended with these terrible kill squad witches set upon someone. No matter what he did, or how much evidence he produced, they always took over. He'd actually become very picky over the past few years about what cases his department actually took. Only finding time and resources for things that involved a lot of destruction and death. Not that it often justified the ends the Dominion required.

"Mike will take you to the new office. Familiarize you with the basics," Max said. "If you'll bring your Dominion laptop, our people will begin retrieving data from it and give you a new one."

"Did you just take over the world?" Sei wondered.

Max gave him a small smile.

"Let me give you a ride. We can get your laptop later. But maybe call your fae buddy to you?" Mike said.

Bryar was stalking the scattered bones like he was waiting for them to rise so he could hack at them again. Everyone gave him a wide berth.

"Bryar?" Sei called. The fae turned his way, examined him for a minute then bounded over. Everyone in the room tensed. Having Bryar in full armor wielding a giant sword looking a little like some sort of Goliath headed their way, was a bit more than a little intimidating.

"Can you head home and look after the kids?" Sei knew there were more death squad witches. Probably over a hundred if he recalled the ranks. The Dominion tried to keep their names and faces quiet, using them as sort of assassins sometimes, to sneak in and take a witch from their home. Though the deaths were never quiet.

He knew his wards would keep them out of his house and properties. But for how long?

Bryar took off his helmet, his face smeared with clay. "No more battles today?" He sounded disappointed.

"Not here at least. But those witches might target Jamie or Kelly, the twins, or even Kaine."

Bryar snorted. "Stupid mortals. You and yours belong to us. Kaine is ours."

"He is," Sei agreed. "But maybe he needs you to be a dad for a bit, yeah? Since I can't go home right this second?"

Bryar shimmered with magic, changing from his warrior form to something not all that different from Seiran, even dressing in pajamas and slippers, his hair bound up in an elaborate ponytail. Though the images on his PJs were some sort of creepy looking duck with fangs thing. Seiran smiled instead of asking. Bryar put his hand over his heart, as if that was where fae hearts were if they had them, and bowed slightly. "I go to guard the prince."

"Thank you," Seiran said. And that fast, Bryar was gone, stepping through a tear in the veil and closing it behind him.

"People underestimate you," Mike said mildly.

"They do," Seiran agreed. "We are going somewhere?"

"Yep. You can clean up there and I'll show you your new workspace."

Seiran's mind was reeling. "I…" But he didn't know where to begin, so he followed the vampire, who was one of Gabe's most trusted people, out to a waiting car. In fact, Seiran had trusted Mike for years. And there were too many questions in his head to even find a place to begin. And the sense of anxiety sat like a lump in his stomach. Worry for his kids and the Dominion rising to smash them all like flies.

THE BUILDING they drove to was very innocuous. It looked like every other high-rise around it. The parking garage the same, though entry only allowed after passing a heavily guarded checkpoint. It could have been a building for the wealthy and elite rather than some secret society Max had created.

They entered through a lower-level blast door, Mike having to scan his palm to get in. Seiran frowned at that, thinking of a dozen ways from movies it could go wrong. But maybe he had an overactive imagination.

"We'll get all your details registered and set up once you're clean," Mike said as they entered the building. The first hallway was bland enough, but filled with security. Vampires, humans, and witches, all genders and abilities.

"What if someone cut off your hand to open the door?" Seiran wondered out loud.

Mike laughed. "It's spelled. Without my life-essence and actual signatures, it won't work. Sort of like a magical checkpoint, though it's not checking my magic so much as my soul. Or whatever you want to call it. But good thought. I'll have security double-check."

"Hopefully not by cutting off people's hands."

"Yeah, I don't think that will be necessary."

There was a giant wall carving that said AF in fancy script on the wall behind what appeared to be a sort of reception area. Though instead of a check-in, it was more guards.

"Heard the order came down," one of them said to Mike. "Looks like we are finally doing this." He nodded at me.

Doing what?

"We've got over a hundred bodies in the past week. Even for the Dominion it's a bit excessive. The government had to act," Mike responded. He waved a hand at me. "I'm taking Rou up to his onsite apartments, then on a tour of his space. We'll have to get his data updated and logged."

"I'll let the spec team know. Have them meet you in the Investigations Unit in an hour or so."

"Thanks," Mike said. He directed Seiran to follow him to an elevator. "You're very quiet," he remarked as they got in and the door closed.

"Tired and overwhelmed." Grieving.

"He'll be back."

"Sure," Seiran agreed. Not really believing it. "All this is real?" They stepped out onto a floor, after Mike was scanned again, that appeared to be living spaces. Perhaps even vampire ones as the heat of the sun was completely absent from the windows, even though the hallway was filled with uncovered panes of glass. None of this looked new.

"Welcome to the Arcane Fellowship," Mike said.

"What is this place?"

"Exactly as it sounds. We study the unknown. All of it. Not only witch magic of the darker kind, like the Ascendance did decades ago. But vampire nuances, like those that make up some of the most powerful vampires, like Max and Gabe. And even fae magic. Though I suspect our studies in that direction will grow in leaps and bounds now that you're here. We've not had many of their kind willing to work with us. Only those of mixed pedicure like your Kaine."

Seiran was intrigued. "You have fae working here who are part witch?"

"Yes, several actually," Mike agreed. He guided them down the long hall and around the corner to a door, where he took out a key. "You'll have to put your hand to the door. I hope the signature is still the same."

Seiran watched as Mike put the key in the lock and then a symbol appeared in the center of the door, a circle surrounded with points. It reminded Seiran of something he'd seen in a book of old Druid magic. Mike motioned to the symbol, and Seiran put his palm to the door, expecting something, but only felt the mild edge of magic run through him. Then the door clicked open.

"You'll have to invite me in if you want a tour," Mike said. "That's standard for all onsite apartments. But this is where you'll go if you can't rush home during a case. It's a good place to rest, and eat, or take a break. There is a bunkhouse a few floors down that have pods just for sleeping, but since this is your space, I think you'll find this a bit more comfortable."

Seiran stepped through the open door. He actually felt the tugging of wards as they recognized him. Strong, though not cast by him.

The space was like stepping into a time warp. Back to when Gabe had moved into that first underground space rather than the decorative loft he'd used as a front before their relationship had become more permanent. The entire space had the same layout and colors, large kitchen, small half bath near the door. Master bedroom and bath in the back, and small sitting area filled with shelves ready for books. Gabe had designed that first apartment for Seiran's comfort more than his own. This place had giant windows, though the blinds between the glass were closed, and they had to be the sunlight resistant ones since Sei felt no heat or warmth from them.

Mike stood outside the door while Seiran explored. Sei's heart ached. Too many memories, but this wasn't the same place. The bed was the same style as they used to have. The bottom, a box that could be opened to hold grave dirt. "This looks like Gabe's old place," he said quietly.

"Because it belongs to both of you. Once you're showered, I'll take you upstairs to your office. We can schedule a crew to come in and stock the pantry, make the bed, etcetera. Gabe wanted to ensure you were comfortable if you had to work long hours. We can get the kids registered too. No reason they can't stop in. We just ask you keep them to the lower levels. The living spaces, cafeteria, workout spaces, and there are a few game rooms. No civilians above floor fifteen."

Gabe? How had Gabe known about any of this? He'd been in the ground for almost fifteen years. "I'm confused."

"About?"

"Gabe?"

"I suspect as soon as he's back he'll be on the board with Max and Lily."

Seiran gaped at Mike. "What?"

"What, what?"

"Lily? Max? Gabe had a part in creating this?"

"Gabe started the process after you reclaimed your father's house and took control over the Ascendance years ago. Max liked the idea of shifting goals. Your aunt had ideas that she could not implement in the Dominion. When she retired from the Dominion, she began working here. Building up the library and overseeing research. Sadly, Gabe went to ground before most of this was finalized. But this whole building used to belong to the Ascendance."

Seiran was reeling. The Ascendance had been an organization not all that unlike the Dominion. A coven of witches, mostly male run, who used to manipulate and gain more power for themselves, no matter the cost. He had thought he'd unraveled the organization, but maybe had failed in more than one thing.

"This was the Ascendance?"

"Was," Mike agreed. "Now it's the Arcane Fellowship. Specializing in education, research, and community. Sounds really fluffy, and mostly is, but there are some very powerful witches here. It took a long time to weed out the bad ones and restructure."

"Are they stealing power for themselves?" Seiran demanded.

"No. The groups are heavily monitored for that." Mike pointed toward the back where the master bath was. "Get cleaned up. There should be some clothes in the drawers, just standard fair, jeans and whatnot. I'll show you around. I think that will give you a better feel for all of this."

"Gabe was a part of this?"

Mike nodded. "He got the ball rolling. That last time he came back, after being shot in the head, I think he was already starting to really have trouble. Put us to work on this and began recruiting to help the change. Your aunt Lily, and your mom, as well as Max, all joined up rather fast. Though I think Gabe had gone to ground around the same time. Sam has been working here almost a decade."

"And never thought to mention it…" Sei grumbled as he headed toward the shower. He was going to have words with that vampire asshole.

"We were trying to gain inside information," Mike said. "Having some members within the organization made sense. Tanaka thought telling you would make you abandon the job before we were established enough to make the power shift." Mike sighed.

"Not all of us thought that it was a good idea to keep you in. But her attention has been on protecting the next generation."

"Not me," Sei said. Never him. He would have left. To be free of the guilt and monstrosities they'd forced him to be a part of for years? He sucked in a deep breath, not bothering to invite Mike in. Sei needed some time with his thoughts anyway. There was anger boiling, as well as the grief, and a healthy handful of self-pity. But he had a lot of questions that needed answers, and at least somewhere to start. Would they kick him out if he told them he had no plans to jump in with both feet and trust another organization with magic and political power? He was done being a pawn for anyone. Dominion, Arcane Fellowship, or whatever the fuck they wanted to call it.

He turned to the door. "I need a little time."

"Sure," Mike said. He held up his phone. "Send me a text when you're ready, and I'll show you around. I'll be down a few floors."

Seiran wasn't sure he was ever going to be ready, but he shut the door and headed to the shower. Tired, but on pins and needles, his heart aching. No one needed to see him cry in the shower when he could almost feel Gabe's arms around him again.

He dressed in a half fog, slowly, thinking maybe he should lie down and try to sleep, but his nerves were on fire, and he kept seeing Gabe's burned face. They had wanted that for him, hadn't they? The Dominion. And then what of his kids? Kill them? Lock them away? Or use them as puppets? It was too much all at once, and not nearly the answers he needed. And he was so fucking tired of having the world on his shoulders alone.

He stood in the bedroom, identical to a place he'd left behind because the memories had hurt so much, and hugged himself. Wishing it were Gabe holding him. He could go home. Leave all this behind, abandon all of the politics of magic. But they would never stop hunting him. Power sought power, and that was the ultimate sting of all this mess. No matter who won, he lost. He would always be controlled by someone else.

Seiran sucked in a long breath, centering himself, and trying to shove away the melancholy. His life wasn't all that different from anyone else's. He felt oddly balanced still. Like Gabe's short presence had given him a bit of extra strength. The Goddess still called to him, but it was distant and faint.

He didn't think for one minute he could actually rest here. Not without his wards in place, his kids close by, and the fae at his back. Funny how much those little things had come to mean to him over the years.

Again, he stood at the threshold of change. Would anything actually shift for the better? What choice did he have? Move forward? Walk away? Run for his life?

He picked the only one he'd ever really found as a choice in his life, and moved forward, heading for the door, sending Mike a text, and hoping whatever was to come, he could keep his family safe.

CHAPTER 29

He followed Mike on the tour, in silence, listening with only half an ear as Mike explained the places they passed. The building was huge, and actually had a dozen or so tied to it through walkways, all with screening checkpoints.

"Your job is to give witches tours?" Seiran asked.

"My job is enforcement," Mike answered. "Most vampires are on enforcement at least half the time. From guard duty, to protecting the investigators."

"That sounds boring. What if a vampire wants to be an investigator?"

"There are more than a handful, but they get enforcers with them out in the field too. Vampires might be strong, fast, and hard to kill, but there are plenty of witches who know how to unravel us. I'm not a fan of puzzles myself. Point me in a direction, and I'll make something happen, but don't ask me to pick the direction."

Seiran studied him, a little surprised. "Never took you as much of a follower."

Mike grinned, showing a bit of fang. "I'm not. I'm just more likely to kill everything and let whatever god of the moment sort it out." He pointed at Seiran.

"I'm not a god."

"Godlike powers anyway. Let me show you to your new work space."

Seiran didn't appreciate that they had to go up and up and up to get there. His office was a giant thing near the top of the building that felt too far from the ground, and a bit cold and sterile. Emmaline looked as shocked as he felt when she'd been shown inside.

"What the fuck, right?" Seiran asked her.

"I don't know where to start." She had huge eyes as they were led to a department of investigators and introduced to at least ten times the number Seiran had ever been allowed. Humans, witches, vampires, shifters, and the handful of fae Mike had mentioned.

The research was endless. Seiran demanded access to everything, and was surprised when he didn't meet any barriers. In fact, everyone jumped to obey, which felt very weird. They all treated him with respect, saying, "Yes, Sir, right away, Sir."

He had a new computer, all his scans finished in minutes, and access to the vast and very well-organized libraries, both on-site and digitally.

"Everything is scanned and backed up for search, or you can view the actual text if it's on-site, order it to site if it's not, or even request a retranslation," someone was telling him. Far beyond the troves he used to have, he couldn't imagine knowing the archives here as well as Page had the Dominion ones. "There is a directory of texts by keywords as well. And if you can't find a text, there is an R&D department that might be looking into it. They are always accepting recommendations as well."

To say Seiran was shell shocked was a bit of an understatement. Reports began to trickle in of all the fires, burned witches, and property seizure that was finding more bodies, dark magic, and hints of a long history of buried problems. All of the bodies, vampire, human, witch, and their history, began to pile up. The massive team of investigators were working on sorting out who belonged where and reporting to Seiran on their findings.

For the first time in his life, he felt like people actually saw him, beyond his family. And it didn't feel like fake respect. He'd even had a handful of them act very shy and awkward, more like he was a celebrity, than a department advisor, as he was now labeled, simply because he was the Pillar. It was weird, but Seiran was too overwhelmed to really let it bother him.

The President made an address indicating his support. Congress was not so cut and dry. Lots of bluster and talk of overreach, but more than half of the sitting members of Congress were either related to a high-level Dominion witch, or in the pocket of them. The system built to give them power was crumbling, but it wouldn't be an easy change.

Seiran had a feeling another war was on the horizon. Perhaps a civil one as the vampires stood ruthlessly against the witches in this. He felt a little torn, his lifetime of indoctrination making him feel like he was betraying everything he knew. But he'd be lying if he said he wasn't relieved. Not only at the possibility that he would no longer be considered part of the legalized death end of the Dominion, but that maybe his kids would have another opportunity in life, beyond being a cog in the wheel of rich people's power.

"We'll want to screen the new additions," a man by the name of Detrick Jacobson told them. He'd been introduced as lead administrator over the investigations department. "Advisor Rou will have final say, of course," Detrick added.

"My investigators?" Seiran wondered.

"Those you think you can trust and who are willing to leave the Dominion. Unfortunately, we will have to monitor everyone to ensure they are not providing information to the Dominion. Transition like this is rarely easy or straightforward."

"Including me?" Seiran asked. He had no intention of ever being involved with them again if possible.

"Yes, and I apologize for that. We are honored to have the Pillar of Earth on our side. But we have long been in opposition to sitting power, and find ourselves a bit more cautious than most."

Seiran sighed. "I'm not sure I trust any of you anymore than I trust the Dominion." Emmaline nodded her agreement.

"That's justified," Detrick said. "I hope time will help with that. We have a lot of information coming in right now, so there is a ton of ground to cover. We will need more investigators, but we work with what we have."

"You have more than we ever did," Emmaline grumbled.

"By at least ten times," Seiran agreed. He had a dozen investigators he thought he trusted. Those like Emmaline, who really took their work with a global full colored view, rather than rules set in black and white. Many more were very rule bound as the Dominion preferred. He hoped at least a few were willing to make the change.

The following flow of information was so intense that Seiran's head spun with all of it. He admitted the exhaustion was getting to him and he floundered in the wake of the intensity of it all. The list of names, witches burned to death, flickering through a screen of information, was the only thing keeping him on his feet. Four Directors, including Han, were dead. Many members of their families, now identified as one of the largest covens in the USA, were also dead or injured.

He felt a little sick. He hadn't meant to kill anyone. But that was the way of things, wasn't it? Their spell, he reminded himself. Not his. If it had hit him, bounced from Gabe to him, would it have hit the kids? That was the only thing keeping him from dissolving with guilt. That, and memories of Gabe's burned body as they laid him on the ground.

It happened to him often enough, this sort of backfire of power. And he had never really stopped having nightmares about his first kill, a man named Brock, who had raped him and tried to murder him to steal his power. Seiran had instead performed the ritual to accept the power of the pillar. Unsanctioned by the Dominion, of course. But the earth had accepted him in a blaze of power. The Dominion had been trying to get rid of Seiran ever since.

He walked in a daze, trying to follow the endless data, but swaying a little on his feet. Seiran felt a hand on his arm and flinched, turning, ready to yell at someone for touching him, but it was Sam.

"Looking like shit, Ronnie," Sam said.

"Fuck you," Seiran grumbled.

He grinned, not at all offended, then folded his arms across his chest. "Sounds like until the big guy is back and trained, I'm on your six."

"What?" Seiran snapped.

"I am your enforcer," Sam said slowly.

"You're going to what, scare people into talking to me? I don't need a guard." Seiran put up his hands and wiggled his fingers, plants growing around them in delicate flowers. "Pillar."

"It's the rules. Every investigator gets an enforcer."

"Can't I have Mike?" Seiran wondered.

"You trust Mike more than me to watch your back?" Sam sounded offended.

"I'd trust him to start less shit."

"Point," Sam shrugged. "But nah, he's only part time enforcement. He's got businesses to run, at least until Gabe is back at capacity."

That was another fist to the gut. Would Gabe be back any time soon? Seiran didn't want to think about it. Between the exhaustion and grief, he was barely holding it together.

"You need some rest?" Sam asked.

"Probably. But it's not going to happen right now." Every time he closed his eyes, he saw Gabe's burned face. Better than the original betrayal at least. Eventually Seiran would collapse and sleep.

"What if you went home and hugged your kids?" Sam said quietly as he stepped in close. No one else was nearby. It was sad how well Sam knew him. But going home meant falling apart. Was he ready for that?

"Not yet," Seiran breathed out an unsteady breath. "I just…"

"Okay. How about we go look at that cabin then? I'll drive. There's some interesting shit coming up in the evidence our peeps are documenting."

"Don't think I'm not mad at you for not telling me about this stuff."

"I did tell you, Ronnie. I think you asked me what the fuck I did for Max, and I said *I'm an enforcer*."

"For a secret witch organization?"

"We aren't a witch organization." Sam put his hands to his chest. "Vampire. Lots of fucking vampires here."

"And witches."

"And shifters. Stay away from the workout rooms if you don't want that stink of sweaty dog to linger with you." Sam shivered. "Now are we going, or do you need me to knock you unconscious for a while?"

"As if you could."

"Try me, Ronnie."

"Fine, let's go." Seiran followed Sam, hoping that he didn't come apart at the seams before he could catch a break. The names kept scrolling across the screens, dead witches, witches in custody for Crimes Against Humanity, and those wanted for questioning. It was too much, and he needed to get away, even if it was just to bury himself in another mystery.

CHAPTER 30

Gabe woke feeling like he'd had a long nap. A cool swath of earth cradled him, but he was aboveground, not floundering below it.

He stretched, working out the aches and taking in the scent of earth, flowers, and green. He was a bit startled to open his eyes and find himself in the arboretum rather than a crypt.

There was a buzz of bees going about their work, and flying balls of color darting too fast to be any sort of bug. The light overhead beaming in to illuminate the space felt warm, but not uncomfortable. Gabe blinked at it all, taking in the scenery and letting his body work out the kinks of having mortal weight again.

Distantly he heard a door open, and thought Seiran was headed his way because he smelled Seiran's blood. But it was Kaine who appeared beside him, in his fae form, the pretty ethereal man, rather than the wide-eyed child.

Gabe tried to recall if he knew the details of Kaine's creation, but if they'd been shared with him, he'd forgotten them. Though, thankfully, all his other memories seemed to be in place.

Kaine set a cup down on a bench and held out a piece of fabric.

Gabe frowned at it for a minute, then reached out to snag it from Kaine's grasp. A robe.

"Thank you," Gabe said, slurring a bit. He felt well rested, but it would take blood and some movement to get the last bit of stiffness out of his joints and brain. He tugged on the robe and slowly found his way to the bench, a bit reluctant to leave the cool draw of the soil. He recalled the burns. That memory would hurt for a while. His skin was whole, and as it had been since the day he'd died his first mortal death, more than two thousand years prior, but the lingering ache etched into his memory would take some time to fade.

Kaine picked up the cup and pressed it into Gabe's hands. "I warmed it. It's only a few days old. Daddy tries to keep a bit stocked."

Gabe accepted the cup and expected it to be regular blood, with maybe a touch of Seiran's since it smelled like chocolate cake and strawberries with a hint of vanilla honey. But when he put the cup to his lips and took the first sip, he knew it wasn't a spiked version of Seiran's blood. It was Seiran's blood. Not fresh, but holy fuck the punch through his veins had Gabe spinning as his nerves came alive all at once.

Kaine gripped Gabe's shoulder, holding him upright, and keeping the cup from spilling. "It's got a bit of a kick, right?" Kaine's smile was so similar to Seiran's, that Gabe's gut hurt. Was Seiran mad? How long had Gabe been gone this time? Fae didn't age, and Gabe recalled Kaine looking like this when they crossed the veil. Which meant he had really no indication of how much time had passed.

He took another long draw from the cup, letting the sparkles fill his sight, and magic swirl through his body. He squeezed his eyes shut as dizziness came and went. The bond zinged into place, awakening and stretching much as he had, like muscles too long unused. He could feel Seiran through the bond. Not close, but not across the world or anything. It wasn't at all withered or stretched like it had been.

"Maybe Daddy can forgive Grandma. I miss Grandma," Kaine said wistfully.

"What did Tanaka do now?" Gabe wondered, taking his time to work through every drop. Too soon the cup was empty. He craved more, though didn't need it.

"Didn't tell Daddy about the secret organization she was a part of to take down the Dominion."

Gabe's memories chugged into place. *He* had helped found a new organization. Though he could only recall having a meeting or two to get it started before he'd gone to ground the last time. Had they made it happen without him then? He hadn't invited Tanaka in, but he'd never trusted her enough to actually look after Seiran's best interest.

"How long was I down?" Gabe asked.

Kaine shrugged. "Time is weird here."

"Time is weird across the veil," Gabe corrected.

"Nah. There is no time across the veil." Kaine took the empty cup and got up, offering a hand in support. "Maybe get cleaned up?"

"Seiran isn't home?"

"He's at work."

"At the Dominion?"

Kaine snorted. "No. At the Fellowship."

Gabe was confused again, but he would ask more questions later. "I'd love to shower. Can I enter the wards of the house?" He glanced around and the external barriers that had wrapped the house in plants were gone, at least from his view out the windows. The sun was bright overhead, though didn't hurt, even while he felt the heat of it. A perk of being bound to the Pillar of Earth he supposed. Vampires didn't burn in sunlight, not like legends rumored. But it could drain them, and make their bones ache. He didn't feel tired at all and the stiffness likely came from his resurrection.

"Sure," Kaine said and bounced toward the main entry Gabe recalled leading to the kitchen. He followed at a gentler pace, his body still slowly acclimating to movement. When he reached the door, he tensed, expecting a ward, but finding nothing that pushed him back. And the kitchen was unchanged. If it had been a long time, either their decorating tastes were the same, or they hadn't cared enough to change it.

As soon as Kaine entered the kitchen he returned back to his child form. Looking about ten or so. Maybe Gabe hadn't missed much time. He tried to remain hopeful.

Kaine put the cup in the sink, running water through it for a few seconds, then heading to the basement door. "There's more blood in the freezer. Not as fresh as the stuff I gave you. I took the packet off the top when the garden alerted me you were there."

Gabe heard footsteps coming down the stairs and a few seconds later the male of the twins appeared in the doorway. He blinked wide eyes. "Kaine? You didn't wake the vampire, did you? And why is he here instead of at the crypt?"

What was his name? Mizuki? But Gabe recalled Seiran calling him Ki. Crazy how both Seiran's boys were gingers, though Kaine's hair was more fresh blood red, than the carrot of his brother's. He recalled the girl had dark hair like Seiran's. Mizuki didn't look any older either.

"I didn't wake him," Kaine protested. "The garden told me he was there."

"I'm going to go shower," Gabe said carefully. "And maybe find my phone so I can call your dad?" Wasn't he supposed to play a dad role too? Those were boundaries he was going to have to work out with Seiran. As long as he didn't find himself kicked out for having to go to ground again.

Ki looked suspicious. "I'll call him while you're in the shower."

"Okay," Gabe agreed. He headed for the basement door, wondering if there was destruction from the fire he had to worry about cleaning up. But as he descended the stairs and flicked on the light, the rug was gone, the bed looked undamaged, made up like a magazine shoot, and the floor was clean, no sign of water or fire damage.

He found clothes and headed to the shower, needing to feel the warmth over his skin to chase away the lingering chill of going to ground. When he stepped out, and dressed, it was with thought as he tried to recall everything that happened. They'd been attacked. Something aiming a fire spell at Gabe through the link of his zombies, to reach Seiran? Or just take Gabe out again?

The warmth of the water had helped awaken his stiffened nerves and he felt the bond tightening. Not closing as much as a feeling that Seiran was getting closer? He had to work not to reach for Seiran. He didn't want to interrupt him while he was driving or something.

The Fellowship? What was that?

He tugged on clothes with slow intent, mostly to keep himself from racing out to find Seiran and decimate anyone who tried to harm them again. He had a lot of questions about the time missed, and wondered if they'd settled into another rut with the Dominion still in power. He had never hated them as much as he had that first moment when Tanaka had threatened to lock Seiran away for life. And even if she wasn't working for them now, he had no plans to ever forgive her. No one could hold a grudge like a vampire. Of that he was certain.

The door from upstairs opened, and footsteps raced down. Gabe turned, expecting to find one of the kids, but it was Seiran.

One second, he was across the room, the next he was in Gabe's arms. Gabe catching him and holding him tight.

"Please tell me you fucking remember me?" Seiran demanded.

"I do," Gabe agreed and silenced his next question with a kiss. It was a long and slow kiss, devouring, as well as sweet. Need building. Their bond collided and solidified, coming together as gentle laps of power instead of a turbulent tide. All the jagged edges of memories and questions soothed into an overlapping sense of unity. This was how they should have been from the start, Gabe thought.

He'd been unraveled too far. Worried that letting Seiran in would scare him away. Instead, he'd left Seiran vulnerable. He'd been so stupid. Gabe longed to throw Seiran down on the bed and memorize him all over again, while apologizing and trying to earn forgiveness. But he settled for a hand in his hair, Seiran's legs around his waist, and one hand on Seiran's ass.

Gabe tottered backward until they both landed in an armchair. Since his arms were full, he didn't care. When the kiss finally ended, Seiran held tight to Gabe as though unwilling to let him go.

"You couldn't have clued me in?" Seiran demanded.

Gabe blinked, looking around on what he was to have clued Seiran in on. Him coming back? He didn't really get advanced notice on that. "Huh?"

"The Arcane Fellowship?"

"I don't know what that is," Gabe admitted. Was he still missing bits of his memory?

"The organization you helped turn the Ascendance into?" Seiran tugged on Gabe's hair until their eyes met. "Secret society of witches, vampires, shifters, oh my? Not so secret anymore."

Oh. "Is that what they named it?"

Seiran made a rude noise at him.

"I don't think I was there for the naming," Gabe said.

"Apparently not. Could you have maybe let me know?"

Gabe tried to recall the details of the organization, but they were sparse. Like he'd drafted an idea, got together a handful of his most trusted vampires, but that was all the further he'd gotten. "I'm not sure I was much involved."

"Your money funded it."

"Okay, but I was in the ground. Who had control of my money?" Gabe threw back. He didn't want to fight with his witch, but would if he had to. And he had to admit the intensity of the gaze and scrutiny Seiran had on him, made him a little hot.

Or maybe that was just Seiran's blood running through his veins. Not that it mattered, he'd take the fiery passion any way he could. It was one of the things about Seiran that had always appealed to him.

"Max." Seiran cursed. "That..." He made to get up, but Gabe held firm.

"He's always been a bit on the manipulative side. Even when we were humans." Gabe recalled back to Max's mortal days. He actually didn't really miss being in that storm. There was always a new city to conquer, an organization to plunder, and riches to obtain. Gabe hadn't really needed any of that. He'd been more about the adventure, discovering new places, and learning everything about new cultures. "Was I gone long this time?"

"Are you all healed?" Seiran asked. "Memories where they are supposed to be?" His gaze looked over Gabe, letting go of his hair long enough to tug at Gabe's shirt. But all the damage from the fire was gone.

"Yes. A little stiff, but otherwise fine. Memories seem to be there."

"But you woke up in the garden? That's bizarre. But we put the grave dirt from the bed there. Wasn't sure if we should carry it all the way back. Do you need more blood?"

"Kaine gave me some of yours that was in the freezer."

"Yeah. Figured I'd save some for a bit. Just in case."

"Thank you."

"How do you feel?"

Gabe thought hard about that. "More me? Less like I was ripped early? More in control. Even the hunger when I woke was only passing. Necessary."

"The revenant isn't pulling at you?"

"No," Gabe agreed. It was silent. Always there as was the nature of a vampire, but not the beating presence it had been.

"It's been about two weeks," Seiran said. He looked tired, like he'd barely slept. "Not long..." But still hard, Gabe could hear that in his voice. Maybe he hadn't been pulled that early last time, or something about resting in the garden this time with the bond renewed had better helped his regeneration.

"Kaine said you were at work? I didn't mean to interrupt your day."

"I'm going through evidence. Endless fucking evidence. I'm a thousand years behind. And learning things I didn't want to know."

"Okay. Like?"

"Like some vampires don't die even if you behead them?"

Gabe flinched. Yeah, false rumors spread easily enough. Vampires were hard to kill in general. Beheading slowed them down enough for fire to really destroy them before the earth could rebuild them. Total body destruction, really, it was a bit of a crazy balance. "Only way to really kill a vampire is by burning it to ash. Usually, aboveground. Good luck getting them to stay there that long."

Seiran was silent for a minute contemplating. "Is Tresler really dead?"

Gabe tried to recall what he could, but he'd only heard about Tresler's death. Whatever tie the old vampire had over Gabe in the past was gone. "I don't know. You were there, I wasn't."

"Technically, I was dead. Shot in the head. Sam burned it all down that day. The earth tried to take him back, but Sam burned everything. How the house didn't burn down…" Sei shook his head. "That guy is like a hammer to the forehead. Nothing delicate in his magic."

Gabe laughed. "Yeah? You're one to talk."

"Hey!"

Gabe curled himself around Seiran in the chair, reveling in the feeling of him being there. His memories back in place made him breathe in deep, the scent of Seiran, the pulsing beat of their magic settling together, and even the sound of his heartbeat. However, he had a feeling something was up. "Why the question about Tresler?"

Seiran tensed in Gabe's arms, then curled in to rest his forehead on Gabe's shoulder. "Just hold me a little longer, then I'll tell you, okay?" There was a hint of a tremble in Seiran, some of the confidence vanishing beneath a tide of fear.

"Sei?" Gabe whispered, holding him hard enough to hurt. Whatever was bothering him was big.

"You know how there were three souls in the golem, and we couldn't find the body for the third?"

"Yeah?"

"The body was Matthew's."

Gabe blinked, processing. Not possible was his first thought. Beheaded, and exploded, the entire site now a field of nullification. However, if there had been enough of the body intact… put in the ground and resurrected? Possible.

"You're certain? You have the body?" He could kill it for sure. End that vampire as he had thousands in the past. It was something necessary as a sire and master vampire, but in this instance, he would enjoy it. The man who had abused Seiran as a child, manipulated Sam, and had tried again to take Seiran from him, he deserved to die a slow and painful death.

Seiran wouldn't look at him, his gaze going blank and finding a spot of nothing on the far wall to stare at. "We only have pictures. Video. Some security footage."

"You don't know if it's really him."

"It's him," Seiran said firmly, an icy hand forming like a fist around their bond. Gabe flinched as it cooled the fire, but felt sharp enough to cut. His rage, he realized, not Seiran's who was all heat and life, but the cold touch of the grave.

"But the soul is in the golem? We could release them."

"Which would free the revenant to control the body." Seiran sighed and finally shifted his tired gaze back Gabe's way. "We think they are using Matthew's body as a vessel for a demon."

"Who's we? I've seen demons before. It's not pretty." Gabe recalled that Seiran had said he'd encountered one before too.

"Sam. He's been my enforcer, at my back until you can fill that role. I guess if you want to. I mean, maybe you want to go back to business or something instead of following me around."

"I have no intention of going anywhere without you again." And Gabe's first goal would be to put down Matthew Pierson once and for all.

"Then best get training. Sounds like there is a course you have to complete before you meet the requirements to be my backup. Sam says it's intense."

"To Sam, anything beyond playing a video game is intense."

A smile touched the edge of Seiran's lips. He still looked way too tired.

"When was the last time you slept?"

"I sleep. I come home, hug my kids and fall into a coma for about three or four hours."

Gabe groaned. Back less than an hour and he had a dead man to rekill, an organization to take over, or several of them, and a lover to retrain. "You're a lot of work."

"Yeah? Maybe you'd like to go back in the ground?"

"Fuck that," Gabe said. "I have an empire to rebuild."

"Everyone said you were sort of the anti-king. Didn't want to be in charge."

"Who told you that?"

"Max. Mike."

"I'm not anti-power, only anti-media spin. Let's work on ruling the world from the shadows, okay? It's what I do best."

"I just want my family safe," Seiran admitted.

Gabe wrapped his fingers through Seiran's hair, missing the length, but enjoying the texture. "We'll work on that. Are the Dominion still after us? I noticed the house was open."

"Always and probably. It's complicated. Long story short, the Dominion has been declared a cult. A lot of people died when I reflected their spell back at them. The government has been arresting members, mostly high-ranking officials, but they haven't gotten them all. And we can't completely trust the government. I think they are more on board with all this because they got to seize assets and money, rather than the loss of life raising their ire."

"Sounds about standard for any government," Gabe remarked.

"The evidence is basically war crime level. Not sure how else to describe it. They have copies of my original reports. Video evidence from cases I worked and I have no idea how they got it. Someone on my team was recording everything, copying everything, reporting on everything."

Which meant Seiran felt betrayed, even if it was for a good reason.

"I'm sorry I wasn't here."

Seiran's gaze flashed with rage as he met Gabe's. "You need to do better. Talk to me. Tell me if you're struggling."

"I will do my best to be better. Can you say the same?"

"I'm not hiding things from you."

"But you are from your family. No more death wish. No more throwing yourself at the problem without regard to who you leave behind. You have kids who need you. I need you." Gabe let out a breath, and with it the anger. There were a lot of places to direct that rage right now, but it didn't need to be between each other. "This thing with Matthew scares you. But you're not that kid anymore. Remember?"

"And if he's a demon now? Demons are…"

"A nightmare," Gabe agreed. "But we'll handle it. We've got allies and resources."

"Fucking fae," Seiran grumbled. "Acting all high and mighty now that the Dominion is on the out. Trying to use me to gain more legal foothold. I am not a political pawn."

But he was and always would be. The bane of being a Pillar. He could fade or burn bright, but the choice would never be his.

"Kaine wants you to stop being mad at Tanaka. Says he misses her," Gabe added.

Seiran cursed again. "She did all this! Had a hand in it all. And didn't tell me. What is it with people not talking to me?"

"I'm sorry," Gabe said. "For my part, I think I was hoping to have something more established before sharing? I didn't want the Ascendance to change names and then lay that mess at your feet to build from the ground up. But Tresler took over my mind before I could really make anything happen."

"You remember that?"

"I do. It was slow. Like slugs in my veins." Gabe shuddered. "It took a long time for me to recognize what was happening."

"And by then it was too late?"

"Lots of patchy bits near the end. Sorry. What about the spell? The fire?"

"Sent by a coven. Several board members were in that coven. People I had worked with for years. I directed the spell back at them. A lot of them died, they were unable to stop the spell they started. They sacrificed the two boys who had messed with the golem to fuel the spell."

"And the rest?" Gabe hoped they were not still out there, hunting Seiran. He could handle whatever came his way. But what if the kids got caught in the crosshairs?

"Some have been arrested by the military. Max has people from the Arcane Fellowship questioning them. What a terrible name."

"Max?"

"Arcane Fellowship. It sounds dark and fluffy all at once."

"Again, pretty sure I wasn't there for the naming."

"Anyway, I'm not sure they are all contained, which is why everyone is to be cautious. Jamie and Kelly are home with the kids. Everything monitored by the fae. I've been looking at the Fellowship too," Seiran said. "Digging through files, meeting people, letting the Goddess search them. Found nothing."

"Like the Ascendance, you mean?"

"That same intent, to corrupt power? All those around me so far, all those I've met? It's more a curiosity. A desire to learn. Maybe they are limiting who I meet? I trust no one."

"I'm sorry I had a part in that. I can only promise to do my best.

A couple millennia of habit will be hard to break, but know that I will answer if you ask, even if it takes a bit for me to figure out what I'm thinking and feeling." Gabe opened the bond wide on his side and left it there. "Open the bond."

He felt Seiran release his grip on it, and the tie between them blossomed like a flower opening, awakening them both to each other's senses. Seiran was hungry, but ignoring it in favor of sitting there in Gabe's arms.

"Eat something," Gabe instructed.

"You still ache," Seiran said.

"Yeah, that's normal. It will fade. Faster the more I move."

Seiran sighed thoughtfully and a bit needy. "I missed you."

"I missed you too." Gabe said again. "Love you." He felt the words settle through him solidifying their bond. He couldn't recall feeling this at peace in a long time. Rested and bonded, he was ready for whatever was coming his way. They'd have to work at balancing their powers, especially now that Gabe had no intent of hiding his any longer. But as long as the world didn't explode, they had plenty of time.

"I love you, too," Seiran said. "Not forgiven though."

"That's okay," Gabe agreed as he picked up Seiran and headed for the bed. "I've got some great persuasive techniques."

"Yeah?"

"Be happy to demonstrate."

Seiran sighed. "You're too pretty to hate."

"You like me for more than my pretty face."

"It *is* very appealing. Body isn't bad either."

"My my, Mr. Rou, are you claiming you only want my body?"

Seiran made a pained sound, his legs tightening around Gabe's waist. "Maybe for a few hours at least?"

"I thought you were researching?"

"A break wouldn't kill me, and then maybe a nap?"

Gabe smiled. "Sounds like a plan."

EPILOGUE

Page arrived with a military escort. He had expected execution instead of receiving a room not unlike a posh apartment. It was the nicest living space he'd ever had with a full bedroom, bathroom, and living room, no kitchen or even hot plate like his dorm had. He suspected that would have been a safety issue. There were also wards everywhere, etched into the walls themselves. And the fact that they locked him in was certainly an indication he wasn't free to come and go as he pleased.

He'd been allowed to call his mother, informed that all lines were recorded and monitored. He even had limited Wi-Fi access to the news. No social media allowed. It felt weird to be so silent online. But Page had to admit he didn't have a lot of friends who weren't across the country or the world. He had spent the past six months hiding. His family blackmailing him, threatening him and his mother, and he'd tried to lose himself in the shadow of Seiran Rou, Director of Magical Investigations.

No one had noticed him there, Seiran's power eclipsed them all, and most brushed him aside. Page was really glad he didn't have to worry about a role like the Pillar. Magically chosen to be a political pawn. What a nightmare.

Page's first week in lockdown, however nice his cell might be, was spent in and out of questioning. He'd been led to a dozen tiny rooms, all etched with nullifying symbols and that weird ache in his bones that told him magic would be harder there. The first two questioning sessions he'd been locked in one of those by himself and questioned through an intercom system.

Trying to understand his state of mind, perhaps?

Seiran had been his third interview, sitting down with Page on the couch in Page's room, aka cell, to ask things. He did record the session, both on his computer and an audio device. Page had seen both used enough to know how they worked. The questions from Seiran had been mostly benign. A lot about Page's mental health.

The hardest to answer had been one Page still lingered on. Was he still suicidal?

The answer was maybe?

Page teetered between depression and hope most days. Reflecting back on the things he'd been a part of made him feel used, worthless, and morally bankrupt. He could spend hours trying to think of different ways he could have changed things. His family might have killed him for it, but that didn't seem to matter much now. He expected the execution order to come at him any day.

Yet as each day stretched on, he began to think maybe not? But that made no sense. Witches died. It was how the Dominion worked. The rich and powerful ruled with an iron fist. What was okay for them, was not for the rest of the world. And Page had never been part of the elite.

His mother had cried when they talked the first time. It had been all Page could do to hold himself together. She blamed herself. But she'd done the best she could. Now their conversations were more mundane. He tried to call her at least every other day. Sometimes the questioning got to be a lot, and he just wanted to sleep. Hearing her voice soothed him in a way that he couldn't really explain.

The last two days had been quiet. No one in to take him to another meeting, and the only time he saw anyone was for his meals, which were delivered by the guards. After two and a half weeks of endless meetings, interviews, and medical reviews, the alone time was eerie.

He wished he had something to read. Other than the news.

The first few days there had been endless stories about witch families mourning loved ones, pointing the finger at the corrupt Pillar of Earth for their murder. And then the truth began to arise. Symbols, ceremonies, bodies, and long histories of phone conversations all with the intent to put the Dominion back the way it was. No men. In fact, all men born with magic would have been killed. Sacrificed it seemed, to fuel magic back to the female members of the families.

When that story leaked, Page had felt a roll of fear in his gut. He'd never asked for any of this. And had been young when his powers first began. They'd have killed him if they could. Wanted him dead. Thought he was evil.

Was he evil? He didn't feel that way.

Then the stories of abuse began to be published. Men with magic, or even women with the sort of dark powers Page had, coming out to tell stories of how they were treated by their Dominion families. It mirrored mistreatment from the Christian Churches. Family members burned quietly in a backyard to prevent the media from finding out. Others ostracized or running for their lives.

Every day there were more interviews published. The Dominion tried to debunk a lot of it, making wild claims, but the evidence didn't support what they said. Originally, the media resisted, not certain it wanted to be part of the smear suddenly staining the Dominion which had held its purse strings for years. But the volume seemed to be overwhelming enough that they had caved and began publishing more and more.

Page wondered if he'd be asked to tell his story to the world.

Compared to some it didn't sound all that bad. The threats and blackmail little more than a blip to torture, rape, and murder. But he wasn't ready. Hard enough that he judged himself harshly for the things he'd done.

The students who had used the golem were all dead. Murdered by their families. The Dominion claimed they were honor killings. The government disagreed. Page had been accused of killing Steve, though Page hadn't touched him.

Page still struggled with the memories of freeing the vampires, thinking he was helping, and what they'd done to the golem he created. The violence and assault bothering him more than his role of actually transferring the souls. He'd messed that up too. Tying them together somehow.

He'd been asked to give blood to the golem again, to try to control it? He had, and hadn't seen it since.

Now he paced. Who knew a couple days of almost complete solitude would unravel him? He had always been a bit of an introvert, preferring books over people. It was why he'd loved the job in the archives. What would happen to all those books now?

He sighed and paced some more, feeling a bit caged. It would be hours before they brought him food again. And he was tired of reading the news about the world and not seeing it. He couldn't help getting a little angry. Wishing they would decide what to do with him already, rather than leave him here.

Page paced for another hour. At least he was getting exercise. Then he dropped down onto the couch and stared at the art on the wall. Very mundane, almost bland. The entire apartment, while high end in décor, was all very stark and lifeless. Grays and browns, instead of vibrant color. But Page was really beginning to crave the touch of others. That wild burning ember in all people, that he'd been able to feel since he was a child, made more sense knowing the little he did about his powers now.

The vampire Gabe had called him a summoner. His power strong with life essence. Not the same as a necromancer. It was why his Mattie had been there when they killed her in front of him for the second time. He'd pulled her soul back, not really realizing it.

Maybe he was evil. That really did sound evil. Manipulating souls.

The door opened and Page jumped to his feet, startled.

He went through a half minute of rolling emotions, unsure whether to be terrified or happy to see someone, even if it was the vampire Sam. Page knew he was powerful, and often worked as the strong arm to the vampire leader, Maxwell Hart. Did that mean he was here to take out Page? Was this to be his end?

"Come on, Page. We have shit to do," Sam said as he waved toward the door.

Page sucked in a deep breath and headed Sam's way, ready for the end if that was to be his destination.

"Grab your shit. You won't be coming back here."

Page paused. "What?"

"This is the detention wing. We're moving you up a few floors."

"I don't understand."

Sam cocked his head to the side. "Did you want to remain locked up forever? Or work through this bullshit you were born with?"

Page gaped at him. "Um, work through it if I can, but is that allowed? I mean, I'm evil, aren't I?"

Sam laughed. "I'm evil. You're just a kid. Get your shit. The big guy wants to see you." He folded his arms across his chest and pursed his lips like he was annoyed to still be waiting.

Page looked around. He didn't really have anything. They'd given him the clothes, little more than scrubs, and the laptop wasn't his. He hadn't even had his phone. "I don't really have anything. When they escorted me here, they didn't say I could take anything."

"I'll send someone to get your shit then." Sam stepped back from the doorway and there were no guards in the hall.

"I'm not going home then?" Page's stomach ached.

"I think once you see the digs here, you'd rather stay on the Fellowship's dime. Since you'll be working here, it's easy access." Sam narrowed his eyes, his gaze intense. "There will be rules of course, and you will be monitored. Just because everyone thinks you're not a major risk doesn't mean you can run around wild. You'll have therapy to complete, regular assessments like the rest of us."

"Working?"

"The Dominion is no more, my friend," Sam said as Page stepped into the hall beside him. Everything felt very still and quiet. This hall did look a bit like a prison. "And your old boss works here now."

"Will I be working with Director Rou again?"

"He's not Director here. More a minister of investigations. But no, you'll be working directly for Hart. At least until your powers are better under control. Classes will be required. I think Hart said he called in a couple of your kind for specific training." Sam led him down the hall to the elevator.

"There are more like me?" Page was shocked.

"Not a lot, but yeah."

"I'm not evil?"

"Kid, do you kill puppies or babies to gain power? Rape people? Randomly steal from anyone you can because you hoard wealth? Torture vampires until their revenant takes control to use their power to create golems?"

"No, gross. Who would do that? I mean, I didn't torture those vampires…"

"Parts of your family," Sam said as he put his hand in the scanner and the elevator opened. "Since you don't have any shit to move, I'll take you right to Hart."

Page didn't like the sound of that, but followed Sam into the elevator.

They went up, and up, and up. Finally, the elevator opened to a reception area, and it looked like a very posh lawyer's office. The woman behind the desk smiled at Sam and nodded. No one else was around.

Sam led Page through a side door and down a hall. Page trembled with anxiety. What would a vampire as powerful as Hart want with him?

They entered the last door at the end of the hall and Page stopped, feeling his stomach flip over. The room was dark, lit by candles. A slab sat in the center of the room and the burned body of Steve lay on it. Page gulped, forcing back bile. The smell was a lot to take in with the sight. How he knew it was Steve, he wasn't certain. Only that he could *sense* it. The golem, Forest, also sat in a chair off to the side, unmoving, and looking mostly human.

"Good, let's get this over with," Hart said as he entered the door behind them and closed the door. He was as Page had always seen him on TV, beautiful, polished, and terrifying all at once.

"What?" Page asked.

"You're going to release the souls in the golem," Hart said. "And replace them with Steve." His gaze stared at the body with a cold intensity Page was glad wasn't directed at him. "We have a lot of questions for Steve. No reason to let the vampires continue to suffer."

"Except Pierson," Sam grumbled. "He deserves to suffer."

Hart's gaze landed on two other witches in the room, both male, one older and looking a bit like Santa Claus, the other Middle Eastern. "My goal is to unravel them. Contain that one."

"It is very faded," the Middle Eastern man said with a heavy accent. "Might not be enough left to matter."

"Just means they tortured him a long time before that one released him," Santa Claus said motioning at Page. "Heard tell he was supposed to have been dead over a decade. That's a long time to torture a vampire."

"A lot of wasted power," the other added.

Page had no idea what they were talking about, but it sounded awful.

"Not long enough," Sam said. He picked up a piece of pottery off a nearby shelf. "You sure this is gonna work? Genie in a bottle style?"

"It will work," the Middle Eastern man said.

"Not our first rodeo," the other added as he held out his arms for the piece Sam had. Sam gave it to them, and they set it on the floor near the golem.

"What if the soul is released?" Sam asked. "Does the demon unravel then?"

Demon? Page's eyes widened. He'd read the report long ago about Seiran's one encounter with a demon. It had given him nightmares for weeks. Was there a demon in the golem?

No way. He'd have sensed that, right? He was supposed to be able to control demons, but would that be instinct? The releasing of souls had been instinct and look how he'd messed that up.

"If a demon has control of Pierson's body, it would have already broken free of the bindings the coven set on it. Too many of them are dead to control it."

"We have a demon out there raging somewhere?" Sam sounded pissed, and more than a little put out. "This piece of shit just keeps on giving, doesn't it? Can we put it back in a body so I can kill it over and over again?"

Hart gave him a wry smile. "Possibly. Let's see how the baby summoner does with shifting these around first." He turned his gaze toward Page, and he felt that heat settle on him. Not unfriendly, but not benign either. Page gulped and sucked in a hard breath as he fought not to get lost in dark smokey eyes and power.

Want to read the story of Kaine's creation? Join the mailing list and get it for free.

LETTER FROM LISSA

Dear Reader,

Thank you so much for reading *Resurrection*, the first book in the new spin off of the Pillars of Magic series! If you haven't read the previous series, you can grab your copy of Inheritance now.

Be sure to join my Facebook group Lissa Kasey's Mystical Men, for fun daily polls, writing snippets, and updates on new releases to this series and others. For a sneak peek at my work before it's published join my Patreon group. Patrons receive three new chapters a week and many other perks. For monthly updates on what's coming out and character shorts subscribe to my Newsletter. Also check out my website at LissaKasey.com for new information, visiting authors, and novel shorts.

If you enjoyed the book, please take a moment to leave a review! Reviews not only help readers determine if a book is for them, but also help a book show up in searches.

Thank you so much for being a reader!
Lissa

ABOUT THE AUTHOR

Lissa Kasey is more than just romance. She specializes in in-depth characters, detailed world building, and twisting plots to keep you clinging to the page. All stories have a side of romance, emotionally messed up protagonists and feature LGBTQA spectrum characters facing real world problems no matter how fictional the story.

ALSO BY LISSA KASEY

Also, if you like Lissa Kasey's writing, check out her other works:

Simply Crafty Paranormal Mystery Series:
Stalked by Shadows
Marked by Shadows

Kitsune Chronicles:
Witchblood
WitchBond
WitchBane

Survivors Find Love:
Painting with Fire
An Arresting Ride
Range of Emotion

Hidden Gem Series:
Hidden Gem (Hidden Gem 1)
Cardinal Sins (Hidden Gem 2)
Candy Land (Hidden Gem 3)
Benny's Carnival (Hidden Gem 3.5)

Haven Investigations Series:
Model Citizen (Haven Investigations 1)
Model Bodyguard (Haven Investigations 2)
Model Investigator (Haven Investigations 3)
Model Exposure (Haven Investigations 4)

Pillars of Magic: Dominion Chapter
Inheritance (Pillars of Magic: Dominion Chapter 1)
Reclamation (Pillars of Magic: Dominion Chapter 2)
Conviction (Pillars of Magic: Dominion Chapter 3)
Ascendance (Pillars of Magic: Dominion Chapter 4)
Absolution (Pillars of Magic: Dominion Chapter 5)

Pillars of Magic: Dark Awakening
Resurrection (Pillars of Magic: Dark Awakening 1)

***

Evolution Series:
Evolution: Genesis

Boy Next Door Series:
On the Right Track (1)
Unicorns and Rainbow Sprinkles (2)

Manufactured by Amazon.ca
Bolton, ON